Macchiatos, Faerie Princes,

and Other Things That Happen at Midnight

The Leyward Stones, Book 1

Crystal Crawford

© 2021-2022 Crystal Crawford, first published in serial format on Kindle Vella as Part 1 (Episodes 1-37) of *Macchiatos, Faerie Princes, and Other Things That Happen at Midnight (The Leyward Stones, Season 1)*.

E-book and paperback formats published in 2023.

All Rights Reserved. No part of this publication may be reproduced, distributed, or transmitted in any form or by any means, including photocopying, recording, or other electronic or mechanical methods, without the prior written permission of the publisher, except in the case of brief quotations embodied in critical reviews and certain other noncommercial uses permitted by copyright law. For permission requests, contact ccrawford@ccrawfordwriting.com.

This is a work of fiction. Any resemblance to actual events or persons, living or dead, is entirely coincidental.

Cover art by Jason Crawford / Fierce, Inc.

CONTENTS

CHAPTER 1

THE STRANGER IN THE CAFÉ

I've always been careful, anxious, slow to trust. I come by it honestly—my parents aren't social butterflies, either, though they're masters at conflict avoidance, both within our family and outside of it. *Keep the peace* and *Better safe than sorry* are both such family mantras, I'm surprised we don't have them framed on our living room wall. We're not exactly a family of risk takers. So it's no surprise that the few times I pictured what my final moments might look like, I imagined myself living a long life and fading peacefully into old age, breathing my last breaths like falling asleep, tucked safely in a comfy bed.

I never imagined this.

As the writhing vortex expands in front of me, sucking me toward it, I realize nothing about this moment is *at all* what I expected. I'm at peace with dying to save those I love, but as the black abyss swallows me, one final, panicked thought tremors through me: *Will I be enough to save them?*

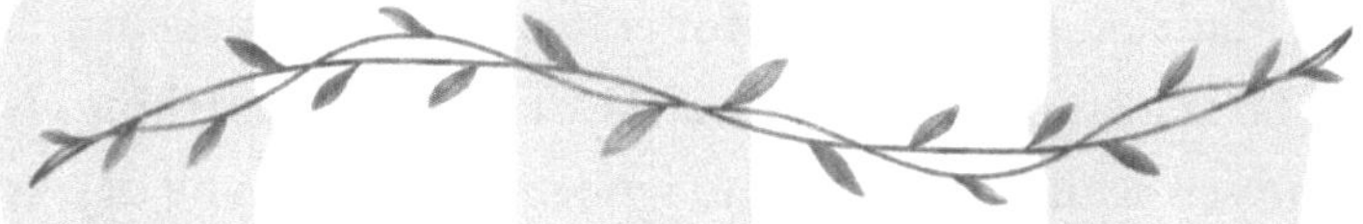

Two Weeks Earlier

The popular kids were here again. If I hadn't been able to tell by their raised voices and exaggerated laughter when the café door dinged open, I'd have known it by the orders the cashier, Larissa, called back at me a few moments later: "I need four medium, non-fat, soy milk macchiatos with two caramel shots each!"

I sighed—Madison and her friends' signature order. My stomach tensed, and I briefly wondered how long I could hide in the kitchen without Larissa or my boss, Gary, coming to look for me.

I unwrapped four cups and lined them in a row on the counter, poured two steaming-hot shots of Gary's signature espresso into each, then pulled the soy milk from the fridge and dumped it into the small frothing pitcher. I had just grabbed the steam wand to froth the soy milk—a process I was still perfecting after a week working here—when Larissa's cheery voice called back, "Ayla, make sure those caramel shots are stevia only, none of the corn-syrupy stuff, and make it quick, please!"

A smile tugged at my mouth despite my anxiety. I knew Larissa had repeated Madison's order word for word for her own amusement, but also for mine.

I could picture Larissa's faux-innocent face as I heard Madison's voice rise from the front counter. "Are you making fun of me?"

My shoulders tensed. A confrontation with Madison Kane was the *last* thing I needed today. It was bad enough that the week after I got hired at Gary's Café, Madison and her friends decided the one coffee shop in Havenridge that had been hiring for after-school and weekend jobs was their new favorite afternoon hangout. Or was that intentional? I wouldn't put it past Madison to come here for coffee simply to make my life more miserable. I'd at least hoped on a Saturday she'd have something else to do, but here she was again. As if trying to ignore her icy glares all day, every day at school wasn't torture enough.

Larissa's response was too quiet for me to hear over the strange ambience music Gary broadcasted through the overhead speakers, but based on Madison's clipped, "Whatever, just tell me when my order's ready," I assumed Larissa had diffused the situation.

I squirted in the caramel shots, finished scooping milk foam onto the top of each macchiato, snapped lids on all four cups and stuck them in a drink carrier, pasted on a smile, and stepped out into the front area.

Madison's glare hit me like a slap in the face the moment I emerged, sending my pulse racing. She flicked her glossy blonde hair over her shoulder and leveled her perfect green eyes at the drink carrier in my trembling hands. "It's about time. What took you so long?"

I shrugged, frozen in the kitchen doorway as my brain sped through clever responses, failed to find any, then realized the moment had passed and we were now in awkward silence territory.

Madison's trio of best friends—Ashley, Ansley, and Sasha—clustered behind her, tittering and whispering to one another behind their hands, their gazes flicking to me every few seconds. One of them swept her gaze to the top of my head, where a messy bun held my dark hair—which was surely sticking out everywhere, as usual; my frizzy hair had a mind of its own—and rolled her eyes.

I felt my face flush and immediately berated myself for it. Why did I care so much what these people thought of me? But the truth was, I hated for anyone to be upset with me, period. It made me feel like I'd done something wrong. And Madison Kane wasn't just upset with me—she *hated* me. Not that I could blame her. I *had* gotten her perfect brother, Rory Kane, expelled from school last year. It turns out the small town elite don't take kindly to it when you get their star quarterback expelled his senior year and all his choice colleges cancel his athletic scholarships and recruitment offers. *He* was the one who sold answers to the exams, but honestly, I never meant for that to happen to him. If I'd realized what telling his teacher the truth would cost him, I might've answered differently when she asked me what I'd seen in the parking lot. But I hadn't wanted to lie.

Even though Madison and I had gone to school together since kindergarten—like almost everyone in this small town—she and I had never been friends. I wasn't part of the "popular" crowd. Until the end of last school year, she'd ignored me. Now, it was like it was her life's mission to make me miserable.

I swallowed down my discomfort and carried the drinks to the front counter. My smile felt stiff like a mask, but I forced it to hold. "Here you go!" I set the drink carrier on the countertop and backed away a step, scanning the café for any excuse to make a polite exit. Unfortunately, the only other patron at the moment was a quiet, middle-aged guy in the corner with headphones on, typing away on his laptop between sips of iced coffee. He wasn't much help in terms of a plausible reason to extricate myself from this conversation.

There was another awkward moment of silence as Madison waited for me to say something, or maybe tried to decide what new insult she could throw at me—she was always subtle in her torment of me, never anything outwardly cruel that I could report her for—then she sighed and grabbed the drinks. "Let's go."

The four of them bounced out of the café, hair swishing, designer purses slung high on their shoulders.

The bell over the café door dinged as the door shut behind them.

As soon as they were gone, Larissa turned to me. Her green-dyed bangs flopped over one heavily mascaraed eye as she tilted her head. "Okay, spill. What is the deal between you and those girls?"

Larissa was new to Havenridge, at least compared to the rest of us native townies from who-knows-how-many generations back. I'd never even spoken to her until I got the job at the café, but she was kind and easy to talk to. When I'd asked her why anyone would move to a place like Havenridge, her answer was it was cheaper than Miami, which was where her parents had wanted her to go to college. Instead, she'd decided to take a year off to work, chose a random small town within bus distance of the airport, and looked for a job and a cheap place to live. Gary's had been the first place hiring, though she soon got a second job at the hardware store down the street, as well. That had been two years ago, and she was still here, with no plans to move. She said she liked it here, though I couldn't help but wonder what her parents thought.

Larissa's fingers fidgeted with the edges of her green Gary's Café apron, and her dark eyes peered at me, waiting for an answer.

I shrugged.

She put her hands on her hips. "Should I beat them up for you?"

A laugh escaped me. "No. Definitely don't do that." I quickly summarized what happened the year prior with Madison's brother.

Larissa narrowed her eyes in concern. "And you can't, like, apologize?"

"Believe me, I've tried!" I threw up a hand in exasperation. "More than once, especially right after they expelled him. I told her I never meant to ruin his plans for college. But Madison said I should've thought of that before I ran my mouth." I dropped my hand. "'Sorry doesn't *unruin* his life,' I think were her exact words. She's made my life difficult every chance she can get since then, along with convincing most everyone else to pretend I don't exist. Hardly anyone in our senior class will even talk to me."

Larissa's face softened with sympathy. "I'm sorry, Ayla. I know it can't be easy to deal with that. Maybe she'll come around in time?"

I sighed. "I hope so." Not that I was putting much weight on those hopes. I'd resigned myself to just getting through the rest of my senior year and hoping Madison would get into some fancy college far, far away from wherever I ended up going, if I could even save up enough to attend anywhere. At least my two closest friends, Jordan and Reina, still talked to me. I wasn't super close to *anyone*, if I was honest, and didn't hang out much with Jordan and Reina outside of school—but since elementary school they'd been the two who didn't seem bothered by my shyness or awkwardness. Making it through senior year would have been so much harder if I didn't at least have them to talk to.

Larissa patted my shoulder, then glanced at the clock. "I'm sorry, Ayla, but it's time for me to go." She slid past me and pulled off her apron. "I've got to go grab some actual food before I start my late shift at the hardware store." She smiled. "Can't live on pastries and coffee, you know?"

I was pretty sure you could, but I didn't argue. "Sure, no worries. I'm locking up tonight." The café closed at ten, but Gary liked for someone to do a full inventory of the kitchen supplies every night, tidy up, and leave a fresh checklist for the cleaning person who came early each morning, so she wouldn't miss any gum wads stuck in the corners of tables or anything.

Larissa quirked an eyebrow. "You've been taking the closing shift a lot for a newbie. Your parents are okay with you working until midnight?"

"Yeah, sure." I shrugged again. "It's Saturday, so granted I stay awake in church tomorrow, they don't care if I'm here late as long as I check in. They stay up late, anyway." I got paid extra for closing, so I'd taken every late shift I could convince Gary to give me for the coming week—which wasn't many. My parents weren't thrilled that I was scheduled until midnight two nights of the week, but they said they'd let it slide as long as my grades didn't suffer. It helped that they'd known Gary for basically forever. Besides, the café was at the corner of a small intersection outside our subdivision. The stray dog who ran through a few weeks ago, chasing down anyone on bicycles, was literally the most dangerous thing that had happened in this part of town in decades.

Larissa shook her head. "If you say so. But don't push too hard, okay? It's just a job."

"Don't you have *two* jobs?" Now it was my turn to shake my head.

Larissa laughed. "Yeah, but I'm at *least* three years older than you. I'm an adult. Adulting is hard, don't you know that? Enjoy your youth while it lasts." She hunched over, hand on her back. "My aching spine! Oh, to be young again!"

I chuckled and gave Larissa a playful slap on the shoulder. "Whatever."

Larissa straightened. "Anyway, I do need to go." She signed out, then darted to Gary's office and rapped her knuckles on the door. "I'm leaving!"

"See you tomorrow, Larissa," Gary's muffled voice answered through the door.

She grabbed her purse from the hooks below the counter and turned to me with a smile. "Have a good night, kiddo."

The bell above the door dinged as she slipped out, and again as the door shut behind her. The café felt suddenly so much quieter and emptier, despite Gary's eclectic mood music, which still droned some kind of piccolo duet through the speakers above. Laptop Man was nearing the bottom of his iced coffee, but seemed to be in his own little world with his headphones and work. I glanced around, noticing a spill on one tabletop. I grabbed a rag and the spray cleaner. Time to get back to work.

About thirty minutes later, Zach showed up, the skinny, quiet kid a couple years younger than me who'd been working here since last summer. He was pleasant enough, but incredibly shy, and since I'd never been able to get more than a couple words at a time from him in any attempt at conversation, we settled into working in comfortable silence instead.

I worked the kitchen while Zach manned the front counter. More patrons trickled in over the next few hours, ate their pastries, drank their coffees, chatted a bit, then left. Eventually, Laptop Man left, too, and another new trickle of patrons cycled in. Finally, 10 PM hit, and Zach clocked out without saying a word. A few moments later, the cello duel in the overhead speakers cut off, and Gary emerged from his office.

"Long day," he muttered through his hand while covering a yawn. "Got all the inventory checklists updated and ready for you. You gonna be okay locking up?"

I nodded. "Yep. Totally fine."

"Tablet's on my desk if you want music." Gary eyed me seriously. "Don't forget to text your parents."

"I wouldn't dream of it." I reached under the counter and slid my cell phone from my purse. "See? Doing it right now." I tapped out a quick text to my mom—*Gary's leaving. I'll lock the door behind him. Be home after midnight.*

He nodded in satisfaction and headed for the door. "Lock it behind me!" he called out as it dinged shut.

"Already on it." I turned the deadbolt until the lock thunked closed and waved through the glass door. "Night, Gary."

"Goodnight, Ayla." He waved back, then disappeared down the sidewalk. A moment later, I saw his headlights as his car started up and pulled out of the small parking lot.

I stifled a yawn myself and headed to the kitchen to start inventory.

Nearly two hours later, my feet were killing me and my back was aching from stooping to count boxes of napkins in the bottom of the storage closet, but the inventory was done, the tables were wiped, and I was almost ready to go home. I walked to the front counter and bent to retrieve my cell phone, then sank down to the floor, stretching out my cramped legs. *About to sign out. Be home soon,* I texted.

We're still up, my mother texted back. *Your father just got back from the convenience store down the street. Grandpa wanted popcorn.*

I chuckled. Of course he did. Grandpa had been living with us since I could remember, and most of the time we all got along fine, but when he was in a late-night snacking mood, there was no convincing him otherwise.

I dropped my phone back into my purse, but before I could stand, a strange trill sliced through the air.

I froze mid-crouch. Had Gary's weird music somehow turned back on? But no, this had been different, almost like... an electrical sound. My heart raced as I stood, eyes scanning for a sparking outlet, a frayed wire—I don't know what I was expecting.

I certainly was *not* expecting the strange guy I found curled in a ball on the floor by the café door, trembling and clutching his side.

I rushed toward him, though not too close. "Sir, are you okay?" My heart lurched with concern, but my pulse raced with panic. I'd locked the front door, hadn't I? I was sure I had—*How did he get in here?*

He turned his face up at me, and I gasped as his gorgeous, deep-blue eyes locked on mine. He looked to be about my age, though I'd never seen him before. He was wearing strange clothes, like the ones the theater kids liked to wear to the Renaissance Fair a couple of towns over. His brown hair fell haphazardly over one side of his forehead, and his face was just about the most perfect face I'd ever seen on a guy.

"Help me," he whispered.

And then he passed out.

"Oh no. Oh, no no no!" I turned to run back for my phone and call for help, but my foot caught on his outstretched arm. A glass vial clattered from his hand.

A strange, iridescent liquid glinted inside it, and something about it captivated me. I knew I shouldn't—it could be illegal drugs or something—but I reached for the vial. It was warm to the touch, whether from the guy's hand or the contents, I wasn't sure. The stopper was partway pulled loose, like he'd been trying to open it. What if it was a medication or something? Like anti-seizure meds? Heart meds? Without knowing what it was or how much to give him, I didn't dare risk it. I glanced at the counter, knowing I should get my phone and call 911, but something deep within me whispered, *The vial*. I debated only for a second, then clutched the vial in my palm and rushed for my phone.

While I waited anxiously for the call to connect, I hurried back over to the guy and popped open the vial, wafting its contents like Mr. Slate showed us in chemistry class. It had no odor I could detect.

The guy twitched.

I screamed and dropped the vial. It hit the guy's shoulder, dumping most of its contents on his shirt before shattering on the floor.

I jumped backward, but not far enough—a shard of glass jabbed through the bottom of my sneaker as my foot came down. "Ow!" I yelled, yanking my foot up in pain.

"911, what's your emergency?" the voice over the phone asked.

"Um, there's..." I hobbled to the nearest table, sank into a chair, and peeled the sneaker from my foot. The ball of my foot was bleeding, but not badly. Just a small cut. "There's a guy here, and he's—" I looked up, and the words died in my mouth.

The guy had vanished.

Chapter 2

Pomegranate Jam

Sunday morning came too early after my night of fitful sleep, but once my family and I arrived at the small community center where our church met for worship, I was glad I'd come. Our church was a little group, only a few dozen people, but Gary and Mr. Slate and some others I knew from school and businesses in the community were there. Whenever our church met, I always felt safe, like people were happy to see me. And somehow, when we sang and prayed, the worries from outside the building receded a little. Of course, it also helped that Madison and her family were not there. They were part of a larger church that met downtown. Sundays were one of the few times I was almost guaranteed not to run into Madison in our small town, and I was grateful for it.

This morning, however, the friendly smiles that usually greeted me as I entered the community center also held curiosity and concern—everyone had heard about the strange intruder at Gary's Café. I smoothed my frizzy hair down and tucked it behind my ears, wishing I'd gone with a bun today as usual.

Gary was the first to reach me as I stepped through the door. "How are you this morning, Ayla?" he asked, clasping my shoulder and peering at me with wide, sympathetic eyes. "Quite a scare last night. Were you able to get any sleep?"

The police had arrived soon after I'd stammered an incoherent explanation to the 911 operator about a break-in and an unconscious guy and a vanishing man, last night. The officers who responded to the call were probably expecting to have to set up a perimeter and go through hostage negotiations with some kind of crazed intruder, but by the time they arrived, it was just me and some broken glass and my sore foot, which had already stopped bleeding. I could barely even see the cut anymore, though I still felt the tender place when I put weight on it.

I nodded at Gary. "Yeah, a little."

I'd called my parents the moment I got off the phone with 911, and they'd called Gary. All three of them had shown up within minutes. I'd offered to help Gary clean up the broken glass, but he'd insisted I go home and rest. After the police took my statement and made sure I went home safely with my parents, they'd scoured the block and the surrounding areas and even checked the local hospital, but found no sign of the guy I'd seen. The consensus was that he'd been homeless, maybe someone who fell sick while traveling through our town, not anyone who'd meant to rob the café or hurt me.

Gary's smile oozed concern. "Well, make sure you take it easy today. I'm glad you're okay."

I nodded again, and Gary gave me one last pat on the shoulder before wandering off to find his seat.

I still felt bad for the mess he'd had to clean up the night before.

My dad met my gaze across the small crowd and waved me over to where he, Grandpa, and my mom had taken seats near the back row. The faint crow's feet at the edges of Dad's hazel eyes crinkled with the smile he gave me as I took my seat near them. I was thankful my parents shared my disdain for sitting near the front. I certainly didn't feel up to everyone's stares on the back of my head today.

Our church didn't have a formal preacher; we didn't even have a formal sermon. It was more like a group Bible study discussion, though there was usually someone leading it. Today, it was Nathaniel, the owner of the hardware store down the street from the café.

Though I flipped to the passage he called out and tried to focus, my mind wandered terribly. I'd run through my account of the events with the officers several times the night before, trying to be as honest as possible, but after repeating my story a few times, even I realized I had to have misremembered something. Physical, tangible human people don't walk into a café through the brick walls. There was no tampering to the front door, which was still locked after he vanished, but the police thought he may have made his way in through the emergency exit in the kitchen when I wasn't looking and possibly exited the same way, since the door was shut but not clicked closed when they checked it. I thought through the night's events and realized I might not have checked the emergency door when I locked up, and Larissa had used it earlier in the day to take out the trash. The door had no audible alarms on it. I supposed it was possible he'd snuck in while I was focused on inventory and stumbled out again while I was distracted by my hurt foot—at least, that made more sense than any other explanation I could offer. I felt embarrassed about the 911 call, and for apparently not noticing a strange guy walking right into the building, but since then everyone had been so grateful I hadn't been hurt and that nothing was taken or damaged, my embarrassment had faded a bit.

My mom nudged my arm from beside me. I glanced at her, expecting a reprimand for being distracted, but her gaze was questioning. *Are you okay?* she mouthed.

I nodded, but when a moment later Gary passed around the box of hymn books, I grabbed one eagerly, relieved it was time to sing so I'd have something more active to do to focus my body and mind away from my confusions about last night.

Worship ended a while later with a prayer, in which Gary specifically mentioned the young man I'd seen at the café. He prayed for health and safety for the guy, and that he'd gotten whatever help he needed, or would return safely to seek help again, if he still needed it. Something about the sincerity of Gary's prayer, and the genuine *amens* that echoed it, gave my heart peace. The guy I'd seen the night before was not a threat to be feared; he was a person in need of help. I might not have been so quick to believe that, except that I could still feel the pull of his eyes. Those blue eyes held no malice when they locked on mine—they'd been swimming with pain and desperation, shaded with a faint tinge of hope. Those eyes... they were the reason I'd gotten so little sleep last night. Every time I closed my own eyes, I saw *his*.

The assembly concluded, and the casual shuffle of folding chairs and chattering conversations burst into life around me.

My mom reached for my hand. "I promised Marge last week I'd go over and help her replant some azaleas this afternoon. Will you be all right?"

I smiled at her, noticing the dark circles beneath her expertly made-up eyes. "Yeah, of course."

Mom squeezed my hand and smiled back. "There's leftover roast in the fridge. I'll be home this afternoon." She slipped her hand from mine and went to join my dad near the exit, probably repeating a similar reminder to him.

Grandpa planted his cane on the floor and stood up from the folding chair two seats down from mine, grunting as he stretched his back. "Never liked reheated roast." He ran a wrinkled hand over the pale scruff on his cheeks, then his brown eyes met mine mischievously across the empty chairs. "How 'bout I call in a pizza?"

I fought back a smirk as I slid Grandpa my phone.

Dad had either acquiesced to Grandpa's pizza idea, or maybe conspired on it, because he didn't seem surprised when we pulled into our driveway about thirty minutes later to find two hot pizzas waiting on our front porch. Dad helped Grandpa up the front steps while I brought in the pizza boxes.

The pizza was gloriously cheesy, Grandpa's and my favorite extra pepperoni selection from the mom-and-pop Pizza Haven around the block. By the time Grandpa had finished his fourth slice, his eyes were going hazy.

"Time for this old man to take a nap," he muttered. "Tired today."

Dad and I shared a glance of concern. My grandpa was hilarious and loving when he was lucid, and one of the best storytellers I'd ever known. He owned about every type of book known to man, many I was sure no one else had ever heard of, organized two rows deep on the shelves that lined his bedroom. But when he was "off"... he was a little scary, to be honest. Doctors said it was dementia, but Grandpa getting tired suddenly was one of the first signs of an episode coming on. It used to only happen once in a while. Now it happened a few times a month, and lasted for several hours, sometimes a whole day. Those were the nights Dad would sit up outside Grandpa's room to make sure Grandpa didn't run away or hurt himself... or anyone else. Not that Grandpa would ever hurt any of us on purpose. I knew he loved us. He just... wasn't himself sometimes. It wasn't his fault.

Dad rose from his chair, tightening his arms around Grandpa's shoulders to help him to his feet. "Come on, let's get you to bed."

Grandpa stood and let Dad lead him away from the table, but before they reached the hallway, Grandpa turned his head back to me. "Ayla, I've got a sudden craving for pomegranate jam. Do you think you could get me some?"

I gaped at him. "Uh, yeah. Sure." How hard could it be to find, right?

Dad smiled thinly at me. "Thanks, honey. Call me if you need anything while you're out."

While Dad got Grandpa settled in, I grabbed my purse and keys from the hooks by the front door and slipped outside.

The air outside was summer-hot even though it was well into September, typical for Florida. I unlocked my old, beat up, blue-grey 1995 Chrysler Cirrus and slid into the driver's seat. Perspiration sprung up on my face and back from the steamy interior as I gripped the searing leather of the steering wheel gingerly and started up the car, turning the AC on full blast. This car had undergone so many repairs over the years that little besides the body was an original part anymore. I was just thankful it still ran.

It turned out pomegranate jam was harder to find than I'd expected. By the time the sun crested past the top of the sky and afternoon storms threatened the humid Florida air, I had exhausted all three of our town's major grocery stores, our only specialty food store, and two local produce stands. I pulled to the side of the road and texted my mom for help. To my surprise, her reply pointed me in a promising direction: *Try Jim Baker's farm, down the road. Marge says he makes it homemade.*

Mom texted me Jim's number, and to my immense relief, he met me at the gate to his farm with a paper bag of two jam jars and a huge smile. "Glad I could help," he said when I thanked him profusely. "I respect what you're doing, looking out for your grandpa. Tell him I'm happy to work up some extra jars of jam for him anytime."

A flash of lightning sliced the sky, followed by a boom of thunder.

"Better get home quick," Jim said.

I smiled and thanked him again, then slipped into my idling car and hurried for home. The sky broke open the moment I pulled into our driveway, and I made a mad dash for the house, bursting in soaking wet through the front door with my sopping hair dripping on the wood floors.

Dad looked up at me in alarm from his armchair in the living room, but when his eyes fell on the soggy paper bag in my arms, he grinned. "You found some?"

"Yes, finally. Jim's farm." I held the bag up victoriously. "How's Grandpa?"

Dad closed his book. "Okay, so far. Sleeping, last I checked."

Mom emerged from the kitchen with an oven mitt on one hand and her long, dark hair that matched mine tied back in a ponytail. She smiled at me. "You hungry? I reheated the roast."

I changed into comfy sweatpants and a t-shirt, dried my hair with a towel, and joined my parents at the dining table. By the time we finished eating dinner, it had grown dark outside, and I was feeling the effects of my previous night's lack of sleep.

"Your mom and I will clean up," Dad said, eyeing my exhausted face after I'd zoned out during our conversation for about the third time in a row. "Why don't you head to bed? Tomorrow's a school day."

My stomach twisted with anxiety. *Don't remind me.* I didn't mind the academics at all—I enjoyed learning. But the people were another story.

I nodded and rose from the table, then walked to the kitchen, scraped my plate, and slid it into the soapy water Mom already had in the sink. "Thanks. I'll check on Grandpa on my way."

Dad kissed the top of my head as he walked past me. "Thanks, kiddo. Goodnight."

I stopped halfway down the hall that contained Grandpa's and my bedrooms, and eased open his door. He was asleep flat on his back, mouth open, snoring. I watched him for a moment, his chest rising and falling peacefully, then quietly shut the door and tiptoed away.

I stumbled half-awake through a shower and got dressed for bed, set out my clothes and backpack for the next day, and brushed my hair and teeth. Moonlight poured in over my bed through the bedroom window, lighting it like a spotlight. Grandpa liked the house cold, and with the chill from my wet hair and after the long couple days I'd had, the soft, warm comforter and fluffy pillow called to me intensely.

The cut on my foot began aching the moment I curled up beneath the covers and closed my eyes. It hadn't bothered me all day, but I supposed being on my feet so much visiting all those stores might have irritated it. I hunkered deeper beneath my comforter. Sleep quickly took me, but all night I dreamed of only one thing, over and over—the stranger and I standing face to face in a black abyss, his deep blue eyes locked on mine in passionate focus, his lips forming silent words I couldn't understand and his hands gesturing wildly, as though trying to tell me something important.

Chapter 3

Odysseus and Rumpelstiltskin

I turned into the parking lot of my high school the next morning, trying to ignore the glances cast at me from nearby cars. I knew everyone had heard about the stranger at the café. Unusual things didn't happen very often in our town, and judging from the eager curiosity in the stares of the other students milling around the parking lot, I would be answering a million questions about it before I even made it to first period. I wished I could drive back home and crawl into bed.

I'd just pulled my car into an open spot and cut the old Cirrus' engine when Madison Kane swung her shiny yellow convertible into the spot beside me. Her blonde hair looked perfectly windblown, like something from a magazine. *How does she do that?* If I'd driven a convertible, my hair would've been a hopeless mass of tangles. Her gaze slid over to me for only a second before she flounced out of her car and strode right past me, pointedly looking in the other direction. So she'd decided to ignore me today. Well, that was better than the alternative. Maybe today wouldn't be so bad, after all.

To my surprise, no one asked questions, though I continued to feel their stares on me as I navigated the crowded hallway, pulled books from my locker, and tromped down the hall to class. Maybe Madison's directive to pretend I didn't exist was overruling their curiosity. Whatever the reason, I was glad to be left alone.

Relief flooded me the moment I made it to homeroom. None of Madison's posse were in this period, so I had at least a few minutes of solace during roll call and announcements where I didn't have to worry about seeing any of them. Despite homeroom being the shortest period of the day, I was thankful it existed.

Reina rushed at me the moment my sneakers crossed the homeroom threshold. Her sleek red hair was pulled back into a high ponytail, and comfy-looking jeans cloaked her long legs, topped with a faded Beatles t-shirt. Her green eyes sparked with excitement as she pulled me toward the desks. "Tell. Me. Everything."

I laughed. I didn't mind *her* asking questions—she was my friend, not just someone wanting the latest headline. I slid my backpack to the floor, settled into the desk beside hers, and plopped my heavy literature textbook on the desktop. "There's not much to tell. Probably only what you already heard." My eyes flicked to the desk in front of hers, where Jordan had turned sideways when he heard us coming.

"Hey, Ayla." Jordan gave a small wave, and my heart skipped a little at the way his mouth quirked up into a half-smile as he met my eyes.

"Hi, Jordan." I waved back.

Jordan and I had always been school friends, the kind who hung out at school but not much else, but in the past few weeks something had shifted. It wasn't just that he'd changed over the summer. He definitely *had* changed; he'd filled out in all the best ways, lean muscles replacing the scrawny frame which had always been swallowed by his baggy t-shirts and jeans. But it wasn't only that. It was also the way he looked at me now, like he hadn't fully noticed me before and suddenly found me intensely interesting. Before, our conversations had always been casual, mostly kept to whatever was happening at school. He didn't talk much about his life at home, or ask me about mine. But since the start of this school year, he'd been lingering longer in conversations, taking the seat beside me more often than usual, and generally seeming to want to spend more time with me.

"Earth to Ayla," Reina said, tilting her head to stare at me. Her ponytail flopped over onto her shoulder. "Weren't you about to tell me *everything* about Saturday night?"

"Oh," I said, tearing my eyes from Jordan's. "Right."

Jordan settled back in his chair, his gaze immediately going distant, though Reina seemed not to notice. She stared at me eagerly, waiting.

I took a breath and explained. It didn't take long to summarize everything that happened at the café, and by the end of my story, Jordan was sitting on the edge of his chair again, intrigued.

"So they're sure he came in through the emergency exit?" he asked, his caramel eyes narrowing beneath his lowered brows.

"No—I mean, they think so, yes. But I still can't figure out how he walked right past me while I was on the phone. He didn't look in much shape to walk." I shrugged. "But I guess he must have."

"Doesn't Gary have security cameras?" Reina asked.

I laughed. "Um, no. He believes they'd only make him vulnerable to cyber hacks."

Jordan raised an eyebrow. "I mean, he's not wrong... strictly speaking. Though there are plenty of ways to secure them and if he's worried, he could always go with an offline system."

Reina shook her head. "Jordan, our resident tech support." She laughed, but her smile was kind.

Jordan shrugged. "Just saying." He smiled at her, but his eyes bounced quickly back to mine.

Static crackled over the intercom, then the voice of the assistant principal blared through the wall speaker. "Please stand for the Pledge of Allegiance."

Reina jumped to her feet. "Guess we'll have to talk more later!"

Our homeroom teacher, Mrs. Blaylock, called roll immediately after the Pledge and announcements, and the bell rang right after that, leaving us no time to continue our conversation. I reached for my backpack, dread weighing down my stomach at the thought of first-period literature class without Jordan or Reina. I loved literature, but Madison and Ansley were both in that class, along with Madison's male-model-wannabe boyfriend, Trevor.

"See you at lunch!" Reina called as she bounced out into the filling hallway.

Jordan lingered at his desk, standing when I stood. He ran a hand through his messy blonde hair as his eyes studied mine. "Can I walk you to class?"

My stomach exploded into a flock of swarming butterflies. "Um, sure."

He reached for the textbook on my desk at the same moment I did, his hand brushing mine.

He yanked his hand back. "Sorry, I just—you want me to carry that for you?" He gestured to the book. "Your backpack looks heavy enough."

He wasn't wrong about that; my classes were so spread out this year that each morning I had to stuff my backpack with every book I needed from first period until lunch, since I wouldn't have time to return to my locker. He'd never offered to carry anything for me before, though. I hesitated a moment—I could still feel a tingle where his hand had touched mine—then shook my head. "No, that's okay, thanks." Self-sufficiency was good, right? Plus, he had his own books to carry.

Disappointment flitted across his eyes, but only for a second. "No worries," he said. "Let me know if you change your mind." He hefted his own backpack onto his shoulder and gestured toward the door. "After you."

We walked side by side down the hall, neither of us speaking, though we would've had to yell to be heard above all the commotion of kids chattering, hurrying to classes, and slamming lockers, anyway. I felt a strange mix of excitement and nervousness as we walked, and when we finally reached my classroom, I was both relieved and disappointed.

"See you at lunch, Ayla," he said quietly. His eyes lingered on mine, then he turned and melted into the crowd of students hurrying to class.

I took a sharp breath, let it out in a huff, and opened the door to my classroom.

Madison and Ansley were already side-by-side in their desks, with Trevor seated backward in his chair in front of Madison, leaning his elbows on her desktop as the three of them talked. Ansley's eyes cut to me as I hurried inside and slid into my desk, but Madison seemed resolved to ignore me. I hoped that boded well for the trajectory of the rest of my day, since we had two other classes together.

Mr. Yager took his position in front of the whiteboard, pushing his glasses into place on his nose, then smoothing his plaid button-down shirt over his portly belly as he stared at us. After a moment of shuffling as Trevor and any others who weren't properly in their desks turned forward, the room fell quiet.

"Three words for the concept we're going to discuss today," Mr. Yager said. "Law of Names." He scrawled the words onto the board in red dry-erase marker, then turned back to the class. "In folklore, mythology, fairy tales, and even some religions, this is the concept that a person or object can have a 'true name'"—he punctuated the term with finger quotes—"and that the person who knows this true name will have control over the corresponding object or person."

I leaned forward in my desk. This topic was a far cry from the *Moby Dick* excerpts we'd been reading from the textbook, but I'd always found fairy tales, mythology, and folklore fascinating.

"World Myths and Legends Day is coming up next month, and I'll be assigning each of you a presentation topic to prepare for our in-class event for that day." He wrote *October 11* on the board, then clicked the cap of the marker shut and turned back to face us. "In the meantime, we'll be doing a special unit discussing the overlaps between folklore, mythology, and fairy tales—starting with this concept of true names. Can anyone kick off our discussion by giving an example of a fairy tale, lore, or myth where this Law of Names plays an important role?"

To my surprise—and also Mr. Yager's, based on how his eyebrows jetted up into his wrinkled forehead—Trevor's hand shot up. Trevor rarely spoke up in class; literature didn't seem to be a subject of much interest to him. Or at least, turning around to flirt with Madison every chance he got had always been of *more* interest.

Mr. Yager stared at Trevor for a moment before calling on him. "Yes, Mr. Lawson?"

Everyone in the class pivoted to stare back at Trevor.

"Rumpelstiltskin," Trevor blurted.

Ansley giggled, but cut it off short when Madison shot her a warning glare.

Mr. Yager looked intrigued. "Go on," he said encouragingly.

"Well," Trevor said, chewing his bottom lip for a moment in thought. "Knowing his true name was the secret to getting free of the bargain the woman had made. So it must have had power, right?"

Mr. Yager nodded thoughtfully. "That's possible, yes, although some think it was the bargain that carried that power—that if the woman could discover his name in time, he would not take her firstborn child—rather than the name itself. Still, it is interesting that his true name was what he bargained with. Yes, I think that fits our discussion."

Trevor turned a triumphant grin back at Ansley and Madison.

"Good job, Trevor!" Madison beamed at him, and Ansley shrugged.

"Anyone else?" Mr. Yager asked.

I sank back in my chair, hoping Mr. Yager wouldn't randomly start calling on people as he sometimes did, but it seemed my luck for the day had already worn off.

"Miss Rogers." Mr. Yager's eyes landed on me. "You seemed very interested during the beginning of our discussion. Did you have something you wanted to add?"

"Um, no?" I felt the heat rush to my cheeks.

"I'm sure you know at least one example, don't you?" His eyes were kind, but insistent.

He had me there. He knew I was into myths and folklore; those topics had been among the books he'd signed out to me for extracurricular reading from his personal class library earlier in the school year.

"Okay," I said, mind racing. "Maybe Odysseus?"

"Very good!" Mr. Yager grinned at me, then turned his gaze back to the overall class. "Yes. After hiding his identity from the cyclops Polyphemus and giving him a false name as a trick, Odysseus foolishly admits his true name to Polyphemus after blinding him. It is that true name which allows Polyphemus to pray for his father, Poseidon, to exact revenge on Odysseus. Had Odysseus remained anonymous, Polyphemus would not have known whom to ask his father to punish."

Relief spread through my chest that I'd given a correct answer. Hopefully that meant I could resume blending into my desk chair and attract no further notice for the remainder of class.

"Nice one, Ayla," Trevor called out.

My heart sped as I twisted around, expecting to see a mocking expression, but his smile was genuine.

Confused and red-faced, I spun back to the front, catching the edge of an icy glare from Madison as I turned. *Great.*

"Thank you for that... encouragement, Mr. Lawson," Mr. Yager said, seeming a little dumbfounded. "Anyway, we can find this concept repeated in many well-known legends, myths, and belief systems, including the Scandinavian belief that some magical beasts could be defeated by calling their names, and the Irish lore that children who were not baptized at birth were more likely to be kidnapped by faeries and replaced by changelings, which some believe was tied to the fact that such babies would not yet have been formally christened and therefore lacked true names to protect them. Even the Biblical creation account emphasizes the importance of names, with God bringing all the creatures before Adam and instructing him to name them." Mr. Yager popped the cap off his red marker again and turned his back to us as he scrawled on the board—*The beginning of wisdom is to call things by their proper name.* "A quote attributed to Confucius, and a fitting way to end today's introduction, don't you think? Now, let me explain this week's home—"

Mr. Yager cut off mid-sentence as someone knocked on our classroom door.

"Yes?" he replied, striding over to open it.

Mrs. Hale, the office assistant, poked her head in. "I have a new student. Joined this morning."

"Oh!" Mr. Yager stepped back, swinging the door wide. "Come on in, then. Welcome to AP Literature!"

The office assistant moved aside, and I caught my first glimpse of the new student, just the side of his face in the doorway as he turned to answer something Mrs. Hale had asked.

My heart stopped.

The shaggy brown hair, the profile of his jaw, the distinct shade of tannish skin, even the lean, muscular build—it had to be him.

The boy from the café.

CHAPTER 4

CASSEROLE AND AGED PAPER

I t wasn't him, after all. I realized that the moment he stepped fully into the classroom and I saw his round, deep brown eyes, nothing like the thick-lashed, almond-shaped blue ones that had been haunting my dreams. Disappointment dropped like a heavy anchor to the pit of my stomach, taking my fleeting hope with it. For a moment, I'd thought I might get some answers about what happened at the café.

The new kid was handsome, though, and his face bore a strong resemblance to the guy I'd seen the other night. I wondered immediately if they were cousins or something, though that would've been a ridiculous coincidence.

Mr. Yager thanked the office assistant, then closed the classroom door. "Put down your stuff and get comfortable," he said, directing the new kid to an empty desk a couple of rows up from mine. "Would you mind telling the class your name?"

The guy turned to face the rest of us, his gaze sweeping quickly over each row of desks. It seemed his eyes lingered on me for a millisecond, but I couldn't be sure. "Callan Hecklam," he said to no one in particular, then strode to the empty desk and slid into it, setting his backpack on the ground. He brushed his hands on his jeans, and for a moment I thought he might pull out hand sanitizer or something, but instead he turned stiffly forward in his desk.

"Welcome, Callan." Mr. Yager smiled, then walked back to the board. "Now, where were we?"

Word traveled fast in our high school—about everything. The moment I stepped into the cafeteria for lunch, Reina launched up from our usual table, beelining for me through the crowd.

"I heard you had a class with the new kid," she said, tugging me by the hand toward the circular table. "What's his name? Where's he from? Is he as hot as they say?" She plopped into her seat, then unzipped her insulated lunch bag and pulled out a plastic-wrapped sandwich.

"See for yourself," I muttered as a hush fell over the cafeteria.

Callan stood in the doorway, looking lost and overwhelmed. The shocked silence of staring at a new kid lasted only a moment, then the cafeteria burst back into chattered conversations—probably all about him.

"He lives up to the hype," Reina murmured dreamily. She dropped her sandwich on the table and popped up onto her feet. "I'm going to invite him to sit with us!"

"You're what? Wait, I—" But she was already gone. "Of course you are," I muttered to myself as Reina shoved through the milling crowd. I sank into an empty chair and leaned away from the table, trying to see past the rapidly forming lunch line to get a clear view of their interaction near the door.

"Tough day?" Jordan set his lunch tray on the table.

I jumped and turned to him as he took the seat next to me. "What? Oh. No. I mean… no more than usual, really."

Jordan studied my face. "You look stressed."

I huffed a dry laugh. "When am I not?"

Jordan's mouth quirked up into an adorable smile. "You make a good point." He eyed the empty table. "Aren't you eating? Do you want me to get in line to get you something?"

The butterflies in my gut awakened from their slumber. "Um, no, I'll go in a minute. Reina just—"

Before I could explain how or why Reina had waylaid me at the door, her sing-songy voice swept over our table. "Here we are!" She flung a hand out toward the one open spot left at our table and grinned. "We may not be the most popular kids, but at least we're friendly, right? This is Jordan, and you may have already met Ayla—"

"Not officially," Callan answered, his dark eyes locking on mine.

"Nice to meet you." Jordan gave Callan a wave, but then his eyes bounced from Callan to me, and his brows drew together in concern.

"Anyway," Reina sang, seeming not to notice, "have a seat! Did you bring lunch, or do you need to get in line?"

"I'm not hungry." Callan moved toward the empty chair beside Jordan and sank into it, then turned a warm smile to Reina. "But thank you. I appreciate how kind you've been so far."

Reina settled back into her seat next to him and grinned. "My pleasure."

The four of us stared silently at each other for a moment across the round table, like four distinct points of a compass.

I sucked in a breath. "I'd better go get in line. Be back in a few." I grabbed my wallet from my backpack and jumped up from my chair, rushing away before any of them could offer to come with me.

The line moved slowly, and I hugged my arms across my chest as I waited, pondering this strange turn of events and trying to make sense of the emotions tumbling in my chest and stomach like wet laundry in a dryer. Somehow, in three days flat, I'd gone from invisible to the center of town drama... as if I needed more of that just when everyone but Madison was finally losing interest in the scandal about Rory from last year. I chewed my lip, trying to sort through the chaotic, toppling mess inside me. Every now and then, a flicker of panic would ping through, like a loose quarter clanking against the inside of the dryer. What had I gotten myself into?

The line shifted bit by bit, until finally it was my turn to receive a steaming heap of gravy-soaked vegetable casserole and a cold, stiff bread roll. I grabbed a bottle of water from the cooler, paid the cashier, and trudged back to the table.

To my surprise, the mood had lifted considerably while I was gone. Jordan smiled up at me as I lowered my tray and sat down. "Not the most appetizing presentation," he said, gesturing to my tray, "but it doesn't taste that awful." He shrugged.

"Good to know." I grabbed my fork from the tray and poked at the lump of food. I was hungry, and I knew I'd regret it if I skipped lunch, but the tumbling laundry in my stomach made it difficult to want to eat anything. I scooped a bite into my mouth, forced it down, and was pleased to find that Jordan was right. It didn't taste as bad as it looked.

"Callan was telling us about where he's from." Reina grinned and leaned toward me. "He does *martial arts*."

She drew out the last two words like they were a scintillating secret. There weren't many black belts roaming around Havenridge... or any I could think of. I wasn't even sure there was a dojo anywhere. Our town was more of a football and farmers sort of place.

"So, where *are* you from?" I met Callan's eyes, ignoring the anxious fluttering in my stomach as their brown depths locked back on me.

"Orlando." He shrugged. "Ever been there?"

"Only once as a little kid." Orlando was only a couple of hours away. My parents had taken me there to go to Disney World when I was four. I didn't remember it, but they had the pictures to prove it.

The end-of-lunch bell rang, and the cafeteria burst into noisy chaos as students shoved their chairs back from the tables and stood.

Reina sighed. "Time to go." She turned to Callan. "What's your next class? Do you know how to find it?"

"I'm not sure." Callan scooted his chair back and pulled a folded schedule out of his jeans pocket.

Reina leaned toward him. "Here, let me see."

"You didn't get to finish your lunch." Jordan's concerned face pulled my attention from Callan and Reina. "Here, wait." He bent over, digging into his backpack, then sat back up and handed me a protein bar. "Just in case."

Sparks of warmth flickered in my chest as I took the bar from him and smiled. "Thanks, Jordan." I slid it into the front pocket of my backpack.

"You're welcome." He smiled back. "Can I walk you to class?" The only class Jordan and I had together was art during the last period of the day, but his after-lunch computer science elective was around the corner from my next psychology class.

I cast another glance at Callan, wishing for some time to talk further with him, but Reina seemed to have things under control, and maybe I'd have another class or two with Callan before the day ended. If not, there was always after school. "Yeah, sure," I told Jordan.

He grinned. "Great! Here, let me get that." He took both of our trays, scraped them into the nearby trash bin, plopped the trays on the conveyor belt for dirty dishes, and strode back to the table. "Ready?"

Reina looked over at us. "Go ahead," she said cheerfully. "Callan's got history class with Mr. Moore. I can show him how to get there on my way to economics."

Callan's dark eyes met mine again. "I'll see you later? I think I might be in your art class, seventh period."

How did he know what my seventh period class was? Had I mentioned it? Jordan's expectant presence hovered behind me as I felt the blush rise to my cheeks. "Yeah, of course. Jordan will be there, too."

Callan's eyes flicked past my shoulders, locking on Jordan. "Sounds great." His smile seemed a little stiff, though that may have been my imagination.

Jordan's warm hand settled softly on my shoulder, and another tingle shot through me. "You ready?" he asked. "There's not much time left to get to class."

I spun toward him. "Of course. Sorry." If he was walking with me, he needed time to get to his class, too.

"I'm not." He smiled, then slipped my backpack from my shoulder. "You carry too much, too often. Let me take this."

This time, I let him. "Okay."

He settled my heavy bag onto the shoulder opposite his own. His golden eyes warmed from the light of the smile he gave me. "Let's go. I know you hate being late."

We walked to class with our arms nearly touching while my mind raced, trying to figure out if carrying my backpack was just Jordan being a good friend or something else. Jordan attempted to make small talk a couple of times, but the busy halls were so noisy I could barely hear him, and he eventually gave up. By the time we turned into my class hallway, the flopping laundry I'd had in my stomach at lunch had transformed back into ping-ponging butterflies. An improvement, at least, though it still made me want to hurl up the one bite I'd eaten of casserole.

When we reached the psychology classroom, Jordan slid my backpack off his shoulder and handed it back to me. "See you in two hours, Ayla." His eyes held mine for one lingering moment, then he spun and jogged through the thinning crowd in the hallway, disappearing around the corner as the bell rang for class. I startled from my daze and hurried inside.

Psychology and the following class, AP Calculus, slipped past in a haze of lectures and note-taking. I shoved my pencil and notebook into my backpack the moment the ending bell for calculus rang, and hurried out into the hallway toward the outer doors. Humid air hit me the moment I stepped outside. By the time I made it down the sidewalk to the art portable, sticky perspiration coated my face. I tried not to think about what my bun looked like; humidity and my hair were *not* friends. I made a futile attempt to smooth my hair as I strode up the steps to the portable.

The art teacher, Mrs. Flores, greeted me from her desk as soon as I pulled open the portable door. "Free period today." She smiled at me and nodded toward the chalkboard. "Work on whichever of your projects you prefer."

I glanced at the board, which had a cursive, white-chalk version of what she'd told me. I nodded my understanding and slipped past her.

Jordan was waiting for me at the table in the back, where we usually sat together. He'd already pulled both of our art portfolios from the storage shelves and had them ready on the table. He gestured to the empty chair on the other side of me as I sat next to him. "I pulled up a chair for Callan, in case he wants to sit by you."

Right, Callan. But why would he think Callan would want to sit by *me?* I offered a weak smile, unsure of what to say. This day was growing more confusing by the minute.

Jordan smiled back, then slid a charcoal sketch of a rearing horse from his portfolio and pulled his supplies from his backpack. He quickly focused in on his art.

I watched him as he hunched over the sketch, admiring the way his smooth, confident strokes made the image come to life, depth and texture emerging as he shaded and blended. He made it look easy.

He glanced at me from the corner of his eye and a smile tugged at his mouth, though he continued drawing.

I pulled my lackluster acrylic painting from my folder and stared at it despondently, wishing I'd been graced with some level of artistic talent. Painting seemed too messy at the moment, so I returned the page to the folder and pulled out an oil pastel drawing instead, a piece I'd created when Mrs. Flores was teaching us how to make interpretive word art using color and abstract images. The word I'd chosen was in the center of the page, surrounded by an explosion of colors in unrecognizable shapes that I'd meant to be abstract wings: *Hope.*

I glanced at the door, suddenly wondering what was taking Callan so long to get to class. Had he gotten lost? Anxious anticipation settled in my gut. I definitely had some more questions for Callan, but when he arrived, would things be awkward between Jordan and me again? Callan seemed to rub him the wrong way, somehow—at least when I was around. They'd seemed to get along fine while I'd been in the lunch line.

I cast a glance at Jordan, but he was lost in his art, quick flicks of his pencil filling the ground around the horse's hooves with blades of grass so realistic his page looked like a black-and-white photo.

I pulled out my oil pastels and settled in to work on my art piece, deciding I'd just have to figure out how to navigate any weirdness between the three of us whenever Callan showed up.

He never came.

Reina, Jordan, and I looked for Callan after school, but he seemed to have vanished.

"Maybe he had to leave early?" Reina suggested as we stood on the front sidewalk that led to the parking lot.

"Yeah, maybe." I adjusted my backpack strap and glanced at my car. "I need to go, though. I have to work at the café this afternoon."

"I've got to get home and help my mom with some things first, but maybe Reina and I can stop by and see you before closing," Jordan said.

I froze. Jordan and Reina lived near each other and their families were close. They hung out outside of school, but they'd never asked me to join them, other than a few birthday parties Reina had invited me to when we were younger.

I glanced at Reina, but she just shrugged and nodded.

"Um, I—" I forced a smile at Jordan. "Yeah, sure, if you want to." A few days earlier, I'd have been excited at the thought of Jordan wanting to visit me at work, but after the way my last shift at the café had gone, I was hoping for a quiet work-shift to study things and try to figure out what had really happened that night. I was also hoping Callan would show up and explain to me why his face looked so much like my blue-eyed stranger... though I supposed that was too much to ask.

Hesitation slipped over the eagerness in Jordan's eyes, and I immediately regretted my ambivalent response. "You know, I've got a lot of homework tonight," he said. "Maybe another time." He smiled. "See you tomorrow, Ayla." He gave a small wave, then headed toward his truck.

"Better go; he's my ride." Reina bounced away behind Jordan, waving back at me over her shoulder. "See you tomorrow!"

"Bye," I called after her, and headed for my car.

My shift at the café trudged by like the thick sludge at the bottom of a pot of old coffee. It was Larissa's day off, and Gary had left to run errands, so it was just Zach and me manning the café. I did my calculus homework between customers, but by dinnertime the traffic into the café was so slow, I'd run out of math problems to do. I grabbed the rag and spray cleaner and walked around cleaning the tables more times than they needed to be cleaned, while Zach stood at the register and picked at his fingernails. The trickle of customers tapered off further until I grew exhausted with the boredom and grabbed Gary's tablet from his office. Even warring piccolos were better than the stagnant silence between customers. How Zach didn't fall asleep right there at the register, I wasn't sure. Time ticked slowly along, and Reina and Jordan never stopped by. The only highlight of my night was that Madison and her posse didn't, either.

By the time Zach left and closing time came, I was itching to get home. I doubted the empty café held any further answers to my confusion about the stranger, and the sore spot on the bottom of my foot was bothering me again. I just wanted a long, hot shower, a good book, and my bed.

I pulled the protein bar from my backpack and gobbled it, feeling a surge of gratitude for Jordan as it calmed my growling stomach, then grabbed the inventory notebook from Gary's office and opened the kitchen storage closet. I was determined to get through closing as efficiently as possible so I could get home.

It was nearly midnight when I finally finished all the checklists. I did a quick walk-through of the café. The utensil counter was low on coffee stirrers, so I headed back to the kitchen to grab some from the closet.

I had just put on a fresh sterile glove and grabbed a handful of clean coffee stirrers from the box when a familiar electrical trill sent a chill down my spine.

I rushed out into the front area, coffee stirrers clutched in one hand.

A wrinkled paper fluttered to the tiled café floor, like it had fallen from the air near the front door.

I crept warily toward the door, wondering if I could use coffee stirrers as a weapon if it came down to it, and peered down at the paper.

Richly inked calligraphy covered the cream paper, which was aged-looking and torn along two edges as though someone had ripped it from a page of some ancient book.

Better than riches, silver, or gold,

Find what Prince Kaizyn lacks where heart's truths are told.

Buried with treasures, planted deep among flowers,

One word—seek you carefully—carries great power.

What in the world? I dumped the coffee stirrers on the closest table and picked up the paper. A sharp pain shot through the bottom of my foot.

I yelped, but the pain quickly subsided. I held the paper out in front me with shaking hands as I read over it again.

This was not normal. Right? Papers didn't appear from mid-air? Humans didn't walk through walls, either, but—

I shook my head. I was losing my mind. Clearly. That's what this was. Lack of sleep or stress or maybe too many skipped meals. Could low blood sugar cause hallucinations? But then again, I held the proof of my insanity right there in my hand. It was tangible. Did that make me sane or even crazier?

I took a shaky breath, then carefully folded the paper in half and slid it into my jeans pocket. I gathered the spilled coffee stirrers, dumped them in the trash, then put on a clean glove and refilled the stirrers container with fresh ones from the box in the kitchen. I put the box away, double-checked the emergency exit was locked, then signed out, grabbed my backpack and keys, and headed out the front door.

Shower and bed, I chanted to myself as I locked the café door behind me and hurried to my car. Surely, this would all make sense after a hot shower and some sleep. That's all I needed, and it would all be fine. *Shower and bed.*

I hurried home, said goodnight to my parents, then showered and got ready for bed, refusing to let myself think about the paper in the pocket of the jeans hanging over the chair by my dresser. I would worry about it tomorrow, or hopefully *not* worry about it, since my only strategy for coping was to force myself to sleep and pray this all disappeared in the morning.

I tossed beneath the covers for a long while, but eventually sleep took me.

Little did I know, things would make even *less* sense the next morning.

CHAPTER 5

Cold Stares and Hot Grudges

I awoke the next morning to the annoying buzz of my alarm clock and the lingering image of deep blue eyes in my mind. It was still dark outside, as usual—whose idea had it been to make high school start so early in the morning? My natural night-owl tendencies were probably genetic, but I was certain I'd read somewhere that optimal brain energy happened much later in the day for teenagers than 7 AM.

When I stumbled into the kitchen, Grandpa was already sitting at the small corner table, staring out the kitchen window with his elbows on the tabletop and a mug clutched tightly in his hands. The dimmer lamp above the small table was the only light on, casting a mild, golden glow over him. The darkness outside the window was thinning into the grey of burgeoning morning. Grandpa's signature peppermint tea bag rested soggy in a spoon on the counter nearby.

"Good morning," I mumbled as I yanked open the fridge, then squinted my eyes against the sharp light from inside. "Have you eaten?"

After a moment with no response, I peered over at him.

He shook his head, still staring out the window.

"Do you want me to make you something?" My chest tightened with concern. Grandpa was usually far more conversational in the mornings—except when he was nearing an episode. Had Dad gotten up to check on him yet?

Fragments of yesterday's confusions and tension floated in at me and I shoved them away, determined not to think about school, my social life, or my possible insanity until I'd at least had a few quiet moments to finish waking up.

"Toast," Grandpa said, taking a slow sip from his mug. "With pomegranate jam." He still hadn't looked away from the window.

I blinked at him, then pulled a jar of Jim's pomegranate jam from the fridge. "Okay." I tilted the glass jar in my hand. The jam didn't look that appetizing, but I wasn't much of a 'toast with jam' person, anyway. When I ate toast, I preferred butter.

Grandpa glanced over at me. "Thank you, Ayla." He went back to staring out the window.

I swallowed down the anxious lump building in the back of my throat, decided I'd wake Dad before I left so he could check on Grandpa, and got to work making Grandpa's toast.

The tangy scent of the jam was strangely appealing, so I decided I would be adventurous and made myself a slice, too, then grabbed a couple cheese sticks from the fridge to eat with it for protein.

Grandpa and I sat in silence while we ate our toast. His gaze stayed fixed on the sky outside, which was filling with delicate streaks of pink and orange as the sun rose behind the trees. It was beautiful, but as the intensity of the colors and brightness of the sky outside increased, so did the churn of anxiety in my stomach. Sunrise meant it was almost time to go to school, and I still wasn't sure I was ready to face whatever drama the day might throw at me.

I slid a cheese stick over to Grandpa. He set down his mug and tore his eyes from the window, then smiled at me as he reached for the cheese. "Thank you. You're a good girl, Ayla. I love you."

My chest tightened again. "I love you too, Grandpa." I squeezed his wrinkled hand, then went to get dressed for school.

I threw on my day-old jeans and a comfy grey t-shirt with sneakers, brushed my hair and teeth, and was ready thirty minutes before time to leave. I debated reading for a bit, or maybe watching part of a TV show, but I was far too anxious to sit still and focus. Instead, I decided to walk to school. I usually drove for convenience, but the school was only a few blocks from our subdivision, a twenty-minute walk at most. Plus, walking would allow me to cross straight through the Gary's Café parking lot. I wasn't scheduled to work on Tuesdays, and I knew I wasn't likely to see anything just walking past that would help me make sense of the night before, but I hoped that seeing the normal flow of early morning customers driving in and out would reassure me the world was still turning as usual—without disappearing strangers and mysterious notes dropping from the air.

I knocked on my parents' bedroom door before I left.

"Yes?" my dad's voice answered, thick with sleep.

"I'm leaving for school. Walking today. Grandpa's up, and he seems... I don't know, a little strange this morning?"

Dad pulled the door open, peering at me in his checkered pajama pants, with tired eyes and wild hair. "Thanks for waking me. I'll check on him."

Mom rolled out of bed behind him, yawning as she slid her feet into her house slippers and pulled her robe from the chair by the bed. "I'll make breakfast and coffee."

"I made him some toast, and he already drank his tea," I said.

"Oh, the coffee's definitely for me," Mom said, tying her robe over her nightgown.

Dad laughed, then turned to me. "Thanks, kiddo." He squeezed my shoulder as he slid by me into the hall. "Have a good day at school."

I grabbed my backpack—so much lighter now than at school, since most of my books were still in my locker—and headed out the door.

The sun was almost fully risen when I reached Gary's Café. Cars filled most of the parking spots in the small lot, and through the front windows, I could see a half-dozen patrons waiting in line at the counter. Larissa manned the cash register, as usual, and I hoped Gary had scheduled reinforcements. I'd never worked a weekday morning, but I knew they were some of the cafe's busiest hours, lots of people grabbing coffee and pastries on their way to work or school. Life at the café seemed normal enough—no strangers on the floor in health crises; no notes fluttering down at people from mid-air. So far, so good.

Larissa caught sight of me as I walked by. She smiled and waved from inside. I waved back and continued through the lot. I didn't have time to stop without being late for school, and being sent to the office for a tardy slip then having everyone turn and stare at me as I walked in late to homeroom was not how I wanted to begin my day.

As I reached the end of the parking lot, a chill prickled across the base of my skull with the distinct sensation that I was being watched. The tiny hairs on my arms stood on end. I considered speed-walking the rest of the way to school, but beyond Gary's Café, the rest of my route to school was open sidewalk edged by road and woods. If there was someone following me, it was best to learn that now, when I still had a chance of being heard if I screamed for help. I clutched the straps of my backpack and turned around slowly.

Across the parking lot, my eyes met the stare of a shockingly handsome guy who looked to be about Larissa's age, standing between two cars. His eyes were a startling, bright blue, so bright they seemed to glow. His skin was pale but vibrant, his dark hair stood up in messy spikes, and his face was—perfection, like someone had brought a hot anime hero to life and plopped him in the café parking lot. His eyes locked on mine with an intensity that sent a shiver down my spine.

I stared into his gorgeous eyes for only a few seconds before I felt my fear resurge. I tore my eyes away and backstepped, pulse skittering, as I sought Larissa through the front window. Should I run? Scream for help? Maybe he was only a weirdo with super-intense eye contact and I should just keep walking? I glanced back, hoping he was making his way to whatever car was his, or at least no longer staring at me—but he was gone.

I swept my gaze over the parking lot, and what I could see of the inside of the café, but if he'd gone inside, I would have seen him, and he was nowhere in sight.

I spun and left the parking lot, walking as briskly as I could toward school.

I arrived five minutes before starting time, still freaked out and a little out of breath. I grabbed my books from my locker, then plopped into my seat in homeroom as the tardy bell rang.

Reina and Jordan turned to greet me, but Jordan's smile dropped the second he saw my face.

"Are you okay? What's wrong?"

I quickly explained about the guy I'd seen on the way to school, though I left out how attractive he'd been. I also left out the note I'd found the night before—the note I still had in my jeans pocket—because I still wasn't sure how to make sense of it.

Reina sucked in a sharp breath. "You think he was watching you?"

I chewed my lower lip. "No. I mean, he couldn't have been, right? He was probably just getting in or out of his car, but—I don't know. Something about the way he looked at me was... creepy."

Jordan's eyes hadn't left my face the entire time I was talking, and now he leaned toward me. "Let me walk you home this afternoon. Please. Reina drove today, and she's got to get home for a family thing, but I have time."

I shook my head. "No, that's not necessary. I'm just jumpy this morning. And it's not like he tried to follow me when I left. I'm sure it's fine."

"Still." Jordan drew a sharp breath. "It would make me feel a lot better."

Reina nodded emphatically. "Me, too. Let him, please. I would drive you myself, but Mom's car is in the shop and she needs to use mine for an important meeting right after school. She'll kill me if I'm not home in time. Still, I'd rather not worry about my friend getting murdered on the way home. Let Jordan walk you."

I glanced at Jordan, wondering if a murderous psychopath would be all that deterred by a seventeen-year-old boy as my bodyguard. But I figured it was less likely for us to both get murdered. And the thought of having him with me did make me feel more safe.

"Okay," I agreed.

"Thank you," Jordan sighed in relief.

The wall-speaker crackled, and we all stood and turned forward for the Pledge.

After announcements and roll call, Reina bounced away with a wave and smile as usual.

Jordan stood and reached for my backpack strap, a question in his eyes.

I nodded, and he slid the strap from my shoulder, then smiled at me as he swung my backpack onto the shoulder opposite his own backpack, like the day before. I grabbed my literature book from my desk and tucked it to my chest.

We walked to class in comfortable silence, other than the chaotic noise of slamming lockers and conversations and shoes squeaking on the polished linoleum as students hurried to class. I felt Jordan look over at me a couple times, and when I met his glance, he smiled.

His smile melted as we turned the corner to the literature classroom. "Oh. Hey, Callan." His hand came up in a half-hearted wave.

Callan was leaning casually against the wall beside the classroom door. He gave a friendly grin. "Hey, Jordan. Hi, Ayla."

My pulse skipped a little as his eyes met mine. "Hi." I glanced at Jordan, suddenly uncomfortable as they both stared at me. "Um, thanks for carrying that." I gestured to my backpack.

"No problem." Jordan handed it back to me, and I adjusted my literature book to one arm as I hefted the heavy backpack onto my shoulder.

Callan pushed away from the wall. "Should we go in and sit down, Ayla? It's almost time for class to start." He moved toward the classroom door.

I glanced at Jordan, who stood conspicuously silent, watching our exchange. But the crowds in the hall were thinning out and Callan was right. If we didn't all get to class soon, we'd be marked tardy.

I felt Callan's eyes watching me as I turned back toward Jordan and smiled. "I'll see you at lunch?"

Some of the tension lifted from Jordan's forehead. "Of course." He smiled back, then turned and walked away.

Callan was still watching me when I turned to face him.

"You weren't in art yesterday," I said to diffuse the awkward silence. "I looked for you after school."

Callan's eyes softened. "Sorry about that. I had to leave early for something. I should be in art today, though."

Classroom doors all down the hall began shutting—a sure sign the tardy bell was about to ring any second. Callan noticed the same moment I did and hurried inside the classroom. I followed him in, and we both found our seats as the tardy bell rang.

Mr. Yager began class immediately. Today's lecture was much drier—a review of his expectations for the essays he was requiring us to write in preparation for Myths and Legends Day. There was no further chance to talk to Callan during class, and to my surprise, he hurried off the moment class ended without a single word.

"Trouble in paradise?" A snide voice made me jump as I was shoving my pens and notebook into my backpack.

I looked up to find Madison standing next to me. "What?"

"I thought you and the new guy were, like, an item or something." She toyed with a lock of her hair. "I mean, you moved in pretty fast. I'm not sure he's had time to consider his options."

"We're not an item." I shoved my spiral notebook into the overstuffed backpack and zipped it closed. "I barely know him."

Her eyes narrowed in on me like lasers. "That's never stopped you before."

I sighed and shoved to my feet. My face rose to meet hers, though with her model-length legs, her eyes were at least three inches above mine. I peered up at her as I awkwardly forced my arms through the straps of my backpack. "What are you even talking about?"

She took a step toward me, her face nearly touching mine. "Just watch yourself." She turned, flicked her hair over her shoulder, and sauntered away.

What in the world was that? I gaped at her back as she exited into the hallway, the aftershock of the confrontation still trembling through my core, then hurried to my next class.

CHAPTER 6

HEAD BUMPS AND SHOCKING REALIZATIONS

My next period was physics class. Physics was confusing enough on a good day; but this day my brain was swirling with so many thoughts I couldn't focus enough to take notes. Instead, I jotted down a list of all my confusions and worries in the margin of my notebook:

—disappearing strangers

—matching faces

—mysterious riddles on suddenly appearing notes

—hot staring guy: serial killer?

—Grandpa

—Callan: questions

—Jordan: ... questions?

—whatever Madison thinks I did now

—my possible intensifying insanity

I stared at the list. What had happened to getting through my senior year as quietly and inconspicuously as possible? I sighed.

By the time the bell rang and physics class was over, I'd decided to make it a point to ask Callan some more questions about himself. Something about him nagged at me, though not in an entirely unpleasant way. I couldn't exactly ask him why he looked so much like the stranger I'd seen, but maybe I could bring the stranger up in conversation casually and gauge his reaction? I ran my hand over my jeans pocket as I stood to leave. The note inside crinkled, sending a wave of unease through me. I swallowed it down and hurried out into the hall.

History class was uneventful—other than the list of actual events, the dates for which I frantically wrote in my notebook as Mr. Brode lectured. But Reina, Jordan, and I were all surprised not to see Callan when we met up at lunch period afterward.

"Maybe he sat with someone else?" Reina's eyes skimmed the crowded cafeteria as we sat at our usual table. "I'll go check." She bounced away but came back a few minutes later and shrugged. "No sign of him."

Jordan glanced at me warily over his tray of lasagna. "Maybe he had a meeting with an advisor or something? Or tutoring?"

Students were not allowed to roam the school during lunch period, so short of hiding out in a bathroom or leaving campus altogether, tutoring or a special meeting were the best explanations for where he could be. I poked at my lasagna with my fork and nodded. "That makes sense. He transferred in mid-semester; maybe he needed help to get caught up."

Jordan and I ate in silence, while Reina chattered on about the latest episode of Teen Vampires and I pondered why, having just met Callan, I even cared whether he was here at all. Unfortunately, my ponderings were interrupted by frequent, tense glances from Jordan, and by the end of lunch, I still had no better grasp on my feelings.

The bell rang, and Reina pushed back from the table. "Why are you two being so weird? You've barely said a word all lunch."

Jordan's eyes met mine. "I'm sorry. I just..." He stopped. "Something's bothering me today."

Reina's gaze bounced between the two of us, an unreadable expression on her face. "I'm gonna... just... see you this afternoon." She grabbed her lunch bag and backpack and hurried away.

Jordan gave me a weak smile. "Walk you to class?"

If I expected our walk to class to illuminate anything, I was sorely disappointed. More than once while we walked, Jordan inhaled sharply as though he was about to say something, then clamped his mouth shut and kept walking. I wanted to ask him why he was being so weird, but I had a strong idea it had something to do with Callan, and I wasn't sure what to do with that. Honestly, Jordan's sudden, strange distance made me a little angry. Was I supposed to apologize to him for talking to another guy? He didn't own me.

A caustic tension still lingered between us when we reached the door to my psychology class, but Jordan simply said, "See you in art," and disappeared down the hall.

Psychology and AP Calculus crawled by with very little of the information penetrating my scattered brain, then I headed to art, half-expecting Callan to skip that class, as well. Part of me hoped Callan wouldn't be there, so that I could work things out with Jordan. But another part of me was disappointed at the thought of not getting to talk to Callan again before the day was over. What was wrong with me?

Callan was there.

Jordan was not.

I was still glancing at the door every few seconds, expecting Jordan to arrive, when Mrs. Flores announced our project for the day: papier mâché. She assigned me as Callan's guide for the day's class—probably because he was already seated at my usual table—to explain to him what she'd already taught us about creating papier mâché and show him where to find the shared supplies we'd need to create our in-class group assignment.

Callan followed me around as I pointed out the bins of supplies, then waited in line with me at the back table to receive our box of shredded newspaper from Mrs. Flores.

As we headed back to our table and sat down, my gaze caught on Jordan's empty chair beside me. "I wonder where he is," I mumbled to myself.

"Jordan? I heard someone hit him in the head with a door when he was walking down the hallway," Callan said.

"What?" I leaped to my feet, but a startled Mrs. Flores scolded me back into my chair.

"Ayla! What's gotten into you?" Her hand fluttered to her chest. "Sit back down."

"But Jordan—" I began.

Mrs. Flores' brows lowered. "Ah, yes. I heard about that. But I'm sure the nurse has it well under control, Miss Rogers. Please have a seat. You can check on him later."

Was I the only one who hadn't heard? Why hadn't Reina texted me? I sank dejectedly into my chair and pulled my phone from my backpack. *Dead*. Of course.

"Phones away, Miss Rogers," Mrs. Flores called out, pointing to the sign on the wall by her desk, a cartoon picture of a cell phone with a crossed-out circle over it.

I dropped my useless phone back into my backpack.

"I'm sorry." Callan leaned toward me. "I know you're worried about him, but I heard it wasn't so bad. I'm sure he'll be okay."

I glanced at him, and his eyes looked sincere. "Thanks, Callan." I gave him a weak smile.

Callan stared back. "I didn't do anything." He grinned. "Since we're stuck here, though..." He lifted the box of newspaper scraps and bottle of glue in confusion. "What in the world is papier mâché?"

Callan was easy to talk to, when we had something to talk about. After I explained papier mâché to him, we chatted comfortably about ideas for what to make for our joint project. We decided on one, and I spent the next thirty minutes showing Callan how to make a papier mâché bust of Caesar, which—though our final result looked awful—was more fun than I'd anticipated.

I laughed at Callan's frustrated expression when his hands kept getting covered in glue and bits of paper, but rather than getting offended, his warm, brown eyes lit up as they landed on mine. "Thanks for being my group partner," he said, grinning at me.

A warm flutter stirred in my chest. "Yeah, of course."

His eyes held mine for a long moment.

The final bell rang. "Oh, no. Jordan," I said, my eyes sweeping over the huge mess still on our art table.

"I'll clean up," Callan said with a gentle smile. "Go check on him."

I took a quick breath. "Thank you." I gathered my things in a rush, then hurried back into the main hall.

Jordan wasn't in the nurse's office when I got there. "I released him a while ago," the nurse said sweetly, though she didn't offer much else in the way of information.

Again cursing my dead cell phone, I hurried back through the main hallway. I didn't expect Jordan to uphold his offer to walk me home after having his head hit by a door, but I still wanted to see him and make sure he was okay. Would Jordan and Reina have waited for me out front after school to say goodbye like usual? I knew Reina had to get home right away for her mom, and with his injury, Jordan might have needed to get home, too—or to a doctor. And until my phone charged, I had no way of reaching either of them.

When I emerged from the school's double doors and saw Jordan sitting on the front steps, I breathed a sigh of relief. "Jordan."

He turned and looked up at me, then smiled. "Hey." His backpack rested on the step beside him, and he was holding a giant ice pack wrapped in paper towels to his forehead with one hand. He noticed me staring and blushed a little. "Stupid, right? I should've been paying more attention."

I sat beside him on the top step, my leg a few inches from his. "I'm glad you're okay. I was worried when I heard."

"The whole school's probably heard by now," Jordan muttered, slumping a little, then he straightened and shrugged. "Oh well. You ready to go?" He pulled the ice pack away from his forehead as he reached for his backpack.

I winced at the large, purple lump on his head. "Are you sure? That looks painful. Seriously, Jordan, you don't have to walk me home. Can you get a ride? I'll be fine."

Jordan turned to meet my eyes. "I'm not letting a concussion stop me from walking you home."

I gaped at him. "Concussion? Jordan, really, you don't have to—"

"I want to." His eyes were inches away, serious as they held my gaze, but then he pulled back and smirked. "Besides, I can't let you get murdered on my watch. Think what the school gossips would say."

I laughed, and he handed me his ice pack. "Mind holding this for a second?"

I held the ice pack while he put his backpack on and stood, then he stepped down one stair and turned back, reaching out a hand.

I extended the ice pack, thinking it was what he wanted, but he gently grabbed my whole hand and tugged me to my feet.

With him standing a step down, we were nearly the same height when I stood, our faces inches apart. My breath caught.

Jordan's eyes held mine, his warm hand still pressing into the back of mine while the ice pack chilled my palm. Then he smiled, slid the ice pack from my hand, and pressed it to his head again. He stepped down another step, putting space between us. "You ready to go?"

I let out my breath and shrugged. "Yeah, sure."

"You know," Jordan said as we made our way down the steps to the front sidewalk, "I've never been to your house before." He glanced at me, mischief in his eyes. "I know you live in the subdivision by Gary's, but not which street or house. Are you sure you trust me to know where you live?"

I laughed. "Should I not?"

Jordan shook his head, mock-seriousness on his face. "Oh, no, I am entirely honorable. Most of the time." He smirked, then laughed. "Okay, all of the time. I am about the least dangerous person you could ever have know your address."

I smiled at him. "I thought so."

He fell quiet for a moment as we headed down the sidewalk that led around the parking lot, toward the gate that marked the edge of the school campus. "Do you even feel safer having me with you? I'm not a martial arts expert like Callan."

I turned to look at him, but he kept his gaze fixed straight ahead as we walked.

"Yes, I do," I said, and I meant it. Jordan wasn't a huge guy, but I'd had PE with him many times over the years, and he'd always been strong and fast. I hadn't attended any of the baseball games since he'd joined the team last year, but if his sudden influx of muscles over the summer was any indication, training for the games had only made him faster and stronger. And more importantly, I trusted him. I knew he'd do whatever he could to protect me.

"Thanks." Jordan glanced over at me as we exited the school grounds and continued down the sidewalk, seeming embarrassed for having asked.

I got the impression he assumed my response had been obligatory, just empty flattery. But short of suddenly fawning over his muscles—which would have been awkward in the extreme—I wasn't sure what else to say.

"Callan bothers you," I said instead, then immediately wished I could pull back the words. Why hadn't I complimented his biceps?

Jordan's sideways glance was wary. "No." He huffed out a sharp breath. "I mean... yeah, a little."

I turned toward him, surprised by his admission. "Why?"

Jordan stopped walking.

I stopped beside him as he turned to face me.

He lowered the ice pack from his forehead, and his caramel eyes locked on mine with a guarded intensity. "I think you know why."

CHAPTER 7

ICED COFFEE AND BROWNIES

I think you know why.

Jordan's words hung in the air, his face a breath away, his eyes flicking between mine like he was trying to read my soul.

Butterflies exploded into chaos in my stomach while all coherent thought vanished from my brain. "Oh."

Jordan let out a soft laugh, then shook his head and stepped back. And like that, the moment had vanished.

I stared at him in confusion, unsure what I'd said or done to ruin the moment—or how to get it back.

He gave me a gentle smile. "Come on, let's get you home."

We continued the walk in a somewhat-tense silence, Jordan asking questions here and there about how much homework I had, and what he'd missed in art class. I avoided all mention of Callan as I explained the papier mâché assignment, then swiftly redirected the conversation to asking Jordan how his earlier classes had gone.

"Fine," he laughed, "until I got hit in the head by someone a little too eager to get to the bathroom."

"They really should make the doors open *in* rather than out into the hall. I never realized what a hazard that is, but I'm surprised people haven't been concussed more often, now that I think about it."

Jordan laughed again. "Then people *inside* the classrooms would be getting concussed." He glanced at me with a smirk. "Maybe I'll come in early one day and remove all the doors."

By the time we reached the Gary's Café parking lot, the tension between us had eased considerably. His head also looked a little better—the ice seemed to have reduced the swelling, though he still most definitely had a purple knot on his forehead.

Jordan stopped as we crossed the front windows of the café, tossing his disposable ice pack into the trash bin by the front door.

"Do you want to stop in for coffee?" he asked. "Or—we don't have to, if you get enough of the place working there."

I smiled at him. "Coffee sounds great."

Larissa looked up from the counter as we entered, and smiled at me. "Hey, Ayla!" Her gaze bounced to Jordan, and her eyebrow raised. "Who's this?"

"Jordan." He stepped forward as we neared the counter, extending his hand.

Larissa shook his hand and grinned at him. "Nice to meet you, Jordan." She turned to me. "You're not on the schedule today. Are you here to order something?"

"Yes." I pulled my wallet from my bag. "An iced caramel macchiato, for me." I smiled at Jordan. "Order whatever you want, I'll cover it. I get a discount."

"Oh." For a moment, Jordan looked as though he might argue with me, but then he shrugged and smiled back. "I'll have what she's having."

Larissa spun toward the kitchen. "Two iced caramel macchiatos!" she yelled cheerily.

"Got it." Zach's monotone reply floated out from the kitchen.

There weren't many other customers and all of them already had their orders, so Larissa leaned her elbows on the counter, facing Jordan and me while we waited.

"So how do you two know each other?" she asked.

"School." We both answered simultaneously, then glanced at each other.

Larissa laughed. "Well, that was adorable."

"We've known each other forever," I said quickly as a blush rose to my cheeks.

Larissa eyed me, nodding slowly. "Uh huh."

Zach emerged from the kitchen and plopped our drinks on the counter. "Here."

"Um, thanks?" I said, reaching for one of the cups.

"Welcome," Zach muttered, then returned to the kitchen.

Jordan raised an eyebrow as he reached for his drink.

"He's always like that." Larissa shrugged. "He's allergic to words."

I laughed, then turned for the door. "I'd better get home. My parents will worry if I take too long, and my phone's dead so they may have already been texting me."

"Oh!" Jordan said. "Yeah, then we should go."

He waved at Larissa and headed for the door. "Nice meeting you."

Larissa raised her eyebrows again, her gaze lingering on me with a subtle smirk. "Oh, it was very nice meeting you too, Jordan." From her expression, I could tell she would launch a full investigation into my barely existent romantic life during our next shift together. I narrowed my eyes at her and she grinned, then waved at us both. "See you later!"

Jordan held the door open for me and I stepped through—and ran straight into Madison Kane.

She reeled back with a look of annoyance on her face. "Fine, you go first. You're already blocking the doorway."

I slipped past her and out onto the sidewalk, shocked to see she had no posse trailing in her wake. She seldom went anywhere without them.

Jordan seemed to notice the same as he joined me on the sidewalk, still leaning inward to hold the door open for Madison.

He was too nice; I'd have let it close on her.

"Getting coffee alone today?" he asked casually as she moved past.

Discomfort flitted over her face, then vanished as her usual snobby glare took its place. "What's it to you?" She shoved past him through the door.

Jordan let the door fall shut behind her, then turned to me and shrugged. "You'd think by now she would've run out of reasons to be mad at the world, but she seems to have an unlimited supply."

A twinge of guilt shot through me—I was one of those reasons. Or at least, what I'd unintentionally done to her brother Rory was. And based on our last interaction at school, now she'd found something else to be mad at me for, too, though I had no idea what.

Jordan seemed to notice my mood shift immediately. "Hey, don't worry about her. She's a jerk—always has been, really."

I shrugged off the heavy anxiety Madison's presence always blanketed me with, and refocused on his warm, steady eyes. "You're right." I smiled, determined to focus on the amazing guy in front of me instead of Madison and whatever her deal was.

Jordan stepped away from the front door, gesturing to the far end of the parking lot, where the sidewalk began that led to my subdivision. "Shall we?"

Jordan and I conversed freely between sips of iced coffee on the rest of the walk home, asking simple questions about each other's lives. Though I knew his parents were both accountants, I learned they didn't work together—his dad's muttering while he worked drove his mom crazy, so although they owned a business together, his dad went into the office to work most days, while his mom worked from home. Jordan asked how my grandpa was, offering sympathy when I told him about the worsening dementia. And I learned Jordan had one pet—a pit bull named Champ, who was apparently a lovable goofball.

When we reached the entrance to my neighborhood, anxiety crept back in. Having Jordan next to me made me hyper-aware of details I didn't usually notice — the worn paint on the entry sign, the withered grass in most yards, the general squattishness of the houses. I had only been to Jordan and Reina's neighborhood a few times, when I'd attended birthday parties over the years... but it was an affluent one. Compared to the houses in my subdivision, the homes in theirs were like pristine mansions. Mine was an older neighborhood, and had never been a fancy one. It usually didn't bother me, but I didn't often bring home guests who lived in mansions.

Jordan glanced around while we walked, taking in the neighborhood with subtle interest. I focused on the sidewalk ahead of me, hoping Dad had at least moved the broken lawnmower out of our yard since that morning.

We turned onto my street, and my squat, white house with the too-bright yellow trim glared back at me. The lawnmower was still in the middle of the yard.

"This is me." I gestured ahead as we neared my house.

Jordan's face broke into a grin. "I love it!"

To my surprise, his expression was completely genuine.

He showered me with comments and questions as we tromped up my sloped driveway. "The yellow trim is so cheerful; it's perfect. Did you guys plant those flowers yourselves? They're beautiful. All my mom will let our gardener plant are roses. Oh, you even have a porch swing! I've always liked those. What kind of flowers are these?" He trailed his fingers lightly over a strip of plants by my front porch.

"Mexican heather and hibiscus," I said, staring at the flowers I rarely noticed anymore. "My mom planted them." They really were pretty.

Jordan's phone buzzed from a text, and he slipped it from his pocket, tapped out a quick response, then dropped it back into his pocket and refocused on me. "She's a gardener, right?"

I nodded, feeling anxiety mount again. "Yeah, sort of. She only does it part time, on the side. The rest of the time she's helping with Grandpa."

"That's right," he said. "I knew that. And your dad works for Kane Textiles, right?"

I'd rather not have been reminded that my dad was Madison's dad's employee, but I nodded. "Yeah. He's manager of one wing of their distribution center downtown. He works from home some days, and downtown on the others."

Jordan stepped in front of me, his eyes scanning my face. "Isn't it weird that we've known each other so long but still don't know basic details about each other?"

I shrugged against the lump of anxiety in my chest. "Yeah, I guess it is."

Jordan smiled warmly and took a step closer, inches from my face as his eyes peered down into mine. "I'd like to fix that."

My heart surged into a racing gallop. Was he about to *kiss* me?... Did I *want* him to?

The front door of my house flew open. "Hey, Ayla! Who's your friend?"

Jordan and I jumped apart and spun toward my front porch.

"Oh, Jordan Peters!" Dad said with a surprised smile. "Didn't expect to see you here! It's been ages since I've seen your family. And my, you've grown. How are your parents?"

"Fine, Mr. Rogers," Jordan croaked out, then cleared his throat. "They're good."

Dad glanced between Jordan and me, and from the curious look he gave me, I was certain my slowly fading panic and the blush I felt heating my cheeks did not escape his notice.

"Are you here for a group project or something?" Dad asked, his gaze back on Jordan.

Did he have to make my social isolation so obvious? He acted like it wasn't even a possibility that Jordan had just come over to hang out. Not that he was wrong. I hadn't invited a friend home from school in years.

Jordan shook his head. "I was just walking her home. She had... a situation on the way to school, and I wanted to be sure she got home safely."

My dad stiffened. "What?" He slid his gaze to me. "What happened? Why didn't you call me?"

"My phone died. But everything's fine. I just saw a guy staring at me in Gary's parking lot earlier." I shrugged. "I didn't think it was anything, but Jordan and Reina were worried and Jordan insisted on walking me home."

Dad eyed me cautiously. "All right," he said finally. "But next time, call me from the school office or something. Your mom or I will always come pick you up if you feel unsafe."

I nodded. "I know, Dad. If it happens again, I will."

Dad relaxed. "Okay, then. Well, thank you, Jordan, for making sure she got home safely. Would you like to come inside?"

A little swish of hope surged through my chest that he might say *yes*. As awkward as I had felt moments earlier, I'd enjoyed his company today and wished we could continue talking. We never had time to talk this much at school.

Jordan glanced at me, then shook his head. "No, thank you. I need to get home. My mom wanted my help with some stuff around the house this afternoon." He hesitated a moment. "Actually, if it's okay with you, sir... Could I take Ayla to dinner and a movie tonight?"

That wasn't *at all* how I'd expected that sentence to end.

"I mean—if she wants to," Jordan added, glancing at me.

I schooled my face into an expression that hopefully looked more like polite interest than complete and utter shock.

"It's a school night." Dad crossed his arms, studying Jordan.

"Yes, sir, but there's a special showing of *The Princess Bride* tonight at the theater downtown, and it's one night only. It starts at 9 PM, which I know is late, but—"

No way my dad would let me go out late with a boy he hadn't seen in years, with only a few hours notice, on a *school night*. This would be a quick and definite *no*.

But Dad's stern mouth spread into a friendly smile that made me more nervous. "Okay, sure. Just have her home before midnight," he said, then turned to me. "Assuming you want to?"

What was even *happening* right now? "Um... yes?" I mean, I did want to go—an evening with Jordan actually sounded great—but at the moment, that desire was a bit overshadowed by my absolute, raging confusion.

Dad laughed. "I'll take that lackluster response as agreement."

Jordan turned to me with a shy grin. "I'll pick you up at 7 PM?"

I nodded, too many thoughts flying through my brain to form words.

Dad glanced past Jordan at the driveway. "It's a while until 7... Are you walking home from here? Do you need a ride?"

Jordan shook his head. "Reina texted me a few minutes ago that her dad got home with their other car, so she's going to meet me at Gary's Café soon to drive me home. It's not that far to the café from here; I can walk there."

Dad's eyebrows rose at the mention of Reina, but he shook his head. "Let me drive you at least to the café. I owe you one for watching out for my daughter today. I insist."

I eyed Dad, suddenly panicked that he might be planning to interrogate Jordan about our relationship in the car.

Jordan bit his lower lip as he glanced at me, then turned back to Dad and nodded. "Okay. Thank you, sir."

My dad smiled at him. "Don't mention it."

"I'll come, too," I blurted. I wasn't sure I could prevent my dad from questioning Jordan, but I at least wanted to be there for damage control.

But Dad shook his head. "Your mother isn't back yet from helping Mrs. Johnson with her groceries. I need you to stay here with your grandfather."

Mom always ran grocery trips and errands with our elderly neighbor on Tuesday afternoons; I'd forgotten she wouldn't be home.

I threw out one last attempt. "I can drive Jordan."

But Dad already had his keys out of his pocket and was halfway to his old Honda Accord in the driveway. "I've got it." He smiled at me, then waved for Jordan to join him. "Climb on in."

I stared after them with increasing panic as Dad drove away.

Shuffling footsteps sounded behind me, and I turned to see Grandpa leaning on his cane in the open doorway. "You gonna stand out here with the door open all afternoon?" He stared at me like I had grown a second head. "You'll let the brownies in."

"Brownies?" I studied his face for a second, but his eyes were distant—he was definitely approaching one of his episodes, if it hadn't already begun. He often worried about strange things during episodes, and sometimes got rather jittery. I stepped toward him and shook my head. "No, Grandpa. I'm coming," I kept my voice calm, so as not to upset him further.

Satisfied, he shuffled back inside. I followed him, shutting the door behind me.

CHAPTER 8

THINGS HAPPEN AT MIDNIGHT

I made Grandpa a snack, idly chattering to him about school and my classes to fill the awkward silence. He stared out the window as I spread jam on his toast, seeming in another world entirely.

When his food was ready, I got Grandpa settled in the recliner in the living room, set up a TV tray next to him with his plate and a glass of water, and tucked a blanket over his shoulders. "Do you need anything else?"

Instead of answering, he reached for a thick, leather-bound book on the end table beside him. It wasn't a book I'd seen before, but Grandpa had so many books packed onto the shelves in his room, that didn't surprise me.

I clicked the lamp on the table to give him better light. The lamplight caught on a shiny, engraved symbol on the book's cover, a shape like a tree seared into the leather and inlaid with some kind of foil or metallic ink. "What's that?"

Grandpa hugged the book to his chest, covering the etching with his arm. "Nothing. Old book. None of your concern."

The bristling tone of his voice startled me, so unlike his usual demeanor. I took a couple steps back. "Sorry, Grandpa. Nevermind." I studied his face for a moment, but it was locked in a grumpy frown as he glared at an empty corner of the living room. Gusts of anxiety swished through my chest, the first whispers of an approaching storm, as I edged back toward the kitchen. "Are you sure you don't need anything?"

Grandpa's eyes flicked to me, and his face softened. "Good girl, Ayla. Always so good." He smiled, then huffed in frustration and went back to glaring at the empty corner with the book clutched to his chest.

I crept toward the kitchen, not wanting to disturb him further. A sigh of relief rushed through my chest as I heard the front door open. "Dad." I hurried back into the hall between the kitchen and living room.

Dad was hanging his keys on a hook by the door. "Hey, Ayla." He swung his face toward me. "I wanted to—what's wrong?"

I'd never been great at hiding anxiety; I wasn't surprised it was plain on my face. "Grandpa," I whispered, then quietly explained the exchange we'd had.

Dad ran a worried hand over his forehead. "Okay, thanks, sweetheart. I'll go sit with him in a moment." He glanced toward the living room, concern plain on his face, then turned back to me. "But first, we need to talk."

The gusts of anxiety kicked up in a whoosh of panic. "Why?" I headed for the kitchen, buying time for my racing thoughts to organize themselves. Dad had been alone in the car with Jordan—was that what this was about? Jordan and I barely even *had* a relationship for Dad to interrogate him over, and the thought that Dad may have done just that made me suddenly nauseated. Had he asked Jordan about his feelings for me or his intentions toward me? Badgered Jordan over details of our courtship? I clenched my hands into nervous fists. *Please, for all that's holy, don't let Dad have used the word 'courtship.'* I hoped Jordan had a great sense of humor—and a heavy dose of patience, because whatever might have been developing between us was far too new and fragile for a dose of *Dad* that heavy. It might not survive it.

Dad studied my face with intensifying interest. "Emotions are exploding across your face like a fireworks show, right now. What do *you* think I'm—*oh.*" Dad's mouth spread into a smirk as he crossed his arms and leaned against the corner of the kitchen doorway. "This isn't about the boy."

Heat rushed to my face. I yanked open the fridge door and buried myself behind it, nudging random jars around on the shelves without registering what they were. "Okay."

"I'm glad to see you hanging out with friends outside of school." His voice was shockingly calm. "Jordan's a nice kid. Always has been. We can talk about the boundaries of where *that* might be going later—"

I fought back a wince as embarrassment surged in again.

"—but right now," he continued, "there's something else we need to discuss." An edge of firmness crept in on the last word.

I peered over the top of the fridge door, my discomfort warming into curiosity. "What is it?"

"This stranger you said was watching you. Was this the first time?"

I straightened and shut the fridge door; I had no clue what I was even looking for in there. "Yes. I'd never seen him before."

Grandpa's loud snores drifted from the living room, distracting me for a moment.

Dad's eyes wandered to the far wall as he nodded, processing my last statement, then he locked his gaze back on me. "Until we know for sure that it's nothing to worry about, I don't want you walking to school anymore."

I sighed. "Dad, I'm sure it's—"

"I'm serious, Ayla." Dad pushed up from the wall and stepped toward me, posture stiff and eyes full of concern. "After what happened at Gary's, this raises too many concerns. These are the kinds of things parents brush off, then regret forever when something bad does happen. Until we know it's safe, you drive to school and work or be driven, and you go straight there and back, unless we know ahead of time you're making a stop. No walking, especially not alone. Understand?"

"Understood." I nodded, rattled by the intensity of his concern.

Dad's tense posture relaxed a bit. "Good. I know I can't keep you safe and protected every second, but at least if you're in a car, you're a bit less exposed. And call or text us whenever you get somewhere—"

"I usually do, Dad." I shrugged.

"I know," he said. "But now that this—"

"Now that what?"

I jumped as Dad turned toward the hallway, a smile spreading across his profile. "Maria. Didn't hear you come in."

"Neither did Ayla, judging by how high she jumped." Mom grinned at me, then looked back at Dad. "What were you two talking about?"

Dad rubbed a hand over the back of his head. "Ayla may have a stalker."

"What?" I shouted as Mom turned to stare at me. "No, I don't. Just a guy who… looked at me weird." Saying it that way made me even more embarrassed that everyone was making such a big deal out of it. I had probably overthought the whole encounter and now I had everyone freaked out for nothing. "Really, it's not a big deal."

"Jordan seemed a bit more concerned." Dad glanced between my mom and me.

"Jordan?" Mom asked.

Dad smiled and raised an eyebrow. "Ayla's date."

Mom gaped at me. "*What?* I swear, I'm gone one afternoon, and it's like I missed five years. What in the world is happening?"

"It wasn't a date, Mom. I mean, it *is,* but it hasn't happened yet. I mean—" I stammered, then stopped. "Jordan is a friend from school."

"A friend who asked to pick her up for dinner and a movie tonight," Dad added with a smirk.

Mom's eyes studied my face. "Uh huh." She glanced at Dad. "And you okayed this? On a school night?"

Dad shrugged. "He's taking her to see *The Princess Bride.* Besides, it's Jordan Peters."

"Oh, *that* Jordan!" Mom's face lit up. "He's always been a sweetheart. How are Bob and Edna? I should give them a call, catch up."

I dropped my face into my hands. "This cannot be happening right now." I peered out between my fingers. "I don't even know for sure if he likes me… like that."

Mom stared at me. "Of course he does, Ayla. Why else would he ask you out?" She strode across the kitchen, pulled open the odds-and-ends drawer next to the fridge, and slipped something from the drawer. "Here."

I reached out my hand by instinct and she dropped the object into it. I glanced at it, then flicked my face back up to her. "*Pepper spray*?" What did she think Jordan was going to try on me?

Mom shrugged. "In case you do have a stalker."

"Oh." I gaped at her. "Why do you even *have* this?" Mom was so gentle, I couldn't imagine her pepper spraying *anyone*. Besides, how much danger was she going to get into? She hung out with elderly people from church.

"Oh, that's my backup." Mom gestured at the palm-sized tube of pepper spray she'd handed me. "I keep my main one in my purse. And now that you're going more places alone, it's time you did, too. Can't be too safe."

I eyed Mom as I closed my hand over the pepper spray. She was over-reacting—a guy had *looked* at me in a parking lot, that was all. But then I remembered the chill I'd felt from his unrelenting stare and decided maybe she was right. It wouldn't hurt to be prepared, just in case. "Thanks, Mom." I gave her a smile, then walked out to the hooks by the front door and dropped the pepper spray into my purse. I turned back to find Mom and Dad both watching me.

"So, about this date tonight—" Mom began.

I tensed, but Mom smiled. "I hope you have fun. I've always liked Jordan. Did you know his mother Edna and I were on the class party-planning committee together when you were both in kindergarten?"

"Um, no?" I had few memories of kindergarten aside from sharp anxiety tied to the smell of fresh crayons, which for some reason had never left me. I probably sucked at art, even back then.

"Oh that's right, you were!" Dad smiled from beside her. "Bob does taxes and accounting for several of the guys at the factory. Every time I see Bob in town, he asks about all of us, how we're doing. They're a good family."

I gaped at both of them. My first official date—okay, my first date of *any* kind—and they were both totally fine with it? What sort of magic had Jordan worked on Dad in the car? But it was far better than the alternative, so I decided to count my blessings.

"Oh!" I said, remembering my homework. "I've got a calculus assignment I need to do before I leave." I slid my gaze between Mom and Dad, wondering if they were planning to question me further about my sudden dating status—or my possible stalker.

Dad slipped his arm over Mom's shoulders and waved me toward my room. "Go ahead, do what you need to do."

"Thanks." I gave them each a quick hug, then slipped past them into the hallway, grabbed my backpack from the floor by the door, and hurried to my room.

I sank into my desk and pulled out my homework, determined to get it done before anything else distracted me. More than once, Jordan's face floated into my mind, shooting a flurry of anxious butterflies through my chest, but I managed to concentrate enough to get the assignment done. I glanced at the clock above my desk as I slid my calculus book and notebook back into my backpack—5:30 PM. Plenty of time to shower and get ready before Jordan picked me up. The butterflies burst into chaos again at the realization that I was getting ready for a date tonight. A *date*. What would I even wear?

But... it was Jordan. Over the years we'd known each other, he had seen me in ugly PE gym shorts, plenty of jeans and t-shirts, and sopping, frizzy hair from rain. If I dressed up too much, it would be weird. Wouldn't it? I yanked open my closet and stared at my assortment of solid-colored shirts and blouses—mostly in shades of grey or blue or black—and my limited collection of jeans. I had a few dresses and skirts I wore to church, but that seemed too formal. Jeans and a nice blouse would be a good in-between, but... the pair of jeans I was wearing were my favorite pair. Would it be weird to wear them again? I'd worn them to school two days in a row already. Would he notice?

I stood staring blankly at my closet for far too long. The thought of going on a date with Jordan was so incredibly weird, but also—the look in his eyes as he'd leaned toward me earlier flashed to mind, and the butterflies burst into motion again. *I really do like him.* The realization rocketed my heart into strange flutters of nerves and excitement, twisting into focus every-thing that was at stake for this date. What if it didn't go well? Would it ruin our friendship? What if I said the wrong thing, did the wrong thing—it would be humiliating... and then what? I'd still have to see him at school. And aside from all this, what would Reina think? They were close. Had Jordan told her he asked me out? Or worse, what if I'd misunderstood? What if this was a group hangout thing and Reina was invited, too? My heart plummeted at the thought, which only freaked me out further. Why did I care so much?

I was halfway toward reaching for my phone and canceling our date with a text when a soft knock rapped at my door. I jumped and spun toward the door. "Yes?"

"You still want this book?" Grandpa's voice grumped through the closed door.

Curious, I crossed the room and yanked open the door.

Grandpa's dark eyes locked on me, his thick brows drawn downward. "Why'd you open? Could've been anyone. Too trusting. Didn't I teach you better than that?" He shoved past me, his cane thumping the wood floor as he hobbled further into my room.

My startled stare followed him.

He stopped near my bed.

My eyes slid to the book he clutched against his chest with one arm. I expected it to be the book he had in the living room earlier, but it was another book entirely.

He tossed it onto my bed. "For your research. Remember?"

Realization dawned as I scanned the title on the cover of the glossy book—*Encyclopedia of Myths and Legends*. "Oh!" I'd forgotten I had even mentioned my English essay to Grandpa, much less asked him for a reading source, but now I remembered bringing it up in our one-way conversation as I'd fixed his snack. I hadn't even been sure he was listening. I nodded. "Thank you."

Grandpa eyed me, his dark eyes unblinking. "Your date tonight."

I swallowed, my chest constricting with a tangle of anxiety and confusion. "Yes?" Was Grandpa going to interrogate me about my barely existent dating life now, too?

"Be home before midnight." He gave me one firm nod, then strode past me toward the bedroom door.

"Um, yes sir," I said to his retreating back. "Dad already told me to."

Grandpa halted for a moment in the doorway and glanced back over his shoulder. "Things happen at midnight," he mumbled, then spun and hurried away, cane thumping down the hallway.

I rushed to the doorway, my heart fluttering with anxiety I couldn't quite process. "What?" I called after him as he reached his own bedroom door. "What does that mean?"

"I need a nap!" He hobbled into his room without looking back and swung his bedroom door shut behind him.

"O-kay." I stared at his closed door for a long moment then sighed, running a hand down my face as I returned to my room. My eyes caught my still-open closet doors and the time on the clock—6:01 PM. Jordan would be here in less than an hour. I bounced on my toes for a second in panicked deliberation between canceling or going through with it, but the image of his caramel eyes in my mind won out and I rushed for the shower, in a hurry to get ready before he arrived.

After showering, I threw on some simple makeup—natural look had always been more my thing, anyway—and yanked a blue-grey blouse from my closet, one that was comfy but nice-looking and that Mom said brought out the color in my eyes. I dried my wild hair in a rush, debated over straightening it, then decided there wasn't time and pulled it back into a somewhat-neat bun. It wasn't until I went to slip my twice-worn jeans back on that I remembered the note.

How had I forgotten about it? It crinkled in the pocket as I lifted the jeans, taunting me with its ominous mystery. I swallowed down the anxiety it resurrected—that subtle but all-too-important concern that perhaps girls who saw notes appear from mid-air weren't entirely sane—and pulled it from the pocket.

My eyes slid over the words, familiar and yet also as though seeing them again for the first time:

Better than riches, silver, or gold,

Find what Prince Kaizyn lacks where heart's truths are told.

Buried with treasures, planted deep among flowers,

One word—seek you carefully—carries great power.

I clenched the note, puzzling over it, until a sudden reconnection with reality startled me back into awareness. My gaze shot to the clock—6:47. Jordan could be here soon, and I was still standing pantsless in my bedroom. I folded the note and slipped it into the top drawer of my desk, then slid on my jeans and jammed my cell phone into my back pocket so I wouldn't forget it. I headed to my closet to grab my black flats, which would be less casual than sneakers but still comfy if we did much walking. Suddenly something clicked—*Things happen at midnight*. A chill shot through me. Both times strange things had happened at Gary's, I'd been getting ready to go home right at the end of closing. Right at midnight. My black flats dangled from my fingers as I jumped to my feet and rushed into the hall.

"Grandpa!" I knocked on his door more loudly than I probably should have.

Mom and Dad both raced into the hall from the kitchen. "Ayla! Is everything okay?"

Dad's panicked gaze swept the hallway. "Is Grandpa—" He rushed toward me.

Remorse flooded me at the terror in his eyes. "No, no, he's fine—I think. I just need to ask him something."

Dad huffed as he stumbled to a stop. "For goodness' sake, Ayla!" he whispered furiously. "You scared me to death!" He shoved open Grandpa's door. Dad's shoulders relaxed as we both stared at Grandpa, sound asleep in his bed. Grandpa's raspy snores drifted out at us as Dad eased the door shut again. He turned to me, his panicked anger ebbing into concern. "Are you all right? Why were you banging on his door like that?"

I felt heat flood my face. "I'm sorry. Grandpa said something weird earlier, and I wanted to ask him about it."

Dad's face softened. "You know he says things that don't make sense, sometimes." His eyes studied mine. "Did he say something that upset you?"

"No." I stared at my shoes, still dangling from the fingers of my right hand. "He said to be home before midnight."

Dad laughed, and when I looked up, his concern had vanished. "So did I, sweetheart."

I met his eyes. "He said, 'Things happen at midnight.'"

Dad shook his head. "Probably a quote from one of his books or something, honey." A shadow passed over his face. "You know how he gets."

Dad was right—it probably didn't mean a thing. Sadness surged in at how far Grandpa's mind had slipped, along with a flash of embarrassment that I'd startled everyone. I bent down and put on my shoes.

Mom slid up next to Dad as I stood up, resting a hand on his shoulder. Her eyes swept over me. "You look lovely, sweetheart." She gave me a gentle smile. "It's about time for your date, isn't it?"

A new rush of nerves beat its wings in my chest. "Yeah." I slid my phone from my back pocket, my thoughts still swirling around the strange rhyme from the note I'd recently removed from the front one. I glanced at the time on the phone. A few minutes until 7. Jordan would be here any moment.

An idea shot off like a flare in my brain, sending a rush of urgency through my chest. I jammed the phone back into my pocket and rushed for the door. "I'm sorry, I have to go! I need to stop by Gary's before my date."

Mom reached after me as I sped past. "Ayla, wait! Won't Jordan be here any minute?"

I spun back to see both her and my father staring at me in alarm. "Yes. I mean, no," I said, nodding then shaking my head. "I'll text him and ask him to meet me at Gary's. I can ride with him from there."

"Why?" Dad gaped at me. "Did you forget about a shift or something?"

I forced a shaky breath. "No, I just—I need to talk to Gary about my schedule for this week, and I want to do it right away, before anyone else takes the shifts I want."

I tapped out a hurried message to Jordan to meet me at Gary's instead of home, and his reply came back immediately: *Sure, no problem. Already on the way. Be there soon.*

Dad blinked. "All right... Are you sure you're okay?"

I nodded, and this time drew a deeper breath, one that calmed a bit of the nerves as I met Dad's eyes again. "Yes, I'm fine." I smiled at both of them. "I'll be home by midnight. Thanks for letting me go out tonight."

Mom and Dad both relaxed, soothed by my return to normal behavior. "Have a good time, sweetheart," Dad said. "Text us when you're on the way home."

"I will." I nodded, then rushed to lift my purse from the hook by the door. I dropped my phone inside and turned back to Mom and Dad. "Love you both. I'm fine, really." I smiled at them, easing the edge of worry still on their faces.

"Love you too," they both said.

"Be safe!" Dad called after me as I slipped out the front door. "Pepper spray?"

"In my purse," I called back, waving over my shoulder. I slid into my Cirrus and started the engine, then looked up to find them both watching me leave from the door.

My heart squeezed as I backed out. I really did have some of the best parents ever. Which was why I didn't want to worry them over the vanishing man and magically appearing note I thought I'd seen. I could only imagine what doubting my sanity would do to them, especially when one weird guy staring at me in a parking lot had made them so worried. No, first I needed to figure out what I *had* seen, and thanks to Grandpa, I finally had a plan for doing that. I would convince Gary to swap me to closing shift for tomorrow night—then I could see what things really did happen at midnight.

CHAPTER 9

THE DRIVE TO MARIANA'S

Gary narrowed his eyes at me as he leaned his hands on his desk. "No, Ayla. I'm sorry, but no."

"Gary, please." I took a step closer to his desk in the cramped office and steadied my voice, trying not to sound as desperate as I felt inside. "I know you said you didn't want me working closing very often—"

"Not at all, anymore, Ayla," Gary said gently, but his eyes were firm. "Not for a while at least. Your parents called me earlier, told me about the man who was following you. Between that and what happened the other night, we all agreed it's best for you not to be here late alone for now."

"But who's going to close up?" Zach was younger than I was, and Larissa worked several nights a week at the hardware store. And Gary never stayed that late—he was a morning person who started turning into a pumpkin before ten o'clock even hit.

Gary leaned back in his chair. "We've brought on a new employee who can help out. She can't close every night, she's a student like you, but her parents are fine with her closing a couple nights a week, and Larissa and I can split the others."

Dread closed in on my chest. "Who?"

"Madison Kane."

"*What?*" I shouted, then slapped my hands over my horribly loud mouth, hyper-aware there were customers out in the restaurant.

If Gary was startled by my outburst, he didn't show it. "I know the two of you haven't had the best interactions"—Gary's eyes widened as my harsh laugh interrupted him—"but she's reassured me that won't be an issue while you're working. She agreed to keep things professional."

I gaped at Gary, wondering if all the strange things happening lately were a sign I'd stumbled into an alternate reality. Or maybe I'd been cursed—walked under a ladder without noticing? Did breaking a stranger's mysterious glass vial count like breaking a mirror? "Why is it okay for *her* to work closing?" I asked, my hands flailing in the air of their own accord. "Do you not care if *she* gets murdered?"

"Honestly, Ayla." Gary stared at me. "What's gotten into you?" He planted his hands back on the desk and leaned forward. "Of course, I do, but Madison's parents have reassured me she'll be safe. She'll be working here during regular hours as usual, but once I leave for the night, her personal bodyguard will wait in the car outside while she closes up."

I blinked. "She has a *bodyguard*? Why?"

Gary shook his head. "I'm not sure their personal affairs are something we should discuss." He sighed and glanced off, leaning back in his chair. "I've considered hiring a security guard for the café, myself, but... it's not something I can afford right now." His eyes met mine again. "I'm grateful we'll have security here a couple nights a week, even if it's Madison's. Soon after what happened to you, Larissa also reported hearing strange noises around here at night. Perhaps it will deter anyone from targeting us—or any of our employees—if they know we sometimes have a guard on site."

His last comments sent my mind racing in a new direction. "What kind of noises did Larissa say she heard?" I asked, trying to sound casual.

"I didn't press for details. She was a little shaken up by it at first, but afterward said she may have imagined it," Gary said. "But just in case, I stayed to close last night, myself."

"Did you... hear anything?" My voice was steady but my heart was racing out of control, though I couldn't have explained why.

"No." Gary rubbed a hand over his face. "It's always been safe in this part of Havenridge, but who knows if there might be some vagrants making their way through, or something like that. I'd hate for anything to happen to any of you."

My heart slowed at his response—a strange mix of relief and dismay. If I was the only one this whatever-it-was happened to... did that make me special, or insane? I made a mental note to talk to Larissa the absolute first moment I got a chance. Had she seen something, too? The idea sent a strange tremor through me, and I wasn't sure if it was hope or dread.

Gary sighed again, but his eyes were kind. "I know it may not be easy for you to work with Madison. I've tried not to put you on overlapping shifts too often, but when you do work together, I hope I can trust you to keep it professional."

I nodded, resigning myself to my new reality. "Of course." But curiosity spun wild in my mind. Why did Madison even *need* this job? From what I heard, her parents handed her hundred-dollar bills like they were sticks of gum. And if she did want a job, couldn't she have worked for her dad? And why in the world did she have a personal bodyguard following her around?

A knock rapped on Gary's door.

"Come in," Gary called.

The door eased open and Larissa's face poked through. "Gary, I'm clocking out. Zach's got the register." Her eyes slid to me. "Hi, Ayla."

Gary nodded. "Thank you, Larissa."

Larissa smiled, then turned to me. "Oh, and Ayla... that cute boy you brought in here the other day has been waiting outside for a while." She raised an eyebrow. "He's starting to look worried."

"Oh no, Jordan!"

Gary laughed and waved as I spun for the door. "See you tomorrow, Ayla—at the *afternoon* shift."

I waved to them both and rushed out toward the café door, hesitating as I caught sight of Jordan through the front window.

The sun had already begun setting when I arrived at the café, and now it was nearing dark outside, though still plenty bright enough to see Jordan, leaning against his shiny, dark blue Honda in a parking spot near the café door, staring at his shoes.

He was alone—this really was a date. A swirling rush of relief and nerves surged through me. The bell dinged as I yanked the café door open.

Jordan straightened the moment he saw me. "Ayla!" He gave a wave, a flicker of something passing over his face—nervousness? "Hi."

My heart lurched as I took him in. He was wearing an untucked, long-sleeved, black button-down shirt, and his jeans were nicer than the ones he usually wore to school—not that I'd ever seen him in a button-down, either. He typically wore t-shirts or Henley shirts. His hair stood in semi-messy spikes, as usual. I rushed toward him. "I'm so sorry I'm late. I was meeting with Gary, and—"

The stress on Jordan's face faded into a smile. "No worries. I'm just glad you're here. I was starting to think you weren't coming." He paused. "Actually, when you texted earlier, my first thought was that you were going to cancel."

"What? Why would I—" I stopped, realizing I *had* almost canceled. I met his eyes, but he let out a soft laugh, and I wasn't sure if he'd been serious or joking.

His gaze swept over me, and his smile widened. "You look great." He stepped around the car, pulling the passenger door open. "Your chariot, m'lady."

The smell of his cologne drifted toward me as I slid past him, something woodsy with a hint of spice and citrus. Since when did he wear cologne? But it smelled amazing. I glanced up at him, fighting a blush as I slid into the seat. "Thank you."

A genuine grin lit up his face as his eyes held mine, then he shut the door and hurried around to the other side.

I had only a few seconds to attempt to calm—unsuccessfully—the aggressively swarming butterflies in my chest before he plopped into the driver's seat and shut the door. We were alone in a car together, and I was suddenly *very* aware of that fact.

Jordan glanced over at me, a strange nervousness behind the smile in his eyes. "So, are you hungry? I picked somewhere to take you for dinner, but if there's something particular you want, I'm happy to—"

I hated choosing where to eat, even in the calmest of situations. The thought of having that pressure on me right now sent the butterflies into a swirling panic. I shook my head quickly. "Wherever you picked will be perfect."

Jordan smiled at me. "Okay. We're headed downtown, then. The place I chose is near the theater."

The downtown area of Havenridge was about a twenty-minute drive from Gary's Café. We talked very little on the drive over, and I was thankful when Jordan turned on some music, so that the silence between us didn't seem so loud. It wasn't uncomfortable silence—we'd always been good at being quiet in each other's presence without it being awkward—but tonight there was a strange undercurrent to the silence that ramped my nerves up to about a fifteen on a scale of ten. Jordan glanced at me often while he drove, which at least was reassuring because it seemed I wasn't the only one who was nervous.

The sun dipped lower to the horizon as we rode, approaching night by the time we reached downtown. Jordan took us to a little Italian restaurant I'd ridden past hundreds of times in my life but never stepped foot in. A tall streetlight lit the tiny parking lot, and at its rear stood a small but immaculate white stucco building, a cobblestone walkway leading from it to the parking lot through a landscaped garden full of rich grass and spotlight-lit ferns and shrubs. The white and green sign on the building's eaves shone bright against the night sky, with cursive red letters glowing in its center—Mariana's.

Jordan parked next to the row of cars already in the parking lot, near the start of the cobblestone walkway. "A close friend of our family owns this place," he said as he eased the car to a stop inside the parking space and turned off the engine. "I hope you like Italian food."

I nodded, taking in the warm ambiance of the place, but the strange realization that I still knew so little about Jordan grappled for my attention. I could drive all over town and never know if any quaint, perfect restaurant or quirky novelty shop I was standing in was owned by someone who was best friends with Jordan's family, or his neighbor, or even his uncle. Did he even have an uncle?

Jordan turned off the car and peered over at me. "You seem distracted. Are you okay? Would you prefer to eat somewhere else?"

I spun to him. "No, it's not that. It's—" I took a breath, trying to figure out the words for what I wanted to say.

Jordan watched me while my mind raced, perfect patience in his golden eyes, like I could take all the time I needed and he would still be waiting, willing to let me sort out my thoughts. It sent a warm current through my chest, and the butterflies burst out anew.

Which was terrible for my focus.

"I mean, I just—isn't it weird that I don't even know who knows you?" I blurted. "I mean, that I could be anywhere with anyone and they could be like your second uncle twice removed and I would never know?"

Jordan blinked at me. "Yeah, I guess that's... kinda weird."

I sighed. "I'm not saying what I mean. The words aren't coming out right."

Jordan's mouth spread into a smile, then—to my utter surprise—he reached for my face.

My heart raced like it was about to explode as his right hand settled on my cheek.

"Your words are perfect," he said.

"They are?" Heat rushed to my cheeks. What a lame thing to say. What was *wrong* with me?

Jordan's smile widened, and he gave one smooth, firm nod. "They are." He opened his mouth and his eyes flicked between mine for a moment, searching them, like he was trying to decide whether to say something. But he dropped his hand. "Are you ready to eat? It's already close to 8, so we don't have a lot of time before the movie." His voice had a sullen edge, almost like regret.

It sent my nerves spiraling into overdrive. "Jordan?"

Jordan clenched the steering wheel with both hands and stared out the windshield, drumming his fingers on the wheel. He huffed a breath, then turned to face me. "I give up."

I stared at him. "What?"

He ran a hand through his hair, which only made his messy spikes messier. "I don't know how to pretend we're only friends if we're not pretending we're only friends anymore," he said.

I blinked. "*What?*"

He pressed one of my hands between his. His eyes flicked between mine, studying me as he took another breath. "I've gotten good at pretending I only think of you as a friend, Ayla. But I—" He paused. "I don't know how to pretend I don't feel more, not when it's like this." He gestured between us, one hand still holding mine.

The butterflies were screaming now, so loudly I could hardly think. I didn't even know butterflies *could* scream.

He squeezed my hand gently, his palm warm against my mine. "I've had a crush on you for *years*, Ayla. I didn't ever plan to act on it, but this year, it's our last year, senior year, and I..."

He shook his head, then seemed to abandon his train of thought and leap onto a new one. "Do you know how many times I've stood somewhere in this town, unable to get you out of my head, and wondering if the shop I stood in was a place you liked to shop, or if the owners knew you, or if there was any chance I might run into you there?" A short laugh escaped him. "And then, you're here in my car, on a *date* with me, and you say... what you said."

He dropped my hand and pulled back, horror flashing in his eyes. "I'm sorry, that was too much. I shouldn't have said any of that. The last thing I ever wanted to do is make you feel weird or pressured, or—or do anything to hurt our friendship."

His gaze turned pleading. "Ayla, hanging out with you in those brief moments between classes is the *best* thing about school for me, the thing I look forward to everyday. I would never want to ruin that."

He sighed. "This was probably a bad idea. Do you want me to take you home?"

I gaped at him. "*What?*" Apparently, I'd forgotten how to use any other words.

"I'll take you home," Jordan said, turning forward in his seat, but then he sighed and turned back toward me. "I'm sorry, Ayla. This wasn't at all what I intended to say to you tonight. But to be honest, part of me is glad I told you finally—how I feel about you, I mean." His mouth twitched up into a sad smile. "I've been wanting to for ages. I just didn't want to lose you as a friend." His smile vanished. "I can tell this made things weird for you, though, so I'll just take you home."

He was already reaching for the ignition.

I bit back the *What* that threatened to escape my mouth again, forcing my brain to find other words. "Jordan, I don't want you to take me home."

He stared at me. "You don't?"

"...I don't."

His eyes widened with something like hope. "Really? You're sure it's not weird for you?"

I nodded. "I'm sure."

The worry on his face slowly morphed into a smile. "Wow. Well, in that case... do you want to go inside and have dinner with me?"

I smiled back. "I would love to."

His smile spread into a grin. "This time, it's my treat." A snarky glint came back into his eyes. "We *are* on a date, after all."

CHAPTER 10

CRASH AND BURN

The atmosphere inside the restaurant was exactly what I had expect-ed from the outside: cozy and magical. Strands of golden string lights formed a glowing patchwork over the ceiling, with hanging plants and ferns dangling from the corners. Small, white-clothed tables topped with gorgeous red roses were placed strategically throughout the dining space, and gentle music drifted from hidden speakers somewhere over-head, backed by a low chatter of conversations from seated patrons and the sizzle and clanks of meals being prepared behind the doors to the kitchen. The savory scents of garlic and other spices drifting from the kitchen made my mouth water.

A middle-aged woman in a black dress with upswept hair greeted us at the door. "Jordan! I heard you might be coming by." She smiled, her welcoming gaze landing on me before swinging back to him. "Table for two?"

Jordan nodded. "This is Ayla." He gestured to me with a grin. "Ayla, this is Mrs. Lucci. Her grandmother founded this restaurant."

"Very nice to meet you, Ayla." The woman mirrored his smile. "You can call me Marianne."

Marianne led us to an open table in the corner, away from other patrons. "I thought you might like a quiet table," she said with a knowing gaze. "So you could talk."

Jordan gave me a shy glance, then stepped around me and pulled out my chair for me. "Is this table okay with you?"

I sank into the chair and looked up at him. Jordan always treated me with care, but the way he was looking at me tonight, like the mask over his feelings had been stripped away, was still sort of blowing my mind. "Um, yes," I said, blushing as our eyes locked. "It's great."

Jordan tore his eyes from mine, slid around to the other side of the table, and settled into the chair across from me.

Marianne handed us each a menu. "I'll be back soon to take your orders." She smiled, then hurried away to check on other patrons.

Suddenly the weight of our aloneness crashed in on me again, and I yanked the menu up in front of my face, sweeping my eyes over words and photos my brain couldn't focus enough to process. I felt Jordan watching me as I buried my face in the menu. I desperately wanted this to go well—because I liked him and hoped this was going somewhere? Because he was my friend and I didn't want to ruin that? Because both? I wasn't sure, and the confusing swirl of emotions inside me was doing no favors for my mental clarity or my appetite, despite my growling stomach. "So..." I willed my frazzled brain into gear and scanned my raised menu again, overwhelmed by all the choices. "What do you recommend?"

"Ayla."

The gentleness in Jordan's voice shocked me into lowering the menu, and I found him leaned forward and staring at me, his gorgeous face etched in concern.

"I'm fine," I said, and my voice came out a strange mix of defensive and sheepish.

"You forget I know you well enough to read the stress on your face." Jordan's eyes were steady on mine, but the wall in them had gone up again, blocking off some of the emotion I'd seen a moment earlier.

I instantly missed it.

"I know." I sighed and set the menu on the table. This was Jordan. *Jordan*. One of my closest friends. One of my *only* friends. I forced myself to meet his gaze. "I don't know what's wrong with me. I—"

"You're nervous," Jordan said, straightening. He sucked in a sharp breath. "I've put too much pressure on you. On this date." He reached across the table, but stopped himself before touching my hand and pulled back, dropping his hand in his lap. "I'm so sorry."

The heaviness evaporated from his face as he gave me a sweet smile. "I should've been clearer before. I don't expect anything of you. There is zero pressure here. Honestly. Let's just talk, have a good time. See where it goes. No matter what, I'm still your friend if you'll have me. Always."

I studied his eyes, and though I still felt a wall there, blocking out some of what he felt, the smile he was giving me was echoed in his eyes. He wasn't upset with me... but I wished I knew what else he was feeling, the part he was covering over. I nodded slowly, relief bringing a smile to my face as well. "Okay."

I should've done all this before Callan showed up. What if I've missed my chance?

I swore I heard the words like it was Jordan's own voice, but I'd been staring at his face and his mouth never moved.

Jordan's brows lowered in concern. "Ayla, what's wrong?"

"Nothing." I shook my head. "I—I thought I heard something. It was nothing."

Jordan seemed to catch the hint that I didn't want him to pry. He swallowed, then lifted a menu. "I love the lasagna here, but if you like mushrooms, the mushroom ravioli is good, too."

I smiled at him, grateful for the change of topic. "I love mushrooms."

His eyes brightened. "Really? Me too! A lot of people think they're gross."

The next hour of our dinner went smoothly, though more like we were friends hanging out than the intensity I'd felt from him in the car. More than once, I tried to steer our conversation back into that range, to coax back the emotion in his eyes, but I couldn't find a way, and Jordan seemed content to chat like it was nothing more than a casual hang out—though

I did find his eyes lingering on me while we were eating, and felt him watching me anytime I looked away.

The food was delicious—I was glad I'd chosen the mushroom ravioli—and true to his word, Jordan insisted on paying when the check came, even though I offered to pay for my own.

"It's still a date," he said as he slid the money into the leather booklet Marianne dropped off with our receipt, but his eyes lacked the playful glint they'd had when he said it in the car.

Marianne took the payment and smiled her goodbyes, then Jordan pushed back from the table. "Are you ready for the movie? It's almost time." He came around to my chair as I gathered up my purse and stood. He peered down at me, an arm's length away, but a vast distance in his eyes as they studied mine. "Do you still want to go to the movie?"

I'm screwing it all up. How do I fix this?

He watched me, his mouth not moving an inch, but his voice had sounded clearly in my mind.

I swallowed, trying not to let my panic show on my face. I'd thought I was losing it with the note and the disappearing guy, but this was even weirder. Apparently, I was going full-crazy at a rapid pace... though maybe insanity was the sort of thing that appeared slowly at first and then replicated exponentially until it covered all of you, like chicken pox. I'd never gone crazy before; I wouldn't know.

Jordan took a small step back. "I know it's late. Would you rather I just take you home?"

The uncertainty in his eyes made my heart ache, and I decided I'd have to deal with my impending mental breakdown another time, because right now, Jordan needed me to focus. "No," I said firmly, meaning it. "I want to go to the movie."

I really did want to spend more time with him, plus *I think I might be going crazy, can we take a rain check?* wasn't something I was willing to say.

Jordan blinked, then nodded. "Okay, yeah. Let's go, then." He turned for the door, expecting me to follow. "It's a good movie—you've seen it, right?"

I hurried after him and grabbed his hand, pulling him back a step.

Jordan stopped, his eyes falling on our clasped hands before sliding up to my face. "What's wrong? Did you leave something at the table?"

"I want to go to the movie *with you*," I said, shaping each word carefully. "I don't care what movie it is. We could go stare at a blank wall, not saying a word, and it would still be exactly where I want to be tonight."

Jordan froze for a moment, studying my face. Then he raised our clasped hands to his chest and closed the distance between us. I felt his heartbeat steady beneath my fist as he stared down at me, his eyes flicking between mine in that way he had, examining the meaning behind my words. "I'm not asking for anything," he whispered. "You don't have to do any of this."

I met his eyes as they stilled. "I know."

"We could go back to how it was yesterday, like it's always been. I would never hold that against you. I wouldn't even bring up tonight at all, like it never happened."

I nodded. "I know."

"But if we—if we do this, I'm not expecting you to commit to anything. You could see other people, if you wanted to... at least until we..." He took a breath. "Until we figure out what this is, and if it's what we both want right now."

My eyes widened as I imagined him with Reina, or even Madison Kane, taking them out on dates like this, while we both figured things out. "Is that what you want?"

He dropped my hands and stepped back. "What? No," he blurted, then blushed. "I mean, no, not really, but I'm willing to. If that's what makes you more comfortable."

A laugh escaped me—then guilt rushed in as hurt flashed in his eyes.

"Jordan, I only laughed because *of course* that doesn't make me comfortable," I said quickly. "Do you think I'd want to see you taking Reina or

Madison on dates in between my dates with you? Do you know how"—I stopped on the word jealous—"*un*comfortable that would make me?"

True horror washed over his face. "Why in the world would I date Madison Kane?"

I noticed he didn't quite balk at the thought of dating Reina, but I was too afraid to ask why. "I just meant that it would feel weird to me to date you and other people at the same time, and to see you doing the same," I said. "Wouldn't it feel weird to you?"

"Yes, of *course,* but—" Jordan shook his head. "But that's not what I meant. I wouldn't—" He stopped and glanced around the restaurant, which to my embarrassment now had several uncomfortable patrons doing their best to pretend they couldn't hear our conversation. He reached for one of my hands again. "Let's take this outside." He tugged me toward the door.

The warm night air enveloped us as we slipped out onto the front walk, under the glow of the backlit sign on the front of the restaurant. The eaves beneath the sign cast shadows over Jordan's face, darkening his golden eyes.

He turned toward me, one hand still loosely around mine. "I don't want to rush things. I want to do this right. Rather than making it anything official, I think we should date casually first, almost like we're just friends, so there's no pressure. Then you'll be free to think it through and decide if it's what you want."

I stared at him. Did he not think me capable of making that decision without all these awkward boundaries? This date was on its way to crashing and burning faster than a train car full of dynamite.

He swallowed. "I'll tell you up front, I'm not planning to date anyone else right now. I just don't want to put pressure on our relationship when it's still so new. I mean, not that we have a relationship yet, that's not what I'm saying, but I—"

He was making less and less sense the more he talked. I suddenly wondered if he thought I had feelings for Callan, and didn't want to force me to choose before I was ready, but the only evidence I had for that reasoning was the words I'd *hallucinated* him saying, and besides—I wasn't on a date with *Callan* tonight, was I? Was he really that dense?

I put one hand on my hip; my other was still gripped in his. "Jordan."

He stopped rambling as I stepped toward him, his eyes scanning my face.

"Is this because of—" I began, but before I could say anything else, he held up his free hand.

"We can just hang out more, outside of school this time. Friends with a potential for more. That's all I'm asking for right now." He paused. "Actually... that's all I *want* right now."

That rejection stung. I dropped his hand. "*Friends* don't usually hold hands, Jordan." I didn't even try to keep the anger from my voice.

A flash of hurt passed through his eyes. He swallowed and nodded. "Yeah. You're right. I'm sorry." He stepped away, putting a full arm's length between us.

Disappointment washed in over my anger. What in the world was going on with him? The emotional roller coaster of this conversation was giving me whiplash, but if he could wall off his emotions, so could I. Or at least I could try. I imagined my face as a mask of stone, no emotions whatsoever, and when I spoke my voice came out cold. "Are you sure this is what you want?"

He visibly winced, but the flicker of emotion vanished as soon as it appeared, replaced by a mask of calm. He cleared his throat and nodded. "Yes, I think it's what's best, for now. Is that... okay with you?"

Was that *okay* with me? For someone I knew was smart, he was truly being an idiot. I stepped toward him, hurt and anger swirling in my chest. "Why are you being this way?"

"What way?" To my surprise he looked genuinely confused.

His gaze flicked to my mouth then back to my eyes as I stepped closer, inches from his face.

"*This* way." I gestured between us. "Jordan, I feel like we're playing a game I don't know the rules for. I'm *so* confused. Now, I'm not even sure—" I stopped, uncertain how to finish the sentence. I wasn't sure *what*? Whether I still wanted a shot at a relationship with him? That was a lie—I knew I did. But I was no longer sure how he felt about me, despite his confession in the car an hour ago. Had he even meant it? I didn't think he would have lied to me, but at the least, he seemed confused about his own feelings. Or maybe I'd somehow misunderstood him. Besides, the guy I was interested in dating was the Jordan of *before*, not the closed-off, idiotic version of him that was talking to me now. Even him showing up with Reina for a misunderstood group hangout would have been less mortifying than whatever had just happened between us.

Jordan stared at me, a debate warring behind his eyes.

Tell her you're an idiot and you didn't mean—No. If you take it all back, she may agree to date you only because she doesn't want to hurt you. You won't know what she really would have chosen.

I gaped at him, the words in my mind filling in the gaps of the conversation, though I couldn't be sure I wasn't imagining them. Maybe the words in my head were some sort of intuitive inner monologue trying to help me? That was the best explanation I had at the moment, so I went with it. Tonight's interactions did *almost* make sense—sort of—if Jordan thought I cared for him deeply as a friend but was also interested in pursuing Callan. Perhaps Jordan *was* just trying to protect me from the awkwardness of turning him down. It still meant he was kind of an idiot, but at least it would explain his motives.

I swallowed down everything else I wanted to say, and stepped back. "You really think we should just be friends? That's what you *want*?"

He shook his head. "No. I mean, yes, for now, but... I hope not forever. Only until we spend some more time together. Until we can be sure it's the right choice. I mean, we've hardly ever even hung out outside of school. Our friendship is too important to me to rush into anything else, and I never should have dumped all my feelings on you on a first date like this. It wasn't fair, I see that now."

The words I was half-sure I'd imagined echoed through my mind again—if I tried to convince him I did want more than friendship right now, he'd think I just didn't want to hurt him. He'd think it was pity. *Oh, Jordan.* Why did he doubt himself so much? His insecurity made me hurt for him, even just as his friend—a lonely ache I didn't quite know how to fix.

He reached for my hand, then pulled back, then reached for it again, holding it awkwardly like a limp handshake. "I'm sorry, Ayla. I've made this date awkward and ruined your whole night. Are you angry with me? How can I make it up to you?"

The concern in his eyes, combined with the echoing words in my mind, melted my frustration. I sighed. "No, I'm not angry," I said honestly. "Just... surprised."

He stepped closer, within kissing distance, his eyes boring into mine like he was reconsidering his own restrictions. For a moment, I thought he really might kiss me, erase all the nonsense about just being friends, and restart this date how it should've gone. But then he took a deep breath and stepped back and my hope went with him, replaced by a heavy lump of disappointment.

Jordan pulled his phone from his pocket and glanced at the time, and when he looked back up, his eyes didn't quite meet mine. "Are you ready to get to the movie? We'll be late if we don't go now. I mean, if you still want to go."

He smiled at me, but it was brittle—I could see the disappointment behind it.

We were *both* disappointed, and it seemed so stupid to leave things this way. Everything in my mind screamed to tear away the facade and have a real conversation about how we both felt, but the conversation had already gone so horribly sideways, I couldn't figure out a way to reset it that wouldn't just reinforce his belief that I was trying to spare his feelings.

Maybe I should *go date Callan,* I thought, *just to bring Jordan to his senses*. But no—I could never hurt Jordan on purpose like that. He might be an idiot, but he was my friend. Might have been more than a friend, if he hadn't been so stupid about pushing me away. But remaining only friends had been his choice, and I didn't like playing games. Maybe "friends" *was* all we were meant to be.

"I'm sorry about tonight, Ayla," he said again, his eyes wide and vulnerable as they locked on mine. "I'll pay for the movie if you still want to go." There was a trace of hope in his eyes. "Unless you do want me to take you home now?" The hope wavered.

This was going to be really awkward at school tomorrow. That said, his stupid, uncertain face still did fluttery things to my insides. I sighed. "No, it's fine. Let's go to the movie."

Chapter 11

Uh, Maybe?

Talking during the movie would've been rude, but that was no explanation for the silence that followed us after we left the theater. Jordan and I had sat stiffly beside each other for the entire movie, hardly looking at each other, and by the time the movie let out and he walked me briskly to the car, I was dreading being alone with him on the drive home. Just like that, our friendship had been ruined—the very thing we'd both been trying to avoid.

What was I going to do now?

Jordan tapped his fingers on the steering wheel as we sat in traffic a few blocks from the ramp that led us to the interstate out of downtown. The clock on his dash read 11:13 PM.

"Looks like some kind of event at the convention center just let out," Jordan said, glancing at me. "I might be late getting you home. I'm really sorry."

I stared out the car window as I pulled my cell phone from my purse. "It's fine. I'll text my parents to let them know." I tapped out the text and sent it, then we both stared—him at the windshield and me out the passenger window—as the traffic crept forward, smothering each other with awkward silence.

The drive back to Gary's Café, where I'd left my car, felt like an eternity.

Finally, Jordan pulled into the lot and parked beside my Cirrus, then glanced across the parking lot. "There's another car here." Concern laced his voice. "Should I walk you to yours?"

"It's two feet away, Jordan," I said, already reaching for the door handle. "I'll be okay." My eyes caught on the dark SUV, realization hitting me as I pushed open the door. "It's Madison's bodyguard."

"Her what?" Jordan leaned forward, peering past me at the dark vehicle. "And why would they be *here*?"

I sighed, glancing back at him. "She works here now."

Jordan's eyes widened. "*Why?*"

I shrugged. "How should I know? Anyway, I'll be fine. Thanks for the dinner and the movie." I hesitated, a wave of regret washing over me at how the night had gone, and how awkward this would all be at school. "See you tomorrow."

"Ayla, wait."

I turned to look back at him.

"I'll wait until you start up your car, at least. So I can be sure you'll get home okay."

I closed my eyes for a second and drew a breath, then nodded. "Okay, sure."

True to his word, Jordan sat in his car until I was in mine with the engine running, then he slowly backed out of his parking spot, gave me one last, awkward wave, and drove away.

I dropped my head onto the steering wheel, staring off into the darkness of my eyelids as I willed away the reality of the past few hours.

A knock on the driver's side window made me jump and scream.

"Sorry, miss, didn't mean to startle you."

My panicked gaze fell on a hulking, muscled man outside my car window, wearing a black sweatshirt and matching black sweatpants. I slid my hand from the steering wheel and toward the passenger seat where I'd set my purse, doing my best not to draw attention to the movement as I groped for the pepper spray in the purse's outer pocket.

"I'm Miss Kane's security." The guy leaned down to my eye level. "I noticed you getting dropped off—you're Ayla, right? You were on the list of employees."

"What? Oh." Weren't bodyguards supposed to wear suits? I relaxed a bit, but kept my hand clenched around the tube of pepper spray inside my purse, just in case. "Do you need something?"

"Just wanted to make sure you were okay. Heard your car start up, but when you didn't pull out after a while, I got a little concerned. It's pretty late for a girl to be out alone."

I glanced at the dash of my car. *11:57*. I was definitely going to be late getting home, now. I was glad I'd texted my parents ahead of time. We lived close by the café, but it was almost midnight.

It was almost midnight.

My gaze flicked to the front windows of Gary's, a crazy idea crackling like lightning through my brain. I turned to the bodyguard. "Um, actually, I need to go inside for a minute. Is that all right? There's something I... need to do. I'll be quick."

He narrowed his eyes. "I'm not sure that's a good idea."

I turned off the car and yanked my keys from the ignition, holding them up. "I have a key to get in. Gary trusts me. I was only asking because I didn't want you to, like, shoot me or something. I'm not here to hurt Madison."

The guard chuckled under his breath, though his eyes still held mine firmly. "Fine," he said at last. "If you let yourself in with your own key and the owner's okay with that, I suppose it's not a violation of anything. I'm here to make sure no one hurts Miss Kane. But be quick about it. Her shift's almost over, and she'll need to lock up so I can get her home."

I nodded quickly. "Of course."

The guy stepped back.

I swung open the car door and rushed to the front of the café, keys jangling as I scrambled for the right one and jammed it into the lock, then yanked open the door.

"Gerard, what are you—" Madison shoved open the kitchen door and rushed out as I neared the front counter, but stopped when she saw me. "Oh, it's you. What are you doing here?"

My eyes flicked to the clock on the wall. *11:59.* If I was correct about any of this—if I wasn't completely insane, that was—then I had less than a minute to get Madison out of there before something happened I would never be able to explain. "Um, a phone, the kitchen, have you seen a phone? Maybe in the closet?"

"What? No." Madison planted her hands on her hips.

"Could you check?"

"I was just in there."

"Please, Madison? Please go check."

"*You* go check."

"You're the one doing inventory. You don't want me to screw up anything for you, do you? Gary's particular."

Madison narrowed her eyes, then huffed a sigh. "Fine, but only because you're a freak and it'll get you out of here faster."

She stalked back into the kitchen.

I heaved a sigh of relief and spun, putting my back against the counter just as an eerie trill sliced the air.

And this time, I *saw* it happen. The air sliced open with a silvery flash. And then a hot, blue-eyed stranger dropped straight out of the sky.

"Ack!" I jumped back and gaped as he landed on the café floor, stumbling a little as his boots gained purchase. Then his eyes flicked up to me, the same eyes I'd seen that night in the café before he'd fallen unconscious. The eyes that had pleaded while he whispered for help. The eyes I'd been seeing in my dreams.

He opened his mouth, as though to say something, then shook his head and ran at me.

I gasped in alarm but he raced right past me, yanking the "Deal of the Day" chalkboard from the counter beside me and knocking over the cup of pens in his haste to fish out a chalk paint marker.

"What are you even *doing* out there?" Madison yelled from the kitchen. "And I don't see your stupid phone!"

I ignored her, my eyes frozen on the gorgeous stranger, who was scribbling something over the calligraphed coffee special Larissa had written earlier.

He held the chalkboard up where I could see it, his eyes urging me with a wild panic as he jabbed a finger at the words. *Can't talk. One minute.*

"Give you a minute?" I whispered.

He shook his head wildly, then scratched out the words and frantically wrote something else and waved his hand at it, like we were playing a panicked game of Pictionary. *Danger.* He pointed a finger at me.

"I'm in danger?"

He nodded manically, his deep blue eyes peering at me with concern.

"Why?"

He reached for my face, his hand hovering in front of me, and the tender gaze he gave me sent shivers down my spine. Then he sucked in a frustrated breath and bent back over the chalkboard. His hair flopped forward as he wrote, hiding some of his face, but when he looked back up at me, his gaze was urgent. *Tell no one you saw me.* He jammed his fingers at the words as I read. He scrawled again as I watched. *Lives depend—*

He vanished, the chalkboard and marker clattering to the floor.

"What was *that*!?"

I spun to find Madison staring with wide-eyed panic, pointing a shaky finger at the empty air beside me. "A guy, there was a guy, and he—" Her eyes flicked to me. "There was a guy. There was a guy? There was—"

"I think you broke her," a familiar voice said near the front door.

I jumped and turned to find Jordan standing in the doorway.

"What are *you* doing here?" It came out harsher than I meant for it to, but to be fair, I'd just seen a guy vanish.

Jordan let out a nervous laugh, his gaze sliding between Madison, me, and the chalkboard on the floor. "Ayla, I—I only got a couple blocks away before I realized I couldn't leave things like that. I was driving to your house to beg your parents to let me talk to you for a minute, but then I saw your car was still here. I pulled back in just in time to see you going inside. I sweet-talked that bodyguard to let me in here to check on you. But... now I kind of can't ignore the fact that I'm either losing my mind or something very crazy just happened. Did I just see a guy disappear into thin air?"

I stared at him. "Uh, maybe?"

He stepped inside, letting the café door swing shut behind him. "Ayla, what in the world is going on?"

CHAPTER 12

THAT'S NOT AN ANSWER

Jordan's eyes bored into me. "Ayla? What just happened?"

I huffed a nervous breath. "Um... well..."

An ear-splitting scream sliced behind me and I spun, heart racing, to find Madison's perfectly manicured fingernails tangled in the perfectly parted hair on top of her head. "A guy just disappeared into nothing!" Madison shrieked, her words finally seeming to catch up with her.

I turned back to Jordan with an anxious shrug. "Yeah, that. Basically."

Jordan shook his head, his eyes flicking between mine with a blend of panic and scrutiny. "Ayla, that's not—that doesn't make sense."

A short laugh escaped me. "Um, yeah. I know."

The front door behind Jordan whipped open. Madison's bodyguard shoved Jordan aside and rushed in, gun drawn, gaze sweeping the room.

"Sheesh," Jordan mumbled as he caught his balance against the front window.

"Miss Kane!" The bodyguard slowed as he took in the situation, confusion blending with the alertness on his face. "Is everything all right?"

Clearly he'd expected something far more dangerous than spilled chalkboard markers and some rattled-looking teens.

Madison's eyes cut to mine, wide like a startled rabbit, and for one brief moment, I let her see my panic, my pleading. *Please don't tell.* But I had no hope of that—it was Madison.

She dropped her hands and faced her bodyguard. "I'm fine, Gerard. Sorry to startle you. Ayla here knocked over the chalkboard and the noise scared me." She shot a fierce glare at me, then rolled her eyes as usual. "She's a klutz."

Gerard glanced between Madison and me, with an extra gaze flicked behind at Jordan. "Are you certain, Miss Kane?"

Madison smoothed her tousled hair and smiled. "Yes, I'm sure. You can wait in the car. I'll be out in a moment."

Gerard nodded and holstered his weapon. "As you wish, Miss Kane. I'll have it running and ready."

Gerard turned and strode back out the front door.

The door dinged shut. I stared at Madison. "Why did you—"

"Cover for you?" Madison shrugged, her cold glare fading to an expression more vulnerable than anything I'd ever seen on her face. "I don't know. I guess I just... I mean... I did see what I thought I saw, right? It wasn't a trick, or—or my imagination?"

I drew a slow breath, amazed I was even trusting Madison enough to *have* this conversation. But what choice was I left with? I held my gaze steady on hers. "No trick. You really saw it."

Madison burst into tears.

"What the—" Jordan rushed up behind me, his startled face pivoting between me and Madison, who sank to the ground and tucked her knees to her face in a shaking, sobbing ball.

A wave of panicked empathy washed over me, and I dropped to my knees beside her. "Madison, what's—"

My cell phone's loud ring startled me back to my feet. I yanked it from my pocket, dread filling my chest. "My parents."

Jordan's wide eyes caught on mine as I answered the call.

"Yes?"

"Ayla, thank goodness!" Mom's frantic voice blared into my ear. "Why aren't you home yet? Did something happen?"

I paced, staring at the floor. "No, I'm fine, I just—I just went inside Gary's for a minute, to get something from—"

"Come home right now," Dad yelled from the background. "We are going to have a serious talk about what the word *curfew* means when you get here."

"On my way." I swallowed, then hung up and slid the phone back into my pocket.

Jordan's worried eyes were waiting for me when I looked up, and his mouth tilted into a nervous smile. "They're never gonna let me take you on a date again."

Madison's head flicked up, some of her usual judgment spilling back onto her tear-splotched face, though her eyes were swollen and watery. "You two were on a *date*?"

I sighed. "I'm sorry, I can't do this right now. I have to go."

"What? You can't leave *now*." Madison shoved to her feet at the same moment Jordan reached out and placed his hand on my arm.

"Wait," he said. "Ayla—"

I flicked my gaze between the two of them. "Please don't tell anyone what happened tonight. *Please*." I needed time to look into this, time to figure out what the note meant—time to talk to Grandpa. He knew something, I was sure of it now... but whether he *knew* he knew it or possessed a fleeting intuition was yet to be determined. Besides, the vanishing guy had warned me not to tell anyone, and though I couldn't help what Madison and Jordan had seen, something told me to trust the guy who'd vanished—to honor his request.

Jordan dropped his hand. "Ayla, that's not an answer."

The warm spot where his hand had rested quickly grew cold. "I'll explain tomorrow, I promise. As much as I can." I walked backward to the door, holding each of their gazes for a long moment as I moved. "Don't say anything to anyone. *Please*."

They both stared at me, Jordan's eyes troubled and Madison's red-rimmed with tears, then I spun, yanked the door open, and rushed for my car.

My parents were seated beside each other on the living room couch when I came inside, waiting for me.

Dad's lecture about curfew turned out to be more of a brief expression of his disappointment that I'd broken their trust by not coming straight home, especially when I might have a stalker.

"Did your delay at the café have something to do with Jordan?" Mom eyed me suspiciously.

"What? No. He'd already dropped me off at my car, and he thought I was heading right home. The rest was my fault." My mind raced over how to explain things without saying too much. "Gary said strange things have been happening there late at night, and... Madison's bodyguard was there, but I wanted to—I mean, I guess I wanted to make sure things were normal." I excluded the fact that they absolutely *weren't* normal.

"So you went inside instead of coming straight home because you were worried about Madison?" Mom asked.

That made me seem more noble than I was and spurred an instant pang of guilt. "No, not exactly. I guess I was just... curious. And I thought, since Madison's bodyguard was there, that I would be safe. I only meant to be inside for a minute or two, but Madison started talking to me, and Jordan came back—"

"Jordan came *back*?" My dad's voice raised.

"To check on me," I said quickly. "Our... date didn't go well. He was going to come here and ask to speak with me, but he noticed my car was still parked at Gary's."

My parents' stern expressions softened slightly.

"Your date didn't go well?" Mom asked in a soft voice.

Dad wasn't quite as calm. "Did he hurt or pressure you in some way?"

"No!" I blurted. "Nothing like that. We... had an argument, I guess. About whether we should date or just be friends."

My parents' faces both flooded with compassion.

"Do you want to talk about it?" Mom asked gently.

I sighed. "Not right now. Not really."

Mom and Dad shared a glance, but didn't press for more information.

"I'm really sorry I didn't come straight home like you told me to," I said, grateful to change the subject back to my punishment.

My dad sighed. "I appreciate that, but I am still disappointed in your behavior tonight. I was worried enough when I thought you were coming straight home, Ayla. And going inside the cafe to check on 'strange happenings' was beyond reckless, especially with recent circumstances. We talked about the need to be cautious right now." He stood, eyes on me as he offered his hand to help Mom stand, too. "I'm going to assume this won't happen again."

"No, sir." I shook my head. "It won't. Sorry for worrying you."

Mom stood up next to him, looking more exhausted than upset.

They both watched me for a moment, then Dad placed his hand on my shoulder as he passed me. "I'm heading to bed."

Mom followed him with a soft brush of her hand over my arm. "Goodnight, sweetheart. Get in bed as soon as possible, okay?"

I nodded. "Yes, ma'am."

They shuffled through the kitchen and out the other side, toward the hall that led to their bedroom.

I dropped my head into my hands. I hated that I'd worried them—but how could I tell them the full truth? They had enough to worry about with Grandpa, and their jobs, and already thinking I was being stalked. I couldn't add magically appearing notes and vanishing strangers to that until I knew more about what I'd stumbled into. And until I knew why the mysterious stranger had warned me not to say anything. Would telling others put them at risk, somehow?

The intensity of that mysterious guy's deep blue eyes lingered in my mind as I trudged to my room, heart aching, to get ready for bed.

I paused at Grandpa's door. I was certain he knew something, but despite my desperation to talk to him, I didn't dare wake him now. I was in enough trouble with Mom & Dad already. But if by some chance he was already awake...

I eased open his door, peering in. The moon cast a gentle light over Grandpa's sleeping form. Lavender vapor wafted from his bedside oil diffuser and a low rumble of snores drifted out at me. I sighed and shut the door. I'd have to talk to him in the morning.

I had just finished getting ready for bed when my phone rang. I hurried to grab it, not wanting the sound to wake anyone else, but when I saw the name on the screen, I hesitated. Jordan. He *never* called me. We hardly even texted.

I knew he wanted answers about tonight, and I couldn't blame him, but I'd already promised to tell him and Madison whatever I could tomorrow, and I needed some time to think through things before that happened. There was a chance he was calling to talk about our date, but I wasn't sure *that* was a topic I was quite ready to tackle tonight, either. I swiped *Ignore,* put my calls on silent, and plugged my phone in to charge by my bed.

I stared at my desk, then crossed the room and pulled the folded note from its drawer. My eyes drifted over the words again and again, but I found no further meaning from its riddle. Was the blue-eyed guy who appeared to me Prince Kaizyn? Had he left the note for me? Or dropped it the last time he appeared, maybe? He'd warned me about danger—did it have something to do with this riddle?

I clutched the paper as I crossed the room again, then flipped back my comforter. My silk pajamas glided beneath it as I slid into bed. I rolled to the side, turned off my bedside lamp, and flopped back onto my pillow, paper still clutched in my hand. Its words danced through my mind as I stared at the dark ceiling. I had no way of solving this riddle on my own, but I did know one person, other than the blue-eyed guy, who might have answers: Grandpa. I grabbed my phone from my night table, set an early alarm so I'd have time to get ready *and* talk to Grandpa before leaving for school, then dropped back onto my pillow, running the paper's words through my mind until I sank into a fitful sleep.

When my alarm blared the next morning, I almost hit the snooze—until the folded paper crumpled under me as I turned and I remembered why I'd set the early alarm in the first place. The sky was still dark, which wasn't different from usual, but at 5:30 AM the sky still had a deep-night feel rather than the almost-morning hue I was used to. It made me want to crawl back into bed, but answers wouldn't find themselves.

I moved through my usual morning routine in a fog of exhaustion. Teeth brushed. Quick shower since I hadn't the night before. Hair thrown in a bun to air-dry. T-shirt and a pair of jeans for school, though not my favorites, since they still hadn't been washed. Backpack checked for homework and books, zipped and placed by my door. Socks and sneakers. Cell phone. And the note. I slid it into my pocket last, then tiptoed through the dark house to deposit my backpack by the front door before heading to the kitchen for breakfast.

Grandpa would be waking up any moment, based on his usual routine, and my plan was to eat first and have breakfast ready for him when he got up, so I could focus on talking to him while he ate. I would have only a few minutes with him before I had to leave for school, and I wanted to make them count. I fried myself an egg and made two slices of toast, topping mine with butter and setting it aside to melt while I spread Grandpa's toast with pomegranate jam. I prepared two glasses of orange juice, then sat at the kitchen table, eating my own breakfast while I waited for Grandpa to arrive.

He never came. When I couldn't delay more than a few minutes longer without being late for school, I grew worried. It wasn't like him to sleep in so long. He had a morning routine, and rarely deviated unless he was sick. Concern churned in my chest as I crept to his bedroom and eased open his door, hoping to find him up and dressed. Hopefully he was just dragging a little this morning. If so, I could tell him his breakfast was waiting, maybe ask him why he'd said what he did about midnight the night before. The rest would have to wait until later. But when I pushed his door open, his snores drifted out at me. He was still asleep.

A small thread of relief eased through my concern—at least he was okay. But he'd been so tired the past few days, and this was far longer-lasting and more intense than the fatigue he usually showed while approaching an episode. Did that mean this episode would be worse than usual, when it finally hit? Or was Grandpa worn out from something else, maybe fighting off a cold? Either way, I didn't dare wake him—not only did he clearly need the rest, but Grandpa was notoriously grumpy when awakened before he was ready, even on a good day. Any conversation I tried to have with him in that state would be unproductive.

I eased his door shut with a wave of unease, then returned to the kitchen. Mom and Dad would both be getting up in a few minutes, so I scrawled out a quick note for them on the refrigerator to let them know Grandpa had slept through breakfast. I packed up his toast with jam and put it in the fridge in case he woke up soon, then grabbed my backpack and headed to the car.

I was pushing it to make it to school on time, even if traffic was cooperative—so of course it wasn't. I hit every red light between my home and the school, and by the time I idled five cars deep at the final stoplight, notorious for its long red light, I had resigned myself to the tardy pass walk of shame. The school parking lot sat visible in the distance but as unreachable as a mirage as the clock ticked toward the opening bell. I tapped my fingers on the steering wheel, waiting for the light to change—then the hairs on the back of my neck and arms sprung up on end. A familiar chill rushed through me, the feeling of being watched.

CHAPTER 13

CHIVALRY DUEL

The distinct prickling sensation lingered on my neck as I glanced around. Traffic was clear in the opposite direction, and there was only one lane of cars heading the same direction as I was, all stopped behind or ahead of me at the light.

I flicked my eyes to the rear-view mirror, trying not to draw attention to the motion, but behind me was only a middle-aged woman applying lipstick, all visible passenger seats empty. I couldn't see past her van to any of the cars behind me, and the driver of the car ahead of me was furiously tapping out texts on the cell phone he was holding up above the steering wheel. The sidewalk to my right was clear of any straggling students who'd been walking down it the past couple minutes, everyone having already rushed ahead to classes. That left only the woods beside the school.

I peered at them, straining to make out any unusual shapes between the trees.

The driver behind me honked, startling me, and I spun forward to see the light was green and the car in front of me had already moved.

I lowered my foot on the gas and drove the final few yards to the school parking lot, swung into the first open spot I could find, grabbed my backpack, and hurried toward the office for my tardy pass.

When I reached homeroom period, announcements had already begun. I did my best to ignore the glances as everyone turned to see who had opened the classroom door. I hurried to the front, handed my tardy pass to Mrs. Blaylock, and scurried to my desk with my cheeks blazing as the announcements blared overhead.

Reina gave me a quick smile and wave as I sank into the chair beside her. *Everything okay?* she mouthed.

I nodded as Jordan twisted around in his desk.

He peered at me, eyes questioning.

I shook my head, unsure what he was asking but whatever it was, now wasn't the time. I dropped my gaze to my desk.

"Ayla," he whispered, and Reina glanced between us as I flicked my eyes back up to him.

"Mr. Peters!" Mrs. Blaylock's sharp reprimand sliced the air. "No talking during announcements."

Jordan's cheeks flushed red. He turned forward stiffly.

Reina gave me one last sideways glance, seeming curious, then faced forward herself, not wanting to incur Mrs. Blaylock's wrath.

The bell rang just as announcements finished. I jumped up from my desk and grabbed my backpack.

Reina lingered beside me rather than bouncing away as usual. She glanced between Jordan and me again. "Is everything okay? You're both acting weird, and you're *never* late." She pointed a finger at me.

Jordan busied himself tying his shoe, though I wondered if he was stalling, waiting for me to leave so he could walk with me.

"Um, yeah," I shrugged. "It was just a long night, and then this morning, my Grandpa—"

"Oh no. Did something happen?" Reina's face melted from confusion to concern in an instant.

Jordan looked up from tying his shoe, eyes wide.

I shook my head. "No, he's fine. I just needed to talk to him and I waited, but he slept in. By the time I realized he wasn't getting up, I was already running late."

Reina's shoulders sagged with relief, but Jordan still peered at me, seeming to sense there was more that I wasn't saying.

Reina hesitated, her eyes flicking between us, then stepped back. "I need to get to class. We all do. You sure you're both okay?"

Jordan and I stared at each other.

"Yeah," I said, though Jordan said nothing.

"All right..." Reina lingered one moment more, then sighed. "See you both at lunch." She hurried away.

I turned for the door, but Jordan stood suddenly. "Ayla, wait."

I tensed. "I don't have time to talk now, Jordan." I shoved out into the hallway, angling toward my locker rather than turning toward my next class. "I know you have questions. But later, okay?"

"I know, it's just—where are you going?" Jordan caught up, keeping pace beside me.

"I still need to grab my books from my locker." The five-minute transition period between classes was half gone.

Jordan reached for my backpack. "Here, let me hold this. It'll be faster." I started to protest, but I didn't want to make things any more awkward than they already were after the night before. If he was willing to pretend things were normal for now, I'd go along.

I let him slide my backpack from my shoulder but as we neared my locker, I came to a halt. I never imagined myself the object of anything from Madison Kane but bullying, yet there she stood right next to my locker, literally bouncing on her toes with impatience to talk to me.

"Ayla, finally!" she said. I nudged past her to open my locker, but she leaned her arm against it, blocking me. "Where have you been?"

"I don't have time for this, Madison. I'm going to be late."

Her gaze landed on my face, cold as usual. "You promised answers."

I sighed. "And I'll give them. But not now. After school, okay? Please move."

Madison slid to the side, but her gaze flicked to Jordan behind me as I yanked open my locker and grabbed my books. "She already told *you*, didn't she?"

"No, I didn't," I said, slamming my locker shut. I spun to Jordan, who was already holding out his hands to take my books from me.

"Let's go," he said. "If we hurry, you might not be late."

I dropped my books into his outstretched hands, no time to argue.

"Ugh. Fine." Madison groaned and stalked away toward our shared class.

I hurried behind her down the hallway, Jordan by my side. As soon as we reached my classroom door, he handed me my books and backpack.

Madison hurried inside ahead of me, letting the door slam shut practically in my face.

The bell rang as I yanked the door back open. I glanced back at Jordan and winced. "Sorry I made you tardy."

"You should get inside before they mark you late, too. Bye, Ayla." He rushed off toward his class.

Callan's gaze landed on me as I entered the literature classroom.

Madison, on the other hand, had already taken her seat in the back row and resumed pretending I didn't exist. I wasn't going to complain.

"Hurry to your seat, Miss Rogers," Mr. Yager said. "It's time to start."

I hurried toward my desk as most of the class stared at me, my cheeks hot. I hated how I blushed so easily anytime attention was directed at me.

Callan's eyes remained steady on me, and as I slid past him to my desk catty-corner from his, he whispered, "Everything okay?"

I nodded. He didn't look convinced, but as I settled in my chair he turned forward, focusing on Mr. Yager's beginning lecture.

Mr. Yager droned on about Aristotle and Joseph Campbell and the Hero's Journey. Ordinarily, I'd have taken rapt notes, but today I couldn't focus. The folded riddle weighed heavily in my pocket, and my mind kept drifting to Grandpa's strange sleeping habits, tightening my chest with worry. Jordan and I still hadn't had a chance to talk about our awkward date, not that I wanted to, and now with what happened at the café, the date wasn't even the most pressing concern. After school, I'd have to face Madison and Jordan with some answers, and I still had no clue what to tell them. And it also didn't help that every time I blinked, I saw the stranger's face, those deep blue eyes, full of a tenderness I didn't understand. I was exhausted from deep within, a kind of weariness I didn't feel sleep could fix—yet also edgy, keyed up, my heart an engine revving too high but unable to shift to a different gear. How long until it burned out?

"Miss Rogers?"

I jumped, breaking the mindless stare I'd been giving the back of my classmate's head. "Yes?"

Mr. Yager blinked at me, expecting me to answer a question I hadn't heard. Heat rushed to my face.

Callan glanced back at me with a look of concern, then spun forward again.

She knows this. The three-act structure is embedded in every story, even in our very lives. I heard it in Callan's voice, though he was no longer looking at me.

"Well?" Mr. Yager said, looking more confused than upset.

I blinked, but my brain was spinning so chaotically I could hardly think. "The three-act structure is embedded in every story, even in our very lives," I blurted.

Callan flicked his head to the side, his startled face staring at me over his shoulder.

Jumping frijoles, I thought. Were those words from Callan's head?

"Very good, Ayla," Mr. Yager nodded. "That's *exactly* the reason we'll be spending extra time on it this quarter. And your answer is also the perfect segue into what I planned to address next..."

Slowly, Callan turned back forward, his posture stiff.

Mr. Yager droned on, his words blending far into the distance beyond the screaming panic in my head. What in the world was happening to me?

The moment the bell rang, I grabbed my stuff and jumped from my desk, rushing for the door.

"Ayla, wait," Callan called after me, but I sped up, shoving past the traffic jam in the doorway.

"Hey, watch it!" someone yelled, but I ignored them and stumbled out into the crowded hall.

For a moment my brain blanked. Which way was my next class? Where was I even going? But my feet kept moving, needing to get *away*.

Jordan's familiar form turned the corner ahead of me as I barreled down the hall.

"Ayla?" His gaze locked on me. "What's wrong?"

A mix of panic and fondness and confusion washed over me. He always read me so well, always knew when I was upset. But right now, what would I even tell him? Nothing made sense anymore.

Jordan seemed to sense my distress and was at my side in a moment. "Are you hurt? Did something happen? Do you need me to walk you to the nurse?"

I shook my head, still hurrying down the hall with no idea where I was going.

Jordan stepped in front of me. "Ayla. Stop."

I halted to keep from running straight into his chest. He waited, staring down at me, until I forced myself to look up at him.

"Ayla, what happened?"

My brain chose that moment to let every swirling emotion I'd been walling away crash in on me. Tears sprang to my eyes. Stupid, stupid tears. Why did I always cry when I got stressed? "Nothing. I'm just—" I shook my head again, blinking them back. "I need to get to class."

Jordan watched me for a long moment.

The concern in his eyes was too much, after everything that happened on our date the night before, the eye contact too hard to hold. I pinned my gaze on his chest, instead. That didn't help; his Henley shirt fit too well over his muscles, stirring up an attraction I'd decided no longer to have.

"You have physics next, right?" he asked gently.

I nodded, shifting my gaze to the floor.

"Let me walk you." He reached for the strap of my backpack, and when I didn't resist, he slid it off my shoulder and onto his own.

We walked, silent amid the noise and chaos of the hallway, until we reached my classroom.

He handed me my backpack, his eyes lingering on my face until I met his gaze.

"You know you can talk to me, right, Ayla? About anything. I'm here."

My heart squeezed. "Yeah," I said, glancing away. "I know."

Jordan lingered for another moment, maybe hoping I'd offer an explanation, but when I didn't, he stepped back. "I'd better get to class."

I nodded, thankful for how well he understood me in that moment, how he knew not to push... though that made my very *not*-just-friends feelings for him surge back up again. Ugh, stupid feelings. Why couldn't they get with the program?

Jordan studied my face, sighed, and took another step backward. "See you at lunch, Ayla." He walked away, blending into the crowd in the hall.

I gave a deep sigh of my own, then turned and entered my classroom, following the flow of students filing into desks. Hot tears pressed at the back of my eyes, but I blinked them back—crying in class was *not* in my day's plans. I flopped my notebook open on my desk and forced my brain into note-taking mode, determined to hold it together at least long enough to make it through physics class.

Thankfully, the physics teacher rarely called on anyone, and by the time the ending bell rang, my right hand was cramped from writing and my underlying panic had been somewhat numbed by my fresh brainful of formulas.

But when I exited the classroom, Jordan was waiting for me in the hall.

"Are you all right?" he asked, eyes scanning my face.

I nodded and stepped around him, still not ready to form words.

A hand grabbed my arm from the other side, not Jordan's. "Ayla."

I jumped and spun to find Callan beside me, eyes intense on mine.

"We need to talk." He kept his grip on my arm, holding me in place.

Jordan stepped forward, a cold glare aimed at Callan's hand around my wrist. "Hey man, ease off." His voice was calm and measured, but I knew him well enough to hear the thread of anger beneath it. His eyes flicked up to meet Callan's. "Can't you tell she's uncomfortable? Let her go."

Callan dropped his hand. "I didn't mean anything by it." He stepped back, though his gaze was on me, not Jordan as he spoke. "I'm sorry for grabbing you; you didn't hear me call your name."

I narrowed my eyes at him, doubting the truth of that statement, but he genuinely looked remorseful and there had been nothing violent or aggressive in the way he grabbed me, only urgency.

I nodded, but slid away from him. "I need to go."

"Let me walk you—" Jordan and Callan said simultaneously.

I froze, spinning back to catch Jordan shooting a sideways glare at Callan. What was this? Some kind of chivalry duel? I resisted the urge to roll my eyes, though as my gaze caught on Callan's for a moment, something flopped inside my chest. What *had* happened in literature class? With Jordan the night before, I'd assumed it was intuition, but now, with the way Callan had reacted...

Callan held eye contact while Jordan glanced between us, growing tenser by the second.

I took a step backward. "I'm going to be late." I turned and rushed down the hall, praying neither guy would follow me.

I reached my next classroom and slipped inside before either of them caught up to me, if they'd even tried. Though I attempted to take notes, my thoughts were consumed by the fact that drama now bookended every class period, and by the strange reality that Madison was no longer my biggest worry at school—though that could easily change, once I spoke with her this afternoon.

Class ended with both my notes and thoughts in a jumble. I wasn't surprised when I exited the classroom to find Callan leaning against the wall, one knee bent and his shoe against the wall for support—though I was a little surprised not to see Jordan waiting for me, too.

"Hey," Callan said, pushing up from the wall.

I stepped around the other exiting students to face him. "Are you leaving class early to stalk me now?"

Callan smirked. "Of course not." His smirk faded as his gaze bored into me. "We just need to talk."

"About what?" I feigned nonchalance, slipping around him and into the flow of students passing.

He kept pace, glancing sideways at me as we walked. "You know what."

Panic bubbled in my chest. Callan and I were becoming friends, but not close enough for me to tell him I'd heard his words in my head. The last thing I needed was rumors around the school that I was losing my mind. I forced a laugh. "Really, Callan, one stalker is plenty, okay? I don't need another one." I'd meant it as a joke, to distract him, but it came out harsher than I intended.

Rather than get offended, though, Callan stepped in front of me, blocking my way. "What?" His eyes were wide. "You mean Jordan, right? That guy is hardly ever more than a few yards from you, anytime I see you on campus."

This time I did roll my eyes. "Of course not. Jordan and I are... friends. He's not a stalker. But you, on the other hand—"

Callan stiffened, not catching my intended humor. "Ayla, answer me for real. Has someone besides Jordan been following you?"

The urgent concern in his eyes startled me, evaporating any remaining amusement. "Actually, yes. I mean, maybe. I saw a guy staring at me a few days ago, and I thought maybe he was following me. I felt like someone was watching me this morning, too, but whenever I look, there's no one—"

Callan took quick steps backward, face tense with alarm. "I—I have to go."

"What? Why?" I called after him, mind racing through what he could have possibly pieced together from my rambling response. It had barely been coherent.

"I'm sorry, Ayla. We'll talk later, okay?" he called back, but he was already rushing down the hallway, voice fading into the distance.

I stared after him for a moment, then headed to my next class, my stomach churning with worry.

CHAPTER 14

DISTURBANCE IN THE CAFETERIA

When I arrived at the cafeteria the next period, I spotted Jordan and Reina at our usual table. The uneasy feeling in the pit of my stomach hadn't lessened since Callan's strange reaction in the hallway earlier, and it only worsened when I realized Callan wasn't in the cafeteria, either. Was he skipping school? What was going on with him? I couldn't help but feel that whatever it was, it would only mean more problems for me.

The meaty odor of the cafeteria caught my empty stomach halfway between growling and churning. Meatloaf again, most likely. The school meatloaf wasn't that bad, but with the way my nerves were flopping as I made my way to the table, I considered just nibbling on almonds from my backpack instead.

Jordan's eyes found me the moment I broke through the crowd.

"Hey!" He gave me a little half-wave and a genuine smile—as though we *hadn't* had the most awkward date in the history of dates; as though he *wasn't* waiting for me to explain why some dude had vanished into thin air right in front of me. As though he was just happy to see me.

My heart squeezed. Was Jordan putting on a show for Reina's benefit, so she wouldn't suspect anything... or mine, because he could see I was upset? Or was he just that sweet of a guy? If so, I didn't deserve him. Not that I *had* him, exactly... or at all. Not anymore, at least. My stomach sank as the awkward plunge of our first and probably last date flickered through my mind.

Reina turned as I neared the table. She grinned and waved, too.

I returned both their waves with the best smile I could muster and sank into the chair Jordan pulled out for me.

"Meatloaf today," Reina said, and shoved a tray of food at me. "Jordan noticed you were running late, so he got in line for you. He brought his lunch today."

I spun toward Jordan in surprise. "Oh! That was... really sweet. Thank you."

"You're welcome." Jordan smiled at me in a way that made my heart flip—stupid, disloyal organ.

While Reina dug into the dessert on her lunch tray, Jordan's eyes lingered on my face for a moment, and the edge of his mouth twitched down into the slightest hint of a frown. Leave it to Jordan to notice how very *not okay* I was, despite my attempt to seem normal. But also leave it to Jordan to keep his mouth shut because he knew I didn't want attention drawn to it.

A pang of loss shot through my chest. He was such a good guy—*but still only a friend*, I reminded myself, but that had been *his* stupid decision. He'd never given me the chance to choose. A twinge of irritation fluttered in over my sadness.

Jordan peeled his eyes from my face with what seemed a good bit of effort and turned to Reina.

"I haven't seen Callan since earlier," he said to her with a nonchalance I envied. "He's usually here for lunch. Have you seen him?" He took a bite of a peanut butter sandwich, then set it back onto its little baggy as he chewed.

"No." Reina bit her lip as she mindlessly poked at her meatloaf with her fork. "Now that you mention it, I haven't seen him since early this morning. Usually we pass each other in the hall between periods. Do you think he left? Maybe he's sick."

I lifted a forkful of mashed potatoes from my tray as Jordan's eyes flicked to me. "Did he mention anything to you, Ayla? He was acting a little... weird, earlier. Don't you think?"

I realized suddenly that Jordan was fishing for information from me about Callan, trying to feel out my opinion of what happened earlier—and maybe drag Callan under the bus in front of Reina in the process. Was he still that jealous of Callan, after trying to convince me I should date *both* of them? My earlier twinge of irritation heated into full-blown annoyance. I dropped the fork back into my mashed potatoes. "I don't know, Jordan, what do *you* think? You were there."

Jordan had no way of knowing how weird Callan had been about my mention of the stalker later, but I wasn't quite ready to share that.

Reina chewed a bite of meatloaf as she glanced between us, her eyes widening as she picked up the tension. She swallowed. "Um, guys? What did I miss?"

The startled expression on her face disarmed me. She knew nothing of the drama between Jordan and me—I wasn't even sure she knew we'd gone on a date.

I sighed. "Just a little disagreement between Callan and Jordan, I guess. Callan grabbed my arm, and Jordan got protective."

Reina's eyebrows shot up, at the same time Jordan huffed.

"There are these things called *words*, you know," Jordan grumbled. "There was no need for him to lay hands on you."

"It wasn't a big deal." I reassured Reina before her eyebrows disconnected from her forehead and took flight. "It was loud in the hallway and Callan was trying to get my attention." I cut a sideways glare at Jordan. "Jordan overreacted."

Jordan met my glare with one of his own, but then his gaze softened. "I don't like to see my friends manhandled. It looked like he startled you."

My frustration eased a bit. "Really, it was no big deal. I could tell he didn't mean anything by it."

A tense silence settled between us, and my mind raced away, replaying my interaction with Callan about the stalker.

I studied Reina and Jordan's faces as they exchanged glances—Jordan still irritated by his stand-off with Callan, and Reina concerned but confused. These were the two people in this school I trusted most. We didn't hang out much outside of school, but I didn't hang out with *anyone* other than at school or work, and of the few friends I had, Jordan and Reina were my two *best* friends. So why was I keeping so many details from them? Already I would have to be careful about what I shared with Jordan and Madison later, and even more so with Reina—but the stalker wasn't part of the disappearing café guy's warning. Shouldn't I tell my best friends at least *some* of what was going on? At least what I *could* tell them? My life was getting far too weird to manage it all alone.

I took a breath, watching both of their faces for reactions as I said my next words. "Callan's behavior when I was talking with him *later* was much more startling."

They both straightened, full attention on me.

"What behavior?" Jordan's voice was tense.

I immediately regretted saying anything. "Nothing physical," I amended, "but I mentioned the possible stalker I'd seen outside the café and... he kinda flipped out."

Jordan stiffened. "Flipped out?"

I hurried to explain. "He wasn't mean or anything. He kind of panicked and ran away."

Reina and Jordan both scrunched their faces, twin masks of confusion.

"What?" Reina asked. "Why?"

I shrugged. "How should I know?" That was the truth. I had no clue. "Maybe he's just weird."

Jordan chuckled. "He's weird, for sure. But..." I could see he wanted to say or ask something, but not in front of Reina. I wondered if he thought the stalker and what happened at the café might be connected. But I had no reason, so far, to think that they were related—other than as two distinct snowflakes in the blizzard of bizarre happenings that currently enveloped my life.

Jordan sighed. "Maybe Callan was just worried about you?" His face looked like it physically pained him to say that.

I bit my lip in thought, then shrugged again. "Yeah, maybe."

"But then why run away?" Reina asked.

We all stared at each other.

"So maybe he is just weird," I joked, but Reina was the only one who laughed.

Someone yanked out the chair beside Reina and plopped down at our table. "Hey, guys!"

All three of us gaped as Madison beamed a cheerful smile at us.

Her eyes flitted between the three of us. "What's up?"

Reina, kind and friendly to her very core, was the first to recover. She returned Madison's smile, though I saw the strain of disbelief at its edges. "Hi, Madison! Not much, we were... talking." Reina paused, her gaze flicking toward Madison's usual table across the cafeteria.

I followed her glance and found all three of Madison's posse plus Madison's boyfriend all gaping at Madison as though she'd lost her mind.

I could feel their stares on the side of my face as I forced my eyes forward again. "So, uh, Madison," I said, trying to make my smile match Reina's as Madison turned her attention to me, "what brings you to our table today?"

Madison's stare locked on me with a sickeningly sweet smile. "Oh, you know, just making conversation. Anything interesting happen lately? Any news?" She emphasized the last word.

Jordan leaned forward, his smile forced. "Nothing so far, Madison. Why don't you check back later?"

Madison's smile vanished as she leaned forward on the table. Her eyebrows narrowed as her glare flipped between Jordan and me. "Fine. But I will be waiting for you after school. You will not leave me out of this, understand? You promised." She shoved her chair back, popped up, and hurried away—out of the cafeteria rather than to her posse.

"Where is she going?" Jordan muttered.

No one was supposed to leave the cafeteria during lunch without permission, but my concern was focused more on Reina.

"You two have some kind of secret arrangement with Madison?" She glanced between Jordan and me with a mix of hurt and confusion, then her gaze settled on Jordan, and the hurt seemed to deepen. "What are you not telling me, Jordan?"

Jordan and Reina were closer friends than I was with either of them—they lived next to each other, their families hung out, they even rode together. Suddenly, despite the secrets Jordan and I shared, I felt like the odd one out.

Reina glanced at me. "And you know about it, too?"

Reina seldom got upset, and the look of betrayal on her face sent a flurry of panic through my chest. I'd never meant to hurt her.

Reina fluttered her hands as though waving away her reaction. "It's fine; it's okay." She seemed to make an effort to rein in her emotions to make that statement true, but her voice did *not* sound fine. "You're both allowed to have your secrets, even with Madison."

Jordan's face softened. "It's not like that, Rei."

I felt an irrational stab of jealousy at his pet name for her, but I swallowed it down.

Reina narrowed her eyes at Jordan, and suddenly her face looked pleading rather than angry. "Then what is it like?"

Jordan cut his eyes to me, which was everything Reina needed to see that *I* was the one controlling this secret, the one setting the rules.

Reina's gaze flipped to me, her mouth tensed into a nervous pucker.

I wanted to tell her everything in that moment, I swear I did—but I had no idea how seriously the vanishing guy took his rules, or what type of danger I was in, and I couldn't bear to bring any more of my friends into something that might end up getting them hurt. But still—it was Reina...

I hesitated a moment too long.

Reina sat up as straight as a rod. "Look, you can have secrets. It's not about that. It's just..." She sighed. "You two have been weird all day. I knew you were keeping something from me, and now, even Madison is in on it. And I just—"

"We went on a date last night," Jordan blurted.

Reina and I both gaped at him.

"Ayla and I, I mean." He held his hands up defensively. "Not Madison. Definitely not with Madison."

Reina glanced at me, then back to Jordan. "You... what?"

The shock and confusion on Reina's face morphed into a hurt even deeper than earlier, and suddenly I realized I'd gotten Reina and Jordan's relationship very, very wrong... at least Reina's side of it.

"I'm sorry, Reina," I said, desperately trying to bandage the gaping wound in her expression. "We should've told you. We should've—" What, asked her permission? Not done it at all? I floundered, helpless as a fish on dry land.

But Reina was already shoving her chair back. "I have to go." She grabbed her lunch tray and backpack and rushed away from the table, pausing only to dump her dirty tray on the conveyor belt and mutter something to the faculty attendant at the door. The attendant nodded and Reina shoved open the exit door and hurried out of the cafeteria. The door clanked shut behind her, barely audible over the chatter from the surrounding tables.

Jordan and I met alarmed stares over Reina's empty chair.

What had we done?

CHAPTER 15

THE PHONE CALL

"I ... should've handled that differently," Jordan said quietly.

Jordan and I weren't even together in the couple sense, but the possibility we *could* be together, the realization that deep down I might still *want* for us to be together, sank a pit of guilt deep into my chest. I could never hurt Reina that way, now that I knew she must have feelings for him—from the expression on her face, that much was plain. But maybe Jordan's side of things weren't as I'd thought, either. Maybe my intuition about his motivations on our date had been wrong—perhaps I was an old crush and now he *did* have feelings for Reina. Perhaps he'd realized once we were on our date that I wasn't the one he wanted to be with, and *that* was why he'd been so conflicted.

That thought made me feel mopey, which just deepened my guilt. I was a hypocrite. I'd be no happier about Jordan dating Reina than she'd been about him going on a date with me... at least at first. But I could change that, right? I could convince myself to be happy for them, if that's what they wanted. They were my friends.

I eyed Jordan. I was afraid to ask, but I needed to know. I drew a breath. "Is Reina the reason you were so weird on our date? Are the two of you—"

"*What?* No," Jordan said. "Reina and I aren't like that. She's like family. I think she's just upset I didn't tell her about our date sooner."

His insistence that he didn't have feelings for Reina wasn't the relief I'd expected—it only made me more confused and frustrated. "Why *didn't* you tell her about it sooner?"

His mouth dropped open, then snapped shut. "I... I mean, I guess I *was* kind of trying to keep it from her until I knew for sure where things were going—"

At my furious glare, he waved his hands and hurried to explain further.

"Not for *that* reason, though. Mostly because I didn't think *you* would want attention drawn to it. Not until you were sure."

I sighed. He wasn't wrong there. "Okay, fine. But why blurt it out like you did? You blindsided her with it and made it seem like it was part of the secret Madison was in on, which only made things weirder."

Jordan ran a hand down his face and groaned. "I meant to change the subject, so she'd stop asking what was going on with Madison and us. I didn't think you wanted anyone else to know about what happened at the café. You made me promise not to tell, and I was trying to *keep* that promise. In hindsight, though, maybe our date wasn't the best distraction to use..."

"Not to mention we *aren't* actually dating," I muttered with annoyance, "which you didn't bother to explain to her at all, though you made that *very clear* to me last night."

Jordan stared at me with a helpless expression. "Ayla, I'm sorry. You have no idea *how* sorry. About last night, about just now—all of it. Can you and I please just act like our date last night didn't happen?"

He seemed to regret that we'd even *had* a date, which stung.

"Not that I regret asking you on a date," he said like he'd been reading my mind. "I just wish I had handled it differently. I *do* still have feelings for you—like, a *lot* of feelings—"

Excuse me, what? I thought, but before I could reply, he kept going.

"—but I'd like a clean slate for us to navigate whether we take this somewhere more. I turned last night into a disaster, and I hate this layer of awkwardness between us."

I stared at him, still a bit in shock, then sighed. "So do I." But did that mean he *did* still want to turn this into something more? Not that I felt like we could anymore, given how Reina had reacted... Why were relationships so *confusing*?

He slid a hand toward me across the table, though not far enough to touch me. "Can we please go back to how things were before last night? A second chance, starting back where we were *before* I made everything between us so weird?"

I studied his pleading eyes and felt my stubborn heart cave. "Okay," I said finally. "I can try."

He sighed with relief. "Good. Your friendship means too much to me to lose."

Friendship. So we were *there* again. But unless he worked things out with Reina, I was no longer sure we could be anything more. And his friendship really *did* matter to me. I met his gaze. "Same here."

He gave me a tentative smile. "Well, I'm not going anywhere."

I returned his smile, and a silence fell between us.

After a moment, he glanced over at Reina's chair.

"What will you tell her?" I asked.

Jordan looked back at me. "The truth," he said. "About us, I mean, whatever that ends up being. I won't keep it from her again. And I'll talk to her about last night and about what happened here today. Don't worry; we'll work it out. I think she's more angry at *me* than at you."

I nodded, and we both fell quiet again.

If Jordan and I decided we *did* want to become something more, would we even be able to act on it? I wasn't stupid—I'd seen Reina's expression. Jordan said he'd had a crush on me for a long time, but people changed their minds about crushes all the time, and a lifelong friendship like Reina and Jordan's was rare. I knew that regardless of what Jordan said now, there was a possibility, given their closeness, that "working things out" with Reina could end in him changing his mind and dating her. But—I *did* value his friendship. And hers. So if that happened, I would have to be okay with it.

Jordan and I ate the rest of our food in silence.

Reina did not return to lunch.

When the end-of-lunch bell rang, Jordan and I both stood and he reached, almost by habit, for the strap of my backpack.

I pulled away. "No, thanks, I've got it." Sweet gestures like carrying my bag felt like crossing beyond the lines of friendship too soon, which would only confuse me more... plus everything in that *possibly-more-than-friends* zone still felt tainted by the guilt of upsetting Reina.

Hurt briefly flickered over Jordan's face, but then he seemed to understand.

I, on the other hand, was in my own personal torment. I was hurting the people who mattered most to me, every way I turned.

Jordan walked beside me to my class. I could feel the weight of the words he wanted to say, but he seemed to be trying to figure out *how* to say them. I let him linger in silence—I didn't know what to say, either.

A few feet from the psychology classroom door, Jordan stopped walking in the middle of the crowded hallway. I stumbled over my own feet as I stopped and turned to see why, taking a hit on my shoulder from the backpack of someone in the rush of students hurrying to class.

"Ayla." Jordan's face was pleading, and he held his hands out like he was reaching toward a spooked kitten—as though I might run away any moment. "I need to tell you something else about why I was weird on our date."

My pulse sped with nerves, but then the class tardy bell interrupted in an extended, clanging blare.

Jordan jumped. "Oh no, you're going to be late. Come on, hurry!" he yelled over the obnoxious clanging. He grabbed my hand and tugged me toward my classroom.

Had he changed his mind about what he wanted to say? Or was he just that worried about making me late? I wanted to ask, but between the deafening bell, my confusion, and the chaos in the hallway, my thoughts were a scattered mess.

Jordan planted me by my classroom as the bell rang its final tones. "Get in, quick, you're technically not late yet!" He yanked open my classroom door and nudged me toward it.

I stepped inside, and as the door closed, I caught one last glimpse of him over my shoulder.

His eyes were full of regret.

Throughout psychology class, my brain replayed the scenes from lunch and from the hallway over and over, beating me senseless with all the ways I could've responded differently. While hurting Reina *should* have been the biggest element of that horrific replay, in reality my brain cycled more ardently through my last moments with Jordan in the hallway. Why had I let him rush me off to class? I should've stopped him, insisted we talk, and taken my tardy pass with pride. Instead, I was stuck in a class hour that felt like an eternity, resisting the urge to bite my nails down to nubs while my teacher droned on about Freud. I usually enjoyed psychology lectures, but a review of Oedipal complexes offered nothing helpful for my current disaster with Jordan and Reina, and I wasn't in the mood for wasting time.

The seconds ticked by painfully as I waited for class to end so that I could find Jordan and attempt to resuscitate our abandoned conversation. He *would* be waiting in the hallway for me, wouldn't he? He had been lately, after this class. I subtly began packing my books and supplies so that I could make a speedy exit the moment the bell rang.

Finally, the bell rang.

I yanked my backpack from the floor and rushed for the hallway—and an obnoxious blare from my cell phone halted me before I reached the door. I kept my phone on silent in school, with only my parents and my grandpa set as calls that rang through, for emergencies. It was Grandpa's ringtone.

I stepped against the wall, out of the way of the fleeing psychology students, and answered the phone with shaky hands. "Hello?"

"Ayla!" Grandpa's voice was wild. "I need you! Come home, right away!"

My heart surged into a gallop. "What's wrong? Why?"

The call disconnected. I frantically redialed, but no one picked up.

I shoved through the remaining students, the hallway and crowds a blur as I dialed my parents, one at a time. No answers there, either. My anxiety ratcheted up to full-blown panic. Someone rammed into my shoulder as I barreled down the hallway, but I cared only about getting to the doorway, getting to my car, getting *home*.

"Ayla?" Jordan stepped in front of me.

I shoved past him and kept going, too afraid to slow, even for an explanation.

He spun to the side and jogged beside me. "Ayla, what's wrong? What happened?" He peered over at me as we ran. "What can I do?"

Images flashed through my mind of my grandpa and my parents, trapped in a fire, murdered by a robber, dying from poison—I didn't even know what to picture, but every possibility was horrible. "Just get me to my car!"

Jordan nodded and dashed ahead of me, shouldering students out of our way like an offensive lineman, clearing a path for my escape without even knowing the reason. People shouted unhappy comments in our wake, but my world was too much a blur to process them.

I heard the bell ring in the distance as Jordan and I reached my beat-up Cirrus. I fumbled with my keys.

Jordan slipped them from my hand, unlocked the car, then opened the door for me and handed my keys back to me.

"Ayla." He peered down at me as I jumped into the driver's seat and cranked the engine. "What's going on? You're scaring me."

"I don't know, I don't—" I shook my head, fingers digging into the steering wheel as another surge of panic rolled in. "I need to go."

Jordan stepped back, and I slammed the door shut and peeled out—but Jordan threw himself in the path of my car.

I stomped on the brakes. My front bumper nudged him enough that he lost balance, catching himself with a slam of his palms on my car's hood.

"Are you *crazy?*" I yelled, furious in equal parts for him slowing me down and making me almost run over him.

Jordan rushed around to my driver's-side door and yanked it open. "No, but I can't let you drive like this. Move over."

I glared at him. "Jordan, get out of the way! I need to go!"

Jordan's face softened. "Ayla, please. If you left like this and got hurt, I'd never forgive myself. You're too upset. Tell me where you need to go—anywhere—and I'll take you, no questions asked. But *please*, let me drive."

I didn't have time to waste arguing with him, plus he was right. I was so freaked out, I could hardly focus on the windshield or steering wheel, much less the road. "Fine," I huffed, then unbuckled and climbed over to the passenger seat. "Take me *home*."

Jordan's eyes flicked to me in concern as he dropped into the driver's seat and adjusted the seat back to accommodate his long legs. "Okay, home it is."

He swung the car around and sped out of the parking lot, going ten above the speed limit as we hurried toward my house—and whatever I was about to find there.

CHAPTER 16

A CULT OR SOMETHING

Jordan skidded into my driveway a few minutes later like a scene from *The Fast and the Furious*. I leaped out of the car before he'd fully stopped. I heard Jordan on my heels as I shoved the front door open and rushed inside. "Mom! Dad!" I yelled, frantically scanning the living room for any clue to the tragedy that befell them. "Grandpa?"

Dad rushed out from the kitchen, holding a sandwich in one hand. "Ayla? What are you doing home? Is something wrong?" A slice of tomato slipped from the sandwich and plopped to the floor.

My brain stuttered, trying to make sense of my new situation. "You're... eating a sandwich," I said blankly.

Dad stared at me in alarm.

"You're not murdered?" I added. "And Mom? Grandpa? They're okay?"

Dad blinked. "Ayla, what..." He glanced behind me, noticing Jordan. "Of course I'm not murdered. Why would you think that? Your mom's at Edna's planting tulips. Grandpa's napping." He eyed me with growing concern. "Why are you two not in school?"

I sank into the closest piece of furniture—Grandpa's stuffy recliner—and dropped my head into my hands. "Grandpa called, he was panicked, he said—he said to come straight home. When I tried to call back, I couldn't—" My voice broke as the adrenaline wore off and the weight of the imagined disaster sank into me. "None of you answered, and I thought—I thought you were—"

"Oh, honey." Dad dropped to his knees and nudged my chin up with his thumb. His gaze was steady and grounding. "Everyone's okay. Your mother left a couple minutes ago, but she left her phone here to charge. I haven't been able to find mine all day; it's probably dead. And your grandpa—I'm not sure why he called you, but I checked on him a moment ago. He's fast asleep. He probably called you in—in an episode." He hesitated, and his eyes held the weight of what that meant, of how much worse Grandpa was getting. "I'm so sorry, sweetheart."

Relief swept over me, but in the wake of my abating panic I felt very, very foolish—especially that I'd roped Jordan into my overreaction. I looked up at him. "I'm sorry, Jordan, I feel terrible. You're skipping school, and..."

He smiled down at me with such a tender expression that from the corner of my eye I saw my Dad stiffen a little. "Don't be ridiculous," Jordan said. "I'm just glad everything's okay."

Dad cleared his throat. "So, Jordan, you rode with her here?"

I intercepted the shift in conversation. "He drove my car here. When he saw how upset I was, he insisted. He was worried it wasn't safe for me to drive that way."

Dad's parental concern over Jordan's obvious attachment to me melted a twinge. "I see. Well, thank you again, Jordan, for watching out for my daughter's well-being." He eyed Jordan. "I should get you back to school. There's still an hour or so left, isn't there? I need to run an errand, anyway. I'll drop you on the way."

Jordan nodded once. "Yes, sir." Jordan looked at me, but I shook my head.

"I'm still too shaken up." I turned to Dad. "Please, let me skip the rest of today. Write me a note. I promise I'll make up the work later."

Dad nodded. "Okay, you can stay here. Jordan, you ready to go?"

The front door swung open and Mom strode in, soiled garden gloves clutched in one hand and dirt-stains on the knees of her overalls, her hair thrown up in a messy bun with a few rogue, curly wisps dampened to her face by sweat. She took us all in. "What's going on? Why aren't they in school?"

It took only a couple minutes to fill her in, then my Dad politely suggested to Jordan—again—that it was time to return him to school.

"We still need to talk," Jordan said softly as he passed by me toward the door. "When you're ready. Maybe you can call me later?"

I nodded, knowing I still owed him and Madison an explanation. "I have work in a few hours—I'll be okay by then, I'm sure. I just need to breathe. I'll call you after. Madison, too, I guess. Can you let her know I had to leave early?" It wasn't ideal for Madison to know I'd panicked and run home for no reason, but without *some* kind of explanation, she'd think I ditched to avoid talking to her about the café.

As usual, Jordan seemed to understand. "Of course. I'll tell her it was a family emergency."

I smiled at him, genuinely grateful for his steadfast friendship. "Thank you."

Dad opened the front door, making it clear it was time to go.

Jordan followed him out. "See you later, Ayla."

The door shut behind them.

Mom slipped off her gardening boots, then crossed to the recliner. She pulled me to my feet and enveloped me in a hug. "I'm so sorry, sweetheart. That must have been terrifying for you."

"Yeah." My answer came out a little strangled. "I'm okay, now, though."

Mom pulled back, slipping a loose piece of hair behind my ear as she smiled at me. "You want some brownies? I made them fresh a couple hours ago."

"Yes, please," I groaned. "Brownies are *exactly* what I need right now." I followed her to the kitchen.

Mom served me a plate of brownies and sat across the kitchen table from me to sip a cup of coffee, easy silence settling over us as I ate. I was on my second brownie and halfway through my glass of milk when a spark of anxiety reignited in my brain. "Mom?"

"Hmm?" She peeled her gaze from the window, where she'd been watching birds flutter around our front garden.

"Grandpa *is* okay, right? I mean, I know he's getting worse, but it's not... life-threatening... yet. Right?"

Mom set down her mug. "It's probably not going to get better, sweetheart... but he could still have a long time left, yes. But how long he'll still be the Grandpa we know now..." Her face twisted with sadness. "There's no way to predict that. Already he's done better than your father and I expected, when he first came to live with us. He'd already lost several memories, whole sections of his life and work—though I suppose, in some of those instances, it was for the best. Probably his mind protecting him."

I leaned forward. This wasn't a part of Grandpa's story I'd heard before. "What do you mean, protecting him? What happened to him?"

"Well..." Mom bit her lip, seeming to debate something in her mind, then shrugged. "I suppose you're old enough to understand now. You may as well know. Your grandpa used to be in a cult or something."

I shot up, slamming my palms to the table. "He *what*?"

Mom raised her hands defensively. "I mean, from what your father and I can tell. Your grandfather was in some very strange, very secretive group for most of your father's young childhood, and though he came home several times a week, he worked very odd hours and could never talk about what he did. Growing up, your father liked to imagine your grandpa was in the CIA or something, but as he grew older, your grandmother—may she rest in peace—confided that your grandfather's job had nothing to do with the government. He'd been recruited into some strange, exclusive country club type thing as a teenager—their headquarters were top-secret—and trained in all kinds of random skills: martial arts, for one, but also in several very specific academic fields."

"What kind of country club teaches martial arts? Aren't they usually just rich people playing golf?"

Mom laughed. "Country club isn't the right term. It was more like an exclusive college with a fraternity or something, one which controlled what job he took later, where he lived, what he did. Like I said, it was very much like a cult."

"Wow."

Mom nodded. "Your grandmother said it was a miracle your grandfather had even been allowed to marry her. Usually they only allowed dating and marriage with others inside the cult... or at least that was your father's impression. Your grandfather was always pretty secretive about his work, even toward his own family. He got out of it around the time your father and I married, but he always seemed a little mentally scattered, after that, and neither he nor your grandmother liked to talk about it."

I stared at Mom. "Wow. Why did you never tell me this before?"

She shrugged. "It's not my story to tell. Besides, it doesn't really change anything, does it? Sometimes your father wonders if they did something to Grandpa at that place, something that changed him. Grandpa's condition was nothing as bad, during our early marriage, as it is now—but he'd have small moments of confusion, here and there. Or days where he seemed distracted." She gave a sad smile. "Now, of course, it's much worse."

My hands tightened into fists as I imagined Grandpa being tortured by some cult, experimented on, or who knows what. "Has anyone ever looked into it? Tried to figure out what happened to him? Or who these cult people were?"

My mom shook her head. "He made us promise not to—a condition of agreeing to live with us. He'd admitted, finally, when you were a baby and your grandmother had already passed on, that he wasn't good living on his own. But he was all set to put himself in an institution if we didn't agree not to pry into his past, despite how much we could see he wanted to be around us more... especially around you." She smiled. "He's always adored you, your grandpa. The first time he held you, his face glowed like the moon."

My eyes welled with tears.

Mom reached across to squeeze my hand, then sighed. "We knew he wanted to be with family, and your father wanted him with us; he's always loved him! But your grandpa's condition for living with us was that we leave that part of his past in the past—no questions. Some of his many books are from his cult days, too, I believe, but he's never wanted us poking around on his shelves, either. He said he was having trouble remembering that part of his life, anyway, and he'd rather we *all* just forget."

I stared down at my half-eaten brownie, letting that sink in. I had *so* many questions, but apparently those were forbidden. Everything I knew about my Grandpa—his penchant for scholarship, his love of books, his playful, inquisitive nature—felt suddenly foreign in light of this information. How many of those skills or careers had Grandpa picked up from that cult? And what did they *do* there? I'd always assumed Grandpa had gotten his background in literature and research at a normal college, not some strange, hyper-secret cult fortress. Most of the books I'd seen Grandpa read, and the discussions we'd had, seemed normal enough. Yet when he was in an episode, Grandpa's strange mutterings at *times* seemed almost lucid, like he was remembering secrets from another life—

Suddenly I remembered the book Grandpa hadn't want me to touch, the one he'd covered up in the living room when I asked about it... the same night he'd told me "Things happen at midnight."

I jumped up, feigning a glance at the clock on the wall. "It's almost time for school to end... which means I need to get ready for my afternoon shift at Gary's." I placed a hand on Mom's shoulder. "Thanks for the brownies."

She rested her hand on mine and smiled up at me. "You're welcome, sweetheart. I'm glad you're feeling better."

I nodded and rushed away toward my room—then backtracked down the hall and peered around the corner to make sure Mom wasn't looking. When I saw her busy with washing the brownie dishes, I slipped back into the hall and stopped at Grandpa's room. I could hear his snore through the door. *Perfect.* I eased the door open and slipped inside.

Grandpa was sprawled on his back, snoring like a disgruntled hog. Lavender vapor hissed from the diffuser, and the lamp on his nightstand cast a muted, golden glow over the book that was splayed face-up on his chest. His blackout curtains were pulled closed, darkening the rest of the room.

I slipped my shoes off in the hallway then shut the door slowly behind me, careful not to make a sound, and crept across the room to his bookshelves.

The light from the lamp didn't reach far enough for me to see the spines clearly, but I didn't dare turn on any other lights, for fear of waking him. I was here for one thing only—the book I'd seen him reading that day in the living room, the leather one with the metallic tree etched on the cover. He'd gotten defensive when I asked about it that day, which meant there was something in it he didn't want me to know... secrets he wanted to hide. Grandpa had warned me about midnight, which meant he might know something about the riddle and what had been happening to me, whether he *remembered* he knew it or not. I needed to find out what, and that book seemed a good place to start.

I ran my finger down the row of spines, searching half by sight, half by feel as I squinted in the dim room. Grandpa's books were layered two rows deep on his shelves, but he'd had that book out recently, so it wasn't likely to be buried in a back row. It was likely to be in the front somewhere, or maybe on his dresser or—

I turned toward his bed, studying the book splayed open on his chest more closely. It *did* have a leather cover, though since it was pages-up, I couldn't see whether it had the tree engraving I remembered. I padded in my socked feet to the side of his bed and reached slowly toward the book.

My fingers were inches from its cover when Grandpa shot up, stiff as a board, and launched himself at my throat.

I scrambled backwards, knocked off balance as he threw his weight into me, hands grasping at my neck.

"Grandpa! Stop, it's me! It's Ayla!"

He shoved me backward until my spine hit his bookshelves. His eyes were dark and wild—not *his* at all—and his teeth were bared in a grimace. His fingers tightened around my throat, straining my air supply.

I yanked at his hands, but he was stronger than I expected, and I couldn't break his grasp. The room began to black in around the edges. "Grandpa," I wheezed with the last of my breath. "Please! Stop!"

His eyes popped wide. "Ayla?"

He dropped his hands and scrambled back as I clutched my throat and gasped sweet air.

Still terrified, I darted for the door. "Mom! Mom, help! Grandpa's—"

He dashed in front of me, slamming his body into the back of the door and planting his arms against the door frame. "You're not going anywhere, *child*." His voice carried multiple timbres, like a whole chorus of voices spoke in unison with Grandpa's own.

Shivers raced down my spine. I stumbled back a few steps, until my back bumped the bookshelves again. There was nowhere else to go.

Grandpa's expression turned wild and menacing again, not *his* at all. He sneered at me. "You and I, my dear, need to have a little chat."

CHAPTER 17

THAT ESCALATED QUICKLY

"**G**randpa?" My voice came out as a squeak, but as his eyes bored into me, I was suddenly certain this was *not* my grandfather. I pressed into the shelves behind me. "Who are you?"

His lips curled up into a sneer, an expression Grandpa had *never* made, and which, on his familiar face, chilled me to the core.

I screamed. "Mom! Dad! Hel—"

The not-Grandpa shook his head, sneer still in place. "They won't be coming to help you."

My stomach dropped like a boulder shoved over a cliff. "What did you do to them?"

He took a step toward me. "What you should be asking is what I'm about to do to *you*."

I ducked as he reached for me, dodging past him, but he twisted after me and grabbed my arm with one hand.

"Ah!" Pain sliced through my foot, right where I'd been cut by glass from the dropped vial. I collapsed to a crouch as the pain spread into my calf muscle, seizing my whole leg in a massive, blinding cramp.

"Gah!" I felt his hand jerk away.

The pain faded immediately, but when I whipped my face up, his glare sent a new shiver of fear through me.

He let out an enraged growl and dove for me.

His arm slammed into my chest, knocking me into the bookshelf. A new jolt of pain shot up my spine as books rained down around us, but it was nothing compared to the agony that sliced through my foot and leg again. I felt his breath against my face as he let out a howl of pain, then he recoiled.

The pain vanished as soon as he stopped touching me, but it took him a split-second longer to recover. I took my chance to dash around him, but I stumbled over the spilled books.

He raced around and leapt in front of me, stopping just shy of touching me, keeping himself between me and the door. "What did you *do?*" He spat each word separately as his glare burned into me, wild with rage. His breaths came in heavy gasps.

Grandpa's window was behind me, now, a couple feet away, but there was no way I could open it and get out before this *not-Grandpa* caught me. And he was still blocking the door.

He stepped toward me. I took a step back, but any further and I'd be trapped against the window like I'd been against the shelves.

Grandpa's face flickered.

His face flashed from Grandpa's to one with pale skin, to Grandpa's again, and then—

I gasped as the face settled on an all-too-familiar one with perfectly chiseled features, dark hair, pale skin, and eyes so blue they glowed.

The stalker from the parking lot.

His eyes widened with alarm at the same time mine did, then his face melted into a smirk that was more frightening than the glare. "So the game is done." He shrugged. "No matter." He took another step toward me. "Whatever you did, it won't protect you." His face twisted into an expression of such pure hatred, it sent my stomach swirling. His fists were clenched tight, his whole frame trembling with anger. "You *will* get what you—"

Ayla, get down!

I jumped as the words came into my mind, clear as a bell—in Jordan's voice. "*Jordan?*"

The pale man blinked, surprised, then the voice shouted in my mind again.

Ayla, now! Duck!

I ducked.

The window behind me shattered.

I crouched tighter, arms protecting my head, as glass rained down around me.

Something sailed over me and the man let out a shocked *Oof!* as the thing crashed into him. I heard him hit the ground.

The man yelled in fury as arms yanked me upward.

I thrashed against them and turned to kick—but it wasn't my attacker who had grabbed me.

"Jordan?"

I got a glimpse of his face as he shoved me behind him, then—

Thump.

I stared over Jordan's shoulder as a female figure in silver clothing slammed the end of some kind of weapon into the man's head again where he'd fallen to his knees. He sank to the floor, limp. The girl's red-haired ponytail swung across the silver plating on her shoulder as she turned and stepped over him.

"*Reina*?" I gasped.

She slid a sword—a *sword!*—into a sheath on her belt and stepped away from the man's body. Her gaze bounced to my face then away again, not quite meeting my eyes.

Some kind of silvery beast pounced around her feet, nearly as tall as her waist.

Jordan spun around and took a step back. His eyes sped over me, scanning me. "Are you okay?"

He was wearing lightweight, silvery armor across his torso and hips, with a long-sleeved, leather-looking tunic beneath it, and leather pants and combat boots—just like Reina. He clutched a dagger in one hand. His other hand was outstretched toward me, his legs poised in something like a guard stance.

The silver beast rushed toward us and I tensed to scream.

"Champ! Sit!" Jordan yelled.

The beast dropped into an obedient sit next to Jordan's legs, staring up at me with big, brown eyes. *Pit bull* eyes. It was a dog—in body armor. Its mouth dropped open into a goofy grin, and its tongue flopped out the side of its mouth.

I stared at it. At all of them. *"Jordan?"*

His eyes met mine, then he straightened, dropped his arms, and slid the dagger into a sleeve at his waist. His cheeks flushed. He ran one hand up the back of his hair and gave me a nervous half-smile. "Um, hey, Ayla. Are you... all right?"

I gaped at him in one pure moment of shock, then I screamed. "What is *happening* right now?"

Something slammed into the bedroom door.

The unconscious man's pale face lolled to the side, dark hair flopping across his forehead, as the door shoved against his crumpled body. His eyes were still closed, thankfully—just thinking of their startling blue gave me chills.

"What is so *heavy* against this—oh." A middle-aged woman in a brown leather jacket and tight leather pants slid through the narrow opening she'd made with the door, then yanked her weight against the door to pull it further open, and a man stepped through behind her.

"Mr. and Mrs. *Peters*?"

Jordan's parents stepped over the unconscious man's body and stood side by side, facing me in matching, brown leather outfits. Mrs. Peters' was a bit more fitted, and she wore knee-high combat boots. Mr. Peters' boots stopped at the ankle.

All words failed me. I'd never seen Mrs. and Mr. Peters in anything other than a pencil skirt and dress pants, respectively.

Mrs. Peters moved around Reina and stopped a couple feet behind Jordan, studying me with a sympathetic smile. "Ayla, sweetheart, are you okay?"

"Of course she's not okay," Mr. Peters grumbled from near the doorway. He stared down at the man's body in disgust. "Do you *see* this? How did a pure Selkblood breach the barrier?"

The room began to sway. The scar from the cut on my foot sent waves of pain slicing through my leg. My head throbbed.

Jordan lurched forward and grabbed my elbow. "Ayla, are you all right?"

My vision blurred. *You're in shock*, I told myself, remembering my Health 101 lessons from school. "I need to… sit." My legs were already turning to jello. I felt Jordan's hands supporting my arms, keeping me from altogether collapsing as I sank cross-legged to the floor.

"Mom—" Jordan's voice sounded distorted, like through water. "Mom, I think—"

Across the room, I saw the blurry form of Jordan's dad lean over the unconscious man and reach for his arm. "Help me get this jerk to—oh!" He jumped back. "What the—get back. No one touch him!"

The unconscious man's body warbled, popped and sizzled like Pop Rocks, and melted into a puddle of goo. I wasn't sure if I'd actually seen that, or if I was beginning to hallucinate.

"Oh, wow, that escalated quickly," I heard Reina mutter. "Ew."

A rush of panic for my family sped through me. "My parents. Grandpa." My tongue felt thick and fuzzy, like it wouldn't do what I wanted, and the words came out slurred. The room began to black in from the edges. I blinked, forcing my eyes to focus.

Jordan's face appeared in front of me. "Ayla? Ayla!"

Two more faces appeared on either side of him.

"Ayla." Mrs. Peters' hand gripped my shoulder. "Did that man touch you? Ayla, did he *touch* you?" Her words sounded both far away and too loud at the same time.

A soft moan escaped me as I clutched my throbbing head. The room blurred and swayed. I felt myself slumping backward as my eyelids slipped shut, too heavy to reopen.

"Get her to the Hub," Mr. Peters said. "Hurry."

I felt strong arms sweep under me, then the scent of Jordan's cologne enveloped me. He tucked me to his chest and stood.

"Hang in there, Ayla," he whispered near my ear. "Please."

A dog barked.

I heard Reina yell. "Hurry, let's go!"

Jordan clutched me against him and lurched into motion. Something crackled like a snap of lightning. Cold air whooshed through the room.

The darkness took me.

Chapter 18

Kind of a Lot to Explain

I opened my eyes to blinding fluorescent lights, then immediately squinted them shut again. I could feel a soft surface beneath where I lay. Memories from the attack in Grandpa's room flooded in at me but I pushed them away, not yet ready to face what they might mean.

"Ayla?" Jordan's voice was much calmer now than it had been before I passed out. I heard a chair scoot across a hard floor.

I forced my eyes back open, blinking as they watered from the bright light. When my vision cleared, I tipped my head to the side and found Jordan sitting in a chair beside my bed, his golden eyes narrowed with concern. He wore his normal jeans and t-shirt, now, rather than the strange leather and silver armor I remembered from earlier. Unless that had all been a crazy dream. I hoped at least *some* of that had been a dream. The memories flashed in again, but I shoved them away.

"How are you feeling?"

I tried to ignore the fact that my mouth tasted like an old sponge and I probably had hospital hair, and forced a smile. "Okay, I guess."

I glanced around at the room as my eyes adjusted further. I was on a cot against the back wall of what looked like some kind of lab. The room was large and sparse, with metal counters along its white walls, and cabinets and drawers beneath those. A metal examination table stood in the center of the room with a tray of instruments beside it and a movable light hovering over it from the ceiling. A pedestal sink stood in the corner near the door. To my relief, I was still wearing my own clothes. A starched white sheet covered my legs.

I sat up and shifted the thin pillow so I could lean against the wall. "Where am I?"

The door on the far wall slid open, and a tall, muscular, dark-haired man stepped inside. He wore jeans and a black shirt with an open lab coat over it, his face buried in a clipboard. "You're in the Hub infirmary," he said. The door slid shut behind him. He looked up at me.

I stiffened and scrambled back against the wall.

"Ayla?" Jordan was on his feet in a second, hovering over me. "What's wrong?" He followed my gaze to the doorway, but already I realized my mistake. The man gaping at me from the door was dark-haired, pale-skinned, blue-eyed... like the stalker... but the blue was less bright, the face older and a bit wider, the eyes kinder. It wasn't him.

Heat flooded my face. "I'm sorry, I'm fine—I just thought—"

Jordan leaned back, though he was still tense. "This is Doctor Harlowe." His eyes were sympathetic as he gestured toward the man at the door. "He's the one who treated you when we arrived. Without his antitoxin..." He trailed off, but the implication was clear; this man was not here to harm me.

The man by the door lowered his clipboard. "Forgive me. I should've realized the resemblance between myself and your attacker might upset you. I can step outside, if you'd like, give you a moment..."

I shook my head, feeling embarrassed both for overreacting and for projecting my panic onto some poor, innocent doctor who'd saved my life. He couldn't control what he looked like. "No, it's fine."

Jordan sank back down into the chair beside the cot. His hand hovered, then rested on top of mine. "Would you like me to go, so you can talk to the doctor?"

"No," I said a little too fast. I slid my fingers into his. "Please stay."

A smile teased at the side of Jordan's mouth. He tightened his hand around mine. "Okay."

I looked up at the doctor and cleared my throat. "So... how am I?" As the doctor turned his kind eyes on me, Jordan's use of the word *antitoxin* sank in. I'd thought I was suffering from shock, but that didn't involve toxins. "What *happened* to me?"

Doctor Harlowe crossed to the foot of my cot and clasped his hands, one still holding the clipboard, in front of his waist. "A heavy dose of active Veil-Dearg toxin, secreted from its pores, which absorbed into your skin on contact. Specifically, the toxin of a *male* Veil-Dearg. The females aren't poisonous to the touch—though *I* never want to meet one again." He shuddered. "They're terrifying."

I blinked. "What?" If Jordan wasn't here acting as though everything this man said was true, I'd have assumed this guy was a raving lunatic. But I trusted Jordan, and he *was* acting as though it was all true. I wasn't sure what to make of that.

Memories swam back in, Jordan's dad staring down at the unconscious man—I turned to Jordan. "Your dad called it a Selkblood. He said it breached a barrier. Jordan, what is going *on*?"

Jordan rubbed the back of his head with the hand that wasn't holding mine. "There's... kind of a lot to explain."

"It's fairly simple, actually." Doctor Harlowe shrugged. "Selkbloods are Fae, gifted with projection and perception manipulation, but this was something else entirely. Dark Fae magic. The Veil-Dearg's body was used as an avatar with the Selkblood's consciousness channeled into it, so the Selkblood could shift appearances at will. With an avatar, he could take risks he wouldn't have necessarily taken in person. Like impersonating a retired LeyGuard and infiltrating his household."

I'd only followed about half of what he said, and most of that sounded like insane ramblings. "So that—that really *wasn't* my grandpa?" Relief flooded me... mostly since I'd seen that thing, whatever it was, melt into a puddle of goo.

"No." Doctor Harlowe's face turned down in a frown. "I wish to the Void the Selkblood behind this had been caught." His voice turned cold as ice. "He deserves to hang for what he's done."

I still wasn't sure this doctor wasn't crazy, but fear plunged through my chest at his last sentence. *For what he's done.* His words implied something much worse than a near-miss poisoning. *My family.* My throat went dry, but I forced the words out, anyway. "Where are my grandpa and parents?"

Jordan and the doctor exchanged glances, which only ratcheted my fear up to panic.

I clenched Jordan's hand until my fingernails dug in. "Tell me what happened to them."

Jordan slipped his crushed fingers from mine and cupped my shaking hand between his own. The pity in his eyes sent tremors of dread through me, but to my relief, he answered me. "We think they've been taken."

"Taken." I said the word slowly, but some of the panic subsided... because *taken* wasn't *dead,* which meant there was hope. My brain was already on to logistics. "Who took them? Where were they taken?"

"The Selkblood or those working with him, we think," Doctor Harlowe said. "And we aren't sure where."

I drew a shaky breath. "But that's—that's not so bad, right? If they're still alive, we can find them and get them back. My mom was in the kitchen moments before that thing attacked me, and Jordan arrived soon after that. My dad was *with* Jordan a little earlier, driving him back to school. None of them could've gotten far, right? And Grandpa—" I stopped, unsure exactly *when* Grandpa would've been taken.

Jordan and Doctor Harlowe shared another glance.

"Stop doing that." I yanked my hand from Jordan's. "Just tell me what's going on!"

Doctor Harlowe sighed. "Ayla, what little of your altercation Jordan and the others witnessed indicates that the Selkblood was able to channel your grandfather's appearance, perhaps even some of his personality and habits. Yes?"

I thought back to my interaction in Grandpa's room. "Yes. At least... some of it."

"And is there anything else you noticed? Did your grandfather have any inclination that he was being watched, before this? Or that your family was being monitored?"

I shook my head. "I don't think so. I'd seen the guy following *me* before, but Grandpa never mentioned anything. He wasn't acting like himself, though. Hadn't been for a couple days."

Doctor Harlowe's eyes widened. He leaned forward. "For how long, exactly? Be precise."

I thought back. "I don't know. Since Sunday, I guess. The day after I—" I stopped. *The day after I first saw the vanishing guy in the café.* The next day, Grandpa had gone to lie down after church, and he'd been acting weird ever since. Chills shot through me. "It's Wednesday. Are you saying my grandfather may have been an imposter *for the past four days?*"

"It's certainly possible," Doctor Harlowe muttered.

"And it's Thursday," Jordan said softly. "You were unconscious for several hours, and it's after midnight now."

My hands shot up into the air. "I missed my shift at the café!" I was losing my grip, the panic zipping through my veins like electrical currents, every bit of me frayed and sparking.

Jordan flinched. "I'm not sure that's the thing to worry about right now, Ayla."

"*Everything* is the thing to worry about right now!" My lungs constricted, like I couldn't catch a full breath. A sob burst out. "Where is my *family?*"

"I'll grab a sedative," I heard Doctor Harlowe say, but Jordan interrupted.

"No, wait." He placed his hands on my shoulders and leaned in, staring right into my eyes. "I've got you, Ayla, okay? I am going to find your parents, and your grandfather, and I'm going to bring them back to you. I promise."

My heart tightened, but the panic loosened ever so slightly.

"Don't make any promises you can't—" Doctor Harlowe began, but Jordan's gaze on mine only grew more intense.

"I *promise*, Ayla. I will do whatever it takes to bring your family back to you."

Doctor Harlowe sighed and retreated to the door. "I'm going to get Chairman Hart. She'll want to discuss this new development with Ayla."

A frantic question raced into my mind. "Wait," I called out.

Jordan dropped his hands and moved back so I could see Doctor Harlowe clearly.

I turned to Doctor Harlowe. "At one point during the... attack... he acted like he really saw me, like himself. Like Grandpa was in there, trying to resist whatever had control of him. But only for a moment. How is that possible, if—if it wasn't him?" I stopped as the image of the Selkblood's body sizzling and melting into goo swam back into my mind. I forced away even the *possibility* that body had been my grandfather's.

Doctor Harlowe raised his clipboard, then tapped his pen against his chin as he stared off in thought. "That's interesting. I've heard of sources being able to intercept the conduit, but that means the source must be nearby. Not at all what I was expecting. And to manage an interception of an avatar spell, at his age..." His eyes slid back to meet mine. "Your grandfather must still be quite powerful."

I stared, trying to make sense of his words.

He continued. "That bodes well, all things considered. It's possible the Selkblood had to keep your grandfather nearby because he put up too much resistance to channel long-distance." He perked up. "Resistance means he's holding out well. This is good, Ayla. It means he may still survive this."

I felt the blood drain from my face. "*May?*"

Doctor Harlowe's matter-of-fact expression softened a bit. "Well, yes. This type of dark magic can really drain the source. But what you just told me is a good sign. And if he's nearby—I'll let Chairman Hart know. We could get a team out searching within the hour." He hurried out the door.

I turned to Jordan.

He reached for my hand again, squeezed it gently. "We'll get them back, Ayla. All of them."

I knew he meant it, but what if it wasn't something within his power to do? What if it was already too late? I felt the press of tears in my eyes, in my throat, as his golden eyes stared into mine. I took a breath, forced the panic to the back of my mind, and nodded. "Okay."

We studied each other for a moment.

"Where are *your* parents now?" I asked. "And Reina?"

"Mom and Dad are meeting with the Hub council to discuss what happened. Reina's around here somewhere." His expression turned apologetic. "She *was* worried about you, but since no one knew how long it might take you to wake up..."

"No, it's fine." I glanced away. I wasn't sure where Reina and I stood. I still felt bad for upsetting her... but now that I knew she was a sword-wielding, butt-kicking warrior, it put things in a new perspective.

"She'll get over it, Ayla," Jordan said. "I know she seemed upset about our date, but... I know Reina. She won't hold on to her anger for long. She cares about your friendship too much."

I could tell he believed that, but I also knew the betrayal I'd seen on Reina's face was deeper than being kept out of the gossip loop about our date. Still, I hoped he was right.

I turned back to Jordan and studied his face for a moment, trying to see him in the new context of what I'd witnessed in my grandfather's room rather than the normal, everyday look he'd now returned to. I trusted Jordan, but the more I looked at him, the more I realized how *little* I knew about his life. Curiosity took over. "So, when you were in Grandpa's room, the clothes you were wearing..."

"Oh, that," Jordan winced and blushed. "It's standard uniform for lower LeyGuards, the armor and all that. They don't trust us not to get stabbed. It's a bit much, I know."

He was shy about me seeing him in *armor*? I felt a smile creep in. "I liked it, actually."

"Oh." He stared at me, then smiled back. "That's good to know."

I couldn't help but chuckle at how pleased he looked. I was also glad for the distraction this turn of conversation was providing—it was better than melting down into panic again while I waited for Doctor Harlowe to return with that Chairman person. I decided to keep probing. "My question, though, was what do the clothes *mean*? Are you like a soldier in training, or something?"

Jordan shrugged. "Kind of, I guess."

I raised an eyebrow. "That day you walked me home, you told me you weren't a black belt like Callan."

Jordan straightened. "Well, I'm not."

"Then the next day you busted right in through my window wielding a dagger and an armored dog and saved me from being murdered."

He blinked. "I mean, yeah, but... it's still not martial arts. How was I supposed to know what you were into? You seemed to like Callan, at the time."

I stared at him. "Are you serious right now?"

He shrugged again, but the slightest of smirks crept onto his face. "So you're into guys with armored dogs, then?"

His expression was adorable, but I was too distracted by the fact that I still had no clue *at all* what was even going on. "What do you and your family do, exactly?" I glanced around at the examination table, the white walls. "What *is* this place?"

His smile melted into a look of sympathy, as though he'd suddenly realized how clueless I truly was. "Oh. It's—"

The door slid open, and a stern female voice interrupted his sentence. "*That* is not information she's cleared to receive."

CHAPTER 19

COULDN'T HELP IT

A woman strode into the room like she'd just walked off a warrior supermodels runway. She was tall, muscular, and wore a leather outfit and knee-high boots, similar to what Jordan's mom had worn at my house. Her glossy, honey-colored hair hung in perfect, curly waves, and her face was gorgeous—and serious.

Jordan blanched as she stared him down. I expected him to pull his hand away from mine like he'd been caught doing something wrong, but instead he gripped my hand tighter. "Sorry, Chairman Hart. I thought since Ayla—"

The woman smiled, but her eyes continued to bore into Jordan. "Ayla has been through a lot, and she needs to understand the situation—and her position in it — before any sensitive information is divulged."

Some kind of unspoken communication passed between their stares, not exactly a reprimand for Jordan, but something like a reminder, maybe.

Jordan glanced at me, then nodded. "Understood."

The woman's smile warmed. "Good. Go ahead then and get her up to speed."

Jordan took both my hands in his and adjusted in the chair. The nervousness in his eyes sent a tremor of fear through my chest. "What I'm about to tell you, you can only know because of... who you are. *Because* of what I'm about to tell you."

My curiosity surged. "Okay..."

"Nothing I'm about to tell you can be shared with anyone outside of this place, unless you're given clearance to do so. Do you understand?"

Anxiety tightened my chest. "Would there be any reason I'd *need* to tell anyone else?"

Jordan hesitated. "Do you trust me, Ayla?"

I stared into his eyes, and found that despite all logic to the contrary, I did. "Yes."

"Then please trust that I wouldn't ask you to keep any secrets that would hurt you, or anyone you care about. But you have to agree up front, not to tell anyone."

"It's like a verbal non-disclosure agreement," the woman by the door stated. "We cannot proceed without it, but we aren't trying to trick you, if that's what you're worried about."

I glanced at her. She stared back with a blank, almost bored expression.

"Would I be able to tell my parents?" *If we get them back.* I forced that thought away.

"If there's a reason to do so, then perhaps," the woman answered before Jordan could. "We would need to evaluate the risks involved."

"What about my grandfather?"

"He already knows," she said. "Or... he did, at one point. So yes."

He did at one point. Was this place my grandpa's crazy *cult*? That thought was honestly terrifying, but I trusted Jordan, and I wanted answers... so I shoved that particular panic aside. Still, I hesitated. Was I really *ready* for whatever answers this might bring? My curiosity had intensified, but so had the feeling that I was balanced on a cliff edge and one more nudge might push me over into a ravine from which I'd never make it back.

Jordan squeezed my hand. "It's okay, Ayla. Please trust me and agree to her terms, because you need to know what's going on. It's past the point where I can protect you from a distance. You need to understand what's happening, so I can keep you safe."

I refocused on Jordan. His eyes were so intense, they made me believe he would do just that—keep me safe—no matter *what* he was about to tell me. I nodded. "Okay. I agree to the non-disclosure terms... so long as *not* telling doesn't put anyone's life at risk."

Jordan glanced at Chairman Hart, and she gave him a subtle nod. He exhaled in relief and turned back to me, still holding my hands tightly. "This is going to be a lot to take in," he said.

I took a breath. "Okay."

"Like, a lot."

Anxiety churned in my stomach, but whatever he had to say, waiting wouldn't change it. I squeezed his hands. "It's okay, Jordan. Just tell me."

His shoulders relaxed a little. "Okay, let's start with your earlier question, about where we are. This is one of the medical rooms at the Hub, the headquarters of the LeyGuard, an organization of which my family and I—and Reina's family—are a part."

I tilted my head, processing his words. "Okay."

"An organization of which your grandfather was once a part—and therefore of which also *you,* technically, are a part, because you're in his direct bloodline."

My heart sped, but I swallowed down my questions, giving him a chance to talk. "Okay..."

"An ancient organization made up of four bloodlines of guardians charged with the sole duty of monitoring, securing, and controlling the LeyGates that allow access between Earth and the realm of the Fae."

"*What?*" I pulled my hands away in shock.

Jordan dropped his grip on my hands the instant I tugged, but his eyes pleaded for me not to retreat. "I know it sounds crazy, Ayla, but it's true. LeyGuards are guardians who keep peace between the Fae and humans, make sure no Fae cross Earthside without permission, and protect our Fae allies from some of the darker, more dangerous Fae, when needed."

I'd assumed I'd still been somewhat woozy whenever I thought I heard that doctor mention Fae, or that maybe he was just an eccentric doctor who liked to use wild metaphors, but here it was again... from Jordan. Was he crazy, too?

I thought of everything I'd seen over the past five days—the vanishing man in the café, the appearing riddle, Grandpa's strange book and his rambling about brownies, the stalker who apparently shapeshifted into my grandpa via avatar then melted into sizzling goo on my grandpa's bedroom floor... and suddenly realized that Fae might be one of the more *reasonable* explanations. Assuming my mind hadn't finally snapped.

"Ayla?" Jordan studied my face. "Are you okay?"

"Fae?" My voice trembled. "For real?"

Jordan inhaled deeply and nodded. "I know it sounds crazy, but I'm telling you the truth."

"I..." I glanced away for a moment, replaying his explanation—and Doctor Harlowe's—in my mind. These Fae didn't seem like the ones I'd read about in folklore or mythology books... but if *real Fae* were actually a possibility, it wouldn't be all that surprising if they weren't exactly like the stories. Myths and legends always morphed from their real-life inspirations over time... but they *were* usually inspired by something real, even if only in part.

I met Jordan's eyes, which were still watching mine closely, and sighed. "I guess I believe you."

Jordan raised an eyebrow. His mouth curved into a half-smile that made my heart do a little flip. "Not the most committal statement of trust I've ever heard, but I'll take it."

I tightened my arms around my chest. "So the people here are *all* part of some group of guardians who protect humans from Fae?"

"And control the LeyGates, and protect our Fae allies from the more dangerous Fae who have turned to dark magic, yes."

"And... my grandpa was one, too?"

Jordan nodded. "Yes."

That *my* family was somehow a part of this was the hardest part to grasp. My dad didn't even like killing roaches, and he was descended from *this*?

I studied Jordan's face. "And... you're one of those guardians, too."

"Yes. Although technically, I'm still in training."

"That... that doesn't mean we're *related*, does it?"

Chairman Hart laughed, but Jordan hurried to reassure me.

"No. Definitely not. We come from different Houses, but even if we didn't, the House lineages go so far back that many of the families in them aren't directly related anymore, at least not in any measurable way. There are many bloodline branches, by this point, inside each House."

I took a breath. "Oh... okay." A new question struck me. "Why were you even at my house when that thing attacked me? How did you know something was happening?"

Jordan tensed, then leaned forward. "You were my mission assignment."

I was his mission? Was *that* why he'd shown more interest in me this school year? I tensed, and he must have seen the shift in my expression, because he hurried to continue.

"But I *asked* for that assignment, and it only began recently."

I stared at him. "*How* recently?"

Worry swept over his expression and he reached for me, stopping just before his hand touched my arm. "You were my friend first, Ayla, I want you to know that. But once I realized you were in danger, I begged Chairman Hart to let my family be the ones to protect you and she agreed."

"Against my better judgment," Chairman Hart interjected. "We usually advise against personal attachments in our missions"—Jordan blushed slightly at the way she said it—"but in this case, it made sense. He was already near you, already in a position of trust. It was ideal."

I blinked. "Oh." I couldn't help but feel a little confused and disappointed. I pulled back some, and he dropped his hand. "But... when... How much of our time together recently was because I was a *mission*?" My voice was a bit harsher than I'd intended, but had *all* of this, even our supposed date, been a ruse to stay near me? That thought hurt more than I cared to admit.

"Hardly any of it, I swear." Jordan's gaze was pleading again.

But did I believe him?

I glanced at Chairman Hart, suddenly embarrassed at how apparent my emotions had become in this conversation. I hated feeling vulnerable in front of strangers. But to my surprise, her expression seemed understanding, which made me feel slightly better.

Jordan gripped my hand, drawing my attention back to him. "Moments after your dad dropped me back off at school yesterday, Reina's parents got a tip about a Selkblood spotted in the area. When we realized it was your neighborhood, I called my parents. My parents contacted the Hub and explained the situation, and they agreed to let us go check it out. We arrived when he was attacking you. We barely arrived in time. If I'd had any idea you were in that much danger—"

He took a shaky breath.

"I'm sorry, Ayla, I should've put it together sooner. It never occurred to me that all the recent stuff happening to you could be connected to any of this. I knew your grandpa was former LeyGuard, but I've known that since soon after we first met in kindergarten."

"You—what?"

"We keep track of our own," Chairman Hart commented from the other side of the room.

Jordan nodded. "But I knew *you* didn't know, and I never imagined your family had been targeted now because of it. There's no reason we know that you *should* have been. I just thought—I mean, pretty girls get stalkers, right? When I walked you home that one day, I had no idea you were being stalked by a *Fae*. And after you got your grandpa's call yesterday, I thought he was ill, like you did. Until we got that tip about the Selkblood, I promise, I had no motive for hanging out with you except that I *wanted* to."

"Then why were you so weird on our date?" I knew it wasn't the most pressing question to ask at the moment, but it slipped out.

Chairman Hart's scowl deepened.

Jordan let out a nervous laugh, but then he glanced at Chairman Hart's impassive stare and blushed. "I—well, honestly, I kind of thought I was too late, and that you had developed a thing for Callan."

That tracked with how he'd acted toward Callan... and with what I'd heard in my mind, though I wasn't quite ready to address *that* oddity yet. Not with that Chairman woman staring at me.

"But also," Jordan continued, "Even though your grandfather had been LeyGuard once, we knew he'd never told his family about it. So technically I wasn't supposed to be *on* that date. That's probably why Reina was so upset I kept it from her, since she's my training partner. She knows we aren't supposed to... get *close*... like that... to people who don't know who we are."

"Oh."

Jordan leaned toward me. "But I couldn't help it, Ayla. I still can't."

CHAPTER 20

CLASS ONE BREACH

My heart did a full somersault at the look in Jordan's eyes.

Chairman Hart cleared her throat.

Jordan pulled back abruptly. "And now that rule doesn't matter anyway, right? Because now you *do* know what we are." He glanced back at Chairman Hart and grinned.

She narrowed her eyes. "There are more pressing matters to discuss right now, Jordan."

"Right." He turned back to me, blushing slightly. "Um, so, there are LeyGates all over the world, and LeyGuards stationed all over the world—but the Hub, where we are right now, is like Central Command." He smiled. "But I have something even weirder to explain to you."

I raised an eyebrow. "...Okay?"

"I'm guessing, just before we busted in through the window, you heard me tell you to duck, right?"

I suddenly felt anxious. "Yes."

"In your mind?"

I hesitated, though I wasn't sure why admitting I heard his thoughts in my head was any weirder than anything *he'd* admitted so far. I nodded.

He smiled. "I knew it! Reina thought maybe you'd seen us there, but your back was to the window, and—"

"Is there a point to this, Mr. Peters?" Chairman Hart interrupted.

"I'm getting there, ma'am," Jordan answered, though his eyes never left me. He leaned toward me. "That type of hearing was a gift of your grandfather's, or so I'd been told. It only tends to activate when in times of high stress, and only with people you're familiar with, but I'm glad it worked." He squeezed my hand.

"A *gift* of my grandfather's?" I stared at him. "What are you saying?"

He held up one hand. Flames flickered on his knuckles and danced over his fingertips, then vanished. He grinned. "I'm saying LeyGuards have *magic*."

I bolted straight up from the pillow. "*What?*"

Chairman Hart strode over to the cot. "That'll be quite enough for right now, Mr. Peters. We're not here for demonstrations, we're here because Ayla and her family are in grave danger."

My shocked awe plunged back into panic and despair.

Jordan's grin vanished. "I'm aware." His eyes met mine. "I'm sorry, Ayla."

My mind was still spinning from what I'd just seen, but I tore my eyes from Jordan to look up at Chairman Hart. "You're going to get them back, right?"

Her stern expression softened with sympathy. "We're going to do our absolute best. Please try to think if there is anything else you could tell us about your interactions with the Selkblood or with your grandfather the past few days, anything that might explain why this Fae targeted your family. No matter how small, it might help."

I hesitated. "When that thing that looked like my grandfather touched me, it hurt him."

Chairman Hart nodded. "Yes, the Veil-Dearg toxin causes—wait, it hurt *him?*"

"Yes." I nodded. "The thing that looked like Grandpa definitely felt pain when we touched. And—and my foot—" I stopped, uncertain how much I should say about the vanishing stranger, but Jordan already knew he existed, and whatever danger the vanishing man had tried to warn me about had obviously already found me. "Every time he touched me, I got this blinding pain right where I'd cut my foot on something a few days earlier, at the café. A vial of shimmery liquid the vanishing guy dropped.

It was like the liquid *called* to me. At the time, I thought the guy had stumbled in hurt that night, but now I think he must have appeared that time, like he did the other times."

Jordan gaped at me. "Wait—the time I was there wasn't the only time? There were more?"

Chairman Hart stiffened. "Jordan, what is she talking about?" Her voice was on the edge between concern and anger.

I focused on Jordan. "Yes. Always at the café, though. The first was last Saturday night; that was the night I got cut. It did something to me, I think. Whatever was in that vial. My foot has felt weird ever since, and I've been having... dreams. And the next day was when Grandpa started acting weird."

Jordan's eyes widened with concern. "Ayla, please, you need to tell Chairman Hart what happened that night, plus the night I was there. And any other times. Anything he said to you. All of it. I know you're trying to protect him, for *some* reason—but Fae aren't allowed to breach—"

"He was *Fae*?" I blurted.

"You knew a Fae *breached,* and you didn't report it?" Chairman Hart bellowed at the same time. She was angry now, for sure.

Jordan answered me first. "Yes, I knew the moment I saw him, though I've never seen one vanish like he did." He turned to Chairman Hart. "I promised Ayla I wouldn't tell anyone. I intended to report it, but only after I had a chance to talk to Ayla—to convince her we *needed* to tell someone. He was only a teen, like us, or close to it, and he didn't register as anyone from the Lock list so it didn't seem urgent, at the time. I figured he'd breached laterally, not over the border. Ayla and I were supposed to talk the next day, after school, and I planned to convince her then."

Chairman Hart glared daggers at him.

He lifted his hands defensively. "I was going to be vague, I promise. I wouldn't have told her about the Hub; I know she wasn't supposed to come here or even know about it. I just... I'd promised, and I couldn't break her trust." Then he added in a quieter voice. "I think the Fae threatened her family if she told."

Chairman Hart turned to me. "Is that true?"

"No! Not exactly. He just... told me I was in danger, and warned me that telling anyone might put them in danger, too." I didn't know why I felt so instantly defensive of the vanishing guy—apparently *Fae*—I hardly knew. But I could still see his deep blue eyes in my mind, and I knew he'd been warning me, not threatening.

Chairman Hart gaped at us both, then refocused her glare on Jordan. "Don't you think that might have been good information for us to know *sooner*?"

Jordan paled. "In hindsight, yes, I see your point."

Chairman Hart sighed. "What's done is done. But now would be a good time, Ayla, for you to share whatever else happened in your interactions with this Fae. Did he tell you who he was?"

"No, but there was a riddle."

Jordan blinked. "A *riddle*?"

I scooted to the edge of the cot, and Jordan moved back to make room as I swung my legs over. I stood, dug the creased paper out of my pocket, and held it out toward Chairman Hart. "It appeared in the café where I work, one night. Like, right out of thin air, near the same place where I saw the guy the other times."

She studied me, then grabbed the paper. It crinkled as she unfolded it. Her eyes sped down over the line, then she looked up at me. "This paper and the style of writing look similar to some of the old LeyGuard archival tomes, but I don't recognize the riddle itself." She folded it closed again. "May I keep this? I'd like to look into it."

I nodded, surprised she'd asked permission, though it did make me like her more. "Yes, of course."

"Thank you. I've already got a team looking into your family's where-abouts, Ayla. Time is of the essence, and we're moving as quickly as we can, but we need to verify intel before we act, for everyone's safety. As soon as we have a lead, I'll let you know."

My chest squeezed with anxiety, but I appreciated that they were already taking action. I nodded. "Thank you."

Chairman Hart turned to Jordan. "In the meantime, since Ayla is feeling better, why don't you give her a tour while I—"

A siren blared from the ceiling.

Jordan was angled between me and the door in a second, dagger drawn. I hadn't even seen him move.

The med room door flung open, and a leather-clad, muscular, dark-skinned man I'd never seen before barged in. "Chairman Hart, I'm sorry to interrupt, but we've got a Class One breach at the southeastern entrance."

Chairman Hart stiffened. "Class *One*? Are you sure?" she called over the alarm's ongoing blare.

The man nodded emphatically. "Yes."

For the first time since she'd entered the room, Chairman Hart looked truly stunned. "How in the world would a Class One Fae know where—" She shook her head. "Nevermind. Bring up the monitor."

I slid toward Jordan and clenched his arm.

He placed his free hand over my hand on his arm. "Stay near me," he called over the siren.

I nodded. I had zero intention of leaving his side.

The other man jabbed some buttons on a watch-like contraption on his wrist, and one wall of the med room transformed into a giant screen.

A male figure stood in a grassy lot, wearing a studded leather vest over some kind of cloth tunic, leather breeches, and thick leather boots. On the screen, the figure slowly removed a long knife from his belt, placed it on the ground, then stepped back and held up his hands. His face flicked up to stare at the security camera trained on him.

Jordan stiffened beside me, at the same moment I gasped. "*Callan?*"

CHAPTER 21

AREN'T YOU GOING TO OFFER THEM TEA?

"**Y**ou *know* him?" Chairman Hart spun toward Jordan with a glare.

"Yes, ma'am." He nodded. "He's... he was... a friend of Ayla's from school."

Chairman Hart's eyes widened as her glare bounced to me. "A friend?"

The alarm was still blaring as her eyes bored into me. My brain stuttered. "I mean, sort of? I don't know him all that well, he's just... I mean... we have classes together, and he seemed... he seemed..."

Chairman Hart decided not to wait for my brain to get into gear. "Ollie, cut the alarm."

The dark-skinned man jabbed buttons on his watch as Chairman Hart pulled a device like a phone from her pocket and swiped her hand over it, replacing the image of Callan with a split-screen of the expectant faces of Doctor Harlowe, a blonde man, and dark-skinned woman with her hair in a tight bun.

"Yes?" Doctor Harlowe's startled eyes on the wall blinked as the alarm continued to blare, then it cut silent, and he visibly relaxed. "Yes?" he asked again.

Chairman Hart pivoted on her heel and strode for the door, calling out orders as she went. "Doctor Harlowe, convene the council. Benton, alert our other waypoints. Natalie, evacuate the upper dorms and move everyone to the safe room... just in case."

Natalie blinked in surprise, but Chairman Hart was halfway to the door with her back to the screen. "Everyone, ma'am?"

Chairman Hart spun back. "Yes, everyone. And you two—" Her stare shifted back to Jordan and me as she stepped into the hall. She pursed her lips. "Stay here."

The door swished shut and the wall screen winked out, leaving Jordan and me alone in the med room.

Jordan relaxed and slid his dagger into its sheath. He stepped around to face me, and his eyes softened as they met mine. "Are you okay?"

I wrapped my arms tight around my chest to quell the shaking from my frayed nerves, and nodded. My brain was still struggling to process Callan as a Fae—I'd taught a *Fae* papier mâché? But I couldn't believe that Callan was here to hurt anyone, and it made my insides squirm to think of them harming him just for showing up here. What if he'd come here to check on me? He *was* a friend, or at least friendly... unless I'd been badly mistaken.

I looked at Jordan. "What are they going to do to Callan?"

Jordan's expression tensed. "They won't hurt him unless he acts first. They just want to bring him inside, to find out why he's here. And *how* he's here." His face shifted into a blend of confusion and concern. "No one besides the LeyGuard should even be able to *find* this place. It's cloaked."

Jordan's posture was stiff, and the tender warmth he'd had in his eyes a moment earlier had evaporated. I chalked it up to stress, but it left me with an uneasy feeling in my stomach. I suddenly realized I was squeezing my arms so tight around myself I was about to cut off my circulation. I dropped my arms, but then they dangled awkwardly at my sides. Sometimes, trying to act normal felt so difficult I wondered if I was really a robot who *thought* it was human.

Jordan took a small step toward me. Something *was* bothering him. I could see it on his face, and it sent flutters of anxiety through my stomach.

Jordan hesitantly reached for my hands, and when I didn't pull back, he gripped them gently and stepped closer. The scent of his cologne enveloped me again as I tipped my face up to him. His face was inches from mine, and I could feel his warm breath against my face as he looked down at me, his golden eyes intense with an emotion I couldn't quite read. "Ayla, I—"

The door flung open and Jordan spun toward it, quickly shifting me behind him.

"Jordan, take Ayla to B-3, immediately," Chairman Hart commanded from the doorway. Her eyes flicked to me with annoyance. "Our intruder refuses to speak to anyone but her."

B-3 turned out to be just off of the lobby on the main floor. Jordan led me out of the med room, down the stairs, and through the lobby to B-3 briskly and without a word... not that I would've wanted to finish our conversation with Chairman Hart staring icicles into my back the whole way, anyway.

When Jordan pulled open the door to B-3 and gestured for me to enter, I expected to find Callan chained to some kind of interrogation table. Instead, I found him kicked back in a fancy leather office chair in a big, open room, with his feet up on the end of a huge mahogany conference table and a steaming mug in one hand.

His gaze met mine, then he dropped his feet and set his mug on the table.

I stood and blinked, unsure what to do next, as Jordan and Chairman Hart filed in behind me.

"I assume you understand I will need to be present for this conversation?" Chairman Hart eyed Callan, then squeezed past me and tapped a button on the wall beside me. The door slid shut.

Callan nodded once, but said nothing.

Chairman Hart pointed to the chair nearest me. "Go ahead, Ayla, sit."

Jordan darted forward and pulled out the chair for me, which I was grateful for since my brain and body were still trying to catch up to whatever was happening and if he hadn't, I would've kept standing there like a lump. I sank into the chair, and Jordan took a seat directly beside me, while Chairman Hart positioned herself at the opposite end of the table, probably so she could glare at Callan more easily.

I stared between Callan and the Chairman, at just the right angle to see them both without much effort... and for them both to stare at *me*, which made me immediately uncomfortable. Jordan was seated so close I'd have to turn to see him, but his presence beside me was comforting—despite the awkwardness and the many confusing events of the past few hours, he was still my friend, and whatever was about to happen, I was glad he was with me.

Chairman Hart settled back in her chair, focused her eyes on Callan with laser intensity, and folded her hands over her stomach. "Well, go ahead then."

Callan glanced at Jordan and me. "Aren't you going to offer them tea?"

His voice sounded so familiar, yet so strange now that I was hearing it in a new context. I noticed a faint lilt to his words that I hadn't picked up before, a vaguely Scottish accent, or maybe Irish? Though it didn't exactly sound like either one. Whatever it was, it was barely perceptible unless I focused on it.

Chairman Hart narrowed her eyes so much I worried her laser stare might actually burn a hole in the wall behind Callan—or in Callan's face. "Sure." She spat the word with no attempt to mask her irritation, then slapped her hand on a button I hadn't noticed, embedded in her end of the table.

A voice crackled from an overhead speaker. "Yes, Chairman Hart?"

"Two more cups of hot tea, please," she grumbled.

"Yes, Chairman," the voice answered, then cut out with a hiss of static.

Callan turned to me. "Do you want honey? Sugar?"

Chairman Hart's mouth pursed so tightly her cheeks turned red.

I shook my head quickly, afraid to anger her further, but Jordan replied from beside me. "I like honey in mine." I turned to stare at him, but he shrugged. "What? I do."

Chairman Hart slammed the button again. "Send some honey, too."

"Right away," the voice answered, then the room fell silent.

Chairman Hart glared at Callan. "Will you be getting on with it now, or do we have to wait for their tea to arrive first?"

Callan winked at me, and I felt Jordan tense beside me.

Callan turned back to Chairman Hart with a grin. "I believe we're ready to begin now."

I was afraid to look directly at Chairman Hart, but I could feel her anger radiating all the way from the other end of the table. "Then *begin*."

"Oh," Callan said. "We already have."

I tensed, waiting for whatever was coming next, but Chairman Hart just kept staring at Callan. "Well?" she demanded.

I glanced at Jordan, but he was looking back and forth between Callan and Chairman Hart, whose attention suddenly turned fully on me.

I turned back to Callan and found him staring at me. *Ayla. You hear me, right?*

I blanched. Had he said the other phrase *in my mind*? I nodded warily.

Callan returned my nod with a grin, then slid his gaze back to Chairman Hart. "On second thought, I think I'd like to wait for their tea."

"Ayla," Chairman Hart commanded. "Report immediately."

I startled and blinked at her. "Wh-what?"

"I'm not blind. He's communicating something with you. Report what you know."

Jordan stiffened. He glanced between me and Callan, then angled closer to me and pivoted in his chair to face Chairman Hart. "She's not an inducted LeyGuard, yet." He glanced back at me. "You're a guest here. You don't have to comply, Ayla, not unless you want to."

Callan let out a small laugh.

Chairman Hart looked as though smoke might come out of her ears at any moment.

The door slid open, and a man darted in with a tray, plunked two steaming mugs of tea, a small jar of honey, and two teaspoons in front of Jordan and me, and dashed back out again. The door shut behind him.

"Answer her if you want to, Ayla," Callan said with a shrug. "I've got nothing to hide at the moment."

Jordan shifted around to face me and took one of my hands in his. "It's up to you, Ayla, whatever it is." His other hand drifted to his dagger beneath the table, which sent a tremor of panic through me. What was he expecting to happen?

I looked back and forth between Jordan's furrowed brows, Callan's smug grin, and Chairman Hart's piercing glare.

"It's okay either way, Ayla." Jordan's hand tightened around mine, easing my anxiety.

I couldn't see any reason not to answer Chairman Hart, so I swallowed down my panic and met her stare. "He asked me if I could hear him. I mean, asked me in my mind."

Now it was Chairman Hart's turn to blanch. She flipped her glare back to Callan. "How did you know of her ability?"

"That LeyGuards have *abilities* isn't a secret to Fae." Callan traced his finger along the side of his mug. "But the rare one Ayla has, specifically, I know from her grandfather. I wasn't aware it had activated, however, until she used it on me in class."

Chairman Hart stared at us, but I had questions of my own.

"You knew my grandfather?"

Callan leaned forward and smiled—not a cocky grin this time, a genuine, warm smile. "I know of him. He's a bit of a legend in our kingdom. He saved the king's life."

I gaped. "What?"

Callan glanced at the Chairman, then turned his attention to me and leaned back in his chair. "Maybe a story for another day, love."

I felt Jordan's hand twitch on mine at the endearment.

Callan continued. "I'm sure the Chairman is expecting me to answer some more *pressing* questions at the moment, but I do have something important to tell you, Ayla, or I wouldn't have come."

I leaned forward. "What is it?"

Callan's brows drew down. His eyes turned serious, and the words that echoed through my mind next stopped my heart cold.

I know where they're holding your grandfather.

CHAPTER 22

LEVERAGE

My heart lurched. "What?"

Jordan's grip tensed on my hand. "Ayla, what is it? What did he say?" He leaned toward me, concerned, but he didn't press for a response. He just glanced nervously between Callan and me and waited.

Do you trust them? Callan's eyes locked on mine.

I looked at Chairman Hart, then back at Callan. "I... don't know."

Callan glanced toward Jordan. *Do you trust* him?

I tightened my hand around Jordan's, his fingers still entwined with mine, and he returned my squeeze. "Completely."

Chairman Hart shifted impatiently in her chair. "Would someone inform me what's going on here?"

I felt Jordan's free hand come to rest on my shoulder. *Ayla?*

It was surreal how clear both of them sounded in my head, but Jordan's voice sent a flutter through me Callan's hadn't. I shifted sideways in my chair to face him.

His eyebrows drew down over his golden eyes as they connected with mine. *Did something happen? Can I help?*

As endearing as his concerned expression was, I still couldn't avoid noticing the way Chairman Hart glared at me over his shoulder. She was clearly furious at losing control of this meeting.

But Jordan never missed anything when it came to me, and this was no exception. His eyes tensed as he realized where I was looking. *Is it her? Do you not trust her?*

I swallowed, searching for a way to ask what I needed to ask that wouldn't anger the Chairman further. "Should I?"

Jordan shifted to face me and took my other hand, too, entwining his fingers through mine to where both our hands rested on my knees. *She wants to help your family, same as Callan. Your grandfather was a hero around here, too, at one point. Someone Chairman Hart personally respected. I'm sure it's the only reason she's allowed this... disrespect... from Callan so far. She believes he may have information that could help, and she doesn't want to risk losing a chance to find your family.* He squeezed my hands. *She's a bit off-putting and harsh sometimes, but she's been a good leader for the Hub. I trust her.*

I gave Jordan a small smile. "That's enough for me."

He grinned in return, and my stomach did a sudden flip—but I tore my eyes from his face and turned back toward the table. Jordan let go of one of my hands so I could turn, but kept the other one tight in his grasp as I faced Callan. "You can speak freely in front of both Jordan and Chairman Hart," I said.

Callan studied my face, as though making sure I was sincere, then nodded. "Very well," he said aloud.

Chairman Hart leaned forward and clasped her hands on the table. "Thank you, Ayla." Her jaw was still tense with irritation, but she no longer looked like her head was about to start smoking. She turned her stare on Callan. "Before we get any further—are our people here in danger?"

"You're in no danger from me," Callan replied. "But I am not the only threat, as I'm sure you're aware."

"My grandfather," I interrupted, unable to wait any longer. "You know where he is?"

Chairman Hart stiffened. "He does?"

"Of course," Callan answered. "Why else would I have risked coming here?"

"How *did* you get here?" Chairman Hart demanded.

Callan shrugged. "I followed Ayla."

Chairman Hart looked unsatisfied with that answer. "You can't just *follow*—" she began.

But I was growing more anxious by the moment. "Where is he? Is he okay? What about my parents?"

Callan folded his hands into his lap. "Your grandfather is still alive, if that's what you mean. But the Selkblood doesn't make things easy on his captives."

I thought of my grandfather's essence channeling into the creature that attacked me, and of what it might have cost him to resist, and shivered. Jordan's hand tightened on mine.

"I lost track of your parents, Ayla, I'm sorry," Callan continued. "I think they've been taken across the barrier. But your grandfather is close. He's being held at Kane Textiles, or at least, I'm fairly certain he still is."

"*Kane* Textiles?" I shouted. Madison's father's company—where my own dad worked.

Callan nodded. "Not the main factory. A side warehouse, one that isn't used much."

"But *why*?" I yelled.

Before Callan could answer, Chairman Hart leaned forward. "How do you know?"

"Because I've been watching Ayla's family, of course." Callan blinked at Chairman Hart like she was dense for asking. "And the Selkblood, as well, once I realized he was following Ayla."

"You were *watching* them?" Jordan bristled. "*Why*?"

But I interrupted. "Grandpa is old, and this could be too much for him, and—across the border? What does that even *mean*?" Callan's strange reaction to me having a stalker made at least a *little* more sense now, but the more I thought about his words, the more panicked I felt. My free hand flailed wildly and my voice ramped up with each phrase, edging toward hysteria. "Why does this guy even care about my family? Why is he *doing* any of this?"

Jordan tugged me close and wrapped his arm around my shoulder. I sank into him, pressing my face into his chest as tears threatened against my shut eyelids.

"We'll get them back, Ayla," he murmured against my ear. "All of them. Don't worry; it's going to be okay." His scent enveloped me, and I breathed it in deeply, finding it centered me just enough to keep me from completely losing it. When I looked up, his golden eyes were locked on mine as though he and I were the only two people in the room—in the *world*. "It's all going to be okay, Ayla," he said. "I promise."

And for some reason, I believed him. I swallowed back my tears and peeled myself away from him to find Callan watching me with an expression of sympathy.

"I'm sorry this has happened, Ayla," Callan said. "Truly, I am."

Chairman Hart inhaled sharply, then slapped the button on the table. "Darcy, inform the council that our target is Kane—"

"I wouldn't do that so quickly," Callan interrupted.

Chairman Hart flicked her gaze up to him. "And why is that?"

"You're experienced in dealing with Fae breachers, but *I* am experienced with this *particular* breacher. And believe me when I say, he is not your typical kidnapper. He is here for a reason, and he will have a plan. Even his traps will have traps. Let me help you, first—I can tell you what I know."

Chairman Hart released the button, and the intercom snapped off with a hiss of static. "Go on."

Callan ran a hand casually through his dark hair, then gestured at Jordan. "The mini-guard here is right."

Jordan tensed at the slight, but Callan just leaned back in his chair, relaxed.

"There's still hope to save all three of them," Callan said, "if we're smart about it."

I was unsure whether to be reassured or frightened further by his statement. His moods were shifting so rapidly, I could hardly keep up.

"What do you mean by *smart* about it?" Jordan asked, his tone suspicious.

"I know what the Selkblood wants," Callan said with a shrug. "And that gives us leverage, if we're careful."

"What *does* he want?" I asked.

Callan met my eyes. "You."

"*What*?" I squeaked, at the same time Jordan demanded, "Why?"

"Ayla is of particular interest to our kingdom, and therefore to him," Callan answered.

"We will *not* use Ayla as leverage." Jordan shifted our joined hands to his lap and peered around me at Callan. "Besides, Ayla's grandfather saved the king's life, sure, but that was years ago. Why would Ayla matter to your kingdom *now*? Why have you been watching her family?" His face tensed. "You're Upper Fae—your people have *always* avoided involvement in Earthside affairs. Why are you helping us at all?"

Callan's face darkened, and for the first time I saw the dangerous glint behind the deep brown of his eyes, the subtle glow to his tanned skin, the otherworldly angles of his slightly-too-perfect face—for the first time since I'd met him, I saw him as *Fae*.

Callan planted his hands on the table and leaned forward. "I have a job to do, too, LeyGuard, but right now, our interests align."

Chairman Hart narrowed her eyes at Callan. "And what job is that?"

Callan smirked at me and winked. "Keeping Ayla alive... which is harder than one might think, but my job now, nonetheless."

My throat went dry. "Keeping *me* alive? Why?"

Callan's smile vanished. "Because I am sworn to protect the crown prince of Teionyr, and if you die, so does he."

CHAPTER 23

BONDS AND CURSES

I surged forward in my chair. "What? How?"

Callan's serious demeanor slipped away as quickly as it had come, replaced by a smirk. "You may want to sip your tea while it's hot because this is going to be a long story." He tapped a finger against his lip and tipped his head to one side. "On second thought, it's not a long story at all. The serum you used to save the prince's life bound your life to his. Now you're connected."

"They're *what*?" Jordan surged forward.

I shoved my tea cup away and pinned the Fae with as stern a glare as I could muster within my panic. "Callan. Explain."

Callan held my gaze. "Prince Kaizyn had a particular faespell with him, a spell intended to be used only by the most intimate of partners—a close friend, family, a sworn guard... a lover. It requires a siphoning of magic from the user, binding their life force to that of the recipient to fuel the healing. Permanently."

I felt the blood rush from my face. "Wh—what?"

Callan's gaze softened. "I owe you a great debt for saving the prince's life, Ayla. The prince himself owes you his life. He would not have survived, had you not broken that vial. But he never intended for you to be the one to do so. In fact, in our kingdom..."

He trailed off, looking suddenly uncomfortable. Between my own anxiety and Jordan's clenched fingers on mine, the tense silence was unbearable.

"Just tell me, Callan." I clenched my jaw.

Callan glanced away and grimaced. "Under the laws of Teionyr, to deploy such a spell with someone outside your own family or sworn guard like this, with the deep connection it forms, especially with someone of the opposite sex..." His eyes locked back on mine. "When between a male and female, the bond can manifest more strongly. It would be inappropriate to marry anyone else while bound in such an intimate way, so in Teionyr, such a bond is tantamount to a betrothal."

Jordan leapt to his feet, his chair flying back. "*What?*"

Callan rose to his feet, too, leaning his palms on the table, but he ignored Jordan and kept his eyes on me. "Prince Kaizyn did not intend to do this to you, Ayla."

I blinked, still clutching Jordan's hand as he stood over me, seething silently at Callan. My breathing quickened, my pulse skyrocketed, my voice climbed toward panic: "Who *was* he trying to betrothe himself to?" Jordan's hand still tight in mine was the only thing grounding me.

"No one!" Callan's voice was insistent, almost indignant. "He was trying to reach your grandfather. The bond is not as intense, when activated between two males, and your grandfather had already sworn an oath to the royal family to protect the prince's life, years ago. It would not have been inappropriate, in such a circumstance, to deploy the spell if your grandfather had been willing. The prince would never have forced him, of course." His voice lowered. "Prince Kaizyn was dying, Ayla. He breached as close as he could get, to what he thought was your grandfather's energy. Instead, he found you."

The memory of those deep blue eyes floated in, and my chest tightened. "He asked me for help."

"For *help*, yes. He could tell you were LeyGuard. He never expected you to open the vial and activate the spell yourself."

A chill shot down my spine as I remembered that vial, how the liquid inside it had called to me. I shivered. Jordan stepped closer and rested his free hand on my shoulder, even though he was still partly bent down to keep hold of my other one.

Jordan glared at Callan over my shoulder. "Then it's not a betrothal. And even if it were, you could hardly expect Ayla to go along with it when she had no idea what was happening."

Callan's eyes darkened. "I'm afraid the people of the Upper Faeside realm may see it differently, especially those in tenuous alliances with Teionyr."

"She saved his life! He *owes* her!" Jordan was angry now, his voice harsher than I'd ever heard it.

Callan stepped back and dropped his hands. His eyes met mine with regret. "On that, you and the prince are entirely in agreement."

Chairman Hart, who had been watching our interaction with tense interest, interjected. "How do you know so much of the prince's mind on these matters? Are you in communication with him? Is he Earthside, as well?"

Callan's eyes met mine. *I can trust her?*

The tone of my response was less than friendly. "I've already said you can."

I am sorry, Ayla. Callan's sincere tone echoed in my mind, and his eyes softened to match. Then he turned to Chairman Hart. "He's not Earthside, no. I've been able to communicate with him only in the same way Ayla did—when he appears briefly through the destabilized breach at midnight. Or when I've risked venturing to him in person, once or twice... in the Veil."

Chairman Hart's eyebrows shot up. "Why the—" She caught herself, then drew on a tight-lipped, all-business face that looked a little like a frustrated ferret, and moderated her tone. "Why would the *sole heir* of Teionyr be camping out in a place like the Veil?"

Callan glared back at her, obviously offended. "It's not like he *chose* to. The High Prince of Upper Faeside would never abandon his duties like that."

Oh, good gracious—now I wasn't just accidentally betrothed to a Fae prince, I was accidentally betrothed to the *High Prince* of an entire Fae realm. Words spewed out of me in a panic. "Callan, please—this is a mistake, you see that, right? I know nothing about Faerie princes or Fae politics or any of this. I helped him, then he reappeared and warned me about danger, that's all. There's nothing else. No betrothal, nothing. I don't even *know* him!"

Callan slipped away from his chair and moved around the table, then knelt in front of me.

I felt Jordan tense behind me, but I kept my eyes on Callan, anxiety swirling in my chest.

"But the prince knows *you*, Ayla," Callan said, forming each word slowly, somberly. "He's been able to feel you, ever since you created the bond. Your latent power, abilities you still haven't embraced yet... the fear you carry inside you, always churning beneath the surface... your compassion for your grandfather, your patience... your courage."

He reached out a hand and rested it on my forearm. I resisted the urge to pull away.

"He admires you," he continued. "He's... quite taken with you, actually."

I nearly fell out of my chair. "*What*?" Jordan's hand was crushing mine so tightly I suspected he had a *different* set of words he wanted to yell.

Callan chuckled. "Who wouldn't be? You're admirable; any male in this room could attest to that." He winked at Jordan, and the blood rushed to my face—while the rest of me was flooded with a fiery emotion halfway between embarrassment and a jaw-clenching desire to punch Callan's nose.

Jordan's hand on my shoulder tightened, probably resisting the urge to do the same.

Callan's face turned serious. "The prince would never wish an unwanted betrothal on you, Ayla. He is a good man. A little too romantic at heart, perhaps, but honorable. He is as horrified at the present state of things as you are. He's thought of little else, besides his own escape, of course, than how to free you from this bond."

Jordan's hand loosened slightly. "Wait... his escape?"

Callan sighed and stood. "Yes. That's what I've been trying to tell you. The prince is not in the Veil by choice. He is *trapped* there—by the same curse that nearly killed him. He is able to breach through to the café for a brief window at midnight, when the Veil is at its most unstable… and even that is only because he breached out so quickly that first night, while the curse was still settling. In essence, he carved himself a tunnel that leads only to the café."

"How is that possible?" Chairman Hart's voice was sharp. "This region has been warded against rogue breaches for decades."

Callan glanced at her. "Had he not had the great Maddox Rogers' energy to target onto, he wouldn't have managed even that. It was a fail-safe, given to him when Maddox swore his oath to protect the prince—a one-way ticket Earthside, for lack of better explanation, to be used only in case of emergency."

Maddox Rogers—my grandfather.

Chairman Hart's silence was so unsettling I turned and leaned around Jordan to look at her. She looked stunned.

Jordan glanced down at me, concern in his golden eyes, then turned to Callan. "Ayla's *grandfather* created the breach in the café?"

Callan shrugged. "Only indirectly. In essence, he gave the key for it a long time ago—it was the prince who opened the door." Callan turned to me. "But I'm sure you noticed, Ayla, that Prince Kaizyn's visits are rushed. Even to that exact location, he cannot step foot out of the Veil for more than one minute, exactly at midnight while the Veil is weakened, before being sucked back. If he attempts to exit the Veil in any other way before the curse is lifted, he will die."

Jordan squeezed my shoulder. When I looked up at him, his face was pale. "And if he *does* die?" he asked in a rough voice.

"Aside from his death likely being the downfall of our entire kingdom?" Callan said with an edge of sarcasm, but then his expression softened. "Aside from that—if he dies, so will Ayla."

The blood drained from my face.

"No." Jordan's voice was firm. "There's got to be a way to disconnect them, to break the bond. *And* the prince's curse."

Callan sighed. "I'm certain there is... but... everything we need to access a potential solution is in the palace back in Teionyr."

"So?" Jordan said. "You're a royal guard, right? Go in and get it."

Callan shook his head. "You don't understand. Prince Kaizyn's uncle, Beirthyr, has usurped the throne of Teionyr. *He's* the one who cursed the prince."

Chairman Hart shifted forward. "Why would he curse his own nephew?"

Callan continued in a rush. "King Veilar fell ill while the prince and his private guards, including myself, were on a mission in the Wilds. We hurried back the moment we heard. Prince Kaizyn went immediately to see him—and the next thing we knew, Beirthyr was on the balcony of the royal palace, declaring King Veilar's assassination... by his only son. By the time we realized what was happening, half of our private guard had been forced into the dungeons for treason, and Prince Kaizyn was nowhere to be found. The three of us who were left ran—keeping our freedom so we could free our prince. But we couldn't find him. The regular Royal Guard under the new king's control spotted us. I made it out of the palace, but that was the last I saw of the other two. We thought the prince might have been captured, but I tracked him to the Veil and realized he'd been cursed. But the people have been told that Prince Kaizyn murdered his own father and fled."

"And everyone just took Beirthyr's word for it?" Chairman Hart asked.

Callan's jaw clenched. "Yes—and no. Beirthyr has had help convincing them, I believe. *Selkblood* help."

I remembered what Doctor Harlowe had said about Selkbloods, that they were gifted with manipulating perception, or something like that, and my heart sank. Not only had the prince been framed for his own father's murder, and been the victim of attempted murder himself, but then some crazy Fae bent people's minds to make sure the prince's own kingdom *believed* his guilt. That was... awful.

Chairman Hart's eyes widened. "Does the Upper Fae Court know of this affront?"

Callan shook his head. "The Selkblood who was after Ayla is named Sevryn—he's a known ally to the Dark Fae uprising... and also a personal friend of Beirthyr's. I've seen them meeting in the corner gardens outside the palace. Now, I hear word he's set up *inside* the palace, as Beirthyr's second-in-command."

"I don't understand," I said. "If Selkblood are so dangerous, why would anyone allow one into the palace? Maybe Beirthyr is corrupt, but wouldn't other people in the palace notice something was wrong? Wouldn't *someone* have tried to stop them?"

"Someone did," Callan said. "Prince Kaizyn did, as soon as he realized what was happening, and that's how he ended up where he is now. There were others who realized it, too... but by then, Beirthyr had such a strong hold that any opposition was arrested or executed. As for the rest of the people..." He sighed. "Selkbloods are tricky. They manipulate emotions. When they want to, they have a way of making people trust them, or simply distracting them until they forget what they're after. There are innocent Selkbloods, of course. But there are also many allied with the Dark Fae. And Beirthyr's connections go deep. They must, or he never could have orchestrated this so easily."

"Lands alive," Chairman Hart breathed.

"Beirthyr told everyone Kaizyn fled," Callan continued. "That he murdered his father, then abandoned his kingdom like a coward. I knew that couldn't be true—but by the time I figured out what had happened, Kaizyn had already been cursed."

"That was the only way Beirthyr could harm him," Jordan muttered behind me, like he was suddenly realizing something. "Because of the Teionyr Seal."

"Exactly." Callan nodded, his eyes hard.

Chairman Hart must have noticed the confusion on my face. "It's protective magic for the royal family," she explained, looking at me. "It prevents them from being assassinated."

"But then how was the prince's father killed?" I asked. "Wouldn't that have protected him, too?"

"There are ways around the Seal," Callan replied. "For one, royals can still die of natural causes... or of magic that skirts around being a direct assassination attempt, like this curse. Whatever Beirthyr did to the king, it took his life." His eyes held mine. "Thanks to you, that was not the case for Prince Kaizyn."

CHAPTER 24

DO YOU EVEN DO MARTIAL ARTS?

A surge of emotion ran through me—relief that I'd saved a life, even by accident; fear about what it now meant for me; frustration and anger at their stupid Fae magic and all its ridiculous rules... so many emotions, all in one tangled, anxiety-churning mess.

"Wait," I said. "There was a riddle Kaizyn left—a paper he dropped for me, something about finding what Prince Kaizyn lacks."

Chairman Hart shifted. "I have it right here." She pulled the paper from her pocket and handed it to Jordan, who passed it around me to Callan.

Callan examined it. "This makes no sense. I've never seen this before, and the prince didn't mention it. Had he left it for you, I'm sure he would've told me."

"Then who did leave it?" Jordan asked.

Callan looked at me. "I'm not sure—could it be your grandfather's?"

I bit my lip, thinking. "Maybe. He's been out of it a lot lately; I suppose it's possible. But it appeared during my shift, right out of the air. How would he have gotten it to the café?"

No one had an answer for that.

My confusion and anxiety hit a peak. I leaned forward, searching Callan's face, trying to find a shred left there of the guy I'd briefly thought was my friend.

"Please, Callan, I just want my family back. I'm sorry about your Fae war and your trapped prince and—well, everything. Your story is *awful*. But I'm not some Fae warrior princess. I'm not even really LeyGuard. And I'm *definitely* not High Prince betrothal material. I just want to find my family, get them home safely, and figure out how to break this bond. If we can help free your prince as part of that, great, but I'm not equipped to deal with a Fae civil war, and I'm not ready to be *betrothed* to anyone, least of all a *Fae*." My voice climbed to heights of panic. "I want my normal *life* back!"

"I'm working on that," Callan grumbled, though his eyes were full of sympathy. "But you see how this all complicates things, yes?"

Jordan rubbed my shoulder, then pulled me close. "I'm here," he whispered. "We'll figure this out. It's gonna be okay."

Chairman Hart leaned forward, tense. "What else can you tell us, Callan?"

Callan tore his eyes from mine, looking back toward Chairman Hart. "We know Beirthyr is working with the Dark Fae. He's up to something—and it can only mean bloodshed and ruin for Teionyr, for all of Upper Fae. But I have no proof, no way to convince the people Beirthyr is corrupt."

"Then we get proof." My heart raced hopefully. "That has to be possible. Right?"

Callan shook his head again. "We can't just march in with evidence, even if we managed to find some. We'd be thrown in the dungeons or hung in the square before we even got a word out." He ran a hand down his face and sighed. "The best way to convince the people is if Prince Kaizyn himself were to return. The people loved Kaizyn. They believed in him. They're confused and hurting now, but if he were to return—there's an uprising, already, an undercurrent of people who suspect Beirthyr's ascent to the throne wasn't entirely honorable, but the prince's absence brings too much uncertainty."

"And you really think his return would make the difference?" Jordan asked.

Callan nodded. "Yes. I know some of them would believe Kaizyn. Even his *presence* back in Teionyr would be a beacon of hope. The people would listen to him. He could spread word outside the palace, rally an army to unseat his uncle, and take back his throne." He looked at me. "And once he does... he hopes he can use the resources in the palace to find a way to break what binds you to him. But only if we can break the curse, first. So long as he's trapped in the Veil, any other plans are pointless."

Jordan leaned forward. "You have a lot of faith in this prince," he said flatly.

Callan stepped forward to match him. "Yes. I do. We grew up together in the palace. Despite our differences in rank, we were friends—family. He always treated me as a brother, and as far as I'm concerned, he's my blood. When it came time to take my oath to serve the heir, as my father had before me, there wasn't even a question. Prince Kaizyn is Upper Faeside's best hope at holding back the Dark Fae uprising, at finally ending this blasted war. But more than that, he is good—through and through. One of the last true Fae of honor. Even if he weren't Teionyrian royalty, I would die for him." His eyes flicked to me, then back to Jordan. "Which is why I agree with you."

Jordan flinched back, surprised. "What?"

Callan's eyes were cold when they fell on me, once again the eyes of a Fae soldier. "The prince's life is connected to Ayla's... so Ayla must be protected at all costs."

Jordan narrowed his eyes. "I thought you wanted to use her as leverage."

Callan hunched forward, eager now. "No, hear me out. I have a plan. As I said, I've been watching Ayla for several days..."

"I noticed," Jordan muttered.

Callan rolled his eyes. "Must you interrupt me every few moments?"

"How did you hide that you were Fae, anyway?" Jordan blurted. "I never sensed Fae magic from you."

I flicked my face to Jordan, surprised that this was something he could sense, but Callan's reply pulled my attention back in his direction.

"I used a faespell to mask the detection." Callan shrugged.

"*What?*" Chairman Hart and Jordan both said in unison.

Callan waved a hand dismissively. "Don't worry, it's rare, and I've used the last of it, now. Only one powerful apothecarist in Teionyr is capable of making it, and no one outside the prince's most loyal Royal Guard even knows about it. We rarely have need to use it. Any LeyGuards who visit Teionyr already *know* we're Fae, and we haven't come Earthside in decades."

"Do you even *do* martial arts?" Jordan called out.

I glanced at him, startled *that* was the question he chose, but he was just glaring at Callan, his face pure exasperation.

Callan chuckled. "Yes, I'm quite skilled... in *our* version of it, at least."

Jordan glowered at him while I gaped between them both, trying to figure out if Jordan was losing his mind.

Callan cleared his throat. "But anyway... my plan?"

"Yes," Chairman Hart said with a sigh. "Go ahead."

"Thank you," Callan grinned, then slipped right back into serious mode. "It wasn't until Ayla heard my thoughts in class, then told me about her stalker, that I knew for sure Ayla must have been the one Prince Kaizyn originally appeared to, and that she was the Selkblood's target. Until then, I hadn't had a chance to speak to the prince for more than a few moments at a time, and I knew only that the girl he'd been bound to worked nights at the café... so I'd been watching Ayla and Madison both. I even watched that other café girl for a while, until I realized from Kaizyn's description of age that it couldn't have been her."

"But now you know," Jordan said. "Why does any of that matter?"

Callan gestured impatiently. "Just listen! If *I* didn't know for sure which girl Prince Kaizyn had bonded to, it's possible Sevryn doesn't either. Madison could still be in danger."

"Oh," I said.

Callan nodded. "Madison seems to know nothing about what's going on, but she's more tangled up in this than she realizes. In my short time watching her, I learned Madison got involved in a dangerous situation, some guy she met at the mall after she and her boyfriend broke up—"

"They broke up?" She and Trevor had still been together, last I checked.

Callan shrugged. "I guess so. Recently. Anyway, she met this new guy, went on a date... it got serious fast, then turned ugly when she tried to put the brakes on things."

"That's why she has a bodyguard," I guessed.

"Yes." Callan nodded. "She had a stalker." He paused, letting his words sink in. "But something doesn't play right to me about this situation, even if it was Sevryn who got involved with her. Soon after they hired the bodyguard, Madison's dad began working strange hours, then suddenly, all kinds of things were shifting around at the factory. He emptied out an entire warehouse, moved a bunch of supplies... and that ends up being the exact warehouse I track the Selkblood to, where he seems to be holding your grandfather? It's strange, don't you think? Madison is clueless, I could tell that much from watching her, but I'm not convinced her father is as innocent."

"What are you saying?" Jordan asked.

"Until we know more about Mr. Kane's awareness, and who else may be involved, we need to move with caution," Callan answered. "It's possible that the Selkblood has taken Ayla's family not only because he suspects Ayla is the bonded one, but also because of what her grandfather *himself* means to the prince—the leverage he represents as a sworn ally to the royal family." He let that sink in for a moment, then continued. "If Sevryn knows for *sure* it's Ayla he needs in order to harm Prince Kaizyn, he may amp up his attempts to find her. We could leak word that Ayla's the bonded one, then watch the warehouse and Mr. Kane... and see what happens."

"You want us to *tell* him to target her?" Jordan yelled.

Callan held up his hands. "Yes... but in the meantime, Ayla will be here—safe. He wouldn't be able to get to her, even if he *did* figure out she'd gone to the Hub. I only found this place because I have something that helps me locate Prince Kaizyn." He fingered a leather cord around his neck, whatever was attached to it hidden beneath his shirt. "The bond between him and Ayla is so strong that I could feel *her* location with this, even through the Hub's wards."

Chairman Hart tensed.

"You're sure no one else has a thing like that?" Jordan asked, his voice suddenly panicked.

Callan met his eyes. "No one. I have the *only* one."

Jordan and Chairman Hart both relaxed slightly.

"And the Selkblood doesn't know you have *me* explaining things to you," Callan continued. "He'll have no reason to expect a LeyGuard team would have pieced together a Fae curse and a faespell bond, deduced his motives, *and* figured out where he's keeping Maddox so quickly."

"We aren't incompetent, Callan," Chairman Hart said dryly.

Callan shrugged. "I never said you were. But the curse Beirthyr used on the prince isn't even common knowledge among the *Fae* population. Sevryn would have no reason to suspect the LeyGuard to know as much as you do now, and that's an advantage." His voice turned eager, moods shifting on a dime again. "I can warn you of the Selkblood's abilities, where I think he may be holding Ayla's grandfather, what I know of his habits, and what he's likely to try to use in attack or defense." He looked at Chairman Hart. "I *do* think you should send a recon to the warehouse, but strategically. Let me brief your team first. They need to know what they're up against."

Chairman Hart opened her mouth to respond, but before she could, the door burst open.

Jordan's dad charged in, breathing hard from apparently running here. "Madison Kane is in the hospital," he panted. "She was attacked leaving work at the café tonight." He glanced at Jordan and me. "Her bodyguard is dead."

CHAPTER 25

THAT CHANGES THINGS

"Attacked by what?" Callan's voice was tense, his whole body taut as he faced the doorway where Jordan's dad had burst in.

A familiar voice drifted from the hall. "All signs point to a Selkblood." Doctor Harlowe appeared in the doorway, and Jordan's dad stepped aside to make room for him to enter.

Callan blinked at Doctor Harlowe, as though shocked by his presence. "Well, you would know."

I glanced at Jordan, confused by what Callan meant. His eyes cut to mine, but before he could say anything, Doctor Harlowe stepped forward.

"Yes, I would." He met Callan's surprised stare with a steady, firm glare, then turned to me.

"Harlowe, I don't think—" Chairman Hart interrupted.

Doctor Harlowe waved her objection away with one hand, his eyes still on me. "I suppose you may as well know that I *am* one, Ayla—if you hadn't figured it out, already."

Fear exploded through my chest, but Jordan's steady thoughts cut through it in my mind. *You're safe, Ayla. He would never hurt you. You're not in danger.* His hand tightened on mine, and he tugged me closer. *I would never let you be in danger.*

That last thought skipped through, words fading as soon as they came, and I wasn't quite sure he'd meant for me to hear it.

My pulse slowed slightly, but it was hard to fight the instinct for fear now that Doctor Harlowe's affirmation brought back into focus all the similarities between him and my attacker—the pale skin, the too-blue eyes, the dark hair. I forced my breathing to slow and met Doctor Harlowe's gaze. "But you—"

I wasn't even sure what my question *was,* I was simply confused, but Doctor Harlowe answered it, anyway.

"I was raised Earthside, by LeyGuards; I'm no danger to you in the slightest. No need for alarm." He smiled gently. "But it does make me somewhat of an expert on Selkblood attacks. And yes, I'm certain this was one."

"Do you mean the poison?" I remembered how quickly it attacked my system, how I'd thought I was going into shock, and felt alarm for Madison.

"No, no," Jordan's dad stepped around Doctor Harlowe and moved toward me slowly, eyes and voice gentle, like soothing a startled animal. "That was the Veil-Dearg toxin. But the Selkblood didn't use a proxy this time; he was there himself... or has other Selkbloods working with him, because this was definitely a *Selkblood* attack." He smiled, trying to reassure me. "But Selkbloods themselves aren't toxic."

"That makes them no less dangerous," Callan interjected, then glanced at Doctor Harlowe. "No offense."

"None taken," Doctor Harlowe replied with a shrug. "You're right."

Jordan leaned down near my ear, answering my unspoken question. "Selkbloods' power to manipulate perception and emotions can manifest as a slightly different gift in each of them, different strengths for how they use it. Some are capable of bending emotion to the point it can distort perception... create illusions from the person's own mind. That makes them *extremely* dangerous, when they have nefarious motives."

"Exceptionally gifted Selkbloods can even make people do things without realizing what they're doing," Callan added.

I glanced at him, surprised he'd heard Jordan's soft comment. Callan's hearing must've been very sharp.

"Theoretically," Callan continued, "a Selkblood could have even made Madison shoot her own bodyguard."

"*What?*" Horror lanced through me as I envisioned all the ways *that* could be used against someone.

"We monitor illusory magic *very* closely on this side of the Veil." Chairman Hart's voice was sharp, and when I looked at her, she was glaring at Callan. "We have wards in place across the city, to prevent such a thing."

"I'm aware," Callan said.

Chairman Hart seemed to be expecting him to elaborate, as I was, but he left it at that.

"Besides, that is *not* what happened here," Doctor Harlowe cut in.

Jordan's dad nodded in agreement. "Both Madison and her guard were attacked directly... *without* human weapons. And *physically*, not through their minds. But when a pure Selkblood goes feral like that—" He paused. "Madison's lucky to be alive."

I turned to Jordan's dad. "What happened? Is she—"

His face softened. "She'll be all right. She sustained a concussion, some scrapes, and a good deal of shock." His eyes tensed. "She watched her bodyguard die, protecting her."

Jordan clenched my hand. "How did he die?"

His father's eyes met his, heavy with an emotion I couldn't read. "It ripped poor Gerard's throat out... right in front of her."

I gasped, instinctively reaching for my throat with my free hand.

"Dark Fae," Doctor Harlowe whispered. "Not all Selkbloods choose to use their gifts in such a way. But those who go Dark..." His teeth clenched, his words trailing off.

Images of vampires shot through my mind, though I knew that couldn't be what they meant. This was something different, something *Fae...* but seemingly every bit as dangerous.

Jordan glanced at me, concerned, then turned back to his dad. "It didn't even try to conceal itself? Or to cover its tracks?" His voice was tight, shaken.

His father shook his head.

"That couldn't have been Sevryn." Callan leaned forward, eyes intense. "He's too careful. He must have others Earthside, working with him... or he's so desperate that he's completely lost control."

Chairman Hart slid her chair back and stood. "That changes things." She turned to Callan. "We can't have dark-aligned Selkbloods roaming our city, especially not a whole group of them. We need to investigate immediately... and we'll need whatever insight you can give us."

For once, Callan's cheeky rebellion vanished. "Absolutely." He nodded. "Whatever I can do to help."

Chairman Hart spun to Doctor Harlowe. "Can you track them?"

"Of course." His eyes widened slightly, as though surprised she'd asked. "Give me an hour, I'll identify their signature." He spun and fled the room, leaving me wondering what *his* particular gifts were.

Chairman Hart turned to Jordan's dad. "Tell Darcy to ready a team to investigate the site of Madison's attack and follow up on any witnesses. Have Natalie return the residents and any guests to Level 2. We need to keep people calm... but let her know what's going on, tell her to stay alert. Have Ollie take a couple guards down to whichever police station responded to Madison's attack, nothing ostentatious, just see what they know. Have Striker go stake out the hospital. And I need *your* team to check out the warehouse Callan mentioned, see how many, whether they're holding Maddox Rogers there, and what they're up to."

"On it," Jordan's dad said. He cut a glance at Jordan, then hurried out the door.

Jordan's hand tightened on mine. "I need Ayla safe."

Chairman Hart nodded. "Of course. We'll make arrangements for her here."

It suddenly hit me what Jordan was saying. I spun to him. "You? No, please—you can't go after them. Didn't you hear what happened to Madison?"

His eyes were gentle as he gripped both of my hands. "My parents and Reina and I are on the Hub's primary recon team, Ayla. I have to go." He squeezed my fingers.

"I thought you and Reina were still in training!"

"Well, yes, but—"

Chairman Hart's sharp voice cut in. "Trainees go on missions. How else do you expect that we train them? The Peters are extremely skilled at their jobs, Ayla, as are Reina and Jordan and the rest of their team. And so am I. I would not send trainees on a mission if I didn't feel they were capable."

Jordan squeezed my hands, pulling my attention back to him. "We have protocols in place for this. It's just a surveillance mission—to observe. We'll be careful." There was no fear in his face, only concern for me. He leaned closer. "I promised you we would get your parents back. Let me do this, Ayla. Let me help." His golden eyes bored into mine with an intensity that made my breath catch.

My heart squeezed. Routine missions went wrong *all the time*... or so it seemed from all the detective shows I'd watched on TV. But this was crazier than TV: it was real... and these were *Fae*. I wasn't even sure yet what all these creatures could do, but I knew enough to be scared about having them near people I cared about. I wanted my family back desperately, but not at the cost of Jordan.

I dropped my gaze to our joined hands.

He squeezed my hands again, gently. "Ayla?"

Jordan was my friend... my *best* friend. More, if I was honest—despite how I'd tried to fight it. And maybe I *didn't* have to fight it, now that so many things had changed... but I'd hardly had time to explore that possibility before he was running off, away from me again, and this time into danger. I forced my eyes back to his, and sucked in a shaky breath. "Would you not go, if I asked you to?"

The steadiness in Jordan's eyes wavered. "Ayla—"

I saw in his eyes that he wasn't asking for permission. He felt he *had* to go, whether because it was his job or because he'd made me a promise, I wasn't sure, but he was going. He just... needed me to understand, to say it was okay for him to leave me here. He was worried about *me*.

Though it terrified me for him to go anywhere near the Selkbloods, and I wasn't comfortable here with a bunch of strangers, I couldn't make him choose between his duty and me, and I also couldn't bear to let him leave with things tense between us, especially with everything else so up in the air. If he could be brave, so could I.

I forced a smile to my face, though I knew it must be a weak one, and nodded. "Okay."

Jordan exhaled in relief. "Thank you. I'll be back as soon as I can, I promise." He squeezed my hands again, then dropped one of them to reach for his pocket. He pulled out his phone and tapped out a text—to Reina; I saw her name on the screen—then slid his phone back into his pocket and looked back at me. "You'll be safe here, Ayla, don't worry."

"Actually, I..." An idea had just occurred to me for how I could occupy myself while he was gone, but I hesitated, wondering if I should even tell him and cause him the worry. But I wasn't sure who to talk to about plans here, other than him, and I also didn't want to deceive him. "I'd like to go see Madison."

Jordan ran his free hand down his face and sighed, as though he was exasperated but not entirely surprised. "Ayla, I don't think that's—"

"Actually, that's a great idea," Chairman Hart interrupted.

Jordan and I both turned to her in surprise.

"We need to know what Madison saw, what she knows." Chairman Hart's eyes were steady as she met our stares, calculating. "Ayla is already close to her, someone she knows and trusts. She could get that information much easier than most, without causing Madison undue distress. Her presence might even be a comfort."

A humorless laugh escaped me. "I doubt that. We aren't exactly friends. At least, we weren't." I hesitated a moment, thinking of that night in the café, of Madison's persistent nagging for the explanations I never gave her... explanations that *might* have made a difference, if she'd known there were otherworldly things going on, that there could be danger. Guilt swelled through me. "But she and I worked together, and... maybe we were coming to a friendship, of sorts. I just need to make sure she's okay."

Jordan squeezed my hand, his eyes narrowed with concern. "What happened to Madison isn't your fault, Ayla." Perceptive as ever.

I drew a shaky breath. "I know." *Sort of.* "I just... I need to see her. Besides, she might know something that could help get my family back."

Jordan let his breath out and leaned back. His eyes studied my face as he gnawed the inside of his bottom lip, obviously still conflicted.

I didn't really need his permission, but I wanted his agreement, the reassurance of knowing I had his support—the same as he'd wanted mine.

"Striker will have eyes on the hospital, and we'll be sending him reinforcements as soon as we can spare them." Chairman Hart nodded. "Ayla will have protection. And a hospital is far too public a place for a typical Selkblood attack. Given the importance of whatever Madison might know, it's not an unreasonable risk for Ayla to make a short visit."

Jordan shifted to look at her over his shoulder. "Who else will you send with her? Practically every Guard who isn't already out on a mission was on the list of people you just told my dad to round up for the new assignments."

"Striker is one of the best—" Chairman Hart began.

"I know that." Jordan raised a hand in defense. "But he's going to the hospital to watch Madison. Ayla will need protection to and from the hospital, and while she's inside. Striker can't be everywhere at once."

A voice spoke from behind me. "I'll go."

CHAPTER 26

BEAT ME TO IT

Chairman Hart, Jordan, and I all turned to stare at Callan, who in all the commotion, I'd forgotten was there.

"What?" Jordan blurted.

"I'll take her." Callan leaned forward, his face serious. "I wasn't planning to let her out of my sight, anyway."

Jordan's grip on my hand tightened.

Callan glanced between Chairman Hart and Jordan. "I'm not Ley-Guard, I know. But Ayla's life is directly tied to Prince Kaizyn's. Do you really think I'd ever let anything happen to her?" His eyes slid to me. "Besides, I kind of like you, Ayla—for a human. I'd sort of begun to think we were friends, and I'd rather no more of my friends get harmed today." He winced, leaving me wondering what he meant by that, then his gaze hardened as it flicked back to Jordan. "I'm quite capable of protecting her."

Jordan stared at him, but didn't contradict him. I wondered, suddenly, what Callan *was* capable of.

"That settles it." Chairman Hart slapped her hands on the table, making me jump. "Callan will accompany Ayla. Striker will be nearby for support as needed." She pinned each of us with her gaze in turn, finishing with Jordan. "Locate the rest of your team and ready yourself; we brief in C-9 in fifteen minutes. Callan, come with me. I need you to tell me what you know." She strode out of the room without a second glance.

Callan raised his eyebrows. "She's a bossy one, isn't she?"

Jordan squeezed my hand again, then dropped it and stepped around me to face Callan.

Before Jordan could speak, Callan held up a hand. "I won't let any harm come to Ayla. You have my word. I'll protect her."

Jordan's jaw twitched. "With your life?"

Callan met Jordan's eyes. "I swear it." He said it like he meant it—like a vow. Which I supposed it was. He'd already sworn to protect the prince, and now that meant protecting me, too.

I stepped up beside Jordan.

He reached for my hand. "You're okay with this?" he asked.

"Yes." I looked at Callan, and found that I did, in fact, trust him. "I'll be fine."

Jordan drew a breath, then nodded. "Okay."

"Callan!" Chairman Hart's sharp voice cut from the hallway.

Callan's eyebrows lowered. "She seems to be under the delusion I'm now one of her employees." He huffed. "But I'm not sure I have the patience to argue with her when I was planning to give her the information anyway, so I may as well go." He tipped his head to Jordan, then to me. "I'll see you in a bit, Ayla." He left the room.

Jordan and I stood, for a moment, as we were—side by side, hands interlocked. The atmosphere in the room shifted, and I was suddenly aware that we were, for the first time in a long time, *alone.*

Jordan turned to face me. "Ayla, I—" He paused, his face a shifting mask of emotions: tenderness, hesitation, concern, uncertainty, and a few more I couldn't decipher.

My own thoughts spun wildly as I stared up at him. There were so many things I wanted to say, to ask—about him, about everything that just happened, about what was about to happen, about *us*. Jordan seemed certain that Reina had only been upset because his dating me was forbidden and he hadn't told her. But that wasn't the case anymore—and everything I'd been through in the past day had only confirmed to me that Jordan absolutely *was* someone I could trust. I couldn't lie to myself and say that my feelings for him were in the friend-zone, anymore. They most definitely were not. I just wasn't sure what to *do* about it.

He stepped closer. His face settled into one final emotion, one that made my heart seize up: sadness. He lifted both my hands, resting them against his chest. "Ayla, I am so, so sorry."

I blinked, surprised. "For what?"

"For all of this. For not putting it together sooner, for not keeping your family safe—for putting *you* in danger." He pulled one hand free of mine and ran it through his hair. His eyes danced away from mine for a moment, troubled.

I squeezed his other hand.

His eyes returned to mine, full of worry. "It doesn't sit well with me, leaving you right now. I need to do my job, to help find your family, and I know Callan and Striker can protect you, but I want—" He hesitated, then reached his free hand toward me and gently tucked a piece of hair behind my ear. His golden eyes searched mine as his hand came to rest on the side of my face. "I want to be *here* for you."

I stared back at his eyes, at the tenderness there, as a kaleidoscope of trust and affection and worry for his safety swirled in my chest. Then I closed the distance between us, rose on tiptoes to wrap my free hand around his neck, pulled his face down to mine, and kissed him.

His whole body went rigid.

Panic spiraled through me—Did he not *want* this? I hadn't even really *thought*, for once, only reacted; maybe I'd misread—I started to pull away.

But then he slid his hand from my jaw to tangle his fingers in the back of my hair, and returned the kiss.

The butterflies that resided continually in my chest around Jordan exploded into a frenzy.

At first he kissed me carefully, like he thought I might pull away any moment, but when I didn't, he kept his hand in my hair but slid his other arm around my waist, holding me firmly as he tilted his face down more so I didn't have to stand on my toes. The kiss deepened, and the butterflies shifted from frenzy into something like a celebration flight, still soaring, but unpanicked, happy—peaceful. The way he held me, the way he kissed me, every movement was gentle, careful, adoring. I'd never felt more protected, more cherished, in my life.

After a few more seconds he sighed and pulled away, resting his forehead on mine.

My eyes were still closed, having squeezed shut somewhere between when I impulsively attacked him with a kiss and when he decided to return it. I was almost afraid to open them, to break the moment. But as my fluttering heart slowed and reality crashed back in and I realized what I'd done, I grew self-conscious again. It was my first kiss—and though I'd never imagined being the one to *initiate* my first kiss, it was everything I could've hoped for and more. But would things be strange between us again, now? And had he even *liked* it? Was it possible he'd returned the kiss only to be polite? And, oh no... how long had it been since I brushed my teeth? His breath had tasted fine, vaguely like cinnamon toothpaste or maybe cinnamon gum, but what if my breath tasted weird? Would he have mentioned it, or would he have been too polite to—

I felt Jordan's head lift away from mine. "Ayla." His breath was warm on my face, still just inches away. "You're doing it again, aren't you? Over-thinking."

"Um... yes?" I muttered, embarrassed that he could always read me so clearly. I blinked my eyes open and found him staring straight into them. To my surprise, he looked completely *happy*.

He gave me a half-smile that made my heart flutter. "You don't need to." He traced one hand along the side of my jaw, his expression something like awe as his fingers trailed my skin. When his eyes returned to mine, the intensity from earlier was back. "You have no idea how long I've been waiting for the right moment to kiss you." He raised an eyebrow, looking amused. "You beat me to it."

"I'm... sorry?"

"I'm not." He grinned, then leaned in and kissed me again.

The butterflies burst into an all-out rave. I was pretty sure they even brought a disco ball.

The kiss was more intense this time, but briefer, and he pulled away again before I expected him to, then wrapped his arms around me and tucked me to his chest.

I could hear his heart racing as he pressed his lips gently to the top of my head. "It's going to be so hard to leave you now," he whispered against my hair, then pulled back, looking down at me. "I really wish we had time to talk."

I tensed as reality crashed back in. "Oh, right. You need to get to your briefing."

He slid his arms from around me and took my hands. "Once I get back, the first quiet moment we have, let's find time to talk—just you and me. About this."

Anxiety reared again, and I glanced away. "About... this?" He'd said he only wanted to be friends, before... then he'd busted through a window, saved me from a madman, and confessed that he still had feelings for me. He'd just kissed me willingly. But that didn't necessarily mean he wanted to be *together*, did it? Maybe this was something more casual, for him. He'd said LeyGuards weren't supposed to get close to people who weren't one of them, and I still wasn't sure I counted as part of any of this—I barely understood what was even going on.

Jordan tipped my chin up to look at him. "Ayla."

I forced my eyes back up to meet his. "Yes?"

His eyes were gentle, adoring. "To talk about *us*, and about what you want. I know there's a lot happening for you right now, and I don't want you to feel pressured in any way, or to feel like anything is moving too fast. I want to know what *you* feel comfortable with, so I can make sure you're happy with things. Even if you want to just stay friends for now, that..." He hesitated, then nodded, resolve solidifying on his face. "That would be fine."

I stared at him. "Oh."

"It's not what I *want*, let me be clear this time." He smiled, though it was a little sad. "But I want you to be happy even *more*. And I know now's not a good time, with your family, and—"

A brief siren blared, almost like a fire alarm, then cut off, followed by a loud voice from overhead speakers. "All strategic teams, report to C-9 immediately for briefing. Repeat: All strategic teams to C-9 immediately for briefing."

Jordan glanced up at the overhead speakers and sighed. "That's me." He squeezed my hands, and his eyes returned to mine with regret. "I have to go. I'll see you soon, okay?"

He slid his hands from mine and stepped back, then turned to walk away.

I lunged forward and grabbed one hand back. "Jordan, wait!"

He turned back in surprise. "Yes?"

I couldn't let him go without saying it, not this time. "I don't want to be just friends anymore."

His eyebrows shot up, and his face broke into a grin. "You don't?"

I shook my head. "No, I don't."

He rushed forward, cupped my face with both hands, and kissed me again.

It was hurried, but gentle this time, full of adoration. He pulled back, grinning as his eyes searched mine. "I love you, Ayla."

My heart stopped.

He smiled. "You don't have to say it back. I wasn't expecting you to. I just wanted you to know." He kissed me gently on the forehead, then stepped backward. "I'll see you soon."

He hurried toward the door, leaving me standing in utter shock.

"Take care of her," I heard him grunt as he rushed out, and I glanced up to find Callan in the doorway.

"Sure thing," Callan called after Jordan, but he was already gone.

Callan's eyes fell on me, reading my face. He crossed his arms and smirked. "So you two have finally gotten over pretending to be friends, have you?"

I felt a blush flood my face as I glowered at him. "I'm not sure that's any of your business."

Callan dropped his arms. "I suppose not. But... I don't suppose you would consider how it makes Prince Kaizyn feel, sitting alone in the Veil, smitten with you as he is, and feeling the rush of your emotions that I'm sure he couldn't help but interpret as what they are." He frowned. "He's probably feeling quite miserable, right about now. It's a good thing that the intensity of that bond doesn't seem to flow both ways, or his misery would be ruining your buzz."

I felt a rush of guilt, followed by resentment at Callan for causing it. I crossed my arms over my chest. "I'm sorry for what's happened to the prince, but I'm not responsible for his feelings. I didn't *ask* for any of this."

Callan sighed and shrugged. "Fair enough. But he is like a brother to me, you know. I can't quite be *happy* about knowing he's about to get his heart broken, even if I understand it."

I studied his face. He seemed sincere. "I guess I can understand that, too."

"I meant it when I said I'd come to think of you as a friend." He smiled. "You're a good person, Ayla. Even though you aren't Fae, you'd make a fine Queen of Teionyr."

I tensed, but he chuckled.

"I know, I know. I'm not saying you *will* be, only that I feel for my poor friend's broken heart." He stepped aside, gesturing to the doorway. "Anyway, if that hulking LeyGuard they call Striker staring at me from the end of the hall is any indication, we've got a wounded Madison to visit, don't we?"

I sighed, then exited into the hall, Callan following close behind me.

Chapter 27

Not One of Them

ulking LeyGuard didn't quite seem extreme enough to capture the man waiting for us in the hallway. He was massive, easily close to seven feet tall, and *solid,* like a human oak tree. His biceps looked thicker than my waist. He was middle-aged, or close to it, and wore a leather outfit similar to what Jordan's parents had worn, but his leather vest was sleeveless, revealing dark tattoos of geometric symbols down his forearms and wrists, and a leather cross-belt wrapped over his chest, holding a knife and a small square of something that looked like sandpaper. A thick layer of stubble covered his jaw and chin, and his dark brown hair was close-cropped but spiked up a bit in the front, speckled here and there with grey.

He leaned against the wall a few paces down the hallway, head nearly brushing the ceiling, fiddling absently with a stray match he held in the corner of his mouth. His eyes were focused but unreadable as he watched us approach.

When we neared, he pushed away from the wall and straightened, and it looked as though his hair *did* touch the ceiling. He pulled the match from his mouth. "You must be Ayla." He nodded once in greeting, then glanced at Callan. "And you're the Fae—obviously."

Callan extended a hand. "Callan."

The man's massive hand swallowed Callan's as they shook. "Striker," he said. "Pleased to meet you."

Callan raised an eyebrow and smiled. "Not all LeyGuards are."

Striker grinned. "Good thing you're with *me*, then." He slid the match back into his mouth and talked around it. "You two ready to head out?"

"Sure, but won't your team need to be at the briefing first?" Callan asked.

Striker laughed. "Uh, no. I *am* my team, at least while my partner's on leave. Unless I'm with him, I work alone. But Hart is sending a couple extra Guards to the hospital once they finish here, for extra eyes. I'll be overseeing them, while we're there."

"So... they're your team," Callan prodded, looking amused.

Striker narrowed his eyes. "Sure, fine, however you want to see it. Just don't tell *them* that, or I'll never get rid of them. Now let's go. We've got one stop to make on Level 2 before we head out: proper clothes." He gestured to his clothes and Callan's and grinned. "Can't blend in looking like we walked out of a fantasy movie."

I followed Striker and Callan back out into the lobby and up a flight of stairs. The landing at the top dead-ended into a wall, with railed walkways heading right and left toward rows of doors overlooking the open lobby courtyard below. I recognized the tinted glass door of the medical wing I'd been in to the right, but we went left instead, toward a row of wooden doors, all labeled with bronze numbers and letters like a hotel.

Striker gestured to a wooden bench against a bare spot in the walkway. "Ayla, you can wait here. I asked one of the girls to grab some fresh clothes for you, too." Then he turned to Callan. "They've already brought up some clothes they think will fit you, something that'll blend in for the age you look. I'll show you where you can change."

"I'd rather not let her out of my sight," Callan said, glancing at me.

I groaned. "Callan, really. What do you think is going to happen to me in the middle of a hallway in *this* place?"

Callan sighed. "Fine, but don't go anywhere."

I raised an eyebrow. "I wasn't planning to."

Callan nodded, then hurried after Striker as he moved down the hall. I heard his voice trailing off as they turned into one of the rooms. "You aren't going to make me wear *skinny jeans*, are you?"

I sank to the bench and stared through the railing, across the open air to the opposite walkway of doors where I'd originally woken in this place, pondering the way Striker had said the clothes would blend in for the age Callan *looked*, and wondering if that meant he was actually some other age entirely. It was a bizarre and unsettling train of thought, but it kept the more serious thoughts at bay—like thoughts of my family, and what might be happening to them while we all sat here, planning, wasting precious time.

A tinted-glass door on the opposite side of the stairway landing slid open, and I jumped. A girl rushed out, eyes on her shoes, dressed in ordinary jeans and a t-shirt and looking so *normal* it took me by surprise. She hurried across the landing past the stairs and toward where I sat, head dipped and her smooth, dark hair covering part of her face, but she pulled up short as she reached my bench.

"Oh!" she said, whipping her face up to look at me. "I didn't realize anyone was out here."

She had a faint Southern accent, definitely more deep-South than typical for Florida.

She was pretty, and about my age—and unlike everyone else I'd met here so far, she looked as uncomfortable and out of place as I felt.

Her eyes met mine, and she smiled, but I could see her gaze subtly raking over my face, my clothes, assessing me. "Hi. Are you—um—part of the LeyGuard?"

I smiled back. "No." I laughed. "I didn't even know there *was* a Ley-Guard until a few hours ago."

The girl sagged with relief and plopped down on the opposite end of the bench. "Oh, thank goodness. I just wanted a quiet moment, but these people have been analyzing my every breath and eye twitch for the last twelve hours, like I'm some kind of specimen." She turned to me and grinned. "I'm Lena."

"Ayla." I smiled back, immediately at ease with her open demeanor. "So you're not one of them, either?"

Lena laughed. "Definitely not. Well, I mean... not really."

Her face turned uncomfortable, but I decided not to pry—I wasn't *exactly* not LeyGuard, either, except in every way that counted since I'd literally not known it existed until today.

She forced a smile. "I'm here with my... friend," she said, after a hesitation. "And my Pops. My friend was hurt, and—well, it's a long story."

So was mine. "Is your friend okay?"

Lena smiled, more genuine this time. "He will be, I think. I wanted to stay with him, but they said it was time to change his gown and bandages so they ushered me out. Some of them here are quite pushy. They saved his life, though, so I guess this place can't be all bad, right?"

She seemed to be looking for confirmation. I didn't know much about the LeyGuard, but I knew Jordan was part of them, and he would never be part of anything *bad*. "I think so." I nodded. "They saved my life, too."

Her eyes widened slightly at this. "Were you attacked by... um... something crazy? A man on a horse, kind of?"

I blinked. "Crazy, yes. Man on a horse? No. Mine was... well, some kind of *Fae* monster?" I felt insane even saying the word, but she didn't bat an eye.

"Oh, thank goodness for that, at least." She smiled at me, seeming sincerely relieved.

A door across the landing slid open, the same one she'd exited. A woman in a lab coat and scrubs stepped out, looking *almost* like an ordinary human doctor, except for the leather combat boots she wore beneath the scrubs. Her eyes scanned the landing and balcony walkways, then landed on Lena. "He's decent," she called across. "You can come back in."

Lena turned to me. "Nice meeting you."

"You too." I smiled at her. "Enjoy your time with your friend."

She shrugged as she stood to leave. "I'll enjoy it more when he wakes up. Anyway, bye."

She hurried away, and I stared after her, the weight of her words hanging in the air around me. A few hours ago, it had been *me* in a medical room with people waiting for me to wake up. How often did people show up in this place unconscious and nearly dead? I could only hope it was only the two of us, and that her friend would be waking up shortly, healthy and well, like I had.

Moments after she disappeared into the room across the hall, a door in my own hall swung open. "I truly thought I'd escaped all this," Callan sighed, stepping out.

I turned to look at him and smiled. He was dressed like I was *used* to seeing him, in jeans and a long-sleeved Henley shirt, looking every bit the normal teenage boy I now knew he was *not*. But it was comforting. It made him seem familiar enough I felt like I could see him, once again, as my *friend*.

Then Striker stepped out, and I quickly stifled a chuckle. The same *normal* human clothes—jeans and a plain shirt, though his was a solid charcoal t-shirt—looked absolutely unnatural on him, like someone had tried to put everyday clothes on a Viking warrior... or a grizzly bear. His gaze landed on me. "Ready, Ayla? Quinn says she set some clothes out for you down the hall. 12A."

I turned toward where he gestured and saw the bronze marker for 12A a couple doors down from the bench.

"Go right in," Striker said. "She and her roommate aren't there, but she left it open for you."

I stood and crossed to the door. Striker was right; the knob was un-locked. I opened the door and stepped inside.

The lights were on, a funky new-age chandelier near the door, with other lights further inside the living room and in the small kitchen I could see off the dining area, and also coming from rooms down a short hallway. I'd expected something like a hotel room, but this was far too personalized—clearly a permanent living space—and larger than I'd expected; more like an apartment.

Either Quinn and her roommate were very eclectic in their tastes, or there was a discrepancy in decorating styles. The apartment looked like it couldn't decide if it wanted to be a chic, modernist penthouse or a whimsical, beachside art studio. The floors were a dark, wood-look laminate, and every wall I could see was a slightly different shade of blue, ranging from robin's egg to cerulean, adorned with painted-metal seahorses, fish, and other marine creatures.

An overstuffed, sky-blue microsuede couch sat in the middle of a white-shag rug, juxtaposed with a sleek, minimalist coffee table piled with an assortment of sea shells and candles and one open bag of potato chips. One end table was neatly stacked with well-worn books, while the other end table held cups of pens, paintbrushes, and even a cup of used paint water.

What I could see of the kitchen and dining area was all sleek and modern, complete with minimalist light fixtures. An easel stood to the side of the dining room table, empty of any canvases, and on the far wall opposite the dining room, someone had painted a fake window with a view of mountains and sky.

I was still taking in the room, and trying to figure out where I should look for the clothes Quinn had set out for me, when a massive cat strolled out from behind the couch. He jumped up on the back of the couch and settled in to wash his face with his paws. He was a tabby of some kind, but a large breed—and the way he stared at me as he bathed his face was vaguely unsettling.

"I'm... just here to change clothes," I said. It wasn't that strange to talk to a cat—I'd talked to animals in my neighborhood many times—but it still felt like I was invading this girl's private space, even though I had permission... and that this cat was judging me for it.

After another moment, the cat jumped down and sauntered down the hallway, and I figured I may as well follow it in case it was leading me somewhere, like Lassie.

Sure enough, the room I followed it into had an outfit spread out on the bed, close enough to my size to work, and the jeans were even similar to a pair I owned. I sighed in relief, glad, after seeing the unusual style of her home, that this girl hadn't left me something crazy.

The cat stared at me a moment, then flicked its tail and sauntered back out of the room, almost as though to give me privacy.

I shoved thoughts of the weird cat aside and got dressed as quickly as I could, then took liberty to use the bathroom attached to the bedroom since nature was calling, ran my fingers through my wild hair, and hurried out of Quinn's apartment.

Callan and Striker were engaged in semi-friendly conversation, Striker leaning against the wall again, as I stepped back out into the outer hallway, but I couldn't catch what was said. They stopped as soon as they saw me.

Callan smiled as he turned toward me. "You look almost normal again."

I narrowed my eyes. "Thank you."

Striker laughed, then pushed off the wall. "Hart called the hospital. Madison's family has them tightly controlling visitors, but you two are now on the approved list. Let's go."

Tell Her Everything

Other than the portal we took from the Hub—a *LeyGate,* Striker called it, that opened up like a giant hole in the brick wall of the Hub lobby—the trip to the hospital was uneventful. The portal dumped us right into a sunrise-lit field outside of the city, then vanished as soon as we stepped through, leaving nothing but an abandoned, grassy lot behind us.

It was only a quarter-mile walk or so from that field to the edge of the city, where Striker, to my surprise, summoned us an Uber.

"Truck's in the shop." He shrugged when I stared at him, then slipped his phone back into his pocket.

If our Uber driver found our group unusual, he hid it well. He picked us up from the downtown apartment district and delivered us to the inner city hospital with nothing more than polite small talk, which Callan, who'd called shotgun, did his best to return. Meanwhile, Striker watched stoically out the windows from the backseat, turning every so often to glance out the back windshield, and I sat silent across from him, too overwhelmed with thoughts of evil Fae and my family and Jordan and *portals* to make conversation.

When the Uber dumped us out in front of the hospital, Striker bid us farewell. "I'll be nearby if you need me," he said, then disappeared around the side of the building without leaving me any clue as to how I was supposed to call him if I *did* need him.

Callan gestured toward the sliding glass doors to the hospital lobby. "Shall we?"

Getting to Madison's room was easier than I expected, despite the police officer stationed in the lobby and the Bluetooth-eared man standing in the hallway outside Madison's room who looked suspiciously like private security. Whatever Chairman Hart had done to get us approved as visitors, it had worked. We were given visitor badges without any questions and escorted to Madison's hospital room.

Whether Madison herself would be as welcoming was still yet to be seen.

The nurse who escorted us nodded to the private security as we passed, then stopped in front of Madison's door and eased it open. "Madison, sweetheart," she said after peering in and obviously deducing Madison was awake, "you have visitors."

I heard Madison answer: "Oh, okay." Her voice was tired-sounding and scratchy, but even through that I could tell she was surprised.

The nurse stepped back and ushered Callan and me into the room, then left us, shutting the door behind her.

It took my eyes a moment to adjust to the dim light of Madison's room—only a small lamp was on near her bed, and the curtains were drawn over the windows—but when they did, I found Madison gaping at us, half-reclined, dark circles under her eyes, hair a mess, her thin blue hospital blanket pulled all the way up to her chest.

"Um, hi." I smiled. "How are you feeling?"

Madison clutched the blanket with both hands. "What are you doing here?"

My smile faltered, but I forced it back in place. "We came to see if you were okay."

Her eyes bounced from me to Callan and back to me. "Oh." She cleared her throat. "Um, thanks... I guess."

To my surprise, all of Madison's usual arrogant jerkiness was absent from her face and she looked anxious, almost embarrassed. But I supposed no one felt their best facing surprise visitors after having been attacked... and with hospital hair, which I was sure Madison would be horrified to know she had, but I certainly wasn't about to tell her.

Callan stepped around me, moving gingerly toward Madison. "Is there anything we can get you?" The authentic concern in his voice surprised me after the aloof attitude I'd seen from him most of the day—but maybe he was nicer than he'd been letting on in front of Chairman Hart. He had seemed nice at school.

To my even greater surprise, Madison *blushed* and looked away. "Oh, no... I'm okay. Thank you."

I stared between them. Had I majorly missed something? I knew Callan had been watching Madison, too, but I'd assumed it was from a distance. Was there something going on with them?

Perhaps Callan's insistence on escorting me to the hospital hadn't been *entirely* for the purpose of protecting me. I fought back a smirk. *Interesting.*

But my humor was short-lived, as I remembered the reason we'd come. "Madison—" I stepped forward. "We heard what happened after your shift last night. I am so, so sorry."

Madison sighed, then peeled her eyes from her sheets to look at me. Her expression was totally dejected—like the fight in her had died. "You didn't have to come, Ayla. I know you'd rather not be here."

I stepped closer, within reach of the bed. "I want to be here." Surprisingly, I meant it. "Would you rather I leave?" I specifically said *I,* not wanting to lump myself in with Callan in case she wanted him there. Maybe *he* could ask about the info we needed. I wouldn't pressure her to talk to me if she didn't want to. She'd been through enough.

Callan glanced at me with a hint of concern, though whether he was worried about me leaving without information or worried I'd drag him away from time with Madison, I wasn't sure.

Madison met my eyes. "No." She gave me a weak smile. "I know this sounds stupid, given our... history. But some company would be nice." She glanced at Callan. "Both of you."

Callan grinned at her. "As you wish."

Madison's blush returned.

I then wondered if Callan had intentionally quoted *The Princess Bride* or if Fae men were just that cheesy without trying. In any case, Madison was clearly into it.

I braced myself for feeling like a very lumpy, awkward third wheel, but Madison turned to me.

"Actually," she said, uncertainty creeping back onto her face. "I've been wanting to talk to you, Ayla."

I blinked. "Really?" Then I remembered I'd never explained the vanishing stranger. "Oh... right. The thing from the café." I glanced at Callan, wondering how much he'd let me tell her.

But Madison interrupted. "Not about that. I mean... you *do* still owe me an explanation"—her eyes narrowed and the barest flicker of her usual sass reemerged, only for a moment, then she sighed—"but that's not what I meant."

That threw me. "About what, then?"

The door to the room swung open.

I spun around just in time to see a muscular, handsome, blonde guy enter... an all-too-*familiar* handsome, blonde guy. My chest clenched.

"Oh!" Rory Kane froze halfway into the room, taking in Callan and me, then his gaze skipped to Madison. "Sorry, Mads. I didn't know you had visitors. I'll go."

"No, wait!" I'm not sure what possessed me to call for him to stay, other than that I'd had enough emotional distress for one day and I hated the thought of carrying around the freshly remembered guilt of what I'd done to him on top of it.

He paused, and his eyes met mine cautiously. "Yes?"

Now that he was staring at me, I realized I had to actually make *words*. "I'm... I'm Ayla, the girl who..."

He tilted his head. "Yeah, I know who you are."

"Oh." My stomach churned. "Well, I just wanted to—to say I'm sorry for what happened, for how I got you in trouble. Last year, I mean. I never knew it would—I mean, I knew you'd get in trouble but I had no idea they'd—"

Rory raised a hand to stop me. "It's okay, Ayla. I never blamed you for it." He laughed. "Well, maybe at first. But not for long. I'm the one who cheated. Whatever else happened as a result of that is on *me*." He paused. "Actually, I'm glad it happened. Losing my place on the team completely destroyed my plans for college... but because of that, I was forced to examine what I'd done, who I'd become. Who I was *becoming*. I wouldn't be where I am now, if not for that." He continued to smile at me.

The weight of the guilt I'd carried lessened ever so slightly. "Oh. So where *are* you now? I mean, if you don't mind me asking."

His smile widened. "I'm *happy*. I ditched the friends I'd gotten in with, took a year's leave to decide what I wanted to do, and made some new friends... better ones. And soon I'll be enrolling in art school."

I tried to picture the star quarterback of my high school standing at an easel in an art studio and I could see it... kind of.

"He's really good," Madison chimed in, actually *smiling* at me. "Apparently he'd been sketching away in his notebooks for years but had been afraid to show anyone."

Rory shrugged. "The guys on the team always made fun of the art geeks at school." He cringed on the word *geeks*. "Like I said, not the best sort of guys. But now I play football on a community team for the county, just for fun—and those guys are nice. One of them saw my sketchbook in my bag and told me I should check out the art program at Havenridge Community College. I figured, what did I have to lose? But the art director there liked my stuff." He smiled again. "I start this spring."

I was surprised he'd be going to a community college. Madison's family probably could've afforded to send him anywhere he wanted, but maybe it *was* what he wanted. "So you're not... mad?" I asked.

He shook his head. "Not in the least."

I glanced at Madison.

She sighed. "Neither am I, okay? I know I've made a huge deal about it, and I was really mad at first, but that's what I was trying to tell you. I'm…" She drew a sharp breath. "I'm *sorry* for how I've treated you."

If the hospital floor had opened up and swallowed me right that moment, I'd have been less surprised. I stared at her. "Um… thank you."

"I really do mean it," Madison said. "I suppose I haven't been the best person, either, but yesterday I almost *died*, and I—"

Her eyes suddenly teared up, which sent a flutter of panic through me. I stepped toward the bed, but Callan beat me there, and was seated on its edge with an arm around Madison before I made it two steps.

"Shh," he whispered as she cried into his shoulder. "It's all right."

Rory glanced at me, as shocked as I was. He leaned toward me. "Who is this guy?" he whispered.

"A friend from school," I whispered back, certain he wasn't prepared for the full explanation.

He blinked, then smirked. "Oh." He cleared his throat. "I'm gonna go get some of those candy bars you like, Mads," he said more loudly. "You okay here?"

Madison pulled her red, tear-stained face away from Callan. I was pretty sure I saw snot-marks on his shirt. "Yeah," she said, wiping at her eyes. "Just… still processing. It hits me at weird times, sorry."

Rory's face softened, and I remembered that Madison had watched Gerard killed in front of her, and how terrifying that must have been.

"I know," Rory said softly. "Want me to stay? I can get your chocolate later."

"No." Madison shook her head. "Chocolate now, please."

Rory laughed and moved for the door. "Got you covered, sis. Be right back."

Madison pulled back further from Callan as Rory exited, settling herself back against the angled pillows. "I'm sorry." She winced as she caught a glimpse of Callan's wet shirt. "I didn't mean—" The blush came again.

"Don't worry for a moment." Callan's voice was gentle as he tucked a piece of hair behind Madison's ear.

I stood awkwardly, wondering if they'd just forget I was there, and whether I could escape into the hallway before they began spouting sonnets to each other or something. Was this how people felt around Jordan and me? No wonder Reina got so upset.

I felt a pang of regret at my last interactions with Reina, but pushed it away. There was nothing I could do about it right now. I winced. *If at all.* What if Jordan was wrong about Reina only being upset that he hadn't told her sooner? If so, once Reina found out Jordan and I were officially... whatever we were now... I might lose her as a friend entirely. The thought made me deeply sad.

"Ayla?" Madison asked. I glanced up to find her and Callan both watching me.

"Sorry." I shook my head, forcing thoughts of Reina away. "I was just thinking." I moved toward the bed. "But how are *you* doing, really?"

Madison bit her lip. "I see him—Gerard." Her voice was small when she said his name. "Every time I close my eyes. You know he...?"

She trailed, but I could tell from her intonation and expression she was asking if I knew about his death. I nodded. "I heard. I'm sorry, Madison."

She dropped her gaze to her lap, fists curling around the blanket up near her chest. "He saved my life."

Callan glanced at me, eyes wary, then turned back to Madison. "Did you... see what happened?" His voice was tender, and though I was certain he was a good actor when he wanted to be, I was also sure his tone wasn't *just* to soothe information from her. He cared about what she'd been through.

Madison tensed and shook her head. "No. I—I fell. I hit my head. I was in shock. I didn't see anything clearly."

The words came out stilted, like she'd practiced them... or been coached into them.

"Madison." I stepped closer, right next to where Callan's legs hung over the side of the bed. "You saw something that upset you, I can tell." My words were gentle without any effort. I really did feel for her, imagining what her past few hours must've been like. "What was it?"

Madison clenched her jaw tight, and tears sprang to her eyes again. She rapidly shook her head.

I glanced at Callan.

Tell her. His voice sounded in my head. *Tell her everything.*

I raised my eyebrows. "Are you sure?" I whispered back.

Madison flicked her eyes to me, confused, as Callan and I stared at each other.

Callan's reply in my mind was firm. *Yes.*

I wasn't sure whether this was a strategic move, or simply because he couldn't bear to let Madison go on thinking she was crazy, but it was clear from his expression he'd made up his mind.

I nodded. "Okay."

Madison's gaze was questioning as I turned back to her and took a steadying breath. "About that night in the café..."

Her lip quivered slightly. "Yes?"

"I have some things I need to tell you."

Whatever residual animosity there may have been between Madison and me, it dissolved in the wake of the conversation that followed. She listened with a pale face and increasingly widening eyes as I explained everything from the first night I'd seen the Fae prince appear in the café, to finding out my grandfather was LeyGuard and that he and my parents had been captured, to the decision that brought us to come speak to her—everything except her father's potential involvement... well, and the personal interactions between myself and Jordan, which I didn't think were relevant.

But despite the utter insanity of everything I told her, other than gaping at us, she didn't react at all. Even when I outed Callan as a Fae, Madison was so non-emotive that it startled me, and from the look of him, Callan as well.

When I finished, Callan and I both studied her pale, blank face for a moment, then Callan tucked his legs up on the bed and shifted to face her, keeping a careful distance—probably because he, like me, had the increasing feeling she was a ticking time bomb of freak-out, readying to explode.

"Madison?" he whispered. "Are you okay?"

The scream that erupted from Madison the next moment could've shattered the hospital windows.

CHAPTER 29

SANEST I'VE FELT IN DAYS

The door to the room flew open. "Madison? Madison!" Rory came charging in, candy bars spilling from his arms. "What's wrong?"

Behind him, an army of nurses ran toward the room, footsteps pounding down the hallway.

Callan and I shared a look of panic, neither of us sure what to do, then Madison's scream cut off.

She turned eyes of fury on her brother. "Go *away!*"

He blinked and gaped at her, still clutching his candy bars, as two nurses squeezed into the room behind him.

"Madison," one nurse said in that soothing voice only experienced nurses seem to manage. She pushed past me and placed her hand on Madison's arm. "Madison, look at me."

Madison forced her eyes to the nurse, though they were still a bit wild.

"There we go," the nurse said. "You're safe here, sweetheart, okay? You're safe."

Madison's expression melted. "I know, I'm sorry."

"There's nothing to be sorry about, baby," the nurse said. "Do you want something to help you rest?"

Madison shook her head. "No."

The nurse turned back to Callan and me. "I think you should g—"

"No!" Madison yelled.

The nurse jumped and spun back to her.

"No, please," Madison said more calmly. "I want them to stay."

The nurse sighed. "All right. But only for a bit. You need your rest." She squeezed Madison's arm, then moved back to the door. "Push the call button if you need me, okay sweetheart?"

Madison nodded, suddenly the dutiful patient again. "I will."

The nurse left.

"She keeps doing that," Rory muttered, to me I thought, though maybe to himself. "The screaming."

Madison had been just randomly *screaming*?

Rory moved toward the bed. "Mads—"

She turned to him, teary-eyed again. "I'm sorry I yelled at you. I didn't mean…"

He dumped his armful of candy on the side table and hurried to the bed.

I stepped aside to make room as he crushed Madison in a hug. "It's okay, it's okay." He pulled back after a moment and smiled at her. "Got you one of everything." He gestured to the pile of candy bars on the table. "Everything that had even a *smidgen* of chocolate in it."

To my relief, Madison smiled back. "Thanks, Ror."

Rory glanced between Madison and Callan and myself, and seemed to pick up on the strange mood. "You told me to go… you still want me to?"

Madison chewed her lower lip nervously. "Yeah. I mean, if you don't mind? Just for a bit. We were talking."

Rory didn't seem bothered by his sister wanting privacy for a conversation. He nodded. "Sure thing. I've got my cell if you need me." He grabbed a *Milky Way* from the table, handed it to her, and left.

Madison stared at the candy bar in her hands, then set it on her blanket and looked at Callan. "You're Fae?"

Callan's jaw twitched. "Yes."

Madison studied his face a moment, then nodded. "Okay."

Callan and I exchanged glances. "*Okay?*" we said in unison.

"Yeah, okay. I mean… you're not an *evil* one, right?"

Callan shook his head. "…No."

Madison shrugged. "Then okay."

We gaped at her.

She sighed. "Despite my freak-out a moment ago"—a blush colored her cheeks again—"this is the sanest I've felt in days." Her lower lip quivered. "When that *thing* attacked Gerard, then ran off..." She took a breath. "I thought I was losing my mind." She turned to me. "And Jordan is some kind of Fae police? *Jordan*?"

"Yeah, basically," I said, still watching her face for signs of a returning panic.

"And *Reina*?"

"Yeah."

She blinked, deep in thought. "Huh. Wow." Her eyes focused back on me. "I'm so sorry about your family, Ayla."

I gave her a weak smile. "Thanks."

Callan reached for her hand. "I'm sorry to do this, Madison, truly... but we need to know what you've seen or heard. Anything that might help us locate Ayla's family."

Madison placed her hand in his, and he tightened his fingers over it.

"I can try," she said. "But I'm not sure how much help I'll be. I didn't see... all that much." She shivered, then whispered, "I saw Kyle rip out Gerard's throat. With his *teeth*. Like an animal."

Callan tensed. "Kyle?"

Madison nodded. "The guy I'd been dating." Horror contorted her face. "He was—he was—"

"A Selkblood, we think," Callan murmured. "Not human. His real name is Sevryn—I'm pretty sure it was him at this point, though it may have been another Selkblood working for him."

Madison shuddered again. "And all of this... it's all because of some *prince*?"

Callan tensed at her tone, but nodded. "In its simplest terms, yes. At least, most of it. Though we aren't sure why some of their activity seems to lead to properties your father owns... to his company."

Madison's eyes widened. "He's been weird."

"Who?" I asked.

She looked at me. "My father. Ever since... ever since he hired Gerard." She fell quiet.

"Weird how?" Callan asked gently.

"Just... not himself. Snappy. Obsessive. Forgetting things? It's hard to explain, but it's not like him at all. He even tried to fire Gerard days after hiring him, even though he knew... he knew Kyle had threatened me, that I *needed* Gerard." Her voice broke on the last words.

Callan squeezed her hand, then turned to me, his mental words flooding my mind in a rush. *Proxy. Or maybe Selkblood control. Their persuasion can scramble the mind, influence decisions, especially ones tied to emotion. It's extremely difficult to resist.*

I stared at him, eyes widening.

He turned back to Madison. "Your father might be under the influence of the same Selkbloods who are after the prince." He kept his words even, tone cautious. "Whatever he's done, it's not his fault." He said it almost like he was absolving Madison's father of sins, though nothing Madison said her dad had done so far seemed *that* bad, other than trying to fire his daughter's bodyguard while she was still in potential danger.

Madison dropped her gaze to her lap. "He's ruined us." She spoke so quietly her words were barely audible. "He started selling whole shipments of stuff at ridiculous prices, moving things around, canceling orders..." She took a shaky breath. "The board voted him out. They *fired* him from his own company, and he didn't even seem bothered. Then Mom checked the bank." She looked up at me. "It's gone, Ayla, all of it. Other than my and Rory's trusts, which we can't have until we're twenty-one, we have *nothing*. No college fund, no savings... we don't even know what he did with all of it, it's just gone. Mom had to take a job to help us pay the bills. And I—"

My mouth fell open. "That's why you came to work at the café."

She nodded, red flooding her cheeks. "Mom thought he was having some sort of mid-life crisis, or a mental breakdown," she whispered. "We didn't want anyone to know."

Callan shifted forward suddenly, grabbed one of his sneakers, and yanked it off.

Madison and I both stared at him in surprise as he fished something from his sock, then handed it to Madison.

She took it tentatively, looking as though she'd rather not hold something from a guy's sock, even if he *was* a hot Fae soldier. "What's this?" She tilted her palm, studying the flat, coin-like object Callan had put in it. It was smooth and metallic, but the material was a shimmering purple-grey, unlike anything I'd seen before.

Callan closed her hand around it. "It's a talisman, of sorts. It carries a faespell... one which negates Selkblood magic. Take it to your father and place it on him somewhere. It should right him, though you'll have to tell him to be careful not to let on that anything has changed, at least until we're able to get your family somewhere safe."

Madison blinked at him. "Don't *you* need it?"

He gave her a tender half-smile. "Not as much as you, for now. I'll be fine."

I wondered what other tricks or talismans he might have up his sleeves... or in his socks.

Madison smiled back at him. "Thank you."

Callan took a breath. "We think a Selkblood is using your father's warehouses as staging locations, though we aren't yet sure for what." He glanced at me. "We believe he's holding Ayla's grandfather in the one near the docks. We've got a team going now to check it out, but if we could get information from the inside, that would certainly help."

Madison gave a little gasp. "They're releasing me tomorrow, as long as my vitals look fine. Maybe I can get this to my dad, then ask him to help... if I can find him. But I haven't seen him in days."

"Hasn't he been here to check on you?" I asked, shocked.

Her face fell. She shook her head. "Not even once."

My heart ached for her.

Her face brightened a bit, and she clutched the talisman. "But maybe this is why."

I could only hope so.

The door swung open, and the nurse entered again. "I'm sorry, sweetheart," she said, smiling at Madison. "But it's time for you to rest. Your visitors need to go." She moved back toward the door. "I'm going to go grab you some fresh ice water and your next dose of ibuprofen. I'll be back in a few minutes." She slipped back out.

Madison clutched Callan's hand so tightly her knuckles turned white. "You'll come back?"

Callan nodded. "As soon as I can." He slid off the bed, then leaned over and placed a gentle kiss on the top of her head. "You have my number if you need me before then."

I really *had* missed a lot.

Madison peered around Callan at me. "Thank you for coming, Ayla. I hope we can be... I mean..."

I smiled. "We can."

She smiled back. "Good."

I jotted my phone number on the notepad by her room phone, then said one more goodbye and moved for the door. "I'll be right outside, Callan."

I stepped out and closed the door behind me, giving them a minute for a private goodbye... however they chose to use it. The security guard glanced at me, then went back to staring at the walls.

A few moments later, Callan slipped out of the room to join me. "Thank you," he said softly, "for not making a big deal about... that."

"You mean your obvious crush on Madison?" I grinned at him. "Only a total jerk would tease someone about something like *that*."

Callan sighed and rolled his eyes. "Fine, I deserve that, but to be fair, you and Jordan are *sickening* to watch." He smirked at me. "Truly nauseating."

The way he looked at me then, all smirking and jeans-clad and *human*-looking, shifted things between us again. Suddenly, he really did feel like a friend.

I playfully shoved his shoulder. "Whatever. Watching one of my guy friends blink puppy-dog heart-eyes at Madison Kane was *never* part of my life plan, so we're even." I narrowed my eyes. "But maybe you could be a bit less antagonizing to Jordan?"

He laughed. "Where's the fun in that?" Then he smiled. "But for a friend... I suppose I can try."

The double doors at the end of the hallway swished open and Striker strode through, chewing on a matchstick, trying to look casual and failing. The security guard tensed, unsure what to make of him.

"Come on, you two," Striker said when he spotted us. "The hospital says Madison's visiting hours are up; it's time to head back."

"Won't you be staying to protect Madison?" Callan whispered as we reached Striker.

Striker nodded. "Of course. As soon as I get you two back to the Hub. I've got backup eyes on her until then, don't worry."

Callan looked uncertain, but he nodded, and we both followed Striker back down the hall, through the lobby, and onto the sidewalk outside.

Striker handed me a flat coin—similar to the talisman Callan had given Madison, but plain bronze and etched with geometric symbols like the ones on Striker's arms. "This will signal the LeyGate for you. Quinn will be on the other side, ready to open it. You just need to get back to the field we started in." He nodded toward a car pulling up to the curb. "I've ordered a ride to take you to the edge of the city; you'll have to walk from there. You remember the way?"

I blinked at him. "You aren't going with us?"

He grinned and leaned toward us, lowering his voice. "Oh, I am. I'll just be taking my own transportation. I need to watch from a distance, make sure no one follows."

I fought back a wave of unease and closed my hand over the coin. "Okay."

The car pulled to a stop, and Striker gestured us toward it. "In you go."

The ride back to the edge of town was uneventful. Callan rode in the back this time, but to my relief, the driver turned on music rather than attempting small talk with me. A few minutes later the driver waved goodbye and pulled away, leaving us on the last block of the apartment district.

Callan's eyes darted around, scanning the street. "Seems clear." He nodded. "Let's go."

I felt phantom eyes watching us the whole quarter-mile walk to the field, though it was mostly empty, abandoned parking lots and cracked sidewalks, so there wasn't much for anyone to hide behind. I ignored the sensation, telling myself it was just Striker.

When we finally reached the empty field, I stared at Callan. "Now what?"

"I don't know." He shrugged. "You're the LeyGuard."

I decided not to debate him on that point, and instead moved toward where I was pretty sure the portal had originally dumped us out. "Is there some kind of hidden trigger, or—" A sharp wave of tingling energy washed over me, like static electricity, and I gasped. "I feel something. Right here." I pointed to the empty air, exactly like every *other* section of air in the field.

Callan grinned. "I told you that you were LeyGuard. You can sense the LeyGates; it's part of your heritage."

I stared at him. "Say what?"

Callan narrowed his eyes. "You going to gape at me, or signal it to open?"

I turned back toward the humming segment of air, clutched the coin, and lifted my hand.

The humming intensified, then the air split open.

A slim teenage girl with dark hair stood on the other side, a view of the Hub lobby sprawling out behind her. "Come on." She waved us toward her. "Hurry!"

Callan and I rushed forward into the opening.

The brick wall snapped shut behind us as soon as our feet touched the floor of the lobby, and the cold, oddly salt-scented air of the Hub washed over me.

"You must be Ayla." The girl held out her hand and smiled. "I'm Qui—"

A siren blared from the ceiling, then a wall to our right split open like a big dark hole, and all chaos broke loose.

I slammed my hands over my ears as the siren wailed and LeyGuard members poured out of every door, running for the opening, then a cluster of LeyGuards rushed *in* through the portal on the wall... carrying two limp and blood-soaked bodies.

My heart jarred to a stop. "Mr. and Mrs. Peters?" My eyes scanned the crowd for Jordan in a panic, but there was no one else I recognized in the group rushing through.

Doctor Harlowe came flying down the stairs at inhuman speed, shouting orders as he raced toward them across the lobby. "Two units of blood, sterile cloths, runestones, clear me two med rooms, hurry!"

People sprinted off in a half-dozen directions to obey his orders, but my eyes were trapped on the bodies Doctor Harlowe was hunching down next to, pressing his fingers to first one throat, then another. He jumped to his feet. "There's still time. Get them upstairs to Glenda, now!" The Guards holding Mr. and Mrs. Peters hurried toward the stairs with them, while Doctor Harlowe spun toward the portal. "How long have they been unconscious?"

I thought he was still talking about Jordan's parents, until I turned.

"Grandpa!" I rushed toward his limp body, heart in my throat, as a stranger dragged him in from the portal, but Doctor Harlowe put out an arm to stop me before I reached him. "He's alive, Ayla. But unconscious. I need you to give me room to work."

I sucked a shuddering breath and jumped back as Doctor Harlowe dropped to his knees, then tipped Grandpa's face to the side and lifted one eyelid. He spun to the man next to him. "Get him to 8C, start IV fluids. I'll be in as soon as I can." The crowd parted, and I noticed two more bodies being gently placed on the floor—my mom and dad.

I clutched my arms around my ribs, forcing my feet to stay still, not to run in, to give the doctor room. A sob escaped me as Doctor Harlowe dropped down to examine them.

"Stable, as well," he said, and I felt like I could almost breathe again. "Get them into 5C, fluids, and set up the sensors for me. I need to... check something."

Anxiety mounted at his tone, but he spun to me. "I know this is hard, but please, let me get them situated and ensure there are no immediate concerns, then I'll call for you."

I nodded mutely as he raced off, the men carrying my family's limp bodies trailing after him.

I felt a hand on my arm, and looked up to see Callan staring at me with sympathy. "Ayla—"

His gaze locked on something behind me and he gasped.

I spun toward where he was looking, bracing myself for whatever devastating news I was about to face next.

What I found was Reina. Her clothes were torn, hair wild, armor dented, hands bloodied, but it was her face that stalled my breath. Her cheeks were blotchy and swollen, her eyes red-rimmed—she'd been crying.

I felt Callan clutch my hand.

I stared at Reina's face, feeling the world crash down on me, its whole weight crushing in on my chest. "Jordan?" The word came out a quivering whisper.

"We were attacked," she answered in a shaky voice, and the devastation in her eyes tore my heart right in half. "Jordan was taken Faeside."

CHAPTER 30

FALLING APART

Though the chaos of the Hub continued around me, my world stopped moving.

Reina looked away, a flutter of emotion crossing her face.

"Reina, *where's Jordan*?" I asked, desperately hoping I'd heard her wrong.

She flicked her gaze back to me. "This is *your* fault, you know." Her eyes flamed with fury. "He never would've done this if not for you!"

The pain of her words stabbed straight through me. "What?" My voice came out weak, barely above a whisper.

"Reina!" Callan stepped up next to me. "You don't mean that. Think about what you're saying."

"I know *exactly* what I'm saying." Reina's green, tear-filled eyes bored into me. "It was Ayla and that stupid *promise* that made him—" Her words broke off in a choke.

My brain felt like sludge, struggling to process. "What do you mean?" I whispered.

She squeezed her eyes shut, unable to even look at me.

"Reina," I said louder, voice shaky. "What do you mean?"

She spoke with her eyes still closed, her words strained. "We confirmed your grandfather was at the warehouse, but we never expected your parents to be there, too. We were headed back here, to report in, but your parents were bad off, and..." Her cold, green eyes opened and met mine with a glare. "Jordan wouldn't leave. He said he couldn't leave them there because he'd *promised* you he'd save your family, no matter what." Her glare deepened, and her fists clenched at her sides, her body rigid. "He nearly got the entire *team* killed! And now he's—he's—"

Pain stabbed so deeply through my heart it took my breath away. Jordan hadn't been taken by accident; he'd put himself—the whole team—in danger for *me*. I squeezed my arms tight around my ribs. I deserved every bit of the hatred in Reina's glare.

"Reina." Callan's voice was gentle as he spoke this time.

Reina sucked a shaky breath and her eyes tore from mine. "I can't—I can't do this." She took quick steps backward, and her face twisted with more tears.

"Reina." My hand drifted out to her, aching for the friendship I once had with her, for the one person I knew cared for Jordan as much as I did. "Please. I'm so sorr—"

Reina's face contorted with anger and pain. "Just leave me alone." She spun and hurried away.

Callan's hand closed gently around my upper arm. "Ayla. Ayla, please look at me."

All I wanted to do was sink into a tiny ball on the ground and disappear, but I forced myself to turn toward him.

His warm, brown eyes fixed on mine, full of concern. "This is not your fault."

I knew he meant well, but his words were a lie—and that only made me feel worse. Reina's words, and all they meant, were finally sinking in. Jordan was gone. My grandfather and parents were injured. And Mr. and Mrs. Peters—what if Jordan's parents died because he'd tried to save *mine*? The air compressed in on me and everything was suddenly too loud, too bright, the walls too close. My chest tightened. The room swayed.

Callan bent his legs to put himself directly on my eye level. "Breathe, Ayla."

The resonance with all the times Jordan had done the same to calm me down sent a fresh stab of pain through me. A sob escaped me. "It's all falling apart!"

Callan stared into my eyes. "Then let me help you hold it together."

I tensed to pull away, fighting the tears, the panic, the adrenaline rushing through me with the need to *escape*. But there was nowhere I could run to get away from this.

Callan's arms wrapped around me. "Ayla," he said gently. "It's okay. Let me be your friend."

The tears won. I sank against Callan's chest, face buried in his shirt, and let him block out the world around us as my sobs came.

Callan held me until my legs buckled, then he sank to the ground next to me as I buried my face in my knees. He tucked one arm around me and stroked my hair as I cried.

When I was finally able to catch my breath, he leaned in. "Your family is right here," he whispered. "The Hub is the best place for helping them, whatever may have happened to them. And Jordan—"

I gasped as another sob fought its way up.

"Jordan is Faeside," Callan continued, his voice gentle. "*Faeside,* Ayla. Not dead."

I peeled my face from my knees to look at him. I was surprised to find the lobby had cleared out, the chaos of people and chatter gone. It was oddly empty, and quiet.

Callan's eyes locked on mine. "Let *me* make you a promise, now."

"No, please." I shook my head. "No more promises." *No more people I care about getting hurt because of me.*

Callan's brows lowered, and he held up a hand. "Let me finish. I promise I will do everything *in my power* to help you get him back, Ayla. I cannot risk the prince's life nor yours, and I cannot betray my kingdom. My mission to free the prince and secure his safety must come first. But outside of that, you will have every aid I can offer. Your happiness is deeply important to the prince's, and therefore, to me. And besides..." He gave me a small smile. "You're my friend, and I don't have many of those."

The blunt way he stated his promise, making no pretenses about his intentions, was oddly comforting. I took a deep breath and met his gaze with a nod. "Thank you."

A figure moved toward us from my right, and I turned my head to find Reina standing a few yards away.

"Doctor Harlowe sent me." She stared at the ground near us, rather than meeting my eyes. "Your grandfather is awake."

Reina led us to a med room on the second floor, pushed the button to open the door, then left without another word.

I hurried inside.

Grandpa looked worse, somehow, than when they'd brought him in. He was sickly pale, his face gaunt, with dark circles under his eyes. But as he flicked his gaze up to watch me enter, I gasped. His eyes were clearer, more focused, than I'd seen them in years.

Grandpa's face tightened with urgency when he saw me. He gestured an IV-laden hand in the air, waving me toward him. "Ayla, come close, hurry."

As I rushed toward the bed, Grandpa's eyes flicked to Callan lingering in the doorway, and he tensed. "A *Fae*?"

I reached the bed and gently clasped the hand he held out, careful not to bother his IV. "It's okay, Grandpa. This is Callan. He's a friend."

Grandpa's thick brows rose as he met my eyes. "Are you certain?"

Callan stepped forward and clasped his hands in front of his waist, keeping a respectful distance from the bed. "D'lenyi merture iyn Kaizyn," he said.

"Oh." Grandpa's eyes widened. "*Oh.*"

I glanced at Callan in confusion.

My life in protection of Kaizyn, his words sounded in my mind.

"The inner guard oath," my grandfather whispered. "In perfect Teionyrian." A tiny smile flitted to his lips. "I haven't heard that in—well, in what feels like a lifetime."

Callan rushed forward and, to my utter shock, dropped to his knees and lowered his head in a bow. "It is my honor to meet the great Maddox Rogers."

Grandpa winced and waved his hand. "No, no, get up. None of that."

Callan stood, red-faced. "My apologies. I did not mean to offend."

Grandpa chuckled. "I see Teionyrian manners have not changed much in the past few decades. No offense taken. But I'm owed no deference from a member of the prince's inner guard." He grinned. "Even if you *do* look young enough to be my grandson."

Callan laughed, suddenly at ease.

I gaped at the two of them. What was *happening* right now?

Grandpa tensed again. His hand tightened on mine as he turned to me. "Ayla, quickly. I may not have much time."

My chest clenched. "What do you mean?"

"My mind is clearer than it's been in years. Nearly dying has a way of doing that to you, and the runestone they used on me helped, too. But it won't stick. I don't know how long I have before I slide back into it."

A tremor of fear waved through me. "Slide back into *what*?"

His gaze slid to Callan, wary. "It's okay, Grandpa, you can trust him."

He narrowed his eyes at me. "I'm extremely curious how you managed to befriend a *Fae...* But no, that will have to wait for another time. There are things I need to tell you now, while I can." He glanced at Callan again. "Check the hall, will you? I'm sure they'll still eavesdrop if they want to, but I'm an old man, you may as well humor me."

Callan moved to the door, peered out into the hall, then pressed the button to shut it again. "All clear."

Grandpa nodded. "Good." He waited until the door was shut, then his eyes locked on me. "My mind, Ayla, is the thing at play here. It's why I came back addled, why I left the LeyGuard. It's why the Selkblood was after me."

A strange chill ran down my arms at the look on his face, the intensity of his voice. "I don't understand," I said.

Grandpa leaned toward me, eyes intense. "I could feel the Selkblood stalking my mind these past few days. Up until the day he took me, I'd been keeping him at bay. I thought I'd won, that he'd found nothing. In my moments of clarity, that is. The other times are so... so *frustrating*. It's like coming to a room for something important, but you can't for the life of you remember what it was, so you stand there, blinking, deep in fog..." He sucked a breath. "The jam helped, of course, but it wasn't enough to stop him."

I blinked. "The jam?"

"Yes, of course." He waved his free hand dismissively. "Pomegranate jam. Excellent for blocking Selkblood intrusions, particularly if the jam is fresh, and they were picked in season—" His mouth tightened. "But that's not the point, Ayla, the point is that I *failed.*"

Callan stepped closer. "Failed at what?"

"He knows I have it," Grandpa whispered, eyes wide. "The name."

CHAPTER 31

ONE WORD CARRIES GREAT POWER

Callan blanched. "Does he know where it is?"

A humorless laugh escaped Grandpa. "That would be a trick, since I can't remember, myself. This blasted brain." His eyes met Callan's with a look of fear. "But he'll find it, I'm sure. That's what he was trying to get to, why he fought to take over, to be in my room—my journals. He saw in my mind that I'd written it down; he knows it must be in one of them."

I stared at both them, anxiety mounting. "What are you talking about?"

Grandpa lifted his wrinkled hand to the side of my face. "My good girl," he stroked my cheek, his eyes studying mine, and gave me a sad, tender smile. "I'm sorry to say this isn't only about you, Ayla. I know about your bond with the prince—the Selkblood was not very secretive while he held me—but it's bigger than that." He sighed. "You hold the prince's life in your own, and I hold the key to breaking the Seal that protects you both."

I felt my forehead wrinkle in confusion. "The *Teionyr* Seal? The thing that keeps them from assassinating him?"

Grandpa nodded. "Yes. There is one way to break it—the *only* way." He gripped my hand. "Prince Kaizyn's true name."

I blinked as flashbacks of English class surged in—Odysseus, Rumpelstiltskin, Confucius.

"Each royal's true name is given at birth," Grandpa continued, "revealed by magic. Only the mother is supposed to know it." He took a deep breath, eyes distant. "There was so much chaos, that day, the city raided, the palace under siege... We'd just secured the king, and I'd gone to fetch the queen. When I got there, the baby was already coming—there was no time." His gaze slid to meet mine. "Kaizyn's mother died right after his birth... in my arms. She gave his name *to me,* made me swear by magic to protect it."

"He owes you his life," Callan said gravely. "They teach of that day, in our lessons. How you hid him in your coat, got him past the Dark Fae outside the palace, brought him safely to where you'd hidden the king. You saved the entire Teionyr royal line."

I stared at my grandfather, his wrinkled hands, his grey-scruffed jaw, those intense brown eyes. It was the first time I'd seen him clearly, without the fog over his mind, and like this, I could imagine him every bit the brave LeyGuard Callan described. A hero.

Grandpa squeezed my hand. "It was a long time ago, Ayla. I was captured on my way back Earthside, tortured by Dark Fae magic." He shuddered. "I managed to give them nothing, but by the time I escaped, my mind was like swiss cheese. After that, what else could I do? I retired, left the LeyGuard behind, vowed never to speak of it again." His eyes softened. "I tried so hard to keep you and your father free of all this. It seems I failed at that, too."

I tightened my fingers around his, struggling for the words to reassure him. I wanted to tell him he hadn't failed, but here we were, in the Ley-Guard Hub—not exactly a success, if he'd wanted to keep this life a secret. "It's okay, Grandpa." They were the only words I could think of that wouldn't ring hollow, though I wasn't sure they made him feel any better.

Callan startled, making me jump, too. "The true name," he blurted. "It could break a curse, too, couldn't it?"

"A true name could potentially free its owner of a curse, yes... but what curse are you referring to?" Grandpa asked.

"Prince Kaizyn is trapped in the Veil," Callan explained. "Beirthyr has been attempting to kill him, but with the Seal, he had to get creative. The prince cannot leave the Veil for more than a single minute at midnight, or he will die. The people have fallen for Beirthyr's story—they believe the prince killed his own father, that he has abandoned them. They do not know Beirthyr has allied with Dark Fae."

Grandpa's face fell. "King Veilar was a good man. A good king. I'm sorry to learn he was murdered, after all." He took a deep breath. "I suppose I only delayed the inevitable."

"You gave Teionyr a chance," Callan said firmly. "A future. But now, if we cannot save the prince…"

Grandpa's face grew solemn. "I know well what the Dark Fae are capable of. But the name…" Grandpa nodded, his voice growing excited. "That's the whole point of a true name—it can bind or loose magic. There's no reason why it couldn't work on the prince's curse." He paused, then his face fell. "But I'm afraid my mind is useless. The name, if it's still in there somewhere, is far beyond my reach."

I leaned toward him. "You said Sevryn believed the name was in your journals. Could it be?"

"When my mind began to fail, I believe I preserved the name somewhere, but I can't—" Grandpa stared off, his brow furrowed in frustration. "I can't remember." He looked back at me. "I never would've written it in plain sight. If it is in my journals, it would be hidden, encoded somehow… or perhaps disguised as something else." Grandpa stared off. "It might be—blast this old brain, I can't remember." His eyes flicked back to me. "But that one simple word, it could be the key to everything."

A chill shot down my spine. "*One word carries great power,*" I whispered.

Callan gasped and cut his eyes to me. "The riddle?"

Grandpa stared at us. "What riddle?"

I closed my eyes, drawing the words to memory. "*Better than riches, silver, or gold, find what Prince Kaizyn lacks where heart's truths are told. Buried with treasures, planted deep among flowers, one word—seek you carefully—carries great power.*" I opened my eyes to find Grandpa gaping at me. "A paper appeared in the café one night—a riddle," I said. "I thought Kaizyn had left it for me, like a clue, to help me help him. But Chairman Hart said it looked like a page from an old LeyGuard tome. Could it have been one of yours?"

Grandpa nodded thoughtfully. "Maybe. It's possible that riddle was a reminder to myself, of where I'd put the name." He hesitated. "Though I'm not sure how a slip of paper from my books would have made it to the café." He looked at Callan. "Perhaps the prince *did* have it, from old records of mine in Teionyr? The book I recorded the name in could've been one I left there."

Callan chewed his lip. "It *could* be. He never mentioned it, but... maybe. Until I can get back to him and ask, I'm just not sure."

Grandpa leaned toward Callan. "Where *is* the prince?" he asked softly. "Is he safe?"

Callan sighed. "For now. As safe a place as can be managed in the Veil. The longer he remains there, though, the greater the chances they'll find him—or something else will. And now that he's bound to Ayla..."

"Terrible accident, that." Grandpa glanced at me and shook his head. "And with all the relational implications, too... It complicates things greatly."

"You're telling me," I muttered.

"That's the reason Sevryn came for you," Grandpa said, "and the name is why he came for me. And your parents—" He gasped. "This sieve-holed brain! Ayla, child, how are your parents? Are they here? Are they well?"

"Yes, they're here, but—" Grief squeezed my throat. "I don't know. I saw them brought in, but they were unconscious. Doctor Harlowe said they're stable, but they looked so pale..."

Grandpa's face twisted, and he cursed. "That blasted Selkblood." He flicked his eyes to Callan. "It's a veilmist."

Callan stiffened. "Are you sure?"

"Sevryn was still in my mind when he placed it. I felt it. It's a strong one—he had help. It'll be a devil to break." He took a shaky breath. "Runestones won't be enough."

My impatience spiked with my confusion. "What are you talking about?"

"They're in a Selkblood trance," Callan said. His face was pale, his eyes solemn. "Trapped in an illusion of his choosing, like a coma."

"What?" My heart surged in panic.

Callan started pacing. "If the source or combined sources are strong enough, veilmists are nearly impossible to break, unless..." He spun to my grandfather. "Maxim Warwick is still in Teionyr. In hiding."

Grandpa's eyebrows shot up. "He remains loyal to the prince?"

Callan nodded. "With his life. He's risked much for us since you've been gone."

Hope flitted across Grandpa's face. "This could work. How soon can you get to him?"

Callan's face fell. "Beirthyr has taken over the city. Even getting *word* in is risky, these days. It will take time."

Grandpa gripped the side of the bed, his stare boring into Callan. "Do what you must to get word to him. And I need someone to secure one of my journals—the one with the tree engraved. If the name or the clue to finding it is anywhere Earthside, it's in there."

"It's in your room still," I said, "or it was, when the... whatever it was... attacked me."

"I'm so sorry about that, Ayla." Grandpa's face hardened. "It was torture to watch through his eyes as he controlled that abomination, using my memories for what to say, to lure you in, to hurt you—" His face softened. "I tried to fight him."

I gripped his hand. "I know, Grandpa. I know."

He shivered. "Sevryn was using me to lure you out, but also holding me to prod my thoughts more." His eyes locked on mine. "I have the true name, you have the bond to the prince... Beirthyr needs something from *each* of us, Ayla, and he will use whatever leverage he can, take whoever he needs to, to force our cooperation."

My heart lurched as realization set in. "That's why they took Jordan."

Grandpa tensed. "The LeyGuard boy? Oh, Ayla, I'm sorry—I know he was a friend." His voice drifted off as he studied my face. "Perhaps more, if they bothered to take him..." My expression seemed to confirm his suspicion. "Ah. Yes. They'll use that." His face turned stern. "Ayla, you mustn't go after him. Promise me. Sevryn and Beirthyr are ruthless. They'll use him to lure you in, to get to Kaizyn. I can tell he means a lot to you, but no matter what happens—you *must not* go after him. Just stay out of all this; stay as far away from it as you can."

Panic mounted in my chest. "But we can't just let them *keep* Jordan captive!" *Or worse,* a voice in my mind whispered, but I shoved it away. "Please, Grandpa. There has to be *something* we can do to help him."

"He's LeyGuard, Ayla." Grandpa's voice was firm. "They can take care of their own. Let them handle it. They're probably planning a way to get him back even now. It's the way things are done. But you, my sweet girl"—he cupped my face again—"*you* are a warrior of heart, not of weapons and battle. I've worked hard to keep you from this life. Stay here. Let *them* face this fight." He squeezed my hand. "Please."

I glanced at Callan.

Perhaps he's right, his voice sounded in my head. *We should at least see what the LeyGuard has planned. They may have it under control.*

Grandpa stared between us. "The mind-gift. Ayla, you have it?"

"If you mean hearing Callan's thoughts in my mind, then yes."

Grandpa scowled. "So the LeyGuard life was coming for you, anyway." He sighed. "After it skipped your father, I had hoped—" His brows drew together. "But you have a choice how far you go into this, Ayla, and don't let them tell you otherwise. It's enough that you're bound to a Fae, they can't force you to swear in as LeyGuard, too. Unless..." His eyes searched mine. "You *want* to?"

I stared at him. "I—I really don't know. I can't think about that now, not with Mom and Dad, and Jordan, and this... thing with Prince Kaizyn." I shuddered as a vision of his deep-blue eyes appeared in my mind, so vivid, as though he were standing right in front of me. "I see his face sometimes," I admitted. "In my dreams. Sometimes even when I'm awake."

Grandpa's brows shot up. "Interesting."

Callan glanced at me for a long moment, eyes wide. "You never mentioned that."

I shrugged. "We were a little busy."

Callan stared at me a moment longer, then turned back to my grandfather. "If Maxim can break the veilmist, perhaps he can break the bond, too. Then we could work to free Kaizyn without putting Ayla at risk in the process. I've heard of wilder things Maxim has—"

Grandpa shook his head. "Faespell bonds are tricky things, Callan. Attempting a separation would put them *both* at risk. It might be better, for now, to let it lie."

I glared at him. "You want me to leave my best friend captured by Fae, and stay *betrothed* to a *Fae prince*?"

Grandpa's brows pinched down, his eyes narrowed. "If it will save your life, Ayla, then yes. At least until this coup in Teionyr is settled and we can examine the options more carefully."

I stared at him in shock.

He sighed. "I know it's not ideal, but Ayla, you need to stay out of this fight as much as you can. Let the bond lie, let the LeyGuard handle Jordan, let the Hub and Callan secure what's needed to help your parents, and let Callan and the prince figure out how to break the curse, to restore him to power. *Then* we can look at breaking the bond. Until then, you and the prince need to stay *safe*. Anything else is too big of a risk—for Kaizyn, and for you."

I studied his eyes. I knew he loved me, that he was trying to protect me, but if there was something—anything—I could do to help Mom and Dad, to help Jordan, I couldn't just sit here in the Hub and wait. "What if I can't, Grandpa?" I whispered. "What if I can't sit this out?"

His voice wavered. "Then I'm afraid, between you and me, we'll have doomed both our family *and* Teionyr."

CHAPTER 32

NOT THE TIME

*W*e'll have doomed both our family and Teionyr. What was there to say to that?

"That can't be the only answer, Grandpa," I said after a moment. "There's got to be something I can do to help, without literally *dooming* everyone. That's a bit dramatic." I hesitated as Grandpa stared at me. "Right?"

Grandpa watched me for a moment, then shook his head. "I suppose there's no way to know for sure, Ayla, but the more you risk yourself, the more you risk Kaizyn, Teionyr, and your parents and your friend as a result. You have to see that, right?"

Callan and I exchanged glances, but I couldn't tell if he was on my side or Grandpa's. Surely, Callan wouldn't allow me to do anything to risk the prince. But he had promised to help me free Jordan and break my parents from the Selkblood's hold, and there had to be *something* we could do.

I sat beside Grandpa and held his hand for a few moments longer, but I could see the strain the conversation had taken on his energy. His eyes were still focused, but a deep exhaustion had replaced the fervor of moments before. I planted a kiss on his forehead. "Get some rest, Grandpa. It's okay."

He clutched my hand. "I may not be as clear when I wake. I may be... confused again. But you will remember—stay clear of Sevryn and his plans. Let the LeyGuards do their jobs, Ayla. Stay here and be safe."

My chest clenched as I wrestled with how to respond. I knew what he wanted of me, but I couldn't promise that I'd sit and do nothing. Not when Mom and Dad and Jordan's safety were all at risk. "I love you, Grandpa," I said instead, and gave him a gentle hug.

He sighed as I released him. His gaze caught on mine as I pulled away. "You will do what you must, darling, I know that. Just please—be safe." The clarity in his eyes was already fading, replaced with the haze of fatigue, but even so, he saw straight through me.

I nodded. "I'll try."

Grandpa placed his free hand on my cheek and studied my face. His mouth twisted like he was fighting tears.

Panic tremored in my chest—I'd never meant to hurt him—but then he gave me a gentle smile.

"My good, brave girl." He dropped his hand and sank back, asleep.

I slipped my hand from his, watching him sleep with a feeling of growing unease.

Callan moved toward the bed, and I spun toward him. "Please don't tell me to stay here and sit this out," I whispered, trying not to wake Grandpa. "I can't—"

Callan held up a hand and answered in a whisper to match mine. "I wasn't going to. But we do need to find a way for you to help that doesn't put you at risk. You're too important, Ayla. For the prince *and* because you're... you. You have friends, Ayla. Family. They—even I—would hate to lose you."

His eyes were earnest as I studied them. I sighed. "Okay. I'll try."

Callan narrowed his eyes at me, but if that agreement was good enough for Grandpa, it would have to be enough for Callan, too. I already felt on the verge of melting down simply from the time we'd already wasted. If I had to sit here at the Hub, twiddling my fingers for days on end while they all mounted some kind of rescue attempt, I would go insane. But I wasn't eager to throw my life right into danger, either. I would be careful. I just couldn't sit and do *nothing*.

After a moment, Callan nodded. "Trying is the best I can expect, I suppose, given the circumstances. I'll just have to stay with you to make sure you don't die."

There was a spark of humor in his gaze—maybe even a hint of respect. I smiled and stood. "Let's go find Chairman Hart and see what their plan is."

I hit the button on the wall to open Grandpa's door, but I only made it one step before I pulled back, startled.

Chairman Hart stood stiffly against the opposite wall of the hallway, failing to look at all patient. "I didn't want to interrupt your time with your grandfather," she said as my eyes found her face, "but we need both of you in the planning room."

"Thank you," I said, both for her consideration of my time with Grandpa and for inviting us straight in to exactly where I needed to be. I glanced at Callan, but he just nodded. I turned back to Chairman Hart. "We're ready. Lead the way."

Callan and I were ushered to another conference room, where we were introduced to "members of the LeyGuard council"—two of whom were Reina's parents, whom I hadn't seen since that last birthday party I attended when I was twelve. Callan and I were then briskly informed that decisions had been made but Chairman Hart wished to ensure everyone was on the same page moving forward.

I hadn't expected them to involve us in the planning, so this didn't come as much of a shock, but the meeting ground to a halt the moment Chairman Hart said, "Our best strategy, at the moment, is to wait for them to make the next move."

Callan's hand clamped around my arm as I shot to my feet. The chair screeched against the floor as it flew back, but it was barely audible over my yell. "You can't be serious!"

All six adults in the room—Chairman Hart, Doctor Harlowe, two Ley-Guards I'd seen Chairman Hart bossing around while I'd been here but still hadn't learned names for, and Reina's parents—turned to stare at me.

"Excuse me?" Chairman Hart's raised eyebrows were probably meant to be intimidating, but I was beyond caring.

"You're telling me you want to leave Jordan Faeside, possibly in some kind of horrid Fae dungeon or who knows where—plus leave my parents in mind-control comas—and wait to see *what happens*?" I spun to Reina's parents. "You can't be okay with Jordan getting left in danger like this. The Peters are your friends!"

Mrs. Fisher, Reina's mother, stared at her clenched hands on the table, but Mr. Fisher met my gaze. His hair was dark—Reina had gotten her red hair from her mother—but he had Reina's green eyes. "We've agreed to this plan *because* we care, Ayla," he said calmly. "Rash action could mean walking into a trap, *or* could trigger the Dark Fae to retaliate, which would only put Jordan—and the rest of our people—in more danger."

Chairman Hart interjected her agreement. "These Fae aren't likely to harm Jordan. They clearly took him for leverage based on his relationship with you, Ayla. That said, we will need to act quickly on gathering intelligence. Our biggest risk, while Jordan is in their possession, is the possibility of him revealing sensitive information about the LeyGuard and the Hub."

I whipped my face up from where I'd been staring at my lap. "You mean, like, from them *torturing* him?"

She met my eyes with a blank expression. "It's certainly possible, though we have no evidence that is their intention. We have no evidence of *any* of their intentions beyond the most generic assumptions. That's the problem. But Ayla, acting too rashly—as Jordan himself did during the reconnaissance mission—could potentially make things *worse* for him. You're an intelligent girl; surely you can see past your emotions to understand the bigger picture here."

If deadly laser eyes were a LeyGuard power in my bloodline, I was certain it would've manifested in that moment.

Chairman Hart held my glare with one of her own.

Then Reina's dad broke the silence. He turned his gaze to Callan. "You are not under our command, of course, but as an ally we ask that you stand down, as well. Until we gather more information about the Dark Fae's intentions, it's simply too risky to take action."

I looked at Callan, desperate for support, but to my shock, he nodded. "I understand your hesitation."

I glared at him in utter disbelief. "You promised to help me!"

Easy, Ayla. His voice sounded in my mind. *Now is not the time.*

I dropped into my chair and clutched my arms around my chest to contain the whirlwind of panic threatening to burst out of it. My thoughts clamored so loudly I barely heard the hurried exchanges that concluded the meeting, but I did hear Chairman Hart's final statements:

"We'll deploy our allies in the bordering Fae kingdoms and wait for some intel on what's going on over there. Until then, we stay put. Aside from essential deployment teams, the Hub is going on lockdown. Callan, Ayla, we'll set you up with rooms here at the Hub. You can wait in the lobby; I'll send someone to get you when the rooms are ready."

The next thing I knew, we were ushered back *out* of the room by a LeyGuard attendant—like children no longer welcome for an adults-only conversation—handed wrapped sandwiches and bottled water, and told to wait in the lobby.

I stood, staring numbly at the sandwich and water I'd taken by instinct when it was shoved at me, until Callan tugged my arm.

"Come on, Ayla." His voice was gentle, even after I tore my eyes from the plastic-wrapped bread lump to glare daggers at him for betraying me in the meeting. "It's been hours since you ate. Food first, then we'll figure things out."

Eating was the last thing I felt like doing at the moment, but the acid pinch in my stomach betrayed the truth of his statement. I sighed and slid my arm from his grasp. "Fine."

Callan followed me down the stairs to the lobby, where I plopped onto an empty bench. He sat near me but let me force down bites of my bland turkey sandwich in silence while he ate his.

I was a few bites from the end of my sandwich when Callan leaned toward me. "Ayla, you know I'm on your side in this. It just wasn't the time," he whispered.

I wadded up the last bit of crust inside my plastic wrap and turned to face him. "Then when *is* the time, Callan?" I hissed back. "When the Hub finally decides it's no longer too big of a risk to go after Jordan? When he's been tortured for days on end? When my parents are so deep into a Fae-magic coma they may never come out?"

"Ayla," Callan said firmly. He lowered his voice and leaned closer. "I meant it wasn't the time to *say* anything. We're definitely not just staying here."

Hope flickered in my chest. "We aren't?"

He grinned. "Of course not. I can't wait around until the Hub decides what to do. I need to see Prince Kaizyn, and let him know what's happened. He'll know what to do next—we have contacts of our own. He may even have an idea where the Selkbloods are holding Jordan. He hears things, sometimes, in the Veil."

I narrowed my eyes. "And you'll take me with you? You won't just leave me here?"

Callan sighed. "As much as I agree with the Hub council that we need to be cautious, I don't think there's any other way, now. If we're going to get Jordan back, and stop whatever Beirthyr has planned, we need to free Kaizyn. And my guess is we'll have a better chance of that if we work *together* than if I leave you behind." He smirked. "Besides, if I go without you, who will keep you out of trouble?"

I drew a breath of relief. "Okay, but how? The Hub's on lockdown."

Callan's face grew serious. "Yeah, that is a problem. I know a place where we can breach into the Veil undetected, but getting out of *this* place unnoticed is going to be a challenge."

"I can help with that."

Callan and I both jumped. I turned around to find Reina standing a couple feet away.

"Sorry," she said with a wince. "I've been told I'm good at sneaking up on people. It's kind of my thing." She gave me a weak smile. "Hey, Ayla." She held up her hands in front of her. "Don't worry, I won't tell anyone what I heard. I want to help... but I want in. I want to go with you."

I glanced at Callan, wary. Hadn't Reina *hated* me an hour ago?

I'm sorry.

I startled at the sound of Reina's voice in my head.

"You heard me," Reina said, seeming surprised. "Jordan taught me how to project the thought but I wasn't sure—he said it had to be a mind you were familiar with, and open to hearing."

I stared at her, unsure what to say.

She stepped toward me. "I'm sorry, Ayla. I was mad, and so scared, but I never should have blamed you. Jordan did what he thought was right, and he did it because he cared about you, and I guess..." She took a sharp breath, and her cheeks reddened with embarrassment. "I was being stupid. I was jealous, afraid I'd lose my best friend because he suddenly liked some girl but the girl is *you*, Ayla. And you're my friend, too. And I really miss our friendship. I just... I guess I didn't know how to handle it. I'm sorry." She wrung her hands and stared at me, waiting for my reaction.

I studied her face and found that she looked entirely sincere. And who *hadn't* made a mistake since this whole thing started? If I'd told my parents about what was happening sooner, or told Jordan he didn't have to promise me to free them, or told Madison about the Fae sooner, or any number of other things at any point in this entire fiasco, so many things might have ended up differently. "I really miss our friendship, too."

She stood tensely, waiting for the *but...* but I didn't have one.

"I forgive you," I said. "I just want to be friends again, and get Jordan back. I just want everything to be normal again."

Reina's shoulders sagged in relief. "Oh, me too!" She rushed forward and crushed me in a hug. "I'm so sorry, Ayla."

As I sat in the awkward hug, reaching up from my seat on the bench with Reina leaning down over me, a little piece of all that was screwed up in my world seemed to click back into place. I had Reina back—and somehow, that made me feel it was possible we could get Jordan and my parents back, too. Maybe everything would be okay again soon, after all.

Reina pulled away after a moment and smiled at Callan. "Thank you for trying to stop me earlier, with Ayla. You were right—I wasn't thinking clearly. I should've listened."

"I was right." Callan tilted his head and smiled. "It's not often a female tells me that. I think I'll just bask in it for a moment."

Reina laughed, and for a moment, it was almost like things were okay again. Except they weren't. And that fact crashed back in on me a breath later.

I reached for Reina's arm. "You said you could help?"

Reina nodded and leaned closer. "Yes," she whispered, with a conspiratorial smirk. "I know how to get us out of here."

CHAPTER 33

NEVER EXPECTED THE CAT

"Don't worry about the lockdown," Reina whispered. "I have someone who can help us get out undetected."

I raised an eyebrow. "Are you sure we can trust them?"

Reina nodded. "Absolutely." She offered no more detail, but I decided to trust her judgment.

"What about your parents?" Callan interjected. "They're on the council, aren't they? Won't they be upset if you defy the Chairman's orders?"

Reina laughed. "Oh, they'll flip. But they'll also understand why I had to do it... once they calm down." Her face turned serious. "Things have been different around here lately. Chairman Hart is more... cautious. Almost like she's nervous. I *know* something must have her on high alert. Even before the past couple days, she was acting strange, but none of the adults will tell us what's going on. Jordan's parents were the only adults who ever"—her mouth twisted, then she cleared her throat —"who ever told us the truth about what was happening. They'd tell Jordan and me things, even when I'm pretty sure they weren't supposed to. But on this, even they were silent." She fell quiet.

"How are they? His parents?" My voice was weak; I was almost afraid to ask.

Reina smiled gently. "They'll be okay. They lost a lot of blood, and they were both affected by Veil-Dearg toxin. The Selkbloods had another one at the warehouse." She shuddered and forced her eyes back to me. "But Doctor Harlowe says he took care of the worst and now they just need rest; they'll recover." She grimaced. "They didn't take the news well of Jordan being missing, but Chairman Hart has sidelined them. She's forbidden them to even attempt to participate in his rescue; said they need to focus on recovering. They agreed without much of a fight... which was weird in itself."

Callan's eyes narrowed. "And the Chairman isn't always this overprotective of her people?"

Reina shook her head. "No. She's methodical and thorough, she always likes to have a plan, but this is different. It's like she's too uncertain to act on things, like something has her scared. Our recon mission was the first thing she's been that decisive about in days, but that was more like normal Chairman Hart. This decision to wait and see what happens... it's not like her. And it's not like the Peters or my parents not to argue with her for not acting, either. Something is going on."

I thought of the girl I'd met in the hallway and wondered if the unconscious boy upstairs had anything to do with whatever was happening.

Reina shook her head. "Anyway, it doesn't matter—I can't just sit around and leave Jordan over there. I'll probably be grounded for the rest of my life, but I have to do *something*. So what's the plan once we're out of here?"

I swallowed. Did we even *have* a plan? "Well, I mean, I need to get my grandfather's journal, somehow. It may have information we need. And then..." I looked at Callan.

Callan shrugged. "Then we breach into the Veil to meet with the prince." He narrowed his eyes at Reina. "Are you sure you're up for this? An unauthorized breach for a LeyGuard is kind of a big deal, isn't it?"

Reina straightened. "So is watching your best friend get kidnapped by evil Fae." She nodded once, firm. "I'm in."

I never expected Reina's plan to involve a cat.

Within an hour after our conversation on the benches, Callan, Reina, Quinn, her roommate Dove, and I all huddled on the shag rug around their cluttered coffee table while the eerie, massive tabby cut a distrustful side-eye at me from the back of Quinn's couch.

Reina had told Quinn and Dove everything, after assuring Callan and I that she trusted them both completely, and they'd taken the information very much in stride, which only made me wonder again how often crazy stuff happened around this place.

"Foge will help create a distraction," Quinn was saying, gesturing to the cat. "And Dove and I will make sure the way to the southeastern Gate is clear. I'd thought to ask Roinan to help make sure the monitors for the Gate aren't being watched—" She stopped as Reina tensed. "I *know*, you said not to involve anyone else. So I didn't. But it would've made it easier. With just the two of us, it'll be harder to be certain the lobby is clear *and* that no one's watching the monitors."

Dove smiled. "But that's where Fogarty comes in. Don't worry; he'll get the job done."

Dove was a delightfully quirky, petite teenage girl with dark hair and a melodic voice that sounded like it came off a real-life Disney princess... or a whimsical woodland fairy, which given the past few days, I wasn't entirely sure she *wasn't*. She was also the proud owner of that uppity cat, apparently named Fogarty. I was pretty sure he hated me.

At the sound of his name, the cat leapt down from the back of the couch and sauntered over to Dove, who lifted him to her shoulders where he settled around her neck and glared at me like a moody fur scarf.

"Okay, so the diversion is settled," Reina said.

My phone buzzed in my pocket, and I pulled it out to see I had a text from Madison.

Reina continued. "That just leaves how to breach over—"

"Leave that to me," Callan interjected. "I know a place. But we'll need to move quickly, to make sure we're not followed."

"—and how to get whatever book of her grandfather's Ayla needed," Reina finished.

"It's at my house," I said half-attentively as I opened Madison's text.

"That could be tricky," Callan said. "Once we're out of here, time is of the essence. I suppose it can't be helped, but every additional stop we make on the way means more chances for the Hub to realize we're gone and stop us before we make it through the breach."

I held up my phone. "I think I may have a solution for that." I turned the screen toward them, showing them Madison's message:

Hey, Ayla. I'm home now—feeling much better. Callan told me about Jordan. I'm so, so sorry! And how is your family? Any improvements? If there's anything I can do to help, please let me know.

Callan shrugged at my stare. "She texted me earlier asking how things were going. What was I supposed to tell her? But how does that help with the book?"

I stared back, still getting used to his undefined relationship with Madison. "I was thinking maybe she could get it and meet us somewhere?"

Callan tensed. "I don't feel comfortable asking her to go to your house alone. What if they're still watching it?"

"*They,* as in the Selkbloods, or as in the people here at the Hub?" Reina asked.

"Either." Callan shrugged. "Both."

"Well, the worst of the Selkbloods are back Faeside now, with Jordan," Reina said. "They jumped through the breach they'd made at the warehouse. I guess that's why they'd been camping there... it's a latent Leyline, hadn't been used in years. But the Hub re-closed it immediately afterward. It's sealed hard; nothing will be coming through there again without permission."

I had to admit I shared Callan's concern. The last thing I wanted was to put Madison in more danger. Besides, if an unfamiliar girl went poking around my ransacked house only days after my family and I vanished inexplicably, my neighbors were certain to ask questions.

I glanced at Reina. "What's the story they're telling everybody? About us being out of school, me being away from work, my family not being home... there's got to be a cover story, right? The Hub seems to like secrets."

To my surprise, it was Quinn who answered. "Of course. They've already cleaned up the mess at your house. They'll be telling Gary that there was an emergency in your extended family and you're out of town for a few weeks. The same story at school and for your neighbors and church, I believe." She squinted, as if in thought. "I saw someone at a podium, leading a prayer for your family." Her eyes refocused on me. "I mean, you *can* use the prayers, I suppose it doesn't matter if they have the right reasons. God knows, right?" She smiled at me.

I blinked at her. "You saw them? Like you went to my church and watched?" I ran through the days... it wasn't Sunday again yet, I didn't think. Maybe late Friday? Or Saturday? Time moved so strangely inside the Hub, and the lack of windows or sunlight certainly didn't help.

"Oh!" Quinn said. "I'm sorry. Everyone usually already knows—" She blushed, seeming flustered. "I... get visions sometimes. Usually not major ones, just little glimpses of details."

I gaped at her. "Oh." Well *that* was a useful talent. "Thank you... that helps." I chewed my lip, working to piece the new information Quinn had given me into my loosely forming plan. "Callan, you said the Selkbloods don't normally attack with witnesses, right? Except for that one? And if the Hub's watching my house, Madison going in might be strange, but only if we let it be. What if she takes someone with her so she isn't alone, someone neutral but who could protect her, like Gary from the café? He has a key; he's friends with my parents. She could make a big deal of saying I told her she could get something from my house to cloud any suspicion of why she's there if the Hub is watching. The council knows I went to visit her at the hospital, so for all they know, I told her she could borrow my favorite shoes or something, and Madison's skilled enough at being—" I hesitated. "Well, at being *bossy*. She could totally rant out loud about how my shoes aren't as nice as I promised her, or something, and pull it off… then grab the book while she's there."

"It's still not enough," Callan said. "If the Selkbloods were willing to attack in public once before, they might again. They know *you're* the bonded one now, but that doesn't mean they won't try to take or hurt more people we care about, for additional leverage."

"I have a friend on the outside," Quinn said. "Someone I trust. She can make sure no Selkbloods are in the area."

"How would she know for sure?" I asked.

Quinn met my eyes. "She *is* one. The powerful ones can sense each other, like picking up an aura. And also, she's out of that life now, but she still has contacts with some of the… darker ones. She reached out after what happened with Jordan, but there was no info. Whatever's happening, it's not happening Earthside. All her contacts say the group that was holed up near the warehouse is gone."

Callan thought for a moment, then nodded at me. "That could work. I know a safe place near the breach where Madison could meet us with the book. As long as she doesn't go to your house alone."

I typed a quick text to Madison: *I'm so sorry to ask, but there is something I need…*

I typed several more texts, explaining our plan, our concern that she not go alone, and what the Hub was telling people about my family.

Madison's response came back immediately: *Of course I'll help. And don't worry about me, I won't be alone. Rory's here, and he's insisting on going with me. We'll get the key from Gary together.*

I showed her reply to Callan, and he nodded. "Good. He won't let anything happen to her."

The five of us exchanged glances.

"Does that mean we have a plan?" Reina asked.

"I think so." Quinn nodded.

Dove smiled and nodded, and I swear the cat nodded too, though maybe it was just rubbing its face on Dove's neck.

"I'll text Madison the coordinates to meet us with the book," Callan said. "Let's get moving."

CHAPTER 34

QUICK ERRAND

Reina halted outside the door to Quinn and Dove's apartment. "Before we begin, I have a quick errand to run." She glanced at me. "Ayla, do you want to come with me?"

I wasn't certain where she was headed, but I gladly accepted the gesture of friendship. "Sure." I smiled at her.

"Great." Reina smiled back, then turned to the others. "We'll meet you in the lobby in thirty minutes."

Dove nodded. "Perfect. Foge and I will be ready."

The cat stared at me from its perch on Dove's shoulder. Quinn and Dove hadn't said what the cat would be doing to ensure we made it out unnoticed, but Reina had accepted their confidence without question, so I hadn't asked. I was suddenly intensely curious.

"Is anyone grabbing supplies?" Callan asked. "I've got a place near the barrier where we can grab some necessities before we breach, but it's short on food. Reina, Ayla, and I will be in the Veil for a few hours, at least, and I'll need to take food for Prince Kaizyn as well. Some extra snacks and water would be wise."

Anxiety fluttered in my chest at the thought of going into the Veil...was I really about to breach into a different *realm*? I couldn't think too deeply about that one, or it started to feel like I was losing my grip on reality.

"I can help with food. C'mon." Quinn grabbed Callan's arm and tugged him down the hallway.

Callan met my gaze and shrugged, then let her pull him along. "See you in thirty minutes, Ayla."

"Yeah… thirty minutes." I could only hope things weren't about to go horribly wrong.

Reina turned to me with a smile that felt almost like normal. "Follow me."

I followed her swinging red ponytail down the stairs and across the lobby to one of the many hallways which branched out from the courtyard.

While I walked, my mind spun nervously over the realization that not only was I about to enter a *Fae* realm, I was also about to properly meet the prince I was supposedly betrothed to, and would probably have to make conversation with him beyond the chaotic one-minute exchanges we'd had so far. I had a feeling *that* would be incredibly awkward. But that was the plan—find Kaizyn, tell him what's happened, see what he knows, then try to figure out how to free him *and* Jordan. For that, I could muscle through the awkward small-talk… but the thought that I was about to go to another *realm* still felt fake.

Reina stopped at a stairwell door and held it open for me. "We'll have to go down another level. This way."

The stairwell had a strange *Employees Only* feel to it, as though it wasn't used much, but Reina seemed relaxed so I didn't worry. "What is it you need to get?"

She glanced back at me over her shoulder and grinned. "You'll see. Almost there."

A couple flights later we reached a landing with another door, though the stairs continued down beyond that. How many more levels down were there?

"This is the one." Reina pulled the door open. "There shouldn't be anyone down here right now, but if they're watching on the monitors or something, they'll just think I came early to walk him."

"To walk—" But as I followed her in, I realized what she meant. "Champ!"

Jordan's dog jumped up against the bars of his kennel, hopping in excitement on his back feet, tail wagging up a storm.

"Hey, buddy." Reina crossed to his kennel and reached through the bars to pet him.

I glanced down the row of other kennels in the room, all empty except for some kind of large, orange-furred animal curled up in the corner of the farthest one. "Are these for LeyGuard pets or something?"

Reina shrugged as she grabbed Champ's leash from a hook on the wall. "Something like that. Champ is Jordan's pet but also basically his K-9 partner, like some cops have. But he lives with Jordan, at home. Most of the LeyGuards who *live* here don't have pets, other than Dove, but if they did, they'd probably keep them in their rooms. And those of us who live off campus keep our pets in our houses. If we need to be here for days at a time, then yeah, we might keep a pet down here, like a pet daycare. The Hub has a dedicated staff to walk and feed and exercise them, but since Champ knows me so well, I volunteered to look after him while he's here."

Reina tugged open the door to Champ's kennel, and I smiled as he barreled into her, covering her face with kisses as she clipped the leash to his collar.

"So do many LeyGuards have animal partners?" I hadn't seen any animals here before this, other than Dove's cat. "Is that one at the end one, too?"

As if on cue, the animal at the end uncurled, stretched, and stood. I gasped. It was *huge*, but it wasn't a large-breed dog like I'd thought—it was a cat. Or mostly a cat. It looked kind of like someone had bred a Great Dane with a tiger.

Reina lifted Champ's paws from her chest and nudged him back to standing on his four feet, then smiled at me. "That one at the end is some kind of animal the Hub is holding for an ally. To be honest, I'm not sure *what* it is. It doesn't seem to be Fae. The attendant said it's called a siskarone." She shrugged. "It's supposedly very intelligent."

From the way it was staring at me, I suspected she was right.

"Anyway, no," Reina continued, "LeyGuards don't usually have animal partners. Champ's kind of a special case, like Fogarty."

Champ came from Reina's side, tail wagging, to sniff my pants. I offered him my hand, which he sniffed and licked, then I knelt to pet him.

"Oh. Special how?" Champ leaned his wiggling, waggly body into me, knocking me off balance in his excitement for me to scratch him.

"He's unusually bonded to Jordan," Reina said, smiling as Champ flopped onto his back for a belly rub. "Jordan rescued him as a puppy after he found him in a drainage ditch on a run a couple years ago, but when we started training for the LeyGuard, he'd be glued to Jordan's side any time we worked out in the backyard. Once we started sparring with weapons, it got a little uncanny—he'd naturally cover Jordan's flank and move with him, almost like a shadow. Like he knew exactly where to be." She shrugged. "So we trained him. Chairman Hart says she thinks Jordan has a *knack* for dogs, like maybe it's part of his magic—that their bond makes it where Champ can just read him. It doesn't work for any of the rest of us."

I stared into the eyes of the dog flopped on the floor with his tongue dangling out the side of his goofy dog grin. "Huh. Wow." There was *so much* about Jordan I still didn't know.

"That's why Champ's coming with us." Reina dropped to her knees beside me, and ruffled the thin fur on Champ's head. "Right buddy?"

Champ increased his excited body-waggling, still belly-up on the floor, legs kicking the air.

"Is that the same thing that happened with Dove and Fogarty?" I asked.

Reina laughed. "No, Fogarty is special in a *different* way."

I opened my mouth to ask about that, and about Jordan and Reina's magic—I had *so many questions*—but Reina stood.

"We should head up. It's almost time."

My stomach plunged to my feet. "Right."

She pulled open the door, and Champ trotted beside her as I followed them into the stairwell.

I hurried along behind them, anxiety climbing with each new flight of stairs. "Do you think—I mean—what happens if we get caught? If this doesn't work?"

"We'll be in trouble, especially me, but it's not like they'll torture us. It'll be okay." Reina smiled back at me. "Besides, you haven't seen yet what Fogarty can do."

An ear-splitting alarm blared through the stairwell.

"Right on time!" Reina shouted over the noise and grinned. She yanked open the final door of the stairwell, and we rushed out to the hallway with a clear view of the courtyard, a mass of people running and pure chaos.

I gaped as a huge *something* barreled through the lobby toward the courtyard stairs.

"What the—" I yelled. "Is that a *bear*?"

CHAPTER 35

LAYERS LIKE AN ONION

Callan darted up, wearing a black backpack over one shoulder, and grabbed my hand. "Let's go, hurry!"

Reina, Callan, Champ, and I rushed across the chaos of the courtyard to where Quinn waited at the entrance of a long, narrow hallway on the opposite side.

"You still have that token you said Striker gave you?" she asked quickly.

I nodded.

"Good. Down to the end, take a left, you'll dead-end into the Gate. You've got about two minutes before the attendant returns to the control room to watch the monitors."

"But why is there a bea—" I began.

"No time," Quinn waved us down the hall. "Hurry!"

Reina slid around me and she and Champ took the lead.

"Good luck!" Quinn called after us as we sprinted down the hallway.

The sirens still wailed overhead, and the hallway felt unbearably exposed and long, but finally we reached the fork in the hallway and turned a sharp left—

—and ran right into Striker, who was leaning against a plain, flat wall at the end of the hall.

We stumbled to a stop a few feet from him, exchanging panicked glances.

Striker pushed up from the wall and pulled the matchstick from his mouth. One eyebrow cocked as he turned to face us. "Where do you all think you're going?"

Reina straightened and met his stare, her cheeks flushing red. "We're going to find help for Jordan." Her voice was firm but cold, just stating fact. Champ stood stiff beside her, glancing between her and Striker as though trying to assess the threat.

Striker slid the matchstick into the corner of his mouth and chewed on it as he studied her. "I see."

"You *have* to have noticed how weird everyone's being!" Reina turned passionate, arms flailing. "Something's going on, and I don't have time to wait around for them to figure it out, not when Jordan's life is—"

"Okay, okay." Striker held up a hand, silencing her. His lips curled into a smirk. "I never said I was going to *stop* you." He stepped toward us, meeting each of our eyes in turn.

"So you're just going to let us go?" Callan asked in disbelief.

Striker shrugged. "Sometimes you gotta do what you believe is right. But are you sure *this* is what's right? Running off without telling anyone? You could get yourselves killed."

A surge of boldness rushed through me as I clutched the token in my pocket. "We have told someone." I straightened my spine, forcing my gaze to hold steady on his. "We've told *you*."

Striker studied my face, then threw his head back and laughed. "Touché, kid." His face turned serious as he looked back at us. "Listen, though—be careful out there. There *is* something strange brewing, and I don't like the feel of it." He slid a smooth, flat stone from his pocket, almost like a worry stone but with geometric symbols etched into it. He held it out to me. "Take this. If you get in trouble, call me."

I stared down at the flat stone in my hand. "How am I supposed to call you with—"

Silence washed over us as the siren overhead cut out.

"We're out of time, kids." Striker stepped back and slapped his hand to the wall. It split open, revealing a moonlit, grassy field with woods beyond. "If you're still planning to be rebels today, you'd better go."

Reina and Champ rushed through. Callan grabbed my hand and pulled me toward the opening.

I looked up at Striker as I passed him. "Thank you."

He nodded. "Go do some good. I'll be here, keeping chaos from escaping."

I didn't have a chance to ask what he meant before Callan tugged me through the Gate.

I stumbled out on the grass beside Callan, Champ, and Reina. The air snapped shut behind us, leaving only the open field. I slid the flat stone into my pocket beside the token, then looked up at Callan and Reina. "What now?"

"We need to move; as soon as anyone gets back to the control room, they'll spot us here through the hidden cameras," Reina said, glancing around nervously.

"To the woods," Callan said. "Follow me."

Once we entered the cover of the woods, we hiked through the dense trees for what felt like at least an hour. The moonlight filtering through the trees was not enough to keep me from tripping on roots every few steps. We moved mostly in silence, the urgency of escape still hanging over us.

"Do you think we're being followed?" I asked once.

Reina shrugged. "Probably not. They were pretty distracted, and I think we got out of sight of the cameras quickly enough."

We continued in silence. Finally, with a hitch in my side and one too many bruised toes inside my shoes, I stopped to lean against a tree. "I need a minute," I said, sucking deep breaths as Callan turned back to look at me. "How much farther?" It was odd to break the silence, but my words seemed to melt some of the tension surrounding us. We were far enough away, now, that it should be safe to talk.

"We're nearly there." Callan slid a bottle of water from the backpack and handed it to me.

I drank it greedily. Then I flipped my face up to Reina. "Why was there a *bear*?"

Reina stared at me, then burst out laughing. After a moment, she caught her breath. "That was Fogarty." She shrugged. "Told you he was unique. He's a Fae bear, bonded to Dove. The cat thing is just a glamour Dove makes him wear." She smirked. "He hates it."

I blinked at her. "Oh."

Callan handed a bottle of water to Reina as well, and she drank some, then poured a little in her hand for Champ to lap.

"Won't the bear be in trouble after all the chaos he caused today?" Callan asked.

I gasped. "Will they kick him out of the Hub?"

Reina waved my worry away. "No, no, Dove knows how to handle things. She'll just tell the Hub his glamour slipped, and he went for a joy run or something, then promise to do better about keeping him in check." She shrugged. "She's the only surviving child of a major Fae dignitary who died fighting off a wave of village attacks a few years ago. Her presence helps keep peace between the LeyGuard and her particular Fae culture. The Hub were *thrilled* when she turned herself in after hiding Earthside for a while. She's a VIP guest."

"Oh," I said. I was relieved, at least, that Dove and Fogarty wouldn't be in huge trouble for our sakes.

Reina looked back at Callan. "Where are you taking us, anyway? You said you had a place for us to get supplies, but the Hub owns all forty acres of these woods, and in this direction it backs up to the river. What could possibly be out here?"

"My cabin," Callan answered.

I stared at him. "You have a cabin out here?"

He shrugged. "It's more of a shack, really, but I needed *some* place to live."

Reina tilted her head. "Warded?"

"Of course." He began walking again, and Reina and I followed.

Reina laughed. "Only the Teionyrians could pull off a warded cabin in the middle of LeyGuard-owned woods." She grinned at Callan. "Chairman Hart would lose her *mind* if she knew."

Callan grinned back. "Good that she doesn't, then."

Reina raised her eyebrows. "It's good that you guys are our *allies*." Unease crossed her face. "What if there are others who can do what you do?"

Callan gave her a reassuring smile. "I'm certain there are, but warding Earthside undetected requires a bit of extra help, nonetheless. There's a reason we built a shack *here*, of all places. This particular outpost has been here for decades..." He glanced at me. "Since the days of your grandfather."

My chest tightened. "Oh."

"There's a latent Leyline nearby; that's where I've been breaching through. The cabin was set up near it intentionally—it was your grandfather's waypoint for communicating with Teionyr privately during the years he was our liaison... when he needed to."

Reina's eyes widened. "The LeyGuard didn't know?"

Callan shook his head. "Not about this one. The king trusted Ayla's grandfather completely, but he wasn't so certain about *all* members of the LeyGuard. He asked for a safe house, something off the grid, and a way for a messenger to breach through undetected." Callan smiled at me. "Your grandfather obliged. He worked with the king's personal apothecarist to formulate just the right faespell to cloak this place from both Fae *and* LeyGuards, unless they have the key."

My grandfather's secrets had layers like an onion.

Reina whistled. "That would *really* explode Chairman Hart's mind."

Callan stopped and turned to face us, his expression serious. "She can never know. This has been here for decades, and even most Teionyrians don't know it exists. Until the curse, even I didn't know—Prince Kaizyn told me about it. But I can't be the one who ruins things. It has to stay between us."

Reina nodded. "Of course."

Callan glanced at me.

"Who am I going to tell?" I asked. "Besides, it's my grandfather's secret, too. No way I'm ratting on him."

Callan smiled, relieved. "Okay. In that case, we're here." Callan reached for the leather cord around his neck and slid the end from beneath his shirt. A small stone dangled from the cord, black and shiny, held by criss-crossing straps of leather. Next to it hung a thin metal rod, about the length and width of my pinky finger. Callan held that up. "The key."

As soon as he lifted it up, the air next to us rippled, then flattened back to normal—except for the tiny wooden shack that had appeared among the trees. It definitely showed its age. The vertical planks that comprised the body of the shack were green with mildew, and the angled slab of aluminum which served as the shack's roof was crusty with something like white rust. Despite all that, the shack still looked fairly solid—though I wasn't certain it would hold all three of us plus Champ at the same time.

Callan moved toward the shallow porch and climbed the two steps up to the front door. "Come on in. I gave Madison these coordinates, but we're within the ward now—we'll see her before she sees us. We may as well wait inside."

That he told Madison to meet us *here* was a statement to how much he must trust her... or like her. Or both. But I decided not to comment on that part. Instead, I followed him in.

Callan flicked a switch on the wall and light from a dusty ceiling fixture illuminated the one-room shack. It was a bit roomier inside than it had appeared. There was a carpeted living room area with a faded floral loveseat, flanked by an end table with a lamp and a short bookshelf. To the right was a square table with four chairs, and beyond that, a small kitchen area with a sink, fridge, oven, and a row of cabinets. A mattress made up with a quilt and pillows sat against the left-hand wall, next to a closed door which I hoped was a bathroom because I didn't want to use the woods.

Callan crossed to the kitchen cabinets and began shoving supplies into the backpack. "Help yourself to whatever you can find in the kitchen.

Restroom's through that door if anyone needs it," he said, and I sighed internally with relief. "Septic's old; don't use too much toilet paper."

There was something extremely amusing about getting septic tank advice from a Fae soldier, but I had to pee too badly to care. "I'll be right back." I hurried to the bathroom and shut the door behind me.

The bathroom was about the size of a port-a-potty, but far cleaner—it seemed Callan had good housekeeping skills. There was a curtained window over the toilet, then a pedestal sink and a narrow, tiled shower stall with hardly any room between them. I flushed and pivoted toward the sink, where a decorative floral hand towel hung from a brass ring on the wooden walls, coordinated with a fancy flower-shaped hand soap in a porcelain dish on the sink's edge. As I lifted the towel to dry my hands, my eyes caught on something carved in the wood of the wall beside it: *Built by Maddox Rogers.*

I ran a finger over it in awe, then opened the door. "My grandfather *built* this place?" I asked Callan as I came out. For some reason, I'd envisioned him hiring a crew, or something—not physically constructing a cabin.

Callan glanced at me questioningly, then seemed to realize what I'd noticed. "Of course," he said. "He didn't want anyone else to know about it."

Yet another layer to my grandfather's secret past. I hadn't known he *could* build something like this. I glanced around the small cabin, seeing it in a new light, and felt a sense of pride. A thin sprout of confidence pushed up through the mud of my doubts, then unfolded like a blossoming bud. If Grandpa could become a trusted liaison between the LeyGuard and Teionyr, single-handedly save the king and infant prince, construct hidden wards for his Fae allies, *and* build a cabin with his own two hands, then I could travel to the Veil and speak to my accidentally betrothed Fae prince and figure out a way to free him, unbind myself from him, and rescue Jordan and my parents. I was Maddox Rogers' granddaughter. I could be brave, like he was. I could do this.

Reina studied my face from her spot on the lumpy loveseat, Champ curled up at her feet. "You just had an epiphany, didn't you? I can see it on your face."

"Not exactly," I said. "At least nothing that helps us solve anything. I'm just feeling... hopeful, I guess. About our mission. I think maybe we can actually do this."

Reina smiled. "Of course we can. Did you not think so until now?"

I shrugged. "Not really, I guess?"

Callan stared at me. "Then why did you insist on coming?"

I stared back at him. "I had to at least try."

Champ jumped up on all fours, fur bristling. A low growl rumbled in his throat.

Callan clutched the key that dangled around his neck. "We've got company."

Chapter 36

Odd Little Family

Callan yanked open the cabin door, then relaxed and smiled back at us over his shoulder. "It's Madison and Rory. I'll go let them in."

Champ glanced between Reina and the door, still bristled up and uneasy, but obeyed when Reina commanded him to sit.

Callan slipped outside, and as I watched him go, a sudden wave of exhaustion hit me. I sank down onto the loveseat next to Reina.

"You okay?" she asked.

"I think the fact I haven't slept in over twenty-four hours is finally hitting me." I tipped my head back onto the couch and let my eyes fall closed.

"Me too," Reina said. "I wonder if we can catch a quick nap before we head out. I don't want to waste anymore time, but we'll be no good to anyone if we're delirious and dizzy from lack of sleep."

I nodded, eyes still closed. "Maybe just a quick one. Thirty minutes? An hour?"

The door flew open. Reina and I both shot upright as Callan barged in.

"We've got trouble!" he hissed. He pulled Madison and Rory in after him, then spun and slammed the door. Madison clutched my grandfather's journal to her chest, but her eyes were wild, her hands shaky. Rory's face beside her was ghost-pale.

My pulse surged, adrenaline forcing my body into full alert again. "What is it?"

"Shh!" Callan gestured for us all to be quiet, then edged to the window and peeked out through the curtains.

I inched my way over to Madison. *Are you okay?* I mouthed to her.

She nodded, but her eyes were still wide and frightened. Anxiety pulsed through me but I breathed deeply and waited, not wanting to make any noise that might put us in danger.

Finally, Callan sighed in relief and pulled back from the window. "The ward held." He turned to us. "I wasn't sure it worked on Shadowhounds, but they passed right by us."

Reina tensed. "Shadowhounds, here? Why? Did you see their mark?"

"No. But whoever sent them, they haven't been here long—if they'd been out there when Madison and Rory first entered the woods..." Callan's face paled as he glanced at Madison.

"What are you talking about?" I asked. "What are Shadowhounds?"

"Dark Fae creatures—kind of like huge, mutated wolves, but summoned by magic," Reina answered. "They hunt in packs, but they don't just roam and hunt. They have to be *sent*. For a particular target."

"They don't give up once they're locked on something," Callan added. "But they'll also kill whatever else is in their path, if they cross anything. They just enjoy killing."

Madison shuddered and clutched the book tighter.

"What are they after?" Rory asked. His voice was scratchy, and I wondered how he was adjusting to his sudden initiation into Fae and Ley-Guards and apparently mutant killer Fae wolves. From the greenish-pale shade of his face and the shocked expression in his eyes, it seemed he wasn't taking it super well.

"Maybe one of us," Callan said. "Maybe *all* of us. It depends who sent them."

Reina sank down beside Champ, stroking his head. He had calmed some, but his fur was still bristled and he let out an occasional grumbling growl. "They could be after Ayla, because of the prince."

Callan nodded. "There's a good chance." He ran a hand through his hair, leaving it sticking up in strange directions, then sighed. "I know we're in a hurry, but it's best to lie low here for at least a few hours, to be sure they're gone." He glanced at Madison and Rory. "You, too. Please stay here a bit before you try to head home."

Madison nodded. "No problem. I'm not going back out there with those things roaming about." Her wide eyes found mine. "They were *huge.*"

"We're lucky they showed up right when you were crossing into the ward," Callan said. "If they'd seen you before you made it in..."

Madison shuddered again, then her eyes found me. "Here." She held out my grandfather's journal. "This is the right one, I hope?"

I took it from her and traced my fingers over the engraved tree. "Yes, this is the one." I looked up. "Thank you. I mean it. This journal could be really, really important, and I know it was a risk for you to get it."

Madison smiled a warm, genuine smile. "You're welcome."

"Any trouble at the house?" Reina asked.

Rory shook his head. "None at all. Gary bought the story about Madison borrowing something, and she showed him your text saying he could give her the key. After that, it was as simple as going to the house and finding the right book. We had to search through the shelves a bit, but that's all."

Madison grinned. "I did grab a pair of cute boots from your closet on the way out, to uphold the ruse. They're in my car back at the edge of town. Callan said we had to park a ways off and walk here. But I'll give them back as soon as I can."

I smiled at her. "No rush."

Callan glanced at the book in my hands, then his eyes trailed up to my face. "You're exhausted," he said. "Why don't you rest, since we're stuck here a while anyway, and I'll take a stab at the journal, see if I can find anything."

As curious as I was to scour my grandfather's journal, the mention of sleep pulled more strongly at me than any curiosity. I nodded and handed him the journal. "Sounds good."

"You can use the bed over there," Callan said. "The sheets are fresh." He glanced at Reina. "And you look half-dead, too. Why don't you take the couch?"

Reina stood. "Are you sure you don't need rest? You can't have slept in a long while, either."

Callan pulled a blanket from the back of the loveseat and handed it to her. "I'm used to going a while without sleep. I'll need to rest soon, but for right now, I'm too keyed up. You rest, I'll search the book."

Reina nodded and slid down onto the couch, curling onto her side with her legs tucked up to fit into the small space. She pulled the blanket over herself. Champ circled, then settled on the floor beside her.

I stumbled toward the bed against the wall.

"We can help you look through the journal," I heard Madison saying as I kicked off my shoes and pulled the quilt and top sheet back. "What are you looking for?"

"Something that might solve Ayla's riddle," I heard Callan answer. "To help us find where a certain name we need might be written down."

As I slid into the bed and settled back onto the pillow, it occurred to me that he hadn't told her it was a *true* name. Maybe there were still secrets he felt he had to keep from Madison. I wondered if that was because he didn't fully trust her, or to protect her, or maybe just out of loyalty to the prince. But a moment later, Callan was reciting the riddle I'd found, and before he even made it into the second verse, my mind was sucked away by sleep, all further ponderings lost.

T he thin sunlight of early morning filtered through the cabin curtains when I next opened my eyes. I startled upright, disoriented, then remembered where I was. I rubbed the sleep from my eyes and glanced around.

Reina was still asleep on the loveseat, Champ sprawled out on the ground beside her. Madison was curled up on the floor near Champ on a makeshift bed of folded blankets Callan must've pulled from somewhere, with a quilt tucked over her. Rory and Callan were both slumped over asleep in their chairs at the kitchen table, Callan leaning on the table with his head on his arms, and Rory across from him with one cheek flat on the table. The journal was splayed between them.

I eased to my feet and tiptoed to the bathroom to relieve myself, trying my best not to wake anyone, then stepped around Madison's sleeping form to peek out the window.

Champ lifted his head as I passed and peered at me, then stretched and stood.

Judging by the foggy, filtered sunlight outside, it was just after dawn. Champ had been inside for hours; he probably needed to relieve himself, too. But I wasn't about to step outside on my own without knowing the boundaries of the wards or how they worked. I certainly didn't want to start my day getting eaten by some kind of Fae wolf.

Champ pranced and whined, making it clear he wanted out.

I tiptoed over to Callan and nudged his shoulder, then whispered, "Callan."

The chair flew back. Callan leapt to his feet and spun to face me, knife drawn from who knows where, all before I even had time to react.

I yelped and jumped back.

As soon as Callan saw it was me, he relaxed and dropped the knife on the table. "Ayla! For goodness' sake, I could've stabbed you!" he whisper-yelled at me.

Rory grunted and repositioned his head on the table, and Madison stirred and muttered a bit from the floor nearby.

Callan glanced around, then lowered his voice further to avoid waking anyone. "What is it? Did something happen?"

I was still a bit shaken from the lightning-speed near-stabbing, so I just shook my head and gestured at Champ.

"Oh," Callan said. "He needs to go out?"

"I'll take him," Reina whispered from the loveseat. She shoved off her blanket and stood. "Is it safe?" she asked Callan.

"As long as you stay close enough to the cabin."

"How close is close enough?"

"About ten yards?" Callan grabbed the knife and slid it into his belt. "I'll just go with you, to be sure." He turned to me. "The sink water is filtered and there's food and some juice in the fridge, if you're ready for breakfast." He and Reina slipped out the front door with Champ.

I was thirsty and starving, so I dug through the kitchen cabinets until I found the dishes, filled up and swigged down a full glass of water, then yanked open the fridge. I froze—the whole top shelf was full of jars of pomegranate jam. My heart squeezed.

It had been far too long since Grandpa could've been here for them to be his, but it made me think of him, just the same. I swallowed down the ache in my chest for my family and focused on finding something to soothe the ache in my stomach instead.

I pulled out a carton of orange juice—medium pulp, just how I liked it—a carton of eggs, a package of bagels, and a block of cream cheese. I set them on the counter, then peeked out the window.

Reina and Callan were right outside the cabin, still waiting on Champ to finish his business.

I dug through some more cabinets until I found a skillet and some salt and pepper, then set to work frying some eggs.

By the time Reina, Callan, and Champ returned, I had a pan full of eggs halfway done.

"That smells great," Callan whispered, kicking off his boots inside the door.

Reina followed suit, crumbles of muddy soil falling onto the mat from their shoes.

Champ bounded in with no regard to cleanliness, trailing muddy paw prints through the kitchen.

Reina laughed softly, then whispered, "I'll clean that up. Do you have paper towels?"

I reached to where I'd seen them on the counter and handed them to her, then pulled five plates from the cabinet and stacked them on the countertop.

Callan sank into a chair and smiled at me. "I see you've made yourself at home." He shrugged, still keeping his voice low. "I guess this is basically your cabin, after all—your grandfather made it."

That was a strange thought, but not an unwelcome one. It was kind of peaceful out here, in this protected pocket of warded woods. In a way, it made me feel closer to Grandpa.

Rory startled as Champ brushed his legs, then blinked and yawned. "Oh, hey. Good morning."

A moment later, Madison sat up and stretched. "Do I smell eggs?" Her hair was as messy as it had been at the hospital, but mine probably was, too—and right now, none of us cared.

I glanced around at all of us and felt a surge of fondness for this very odd little family I'd found myself with. Reina I could've expected, but a Fae soldier, a trained fighting dog, and Rory and Madison Kane—them I *never* would have imagined. Yet I was genuinely glad to have them all here with me. I smiled at Madison. "Yes. Would you like some?"

She groaned. "Yes, please. And also a bathroom?"

Callan laughed and pointed across the room. "Through that door."

"Thanks." She stood and made her way over to it.

I flipped the eggs, then turned to Callan. "Did you find anything in the journal last night?"

He poked at the journal and shook his head. "No. I have no idea what I'm looking for. Maybe you'd have better luck. You know your grandfather better."

I glanced over at the journal. The pages they had open were a bunch of scribbled notes, interspersed with sketched symbols. I wasn't sure I'd do any better, but I nodded. "I can try after we eat."

I turned back toward the stove, flicked the burner switch to off, and slid an egg from the pan to the first plate. I set that plate on the table and reached for another.

From across the room came the sound of glass shattering, followed closely by Madison's screams.

CHAPTER 37

BREACHES

Callan leapt to his feet and raced to the bathroom, reaching it before anyone else. He yanked the door open and cursed. "They've taken her!"

I caught a glimpse of shattered glass from the window as Callan spun around and shoved past us, rushing out the front door.

We all ran after him.

"Who's taken her? What's happening?" Rory yelled, panicked, as we stumbled out onto the porch. Rory wasn't even wearing shoes.

Callan pulled up short a few yards from the cabin, cursed again, then drove his knife into the ground and let out a wordless yell of fury.

Champ raced past us, fur spiked and barking up a storm, but Callan leapt for him and grabbed his collar. "No! He can't cross the barrier!" He turned to us. "There could be more out there!"

"Callan! What's going on?" I yelled as Reina, Rory, and I ran up behind him.

Reina slid past me and grabbed Champ, taking him from Callan.

Champ continued growling, but didn't try to pull away.

Callan stood and faced us. His gaze found Reina. "Fadehound. It has to be. I couldn't see it, I could only see—" He gestured at the ground, and I gasped as I noticed the drag marks and giant paw prints in the muddy ground.

Reina paled. "How'd it make it through the ward?"

"It shouldn't have been able to!" Callan yelled. "Not if the Shadowhounds can't. The wards allow anyone to go out, but you can only come in with a key. Unless…" He blanched. "Unless it came in when we did, then waited."

Reina gaped. "Why would it do that?"

"What are you talking about?" Rory was wild-eyed, on the verge of losing it. "Who took my *sister*?"

"Not who, what." Reina turned to him. "Fadehounds aren't like Shadowhounds—they're smart. Stealthy. They have to be sent and summoned, like Shadowhounds, but sometimes they go rogue." She turned to Callan. "But why sneak in and wait until Madison was alone? You and I were outside this morning. It could've grabbed either of us. Why did it want her?"

Callan ran a hand down his face. "I don't know." He started pacing, then stopped and looked at me. "Unless it thought she was Ayla, maybe? They're smart, but they can make mistakes."

"Maybe," Reina said. "But Callan, you know, with a Fadehound—"

"I know, okay!" Callan yelled. "Just let me think!"

Dread spread through me. I turned to Reina. "You know with a Fadehound *what*?"

Reina met me with a sad, solemn gaze. "Their breath is toxic, Ayla. Their saliva, too. They're not made for just capturing things. When someone is taken by a Fadehound, they never survive long, especially a human."

"No." Rory's voice shook. He ran a hand through his hair. "No. Why are we just standing here? We have to get her back!"

"I'm sorry." Tears pooled in Reina's eyes as she turned to him. "We don't even know where it took her, and we're not equipped to fight off a Fadehound. We need to go back for help. There's nothing else we can—"

"Yes," Callan interrupted. "Yes, there is. Other help will take too long." He yanked the leather cord from around his neck and thrust it at me. "This key will open the breach. It's just outside the ward, behind the cabin. You and Reina should be able to feel it once you're close. Once you're in the Veil, the stone that's also on this cord will lead you to Prince Kaizyn."

I gaped at him. "What are you doing?"

He drew his knife. "I'm going after Madison."

"Callan, no!" Reina yelled, but he spun on his heel and charged out into the shadows of the trees.

Champ danced and whined, tugging on Reina's grip. Reina stood, bouncing slightly as she hunched over to hold Champ's collar. "I can't—ugh, Callan, you idiot!" She sank back down next to Champ and looked up at me. "We can't go after him. We don't know what else is out—wait, where's Rory?"

Reina and I both looked around in a panic, but Rory was nowhere to be found. I raced back inside and found him shoving on his shoes.

"I'm going after them, Ayla." He stood. "I know I'm not a Fae or a soldier, or whatever the rest of you are, but I can't just do nothing."

Panic swirled and splintered inside of me. My world was careening out of control suddenly, my plans spiraling into chaos.

"You could get hurt, Rory. You could die!" It was all I could think to say.

He met my stare. "So could Madison." He slid past me and out the front door.

I chased after him. "Rory, wait!"

He glanced back at me. "Good luck, Ayla." He darted off into the trees.

Reina stared at me. "What do we do now?"

I clutched the stone and metal rod in my hands—it was my path to Prince Kaizyn, to possible answers, my best chance at saving Mom and Dad and Jordan. But I knew nothing about the Veil, or how to navigate it, and as skilled as I knew Callan must be, I still couldn't just abandon him, Madison, and Rory to face whatever now roamed these woods. I slid the cord around my neck. "We have to go after them."

Reina stared at me, then nodded. "Just let me grab Champ's leash." She dragged him toward the cabin.

I bounced nervously on my toes as I waited for her and Champ to return, but then I remembered Striker's stone in my pocket. I pulled it out and stared at it, tracing my finger over the symbols. He'd said to call him if we ran into any trouble...

The stone warmed suddenly, letting off a vibrating hum, then went cold again.

Reina dashed back out, Champ leashed beside her. "I grabbed Callan's backpack, it's got food and water."

"I tried to call Striker." I held out the stone. "I'm not sure if it worked."

"How long ago did you do it?"

"While you were inside. Maybe a minute ago?"

"Did it warm up and hum?"

I nodded.

Reina chewed her lip. "Huh. Then it worked, but he should be here by now; that's a summon-stone. It's instantaneous."

I blinked at her, shocked that Striker had given me a stone to physically *summon* him to me. Then I sighed. "Well, we can't afford to wait around for him to come." I slid the stone into my pocket.

Reina clenched Champ's leash. "You ready?" Her face held a half-nervous, half-eager expression.

I, on the other hand, was all nerves, but I nodded. "Let's go."

We ran after the others.

A tingle crossed my skin as we left the protection of the ward, then we were standing in the woods—no cabin in sight. "Wow. You can't even tell it's there."

Reina glanced past me and shook her head. "Uncanny. Chairman Hart would be so annoyed by this." She gave me a weak smile as her eyes scanned the surrounding woods.

The early morning light lit the ground near us in patches, but the tree coverage got thicker as the woods deepened, bathing everything in shadows. The others were long gone, the woods silent other than occasional chirps from birds high in the trees.

"There!" Reina pointed at some indentations in the leafy ground to our right. "Footprints. They went this way." She dragged Champ in the direction of the footprints, and I followed. "Listen carefully for any noises, and watch for any movement," she whispered. "There could be more Fadehounds out here, or Shadowhounds, or... well, lots of things."

I tried to ignore the rapid pounding of my heart against my ribs. "What do we do if we do hear or see something?"

Reina glanced back at me and stopped walking. "Run," she said in a louder voice.

I chuckled. "Right, of cour—"

Her eyes sprang open wide. She yanked my arm. "No, right now, run!"

I glanced back and saw the air had split open several yards away, and a giant, black wolf-hyena monster thing was already mid-leap through the opening.

I raced after Reina as fast as I could. My arm slipped from Reina's grasp as I tripped over a root.

She spun back for me and pulled me to my feet.

The monster was nearly on us; there was no way we could outrun it.

Champ snarled and tore free of Reina's hold, then leaped for the creature.

"Champ, no!" Reina shouted, then the air split open and both Champ and the monster were sucked inside. It snapped shut.

"No!" I spun to Reina. "What was—"

The air split open right next to me and sucked Reina in, then snapped shut before I could reach her.

"Reina!" I screamed, then the air split open again, and a force sucked at me from the inside out, like a vacuum pulling at both my body and my soul.

I grabbed at the tree branch nearest me. Its bark gouged my palms as the force dragged them along the rough branch, but I clung as tight as I could. "No!" Fear pulsed through me, but not only for myself. I had people to rescue, people depending on me. This thing, whatever it was, couldn't have me.

The split in the air widened, a gaping black hole in the woods. The pull strengthened until it felt my heart was about to be sucked out of my chest.

I clawed my fingers deeper into the branch, dug my heels into the ground, but still the pull inched me backward.

You are Maddox Rogers' granddaughter, I repeated in my head, summoning all the courage I could muster. *You have people to rescue. You have family and friends to save.* I glanced wildly around the woods, trying to think of something, anything, to help my situation.

The metal rod on the cord around my neck—the key—warmed and hummed against my collarbone inside my shirt, growing so hot it nearly burned me.

I didn't dare let go of the branch to move it off my skin.

The hole's pull intensified, and my grip on the branch slipped. I flew backward into darkness.

I landed on my butt on a stiff layer of nothingness. The last glimpse of the woods winked out in front of me. The ground felt hard beneath me, like packed dirt, but when I looked down, it was nothing but blackness. Everything was nothing but blackness. I couldn't even see my own hands in front of my face.

I stood, slowly and carefully, raising my hands over my head in case I was trapped in some kind of tunnel—but there was plenty of room to stand upright. I didn't dare walk, though, for fear of falling off an unseen precipice. The entire place was darkness, and I felt it closing in on me. I felt suddenly claustrophobic. My breaths came quick and tight. The metal rod on the cord must've flopped outside my shirt as I fell; I could still feel its heat through my shirt. I was glad, at least, I hadn't lost it.

Something rustled to my left.

I spun toward the sound, then questioned whether it had actually come from that direction. The darkness was completely disorienting.

There was a creak like metal hinges, and a small light flickered to life in front of me.

I blinked against its sudden glare, then it came into focus—a lit lantern, dangling in the air a few feet away, at about the height of my waist. My gaze trailed up from there to the clawed, misshapen fingers holding it, then up further, to the hooked nose and wide, black eyes staring up at me over its glow at about the level of my chest.

A wide, thin-lipped mouth split open into a grin, revealing tiny, pointed teeth. "Hello, dear," it crooned in a voice like that of a talking frog.

I screamed and scrambled backwards, forgetting for a moment that I had no idea what else might be around me.

The creature took shuffling steps toward me, closing the distance. "I wouldn't run, dear. No telling what you might find in here."

"Who—who are you? What do you want?"

Its grin widened. "You, of course."

I gasped. The metal rod surged hot against my shirt, burning me through the fabric. I grabbed for it, to yank it off my skin. It seared into my hand.

The air split open wide behind me and weak sunlight flooded into the darkness. I spun and leaped for it.

"No!" The creature dropped the lantern and lunged for me. Claws raked from my lower calves to my ankles, shredding my jeans, slicing my skin.

I crashed hard into the forest floor. The air snapped shut behind me.

"Ayla!" a deep voice yelled.

I glanced up to see Striker rushing toward me through the trees, then the world swam and I passed out.

CHAPTER 38

INTO THE VEIL

I woke up on the bed inside the cabin.

Striker stood from the loveseat as soon as I sat up. "Careful! You've been out a few hours."

"What?" I swung my feet to the floor to stand, but a wave of lightheadedness hit me. I braced my head in my hands until it passed, then looked up at Striker. "We have to go after my friends. Some of them could still be out there!"

"Ayla." Striker knelt in front of me and stared into my eyes. "What happened? I've been searching the woods for you for *five days*."

Dread settled in my sternum. "What?"

"When you summoned me, the stone couldn't get a track on your location and malfunctioned. I went to your grandfather. He told me about the cabin, and I realized you must have tried to summon me from inside the ward, so I came here... but I couldn't get inside the ward without the key. I wasn't sure if you were in there, or if you'd already gone into the Veil... then I found the drag marks. They all led to dead-ends, like they vanished mid-stride. I scoured these woods, but until the air opened up this afternoon and spit you out, I wasn't sure you were still alive." He gave me a gentle smile. "I'm glad you are, kid. But what happened out there? Where are the others?"

"No. No, I was just out there. Reina was with me—" I tried to stand, but pain shot up my legs.

"Easy," Striker said, steadying me. "Those are gonna hurt for a while. Female Veil-Deargs don't have venomous claws, but they still cut you pretty deep. Just shy of needing stitches. They're cleaned and wrapped with ointment; should feel better in a couple days. If it'd been her teeth, that would be a different story."

I glanced down to find my jeans rolled up, clean white bandages around both ankles. I sank back down onto the bed. "Veil-Dearg?" That was the thing Doctor Harlowe had mentioned, what had poisoned me the first time, a *male* one. He'd said the female ones were terrifying. He wasn't wrong.

Striker nodded. "I got a glimpse of the one that grabbed for you as the breach snapped shut. As soon as I picked you up to carry you, this place rippled into view. That key must have some kinda magic—I'm guessing you don't go around opening up breaches on a normal day."

I reached for the corded necklace. The metal rod and stone still hung around my neck, beneath the collar of my shirt—cool against my skin. "Yeah." It was all I could find the energy to say.

Striker didn't pry. Instead, he settled back onto the floor, bent his knees and wrapped his arms around them, peering up at me like a kid ready for story time. "Now, tell me what happened."

I did my best to explain the events of the past few hours... days?... I wasn't even sure anymore. "How has it been five days?" I asked when I finished. "I was only with the Veil-Dearg for moments."

"Time moves differently in certain parts of the Veil," Striker answered, but his eyes were far off. He stood. "Come on, I need to check something."

Striker had me stand inside the boundary of the ward, for safety, as he made a careful circle around it, holding his hands out like he was assessing the air. When he returned, I used the key to let him back in.

"There's a latent Leyline here," he reported. "My guess is it's the same one that runs down past the river to the docks, where the Selkbloods were using the Kane warehouse. That's probably why they gathered there."

My pulse skittered. "So anyone can just come through, anytime they want?"

Striker shook his head. "No. It's not easy to open a breach, even at a Leyline."

I clutched the leather cord. "Callan said the breach behind the cabin opens with the same key as the cabin ward."

Striker nodded. "I figured as much. What I don't understand is who else is opening up breaches here. Veil-Deargs and hounds can't open breaches on their own; they have to use ones that are already there. The Leyline here makes it easier to make a breach, but the LeyGuard has wards all over this region. Nothing should be able to breach through at all, without permission. Your grandfather's key was created as a way around that, but according to him it's one of a kind. Yet the Selkbloods managed to breach through near the warehouse, and from what you said, they were opening pockets at will all over these woods. A lateral pocket, one that moves only Earthside, is one thing... but based on your experience, these pockets are opening directly into the Veil."

A shiver rushed through me at the memory. I hugged my arms to my chest. "What does that mean? Where are my friends? How do we get them back?"

Striker's eyes met mine regretfully. "I'm not sure we can, kid. The Veil's a big place—we wouldn't even know where to look."

I started to protest, but he raised his hands defensively.

"I'm not saying we won't try, Ayla. But we may need to bring in some help."

I stared at him. "We can't tell the Hub." I couldn't explain the gut feeling I had, but it was screaming at me that something was off with the Hub; that they couldn't be trusted.

Striker studied my face, then nodded. "I'd argue with you, kid, but I'm afraid you might be right. I'll have to report Reina missing... she's LeyGuard. But I'm not even sure, right now, if I can trust the Hub to do anything about it. Or if I can trust them at all."

A spear of fear shot through me. "My grandfather, and my parents—"

Striker placed a massive hand on my forearm. "They're fine, Ayla. My partner Brone is watching them—I checked in an hour ago; they're all okay. Your grandfather is recovering well, mostly resting. No change in your parents, though, I'm afraid." He winced.

"I thought you didn't work with partners," I said.

"No, I said I don't work with anyone but Brone. He got back from his trip a couple days ago. I trust him with my life, and right now, he's the *only* LeyGuard I trust." His eyes held mine. "He's covering for me. The Hub doesn't know I'm here. Anyway, what's going on at the Hub is *our* problem. You've got other things to worry about. But you can rest easy about your family. Brone and I will make sure they're kept safe."

I stared at him. "Why are you helping me so much?" I knew it might not be polite to ask, but I couldn't help but wonder what was in all this for him, besides a heap of trouble.

He smiled gently. "Your grandfather did me a huge favor once, when I was just a bullheaded trainee. I owed him. I've probably repaid that debt by now, but you seem pretty brave. For all I know, you're the LeyGuard's next great hero, and I'd hate to miss out on being part of your origin story." He smirked.

I winced. "I'm not sure about that last part... but thank you."

"I'll consider it my good deed of the year." Striker grinned, then chewed his match. "But we've still got a problem. Without something to point us where to look, finding your friends in the Veil will be like looking for a needle in a haystack full of monsters trying to kill you."

I reached for the stone, remembering how Callan told me it would lead me to the prince. "I think I have something that could help with that." I slid the stone from beneath my shirt.

Striker stared at it. "I'm guessing that's more than an ugly black stone?"

I shrugged. "Callan says it leads the way to Prince Kaizyn."

Striker's eyes widened. "Keep that hidden." He nudged my hand back toward me. "In the wrong hands, that map to the prince could mean the end of both your lives."

Fear lanced through me as I shoved the stone back inside my shirt and nodded.

"But if we can find the prince," Striker continued, "he'll know far more about the Veil than we do. The LeyGuard spends as little time there as possible. So do most Fae—it's an awful place. But they at least know their way around in it. He might be able to help you figure out where they were taken. But you shouldn't go alone."

I clutched the stone through my shirt. "In case you haven't noticed, I don't have anyone else." My voice broke on the last word. Grief swam in, pressing tight on my throat. "They've taken everyone."

Striker bent down to my eye level. "You have me."

"You'll come with me?" I stared back at him.

"Into Hell itself, kid." Striker smiled. "You're the chosen one, remember?"

I laughed. "Not even close."

Striker's smile vanished. "Listen to me, Ayla. *You* decide who you are—what you do. It doesn't matter if you're Maddox Rogers' granddaughter, or some random kid we found in the woods, LeyGuard or Fae or whatever. We all have choices. You want to be brave? A hero? Then be one. No one can stop you. It only takes the courage to do what's right, no matter what anyone else is doing."

I stared at him. "And going into the Veil is what's right?"

He tilted his head. "You tell me. Is it?"

I thought of Jordan, of Reina, of Callan and Madison and Rory and even Champ—all stuck in the Veil, trapped somewhere... being used as bait for *me*. And that was the best-case scenario, the one that meant they were still alive. Resolve solidified in my chest. "Yes."

Striker nodded once. "Then that's what we do."

A few minutes later, Striker and I stood behind the cabin, carrying spare backpacks we'd found inside. Striker's was stuffed with food and bottles of water, while mine held some rope, a couple blankets, and a first aid kit. We'd also stuck Grandpa's journal into one of the packs.

"We stay together," Striker said as we neared the humming section of air that signified the breach. "It'll be dark, like before. Lots of dangerous things stalk the Veil. Stay close to me."

"Okay," I agreed. I wasn't sure I'd have the courage to re-enter that terrifying blackness if I were going alone.

Striker glanced at me. "You ready?"

I nodded and reached for the key around my neck. It surged hot before my fingers even touched it, then the air a few yards to our left split open. A breach I *hadn't* made.

Striker spun. "Quick, Ayla, go!" He shoved me behind him as a half-dozen grotesque wolf-things poured out of the new breach. Shadowhounds.

I hesitated, not wanting to leave him.

Striker yanked the match from his lips, struck it against the strap on his chest, and his entire arms blazed into flame. He glanced back at me. "Ayla, you have to breach! Now!"

I gaped at him. "What?" I thought he'd been telling me to run—not jump into the Veil alone.

"They're trying to stop you! You've gotta go through!" Striker slung his arms, and ropes of fire shot out from glowing symbols on his wrists, like flaming whips. He swung and slashed into one of the hounds as it crashed into him.

It howled and caught fire.

Striker swung the other arm, and his fire-whip wrapped around the body of the next lunging Shadowhound. He yanked, and the fire sliced it right in half, both halves smoking and cauterized.

I gaped, frozen in place, as four more Shadowhounds rushed in at him.

Striker yanked the backpack off his shoulder and tossed it to me.

It hit the ground near me, then Striker spun back toward the hounds. His whole body went up in flame.

I screamed, but Striker yelled back at me over his shoulder as he incinerated one hound by crushing it against his chest, then caught two more with his whips. "I'm fine, Ayla! But they'll send more. We can't risk them following you. I'm sorry, kid. I'll find you as soon as I can—but you gotta go. Now!" His eyes found mine. "Go straight to the prince. You can do this!"

I grabbed the extra backpack and slid it on my other shoulder, then sucked a sharp breath and spun back toward the humming air behind me. "You can do this," I whispered to myself. "They need you. You can do this."

I clutched the key. It hummed and seared hot against my hand, almost singeing my palm—and the air split open.

A writhing vortex expanded in front of me, instantly tugging at something deep inside me.

I froze. This wasn't me; I wasn't a risk-taker. I was supposed to die of old age, tucked in my bed, not torn apart by some crazy Fae monsters in a pitch-black Veil.

But even if this was to be how I died, would I do anything differently? This could be my only chance to help my family, my friends—all of them. Going into the Veil alone was crazy... and what if it accomplished nothing? I might not be strong enough to save them. I might not survive more than five seconds back in the Veil, and then I and Kaizyn would *both* be dead. But if I didn't go...

I clenched my jaw. I knew the risks, but I still had to try.

Something exploded behind me. I jumped and spun—the trees around us had caught fire.

More Shadowhounds poured out of the breach by Striker.

"Ayla, now! Go!" Striker yelled.

I spun back toward the breach, then leaped headlong into the darkness.

Epilogue

Jordan

The door at the end of the hall clanged open, and lights flickered on overhead. I threw my hand up to protect my eyes from the blinding fluorescents. It had been days since they'd bothered to turn the lights on down here.

I crouched in the corner and kept my arm over my eyes, feigning grogginess as I listened. Two sets of boots—and something dragging. Another prisoner? If so, they weren't bothering to be gentle. One guard yanked the door to the cell across from me open and shoved someone in. A female voice whimpered as the person hit the hard ground. I cut my eyes over from beneath my arm, but couldn't see much. The cell door clanged shut.

The guards stomped off. The lights cut out. The outer door slammed.

I hurried to the bars of my cell. "Hey, are you okay? Can you hear me?"

A sniffle. Then—"Jordan? Is that really you?" The voice sounded weak, exhausted.

My heart stumbled as I strained my eyes against the darkness they'd been so accustomed to moments before. Slowly, a face took shape, pressed to the bars across from me. A human, not Fae—the first human I'd seen in days.

"Madison?" I gaped at her. "What are you doing here?"

Relief washed over her face, followed quickly by a wave of despair. "I think I'm bait—like you. For Ayla."

My veins went cold. I clutched the cell bars. "Tell me what you know about what's happened since they took me."

Once Madison filled me in, my mind raced. I'd been doing everything I could to learn about the enemy's plan, to play this smart, as the Hub had trained me. Lie low if captured, gather intel, wait for rescue. But if the LeyGuards truly weren't coming...

I slid the hidden runestone from my boot.

Forget reconnaissance. There was no way I would let the Dark Fae use me to get their hands on Ayla. At the next guard change, I was busting Madison and myself out of this place—even if I had to blow a hole straight through their dungeon.

READ THE REST OF THE SERIES!

END OF BOOK 1

(To be continued in Book 2, *LeyGuards, Faespells, and Other Things That Breach the Veil*)

Read the rest of this trilogy!

***Macchiatos, Faerie Princes, and Other Things That Happen at Midnight* is book 1 of a trilogy, and books 2 and 3 are already available for order!** Grab Books 2 & 3 now at the links below!

LeyGuards, Faespells, and Other Things That Breach the Veil (The Leyward Stones, Book 2): **https://books2read.com/leyguards**

Fae Curses, Dark Kings, and Other Things That Must Fall (The Leyward Stones, Book 3): **https://books2read.com/faecurses**

Did you know there will be more Leyward Stones books to come, too?

The *Macchiatos* trilogy is Trilogy 1 of The Leyward Stones series, but Trilogy 2 is already in the works! Subscribe to my newsletter at **http://ccrawfordwriting.com/subscribe** to get updates on my future releases!

ACKNOWLEDGEMENTS

First and foremost, thank you to God, without whom this book would not exist. He dropped this idea into my lap in the strangest of ways, and the journey to figuring out what to *do* with that idea surpassed all my expectations. He took my meager offering of idea snippets, side-stories, and half-baked outlines and—through tons of prayer and the amazing support system He blessed me with—turned those loaves and fishes into a full series. I am forever grateful, and I pray this series honors Him and brings Him glory.

Thank you to my husband, Jason, who—although he disagrees with this amount of *teen romance* in this series (ha!)—was pivotal in the early planning and development of the Leyward Stones world and series lore. So much of this series is owed to the long conversations he and I had, and to his ideas and suggestions (even if I didn't always agree with them!) that honed and sharpened my concept and truly deepened and enriched this story world. He is also responsible for *all* my cover art for this series, and for the LeyGuard House symbols (which don't appear in these books, but I've shared them on my social media and in the Worldpedia on PirateCat Publishing). He tirelessly brings my visions to life, fiercely protects my writing time, and is my never-ending champion and marketer for my writing, an *amazing* father to our four kids, and my devoted partner in life. Thank you, Jason. You are one of my greatest blessings.

Thank you to my kids, who are so patient with my long writing/editing hours during crunch-time before deadlines, and whose enthusiasm for life and boundless creativity are truly inspirational.

And to my parents, who always encouraged my creativity and my writing, even when they thought my ideas were strange.

Thank you to M.J. Padgett, my loyal friend and writing support, whose tireless feedback and late-night brainstorming chats transformed this series completely. (You know what I mean!)

Thank you to the rest of my Alpha team — Christy Freeman, Beth Burnett, and Emily Fertic — for your support, for your endless hours reading this series as I wrote it, for your enthusiastic and helpful feedback, for putting up with me messaging the group chat again and again, and for your Alpha comments that just made me laugh.

And to Lydia Freeman, who is absolutely an Alpha even though she's not officially in the group chat. I *always* look forward to your comments in my Alpha docs.

To my online writing community: To Candice Lisle, whose support of my writing *always* is truly humbling, and to Christopher Henckel for being an amazing crit partner for the shorter stories I wrote in this world. (And to the Crit Quad, in general, for your encouragement and support.) To the rest of the Wulf Pack and especially Wulf Moon, for growing me as a writer *so much*, then celebrating every writing success with me and working to amplify the signal. To Scot Noel, Jane Noel, and DreamForge Magazine—for championing my series in its earliest form on Vella, for giving me a platform to talk about my Vella experiences, and for buying and publishing two Leyward Stones short stories, believing in my vision for this world and bringing it to life in print (and with gorgeous illustrations!) even before the rest of this series had taken shape. THANK YOU, all of you, for the unbelievable support you've given me from every direction. I am truly blessed.

Thank you to Jeremy Reynolds and my other early Patreon subscribers, who read this series in early iterations, and some of whom even followed me over to PirateCat Publishing to continue reading the story when I published it there.

To my Vella audience, for making the initial, serial version of this story such an *amazing* experience to write. To my newsletter subscribers, who patiently waited for the e-book and paperback versions of this series for a *long time,* and still showed up regularly on my emails with engagements and replies and support.

And thank you again to Christy, for being my editor, for being patient with my shenanigans, for being enthusiastic about my books always, for putting up with me and my crazy ideas with grace, and for calling me on all the times I use *being* unnecessarily in sentences. You're the best!

Want to see more from me, outside my published books? Come find me where I hang out online!

If you love **clean young adult fiction** and want a portal where you can read a bunch of my clean YA content, interact with me and other readers, and help me build a community around clean YA fiction, **check out my Story Subscribers portal on my website!** Find out more on the next page, or at **http://ccrawfordwriting.com/storysubscriberscontent**.

If you'd like to receive updates on future releases, behind-the-scenes info on my writing, and personal updates, subscribe to my monthly email newsletter at **http://ccrawfordwriting.com/subscribe**. I never spam my email subscribers—you can expect one email per month, with occasional bonus emails if I have a new release, sale, or something important to share. And you'll even get free story downloads for subscribing!

I'm also on social media! You can find me at:

Website: **http://ccrawfordwriting.com**

Blog: **http://ccrawfordwriting.com/blog**

Facebook: **http://facebook.com/ccrawfordwriting**

Instagram: **http://instagram.com/ccrawfordwriting**

YouTube: **http://youtube.com/ccrawfordwriting**

Or contact me directly through email at **ccrawford@ccrawfordwrit ing.com**. I'd love to see your comments and respond to any questions you might have.

Thank you so much for reading!

Then check out my Story Subscribers portal!

It's a special section of my website where you'll find a collection of stories from me right there online & ready to binge-read! Some of the stories in there are free, and others are behind a small paywall... right now (as of May 2026), that paywall is only $1.99/month to access ALL of my Story Subscribers content. This small fee helps keep my business running... plus my Story Subscribers get access to some *exclusive* content not available anywhere else, like my ongoing serials and bonus side stories set in some of my published story worlds.

Also, EVERYTHING in my Story Subscribers portal is clean and either YA or YA-appropriate in content. **What do I mean by "clean"?** For me, that means:

PG-13 or less for violence (battle violence in the fantasy/sci-fi but no gratuitous gore).

Sweet/wholesome romance (when romance is present) that focuses on relationship and never goes beyond a chaste kiss.

NO profanity (but with an occasional mild euphemism like "dang" or similar, and occasional in-world, made-up "swear" words).

I write from a Biblical worldview (though much of my content is not explicitly religious), and do my best to portray healthy relationship dynamics, especially in parent-child relationships and romantic relationships, which I've found are often quite *unhealthy* in much of the mainstream YA fiction. My characters are not perfect, and do not always make the right choices, but their mistakes are always used for growth. There will always be a clear concept of good versus evil in my stories (especially fantasy!), and they'll always end with either a hard-fought happy ending, or at least a note of hope.

If this sounds like your cup of tea, I'm thrilled you found me—and I hope you'll check out my Story Subscribers content!

Just visit my Story Subscribers page at **http://ccrawfordwriting.com /storysubscriberscontent**to join or find out more!

Crystal Crawford writes clean YA fantasy and clean YA romance (and a smattering of other genres) in Florida, where every natural body of water hides something that could eat you, and if they don't get you, the weather might. She lives with her husband, five kids, two cats, one doofusy dog, and two live-in grandparents, who have all supported her dream of writing and drinking far too much coffee. Her imagination is her happy place! (But a deserted beach is nice, too.) When she isn't writing, she enjoys reading, napping, watching shows with her family, working in the garden, and homeschooling the kids, though most days you'll also find her doing laundry.

ALSO BY CRYSTAL CRAWFORD

The Leyward Stones

Macchiatos, Faerie Princes, and Other Things That Happen at Midnight
LeyGuards, Faespells, and Other Things That Breach the Veil
Fae Curses, Dark Kings, and Other Things That Must Fall
and more books to come!

The Lex Chronicles (Legends of Arameth)

The Edge of Nothing
The Path to Paradox
The Ends of Exile
and more books to come!

Aubrey Lance, S.S. (Supernatural Sleuth)

Season 1: The Vanishings, now available to read in serial format in the forum on my website: http://ccrawfordwriting.com/forum/aubreylance -season1

Secret Messages Sweet YA Romance Series

I'm Not a Stalker
The Five Suspects
and more books to come!

Love and Aliens

The Extraordinary, Extraterrestrial Love Lives of Doppelgangers
and another book to come!

Published Short Stories

- "Our Kind" (a Leyward Stones short story published in DreamForge Magazine) — available to read free at https://dreamforge.mywebportal.app/dreamforge/stories/show/our-kind-crystal-crawford

- "One Shot at Aeden" (a Leyward Stones short story published in DreamForge Magazine) — available to read free at https://dreamforge.mywebportal.app/dreamforge/stories/show/one-shot-at-aeden-crystal-crawford

- "Cheer Hawks and a Side of Murder" (a short story originally published in the Murderbirds anthology by Mike Jack Stoumbos)

- plus loads of other Leyward Stones, Legends of Arameth, and assorted short stories available inside PirateCat!

Nonfiction

- The Unspoken Language: An Animal Trainer's Memoir

- Slap Him with a Fish: a Crash-Course in Fiction Writing

- Put Some Pants on That Kid: a Writing Handbook for High School and Beyond (Student Book and Parent/Teacher's Guide)

- The Other Side of the Law (a co-written lawyer's memoir)

- Unbreaking: How Giving Up Saved Our Marriage (a raw, real marriage memoir)

Find the purchase links to many of the above books all in one place at
http://ccrawfordwriting.com/books

www.ingramcontent.com/pod-product-compliance
Lightning Source LLC
Chambersburg PA
CBHW030150310726
48970CB00005B/1677